# Strawberry Fields

## The Kansas Pirate Series:

## Book II

I0617869

## S.L. Kotar and J.E. Gessler

Ahead of the Press Publishing
St. Louis, Missouri

**Library of Congress Cataloguing-in-Publication Data**

Strawberry Fields
The Kansas Pirate Series: Book II
 / S.L. Kotar and J.E. Gessler / authors
/E.J. Rossi / illustrator

ISBN     Paperback          978-1-950392-02-5
ISBN     KINDLE             978-1-950392-03-2

This story is a work of fiction.  The names, characters, places and incidents are products of the authors' imagination.  Any resemblance to actual events, locals, or persons, living or dead is entirely coincidental.

Manufactured in the United States of America
Ahead of The Press Publishing
St. Louis, Missouri

## Table of Contents

# Summary of The Kansas Pirate Series Books

## Pirate Treasure

## Book I

They said the boy was haunted and the townspeople of Lawrence, Kansas, wanted nothing to do with widower Seth Ward or his two children. In 1857, superstitions run high.

Left alone to raise Patricia and Peter, Seth has been isolated from his neighbors since the death of his wife from a lingering, malignant disease. Nearly at his wits end, a young woman appears in response to an advertisement for help.

Barbara Nelander dared brave the terror of a dead woman's ghost and the haunting of her son because she was not like other women. Born in Nova Scotia, "Nelander," as she was called, had served as a crewman aboard her father's trading ship since early childhood. Used to working in a man's world and handling difficult situations, she signs aboard with the determination to dispel the ghosts of the past.

Transforming the homestead into a figurative pirate ship, she uses her wiles to restore Peter's self-confidence, extract a buccaneer's revenge on those who tormented him and battles drought alongside Seth as the harsh Kansas summer threatens to destroy the family and the relationship that develops between the "captain" and "first officer."

# DEDICATION

"Strawberry Fields"

In its largest context, our book, "Strawberry Fields," is about a vision that became a reality. It encompasses love, hardship, doubt, and faith: the four elements in the life cycle of a dream. John Lennon, Paul McCartney, George Harrison, and Ringo Starr passed through these stages both individually and in a Rock n' Roll band they called The Beatles. In so doing, they shared the journey and changed the world.

Though all the hardship and doubt, their music bestowed love and faith: through that came our writing and through that, this book, dedicated to the everlasting memory of the four lads from Liverpool.

SLK and JEG

# CHAPTER 1

All the wrath of the sea gods, combined, could not have come close to approximating the pain she felt. Barbara Nelander-Ward had prepared herself for the worst, but this agony surpassed her wildest expectations.

Face flushed, heart racing, fists clenched, she stifled one cry but as the spasms came again in fresh waves, she howled an invective.

"Damn!" Ashamed of her weakness, for she was not one to surrender easily, Nelander clenched her teeth, spat, then offered a weak apology. "I am sorry. I had not meant to cuss. But at least," she tried, "I did not put a 'God' in front of it."

The tall, solidly-build man at her side, himself the color of a furled topsail, forced a grin. "That would have been swearing."

"I promised I wouldn't, but you damned landlubbers have such delicate ears."

Her second use of the impolite word went unremarked.

Offering his hand, Seth Ward encouraged her to take it.

"Hold onto me. Squeeze as hard as you can. Concentrate on --"

"Crushing your fingers? That is an incentive, if ever I heard one."

Despite the temptation, she did not oblige. "Go to the door and look out. Just one last time. To see if anyone is coming."

Slipping silently away with the grace of a deer, which belied his stature, Seth crossed the living room and stood in the open entranceway. A breeze blew in from the north, cooling his body, if not his nerves. He might have saved himself the trip. The road leading to the farm had not been traversed in several hours, and that by the doctor. No sign of any wagon, carriage or foot-weary traveler met his eye.

He would have had it otherwise. His wife put a great deal of stock and not inconsiderable faith in the arrival of her friend. As unlikely as it seemed for a woman to travel by herself from the Nebraska Territory all the way to Lawrence, Kansas on a journey of mercy, such events were known to happen.

*But not by an ordinary woman,* he reminded himself. *By an extraordinary one.*

Barbara Nelander-Ward, familiarly called "Nelander" by friends and foes alike, had undertaken just such a trip only five months before. It had been winter, then, but she swore to go, and by God, she had. Making her way across one territory into another, she had sought and ultimately found the temporary home of their former neighbors, Terrance and Beth Windsor and their two sons, Jed and James.

The reunion had not been a happy one. During the summer of 1859 when drought held the land in a viselike grip, burning the soil and parching all living creatures to the point of death and beyond, the Windsors had opted to pack their bags and seek greener pastures. While the Wards held steadfast and ultimately persevered, they had not.

Nebraska had proved greener, but only in a figurative sense, for it did the Windsors no good. Without land to till or money to take them further, they had settled in a shanty town called Snow Bluff.

For all their chance of escaping, it might better have been named Hell's Bottom.

Beth had promised to return in time to assist with the baby's birth, but she had not kept her word. Seth never believed she would. No one willingly returned to a place they had abandoned. Not when their subsequent life had turned to ash.

Resting one hand on the doorframe and stuffing the other in his pocket, his gaze turned from the gently rolling hills to the flag staff planted squarely in the middle of their yard. A black and white standard, stretched to full length by the wind, revealed a startling accurate depiction of a skull over two crossed bones. "Forearms," Nelander had called them.

*Without the hands,* he had thankfully thought at first sight. Seeing skeletal fingers would have been too gruesome.

She called it the Jolly Roger and explained its significance as a symbol of pirates, the world round.

*It is meant to be easily recognizable; to instil fear. Pirates are the scourge of the Seven Seas. They seek booty -- treasure to you. Doubloons and silver and jewels. They attack with bare bodkins and cutlasses, taking no quarter on a resisting crew. They are fierce-looking warriors -- some with eye patches, others with peg legs or hooks for hands. They wear bright red sashes, drink rum with impunity and swear like the devil.*

Or words to that effect.

Nelander had come to him three years ago with a glint in her eye, wearing a seaman's blouse and trousers, slippers meant for the deck of a ship and a navy blue cap covering her close-cropped hair. While she did not have an eye patch, a peg leg or a sash, she did have a salty vocabulary and a tenacity worthy of the buccaneers of old.

It had been she who made the flag. *As a means of instilling pride. A reminder to the townspeople of Lawrence that the Ward family knew how to stand up for their rights. That they were not above a bit of trickery.*

The townspeople had called it "evil," but he understood better.

The lanky "seaman," for such she called herself, first heard of the Ward farm in reference to a job. Seth needed a woman to tend his two offspring. The position had been open for two years. None of the locals had seen fit to apply. The woman who suggested it did so with reluctance. She could not, she said, "Recommend it." Seth Ward's boy was "peculiar." That, she explained, meant "Touched in the head."

As it turned out, such a definition was a kindness.

The farmer offered, she said, "Room and board and a small fee."

He did, in fact, provide Nelander with shelter. But not the fee.

In fairness, she never asked for it.

Seth had not expected to fall in love with the pe-culiar woman who had journeyed all the way from California. Love had been the last thing on his mind. He needed someone to watch his children. "Protect" might have been a better word.

Barbara Nelander had done that and more. She transformed the Ward farm into a ship. Not precisely like the one she lost in San Francisco. That had been a real ship. A "schooner," she called it. She served as second officer aboard the *Bottom Dollar* and knew more of the ocean than any man-jack who ever sailed the briny sea. But knowledge did not translate into acceptance and after the murder of her father, captain and owner of the vessel, she determined to make her way home to Canada. When ready cash ran out over a thousand miles from Nova Scotia, Nelander arrived at his doorstep, looking for a job.

With her nautical ways, tough talk and a propensity for not taking "no" for an answer, Nelander reshaped the farm and its inmates. Patricia and

Peter become "able-bodied seamen," and he, the "captain." Giving herself a promotion, she rose in rank to first officer.

Utilizing pizzoned chili, an eye for men's character and a knack for revealing the world larger than Lawrence, Kansas, his seafarer had put down roots.

"Seth!"

Dr. Hank McTree called from the bedroom. Seth knew what that meant. The baby was about to arrive; his crew expanded by one. That would make five, total. A good, odd number. It suit circumstances well.

Stealing one last glance at the road, he steeled himself, then crossed into the living room. Two pair of wide, round orbs met his, temporarily blocking the path.

"Is it going to come soon, now, papa?"

"Yes," he agreed. "Soon."

"Must be a terrible frightful thing. I ain't never heard Nelander cry out like that."

"There's a lot of pain involved. But it won't take long, now."

"You want I should make her some tea?" Patricia asked. As the older of the two, the ten-year-old spoke first.

"I think that would be a good idea."

"Shall we put some rum in it?" That from Peter, the seven-year-old. "Pirates drink rum, Captain. It makes 'em fierce."

In the present crisis, Seth thought rum might be a good thing.

"You do that. And if Nelander doesn't want it, I expect the three of us could use it."

"Yes, sir."

The boy saluted, then carefully readjusted his eye patch. While generally reserved for "going ashore," he had dressed in full pirate regalia for the occasion. It made him braver. Seth wished he had an outfit to wear, too.

"And don't forget to mark the time," he added, slipping past the crew of the *Pirate Treasure*. "Nelander'll want to hear the bell."

This time, Master Patricia saluted. "Aye, sir. I expect she will."

Marching in single file, the little ones went into the kitchen. After the kettle had been put on the stove, three strong, clear chimes rang out from the yard. Nine-thirty o'clock. Pausing from habit, Seth glanced out the window. Daylight. That meant A.M. and not P.M. He grinned. A man who could rightly interpret 9:30 A.M. by the peeling of a bell could withstand almost anything. It proved his seaworthiness, even if Kansas did lay almost two thousand land miles away from the Atlantic.

And a heap more distant from Nova Scotia, Canada.

Gliding on cat's paws, he edged his way inside the bedroom. The supercharged air smelled of blood and sweat. Familiar with the odor of open wounds and disease, the farmer in him rallied. He had attended enough birthings of cows and horses to recognize healthy from sick. This was a good smell. The promise of life to come.

"Any time now, Captain."

The doctor resorted to his companion's rank rather than his more familiar first name. He meant it respectfully because he knew the farmer would be a help and not a hindrance.

"Tell me what to do."

"Hold her hand. Keep her breathing nice and regular. Remind her to push."

"Push, hell," came the voice from the bed. "I can't push fast enough."

A strong voice. Telling him she had control of the situation.

Grasping her hand, their roles reversed. He squeezed her and she held on. They were like that. A team.

Another groan, then clenched teeth.

"Push."

"It's nine-thirty," she said. "I've been at this seven hours."

"Patricia's making tea. Peter's adding rum."

"Remind me to promote them."

Contractions, wracking her frame. Skin stretched to the breaking point. He wiped her brow.

"Don't suppose you got a calf in there, do you? Or a foal? We could use either."

"I think I'm giving birth to a whale!"

"How long before we can strip the blubber and make oil? Kerosene comes dear these days." A cry, a heave and the top of a head appeared. His heart jumped. "Easy, now. Easy. It's fine. Just fine."

Eyes closed, Nelander worked on the process. She had hoped to have her best friend with her. To share the infant's first cries with a fellow pirate. One she had taken a sacred vow to protect.

Loyalty.

Obeying orders.

Seeking retribution.

Looking for and sharing treasure.

The Four Articles of the Secret Pirate Association of Lawrence, Kansas.

Beth Windsor had broken the first two.

Barbara Nelander forgave her. But only conditionally.

Her friend would have a hell of a lot of explaining to do.

# CHAPTER 2

"Push."

"If I hear that word one more time I'm really going to start swearing. I mean it."

"All right," Seth agreed. "Then row."

"Row?"

"Row." He demonstrated a calisthenics more closely approximating a sit-up. Nelander rolled her eyes.

"What the hell is that action supposed to represent? If a seaman of mine rowed like that I'd keelhaul him."

He grinned. "I'm guessing. I've never actually rowed a boat. I just liked the word."

Holding onto his grin as if that were a life raft, Barbara copied the style, giving a huff and a push each time she rose. Dr. McTree arched an eyebrow, considered, then gave approval.

"Very good. We'll bring this tiny seafarer into the world in no time."

Working through the pain, concentrating on it, pushing and groaning, she had almost lost touch with reality when she heard a voice say, "The head is out. Shoulders next. They're the hard part."

More work. Supreme effort. A radiating agony as her private area stretched, resisted and finally gave way.

"Here we go. Almost through."

Teeth clenched, biting through a cloth someone had put between them, she persevered.

*Row. Row. Row.*

A sudden heave, a sensation of weightlessness, then blackness descending before a cry, a shout and then the wail of a newborn babe. Emotions instantly alert, she struggled, propping herself up by an elbow. What her eyes beheld could, in no other way, be described as a miracle.

A scrawny, pink, wrinkled, bawling whale calf. Only this creature had arms and legs and a head the size of a tar bucket.

Carefully severing the umbilical cord, then tying off the stub at the navel, the physician used a damp towel to wash the infant. By the new mother's reckoning, the operation lasted several bells.

"How is it?" she demanded, growing impatient. McTree beamed with pleasure.

"See for yourself."

Propping a hand behind the baby's neck, he displayed the new arrival for the proud parents.

"A girl."

"She is healthy? She is all right?"

"If crying is any indication, you have a little --"

"Heller on our hands," papa eagerly supplied. Leaning nearer, he watched as his wife accepted the child. A thrill never before experienced ran from the nape of her neck through her toes.

"A baby."

"Here," McTree demonstrated, repositioning her precious burden so it rested more comfortably. "Support the head. She is too small, yet, to hold it up by herself. Good. And now, you must count the fingers and toes. A ritual," he added, "for new parents. So they may see for themselves all is right and well."

Hardly daring to touch so delicate an object, Barbara looked up at Seth. "You do it."

Taking one miniscule fist, he patiently straightened the fingers. "One. Two. Three. Four. Five." Repeating the process, he determined both hands and feet possessed the requisite number. "All there."

"She is perfect, doctor."

"Indeed, she is."

"Is that the new crewmember?" Peter dubiously inquired from the door. Motioning he and his sister inside, Nelander showed off the baby.

"Your sister."

Patricia sighed. "It's going to be a long time before she ever gets to be an able-bodied."

"Not as long as you think," Seth promised. "Both of you started out this way and look how far you've come in only a few short years."

They appeared unimpressed.

"It's gonna be awhile before she rings the bell."

"Or feeds the chickens."

"Or shovels out the barn --"

"Enough! Several weeks, at least. No immediate help with your chores."

"Oh, m'gosh!" Patricia exclaimed, pounding her brother on the back. "It must be past ten. We gotta ring the bell!"

Disappearing from sight, they hurried outside. She pulled the cord twice, then he followed, totaling four bells.

"Ten o'clock," the captain noted. "That is the time we shall use when we make entry in the Bible. "March 4th, 1860 at 10:00 A.M."

"March 4th," the first officer noted. "March-forth. As in, 'move ahead.' I like that. A good date. Perhaps slightly early to be a spring baby, but close enough."

"I think I would prefer a winter baby. This 'spring' has the sound of boundless energy. I have trouble keeping up with one of you -- two will leave me exhausted."

"Better get used to it."

Cradling the newborn to her cheek, she kissed the child, then offered her up. Seth accepted her, bestowed his own kiss, then held her out for a critical appraisal.

"Bald as a buzzard's head."

"Thank you. Could you possibly think of anything less flattering?"

"As hairless as a rattler --"

"Never mind."

"As naked as a top spar without a sail."

"That's better. Give her to me."

She took her back, then groaned. "I feel as though I've been put through the wringer. I've got to get up."

"No, you don't," McTree warned. "Not for a day or two. Your body has been through a terrible strain. Give it time to recover. You must drink a lot of fluids and eat when your stomach settles. And sleep."

His words brought down a ten-ton weight. Lying back, she battled falling eyelids.

"There is so much to do. And I know nothing about babies." A fear settled over her. "Doctor -- feeding and cleaning and raising."

"Captain Ward will help you," he promised, resting a hand on her shoulder. "Thankfully, one of you has experience. But you will find much comes naturally."

"You will stay with us?"

"No. But I will be back this way tomorrow."

Taking his black bag, he gathered what few instrument had been set out, then followed Seth into the kitchen. Gratefully washing his hands, he dried them on a clean towel, then extended one.

"Congratulations, Seth. She is a beautiful baby. And your wife did wonderfully."

"She will be all right?"

"The first forty-eight hours are the most dangerous. But I see no reason for overdue concern. Keep Nelander warm, give her water and good strong broth. Let her sleep. Alone," he warned. Seth colored.

"Yes, sir."

"Two or three months before she's ready for you. She'll let you know."

"Yes, sir."

"Don't mind me. I tell this to all the new fathers. Most of them don't have sense like you. They're impatient." His lips curled. "Too many children in too close a time is dangerous."

"Yes, sir."

"Good. Then clean up the room. Take off the sheets and blankets. Wash them and hang them outside for the wind to blow dry. Mop the floor. It's still cold outside but leave the window open a crack. At least in the day. And Nelander'll be wanting to wash up, too. She'll be awfully sore down there but cleanliness is next to godliness, they say, and I subscribe to it. A sponge bath -- no soaking. At least not for several weeks. I worry about infection."

"Yes, sir."

"The baby will sleep, now. She'll cry when she's hungry. Not too much at first. And don't forget to burp her. You remember?"

"Hadn't thought of it until you reminded me."

"Baby swallows a lot of air. If her stomach gets hard, you'll know right enough. Let me know if she spits up a lot. Most take to mother's milk but there are always some that don't. In that case, you can feed her cow's milk. But breast milk is better. Nelander didn't say she was adverse to that?"

"Never discussed it."

"It's up to her, of course. But I always thought baby animals do better with what's natural."

"I'll mention it if it comes up."

Fastening the latch on his bag, the doctor nodded and walked toward the door. "Thought of a name, yet?"

Seth stopped, hand going to his head. "Funny thing. We never talked about that, either. Guess we were waiting to see if it were a boy or a girl."

"Well, you've got yourself a daughter. Not disappointed, are you?"

"I mighta been, if it had come out a foal or a calf. Or even a puppy. But a baby girl is the most precious thing in the world."

"Glad to hear you say that."

Reaching into his pocket, the new papa offered Dr. McTree a handful of coins. The physician stared at the money, clearly torn.

"I know times are hard, what with the drought and all. No one's paying anyone these days."

"I have it and we're obliged to you. Doctors have to eat, too."

"Won't set you back?"

"I have money for seed."

Choosing two, the doctor pocketed them. "Thank you."

"Don't want my child coming into the world owing."

"You never have owed me, Seth. In fact," he debated, chewing the words before speaking, "it's really I that owe you."

Whether from obstinacy or legitimate ignorance, he made McTree explain. "How's that?"

"I had never seen one man take on an entire town, before. You did that. And with honor."

Twisting his lips into a grimace, the farmer pushed open the door and walked out, leaving the physician to follow. Unlooping the reins of the horse from a split rail fence, newly erected, he maintained control while effecting to check his carpentry.

"I didn't really have time to put this up. Most all winter I've been out in the woods choppin' firewood. Didn't have the strength to do it durin' the summer months; nor into the fall. Not havin' any water takes a toll out of a man."

"It does that." Realizing the farmer would have his say, McTree held back from asking for the reins.

"Or scroungin' the prairie, sawin' up them trees uprooted in the floods."

"Yes. Riding out here, I hardly recognized the landscape. A lot's changed. Had to stop more than a few times to get my bearings."

"Funny," Seth agreed, blowing air through his nostrils. "That's what happened to me, Doctor. All through Belinda's sickness, I had to keep remindin' myself where I was. And what life was all about. I cain't say I always knew." He affectionately scratched the carriage horse behind the ears, seemingly oblivious to the way his speech pattern degenerated. "Week after week, month after month, until I was adrift at sea. There wasn't anything I could do. I was jest helpless, watchin' her die before my eyes.

"A man's sympathy goes only so far, doctor. I suppose you see that in your work. When people first hear of a tragedy, they feel bad an' do what they can to make matters easier. But as time wears on, they sort of become used to it, an' by and by, they get tired of it. It's almost as though they start blamin' the sick person for bein' a burden."

"I have noticed such a phenomenon."

"That's the way the people of Lawrence treated me. In the beginnin', they was solicitous. That wore down to tolerant, then finally outright soreness on the subject. While none of 'em had to deal with what I was facin', jest seein' me became a boil on their backsides."

McTree might have said, *I remember,* but Seth well knew he did.

"After a year or so, their sympathy became, 'When is she gonna die? When is it all gonna be over?'"

"It was a horrible disease that gripped her, Seth -- they were afraid. You can't blame them for that."

"Oh, I blame them, all right. Maybe not for their fear -- fear that whatever she had might sneak up on them one night an' grip 'em -- but for their hardness. It blinded 'em. Made 'em edgy. Like a dog that's bit a toad and got poison in his mouth. He backs off and gets cranky but he still wants to bite. That's the way they was. Still wantin' to bite. They started blamin' that 'toad' -- the woman I loved -- fer all their troubles. So that by the time she got around to dyin' in that horrible way, they was suspicious -- lookin' fer trouble. Too hard, doctor."

"I'm sorry."

Seth backed the horse away from the hitch, but did not relinquish the reins.

"Instead of bein' thankful the good Lord finally took her, all of a sudden it was, 'We don't like the way she died. It wasn't natural. A woman don't jest fall down an old well. She jumped in to end it all." His cheeks flushed. "All those God-fearin' folks started waggin' their fingers, playin 'holy-er than thou.' Suicide, they called it, purposeful' forgettin' all the agony that woman endured. I suppose they thought she shoulda kept on cryin' and writhin' around in that terrible misery, draggin' herself an' me an' her children down wid her."

He began walking, leading the horse down the path. McTree followed at a respectful distance, not willing to get too close while the hurt played itself out. If Seth had anointed him listener for the town and perhaps a representative of their collective guilt, he would bear the burden.

"'We don't want her buried in our cemetery,' they said. Right out. To my face." He bared teeth. "Called for an inquest, they did. All those pious citizens; all them who knew what I'd been through. 'Look into it,' they said. As if their damn kirkyard was a sacred place. Good enough fer hanged men and drunkards but not an innocent woman."

Grasping the reins too hard, the horse balked and whinnied. Seth held his anger in check long enough to assuage the animal with a pat on the neck before resuming.

"An' then it was, 'Mebbe Seth done away wid her, himself. Mebbe he jest got tired of her an' took her out to that well an' pushed her down. Broke her neck. That's murder. Mebbe the sheriff outta look into that, too."

"No one really believed that."

He snorted. "I think they did. Might be some of 'em still do. I don't care. Fer myself, I coulda borne their accusations. But they didn't let it go at that. Once the judge threw out the charges -- against me -- they took up agin' Peter. That, Dr. McTree was a sin."

"Yes, it was."

"He was only a little boy. Jest four years old. He hardly remembered his ma when she was well. Jest her pain an' sufferin'. An' then she was gone. Buried out in my pasture became them damn do-gooders didn't want her buried in consecrated ground. He knew it weren't right. Is it any wonder he took to cryin' for his ma? Went to her grave an' listened to her talk? Tried to dig her up so's he could hear her better?"

"No wonder at all."

"Oh, but doctor, there was a wonder. A great wonder swept through Lawrence. A hell-bent-for-leather wonder. An' they all knew. He was bewitched." Fury welling in his breast, his fists clenched. "Bewitched. That's what they said. Wouldn't have nothin' to do wid me -- or them innocent babes. I couldn't send 'em to school, I couldn't even go to church fer fear they start in on him wid all that devil talk. Got to be so's I couldn't take him into town -- jest goin' in fer supplies was a misery. Everyone starin'. 'He's the father of a bewitched boy. Don't go near 'im. He's got the devil on his shoulder.'"

"They were a bunch of old ninnies; afraid of their own shadow. No one had ever heard of a cancer, before." Putting his bag in the carriage, McTree wrung his hands. "I tried to tell them Belinda suffered from a disease process. No more and no less evil than a burst appendix."

Seth Ward might not have heard.

"They knew I was all by myself; a man wid two young children to raise an' a farm to run. Did any of them come by to offer help? They did not. Did they even make a funeral meal; or stop by after church wid a basket of food? They did not. No, sir. They made some invisible line around my property an' kept away. When I begged fer a woman to come out an' watch Patricia and Peter so's I could work in the fields, did any of them answer it? Hell, no!"

He spat, then ground the spittle into the dirt.

"If it wasn't fer Nelander -- a complete stranger, tossed outta the sea -- I'd be alone to this day. Wid a boy so torn up and confused in the head I had to put a harness on 'im so's he wouldn't run off any chance he had an' go diggin' agin'. It were she that cured him, doctor. Gave us all a new way of lookin' at things. Made us pirates, she did. Made herself a pirate flag an' hung it right outside on a flag pole. The Jolly Roger."

He finally smiled, a wan, weak but intensely meaningful expression.

"Then we got the bell; fer tellin' time. Eight bells fer midnight; one bell fer 12:30. You tell whether it's night or day by lookin' outside." The smile widened. "She dressed Peter up wid an eye patch an' a cutlass and he became someone brand new. A different boy. One wid pride. One who could defend himself."

Pausing to wipe his forehead, Seth turned back and stared at the pirate flag fluttering in the breeze.

"It were she who suggested I put up the hitchin' rail. On my own, I wouldn'ta done it. What do ya say to that?"

"She is a wise woman."

"Wise in the ways of the sea. Wise in the way of people's thoughts. She played mind games wid 'em, doctor. Took her hot spice chili an' made a stew an' took it to the Fair fer the Eatin' Contest. Pizzoned the lot, she did. Made 'em step back. Reconsider. Called 'em out fer what they was -- cowards an' devils. Tolt them that if there was any bewitchin' in town, it was them who was bewitched. Them, wid the hard hearts."

"And they've come around, Seth. It's good you made that hitching post. To let them know they're forgiven. That things are back to normal."

"Oh, doctor," the embittered man protested, but in a soft, frightening manner, "I ain't fergiven 'em. It's all a part of play actin'. I'll never forgive 'em. Not if I live to be eighty. Not fer what they done to my boy. I'll nod an' shake their hands, an' shop in their stores an' sell my crops and we'll show off our new baby at church -- even have her baptized, if that's what Nelander wants -- but I won't fergit. Now -- how's that fer bein' honorable?"

He held out the reins but at a distance, making McTree reach for them.

"I would say you're a prideful man."

"Too prideful?"

"Not that I could blame you."

"That's fair enough said." Allowing the physician to take the lead, he retreated a step, hands shaking. "Don't know why I went off on you like that." Tongue pressed against his cheek, he forced himself to speak properly. "I'm sorry. You were good to us -- Belinda and I. You stood by us. Spoke up at the trial. I always counted you as a friend. You and the Windsors. Losing them was a hurt."

"It's too bad Beth wasn't able to come back to see the baby born. I'm sure she wanted to."

"I didn't expect it -- it was Nelander who hoped. I knew Beth wouldn't come. When a family runs off the land they loved, it's asking too much. We survived the drought. Can't say I coulda done it without Nelander's money, but we saw it through. They packed up an' left. Things have gone bad for them; real bad. They never got that farm in the Dakotas Terrance talked about. Never made it that far. Just to some stink hole in the Nebraska Territory. I don't see as how they can get out. Our good news is just another reminder what they gave up."

"But you tried. You invited them."

"Did more than that." He scuffed his foot, making a small trench in the land. "You know we bought their place.... In case they might reconsider. It's a weight on me, doctor. A debt owin' the bank I'm hard pressed to pay."

Clearing his throat, Captain Seth Ward waved away his own words. "No matter. We'll see it through. There," he indicated, pausing to listen as Patricia rang the bell, making the passage of another half hour. "What we've really gone an' done is increase the property we own. Added to the 'ship' we call *Pirate Treasure*. I expect Nelander'll find buried gold on it, yet."

"If anyone can, she's the one to do it." Holding out his hand, Dr. Hank McTree offered it. "I'm proud to know you, Captain. I said I owe you and I mean it."

"But your words didn't make sense."

"You taught me the power of patience. And love. And about how a man fights back. Not with his fists but from the strength of his soul."

"I had help."

"Then about how a man doesn't give up on life, even with the odds stacked against him." Wrapping the reins around his hand, the physician slowly climbed aboard the buggy. "I'll be around tomorrow, something doesn't come up. You need me -- for anything -- don't hesitate to call."

Finally, Seth grinned. This time, with humor.

"I'll hesitate. But I'll call."

He waved but did not stay to watch the doctor work his way down the road. He had chores to do. But first, he had to go inside. A new mother and a babe were awaiting his kiss.

## CHAPTER 3

"I've brought you some tea." Tiptoeing in so as not to disturb the sleeping baby, Seth handed the cup to his wife. "If you get it down, I've got some beef broth on the stove."

Sipping the beverage, Nelander rolled the hot liquid around in her mouth, swallowed, then quickly finished the remainder. Handing it back, she quipped, "Next time, less tea."

"Too many tea leaves?"

"Not enough rum."

"Ah. That was Peter's idea."

"He is a seaman after my own heart. I predict a great future for that boy."

"As a drunk?"

"A man with a judicious sense of liberally dispensing alcohol has an admiralty awaiting."

Accepting the cup, Seth unthinkingly yelled over his shoulder.

"The first officer wants more tea!"

"Shhh!" Nelander warned, indicating the infant. Startled by his lapse, he jumped, finger to his own lips.

"Shhh. Or damn!" The new parents froze, critically observing their offspring. When the baby did not wake, both heaved a sigh of relief. "Something I'm going to have to get used to. Aboard ship, it's become a habit to holler."

She smiled at his reference, then motioned Peter inside. "I most heartily ratify your choice of drink, young master. More of the same, if you please."

Bouncing on his toes, the boy took possession of the cup.

"I knew you would."

Scampering off, the adults had a moment to themselves.

"You were long bidding farewell to the doctor."

"Had to get a few things off my chest. He approved your hitching fence, by the way."

"Did he?" She guessed the conversation. "He expects we will have visitors?"

"I suppose he thinks we are more acceptable of late."

"I am glad to hear it."

He arched an eyebrow. "Are you?"

"For the sake of the crew. I have found your company more than enough to satisfy."

"Are you sure? I know you miss the Windsors."

"I do. But I must look at them now as shipmates who have signed aboard another vessel. As I should have done when they left. That was my mistake."

The pain hurt and he glanced down.

"You would, perhaps, prefer the company of another woman?"

"You forget. I am not used to women's' company at all. Aside from wishing to share the birth of our child with another, I hoped to learn from Beth. Other than that, I did not view her as a female but as a friend. As for company, I do not feel any great lack. One makes do with what one has."

"That is a lonely thought."

"No more for me than you."

Leaning against the bed board, Seth nodded. "I suppose that is true. I've kept to myself do long, having anyone else here would seem an intrusion. Tragedy teaches self-reliance."

Gently rubbing the back of Nelander's neck, he sighed in contentment. "Dr. McTree did remind me of two things I had overlooked."

"And they are?"

"First, a name for our daughter. What is your preference?"

"I would leave that to you."

"No. It is a mother's prerogative."

"And if I chose a name you do not like?"

"I shall spring up, run around the room several times, bang my head against the wall and convince myself that was my choice all along."

"Who named Patricia and Peter?"

"Belinda."

"Were they called after family members? Her own mother and father, perhaps?"

"No."

"Then I shall name our daughter Paula."

"Why? Has it a significance to you?"

"Not at all. It is a strong name and it begins with a 'P.'"

He missed the obvious. "Why a 'P'?"

"Because both Patricia and Peter begin with that letter. I would not break with tradition."

"Paula Ward. I like it. It has the right... cadence."

"A good word," she agreed. "Cadence. You never cease to amaze me."

"We have both been educated from books rather than teachers. I think of it as another bond between us."

"And the other thing the doctor reminded you of?"

"Baptism."

"I would have her baptized. But not by the so-called Reverend Ginnis. His hands are not clean."

"Who, then?"

"If the Windsors were here, I would ask them to stand as godparents and baptize Paula. But as I have been disappointed in that, you shall do it, yourself."

If she expected an objection, Seth did not oblige.

"I will do it. In three days' time, if all be well."

Nelander inwardly cringed, cradling the baby close. "All will be well. She is healthy."

"She is perfect."

"It is settled, then."

A light knock on the door diverted their attention from a parent's natural fear of early infant mortality.

"I have brung the tea."

"You have brought the tea."

Scrunching his eyes at the correction, Peter and Patricia entered, she carrying a tray this time. Upon it lay a long green stalk.

"There weren't any flowers to pick, it being so early, but I found this," Patricia explained. "It's a wild onion. They're always the first up in spring. I thought because you like onions so well, it would do."

"It is exactly what I would have wished."

"Keeps away the scurvy aboard ship."

"Precisely right. Your townspeople may think it odd to see a woman eat a raw onion, but to me it is not only a delicacy but a necessity. It is a good plant with which to welcome a new arrival."

Grasping the stalk, Nelander put it between her teeth and chewed the end. Patricia winked at her brother.

"See? I told you she would eat it."

He made a face. "Drink your tea before it gets cold."

Nelander tried it and kept a stoical expression. But just barely. "Good," she managed. Peter bounced.

"You liked the first cup so I thought I would add more rum to the second."

"Twice as nice."

Captain Ward tried the concoction for himself and choked. Swallowing some and letting the rest dribble out his mouth, he gasped, "Where's the tea?"

"Oh, it's in there."

"One part tea and nine parts rum."

"Tastes good, don't it?"

"Next time," he grumbled, "make it the other way around."

"We're seamen, Captain."

"Well, don't think you're going to have it like this all the time. Rum is for special occasions."

"Damn!"

"And never mind the cussing." Nelander laughed. The crew shared the private joke, leaving the captain out in the cold. He shivered. "All right. Enough of this frivolity. I've got some cleaning up to do and then we're going to let the first officer get some sleep. Patricia, get me some fresh bed clothes; Peter, a bucket of hot water and some lye soap. Hop to it."

They took him literally and hopped to their assigned tasks. Helping Barbara into a chair, he scrubbed the floor, washed down the bed frame and flipped the mattress. When all had been readied, he helped his wife back to bed. She smiled gratefully.

"Next time is my turn."

The statement gave him a start. "The next time? When I have a baby, you mean?"

"Would if I could, sir, but I meant cleaning out the stall after Bessie has a calf."

"Oh. I am relieved to hear it." Motioning she close her eyes, he crossed the room. He almost escaped unscathed when she remarked, "Damned right you are."

He coughed and ran for cover.


Three days later, March 7th, 1860, a Wednesday, the Ward family gathered together on the porch. The wind blew crisp and clean with a tantalizing reminder that spring lay around the corner.

"Everyone in the wagon," the commanding officer announced. "We're off to a baptism."

"Where are we going, Papa Captain?"

"To a very special place I know." He winked at Nelander. "Do you?"

"I have an idea."

"I said I would take you there when the time is right. Can't think of a better one."

Piling the group aboard, he took the reins and gently slapped them over the horse's back. "Giddy-up, Blaze."

Driving southwest at a slow, even pace, they soon deviated off the road and onto an untilled field. Tiring of the progress, Patricia and Peter jumped down, running ahead. Amid their shouting and cries of "Catch me if you can!" Seth turned to Nelander.

"I want to take you around the long way. Come upon the valley from the direction I first saw it. It won't be covered in green but the creek ought to be flowing. That'll give you an idea."

"It is what I hoped."

Maneuvering further west, then circling around, Seth finally brought the wagon to a halt on the rim of a dale. Long, wide sides sloped down into a flat landscape, perfectly parted by a running stream. To the north lay a natural opening, wide enough to admit several wagons, side-by-side. Opposite, where the valley ended at a sharp "V" grew a stand of weeping willows. Ten yards before the creek disappeared underground at the base of the southern wall, the current ran over a series of rocks, creating a small waterfall.

"This is it. My private corner; one I first discovered when I was a little boy."

Absorbing the vista with a kinship of awe, Nelander trembled with excitement.

"I can see why it appealed to you. Quiet, isolated and... magical."

"It's what brought me back. Otherwise, I probably would have bought a farm closer to where I was born. When I found it had already been sold, I almost didn't stay. Don't know why I did, really."

"On the hope that one day it would be yours. And now it is."

"Ours," he underscored. "If you hadn't talked me into buying the Windsor property, I never would have thought about it."

The reminder that she had asked him to assume a debt on the errant hope the family would return caused pain and she flinched.

"I'll make it right by you. We'll sell the rest of their land... or rent it out. But this, we'll keep."

"Don't know what for. It's pretty but no good for crops."

"Pretty has its own reward."

He made no comment and she knew he saw no gain. But she had made a promise and meant to keep it. Inspiration would come.

She started to get out but he held her back.

"No, Barbara. I don't want you climbing down the hill. Not until you're stronger. I'll bring the wagon through the north end."

Reluctantly acceding to his wish, she nodded and he urged the horse forward so they entered the vale from the broad opening. Putting two fingers to his mouth, Seth gave a sharp whistle, summoning the children.

"We've got a ceremony to perform and then back to work. A farm doesn't keep itself, you know."

Accepting the baby, he assisted his wife from the wagon, keeping her hand as they approached the creek. Descending to bended knee, the pair waited as Patricia and Peter came close behind. After pausing a moment for silent prayer, Seth dipped his hand, cupping as much water as it would hold. Allowing it to warm, he drizzled a stream over the infant's forehead.

"In the name of the Father, the Son and the Holy Ghost, I baptize thee, Paula Nelander Ward."

The mother's sharp intake of breath preceded a kiss on his cheek.

"Thank you for that."

"Paula is part of me and part of you. It is only fitting she carry both our names."

Ignorant of the honor bestowed, Paula scrunched her eyelids and cried.

"Here, let me take her." Quickly pulling the bunting over the baby's head, Nelander cradled her with a proud smile. "I cannot say either one of us behaved any better at our own baptisms."

"Undoubtedly not."

"What about me, Captain?" Patricia inquired. "Did I cry?"

Seth puffed air into his cheeks. "My recollection is that neither of you did anything your first year but cry and eat."

"And something else, besides," Barbara teased. "The end product of all that eating."

"That, too!"

Two grins, two pouts and one sleepy countenance remanded to the wagon.

It had been a good morning. The best, in fact.

Casting a glance behind as they returned by the shorter route, Nelander had a feeling it was only the beginning.

And that they had a long way to go.

Fair weather and foul.

# CHAPTER 4

The remnant of a charred log collapsed in the fireplace, scattering embers over the hearth rug. With a grunt of annoyance, Seth stirred from his chair but Nelander waved him off. Slipping easily off her seat, she stomped the burning sparkles with slippered feet.

"See that you do not burn yourself," he warned. "The soles of your shoes are thin." Peering closer, he hissed in disapproval. "It is the unseasoned wood. Burns unevenly. The sap inside boils and explodes."

"Yes. It is a terrible pity. I see it has left a black mark on this priceless Oriental carpet. I don't know how we shall replace it."

Peter crawled over on all fours to have a gander at the damage. "Is it really an Oriental carpet and what does that mean?"

"It is a rag rug," his father elucidated with less than enthusiasm.

"An Oriental carpet comes all the way from the Orient. Get me the atlas and I will show you."

He eagerly brought out the book which Nelander had given Seth as a wedding present and flipped the pages. Pointing to a large land mass, he inquired, "Have you been there?"

"That is Central Europe. No, on my many voyages I seldom traveled inland."

"Why not?"

"To do so would have taken weeks and my father was never one to dawdle. We spent no more time ashore than to unload the cargo, sell it and take on new. The only exceptions were when the ship needed repairs or upkeep."

"And then what did you do?"

"Occasionally I would take a carriage out into the countryside. Or tour whatever foreign city we happened to be at."

"Name some."

"Here: this is Liverpool. It is a major port in England. England, as you recall, used to be the mother country of the United States. Their armies fought a war against the British so you could be free."

"So you could be free, too" he objected.

"In a manner of speaking; now that I have come to Kansas to live. But I was born in Nova Scotia. That belongs to Canada."

"Didn't they want to be free?"

"I suppose the people there felt they had all the freedom they needed. They were not so heavily regulated or taxed as were those in the Colonies."

"Why not?"

"Money," Captain Ward snorted, folding the newspaper he had been reading and dropping it to the floor. "Politics always seem to revolve around money. Those who have it want more. Like the king of England. Those who earn it want to keep it. Or at least see it invested for their own good."

Detecting a note of frustration, for the issue of money was never far from either of their minds, Barbara redirected her attention to the atlas. "I have been to London and France. But not so far as Paris. That is the capital. And here -- this is how the *Bottom Dollar* sailed from Boston to San Francisco."

Tracing an outline from Massachusetts down the eastern seaboard and then around South America, her finger flew up the Pacific.

"That's a long way."

"It is. And takes many months. That is the reason the cargo we carry brings such a good profit. The people in California must pay for the cost of transport as well as the price of the goods."

"That doesn't seem fair."

"Perhaps not. But if they do not pay for it, who will? Think of it this way," she explained, settling the open book on her lap. "If Mr. Anson at the General Store brings out a delivery of flour and corn meal -- or if Mr. Tinker sharpens the captain's plow and returns it himself, don't we pay them for the service?"

"I suppose we do."

"Why is that?" When he hesitated, she answered. "Because they have gone to considerable time and effort. It is the same with a ship, whether it is owned by a firm or the captain. They must pay the officers and the crew. They have to provide food and drink during the voyage. This is a considerable expense. They must see the vessel is in good operating condition: the hull clean and sound. The sails strong, without rips or tatters.

Then, there are innumerable sundries. Rope. Tar. Fittings. All that must be balanced on the books before they can break even, much less make a livelihood."

"You know a lot."

"I kept Captain Nelander's ledgers. I often saw to the outfitting and bought the cargo. I paid the crew."

"Did you ever not make any money?"

"Yes."

"What happens then?"

Seth leaned forward. "I am interested in hearing that, myself."

Inwardly cringing, she readily explained. "First and foremost, the crew must be paid. It is a bad commander who undertakes a voyage without that much capital on hand, regardless of the outcome."

"What if he doesn't pay them?"

"They have the right of redress. That means they can sue in court for what is rightfully theirs. If no wages are forthcoming, the ship is sold at auction and they are paid from the proceeds."

"You mean the captain loses his ship?"

"The same as if we do not pay the bank," Seth interjected. "They repossess our farm."

Patricia brushed against his arm. "That's what happened to the Windsors, isn't it? They left and Mr. Provost took it away."

"Yes. That is exactly what happened."

"And then we bought it. But they didn't come back, papa."

He did not answer and Nelander went back to the atlas.

"This is the Orient, Peter. I have never been there but had my father lived, we were to sail for China."

"Would you have bought Oriental carpets?"

"I suppose so. That, and tea. And Chinese lanterns and fireworks and all sorts of exotic things."

"Where would you have sold them?"

"In New York City. Or Boston."

"But didn't you ever go home? To Nova Scotia?"

"Of course. My mother lives there, yet. And most of the crew were Canadians. They wanted to return and see their wives."

"I bet you missed your mama."

Nelander hesitated, pursed her lips, then shrugged. "She was, in many ways, a stranger to me. I left when I was five. My father needed me to work aboard ship, the same as your father needs you to help around the farm. Going home was awkward for me; occasionally I stayed in her house, but as I got older, I remained on the *Bottom Dollar,* seeing to preparations for the next voyage. One can never leave a ship without anyone aboard."

"In case someone steals it?"

"That, too. But there are always matters to attend. Harbormasters to settle with; chandlers and the like. Berths to fill."

"Were you ever lonely?"

"That is a hard question to answer. Let us say if I were, I did not dwell on it. I would find solace in my books; or in work. Or by climbing the mast and communing with the sea."

"But the sea cannot talk back."

"You would be surprised. You know Herman is angry when the ruff on the back of his neck raises?" The children nodded.

"Better stay away. He might bite."

"And yet he has not said so. You understand him because you have grown to know his ways. The ocean is much like that. It has no words but it communicates with sound and sight and smell." She drew them nearer, placing her arms around their backs. "Just as Herman's ruff is an indication of danger, so, too, the waves change their shape. In calm, they are low and somewhat roundish. As circumstances alter, they rise, become more peaked. During storm, they are white-capped, as we say, and pointed, like spears."

Feeling his own mood captivated by the vast panorama Nelander painted in living color, Seth joined them, squatting on the floor to equalize his height with the rest.

"Go on," he urged.

She met his eyes and swelled with importance.

"Then there is the wind. At times, as quiet as a church mouse. You lean across the bow and swear a hush has been draped across the watery world.

You become accustomed, you see, to the lapping of wave against wood. And then you hear it; a low, special whisper."

"What does it say?" Peter asked.

"All is well. All is well. And more, besides." Nelander raised a finger. "If you listen closer, you can hear -- or feel, or sense -- I do not know how better to describe it -- the movement of life beneath the surface. Hundreds of millions of creatures; some so small you cannot see them with the naked eye."

"Then how do you know they are there? Besides feeling them?" This, from Patricia.

The seaman straightened, redirecting her gaze to the ceiling.

"You have heard of a telescope?" They had not. "Binoculars, then? Lenses which you put to your eyes to bring the distant close?"

"Ah. Yes." Seth spoke with determination, startling his listeners with his authority. "My younger brother wrote of it. Once. A long time ago. You recall I said he had joined the army."

"Norman."

He nodded. "He had been sent to a fort in the Cimarron. To defend against Indians or Mexicans, I am not sure which. He was a dragoon."

"Explain, please."

"Mounted soldiers who fight on horseback as well as on foot." She motioned her comprehension. "He bought a pair of binoculars at the post. Special lens, like eye glasses, only much more powerful, bring distant objects up close. So that a man may make a determination at a far piece if an object be an outcropping of rock or a buffalo or an enemy."

Other than the name and a casual reference, Barbara had never heard him speak freely of Norman. To do so now thrilled her, for it drew the mysterious brother closer into their world.

"A telescope works on the same principle," she proceeded. "Those who study the heavens use it to examine the moon. And the stars. Did you know," she demanded, eyes twinkling, "there are craters on the moon? And mountains?"

"No!" the crew chimed in unison and stark wonderment.

"On a clear night, if you look closely, you can see the shadows. With a telescope they are revealed with great clarity."

"Do people live there?"

"Not that I ever heard," she chuckled. "But it would not surprise me."

"The Man in the Moon," Seth grinned. "You know," he directed at the girl and boy, "when you were very young, I used to take you out into the fields. We would lie on our backs and stare into the heavens. Without much tryin', we put a face to Old Mr. Moon."

"I do remember that, papa!" Patricia cried. "Old Mr. Moon. And sometimes, he would wink at us."

"I believe he did."

"But I don't remember," Peter cried. "Why don't I?"

"You were a baby. Hardly old enough to walk."

"Let us do it again, Captain. Please. I want to see Old Mr. Moon."

"You are too old for that now," he brushed aside, disturbed, perhaps, by other memories of the time. Kissing her finger then tapping it against his nose, Barbara smoothed over the hurt.

"You have a new child now. And she will want to see the Man in the Moon wink at her. And so will I."

He grabbed her finger, kissed it in return and shrugged. "You were speaking about microscopes."

"It is the opposite theory: using lenses to see that which the unaided eye cannot."

"You mean there are things we cannot see?"

"Most certainly. I was in Manhattan once and I went to the Barnum Exhibition. It was a huge building filled with all sorts of... wonders. Two-headed snakes and displays on magnetism and such. It left the head reeling." She rolled her eyes for the audience. "What caught my attention, however, was this microscope, which magnified everything well beyond what you imagined. I bet I stood there an hour staring at cheese."

"Cheese?"

"Indeed so. It was covered with 'microscopic' animalcules; tiny living creatures too small to be seen without aid."

Peter made a face and ducked back. "Pizzon."

"Apparently not, for after the demonstration the instructor ate the cheese."

Seth grunted. "Must be like chili. You get used to it, you can eat it fine. But on first taste, it burns out your mouth."

"Melts yer teeth," Patricia supplied.

"I don't know. But I brought a cup of sea water with me the next day and stared at that through the microscope. It was filled with similar beasties. It gave me a great reflection on the world in which we live -- how much we do not know." Shaking her head, she resumed her narrative. "Those are what I heard when I listened to the sea. The great and the tiny. The fishes and the mammals and those too small -- by themselves -- to make noise. But gathered in the tens of thousands, who knows?"

"And what else?" Master Peter begged.

"Smell. The sea has a way of communicating by smell. We shall use able-bodied Herman, again. He is always sniffing all over the place. Sometimes, he finds a particular odor which appeals to him and he digs in the ground. Or he smells something on the wind currents and goes off to investigate. Dogs and most animals can identify smells we humans cannot. The first thing they do when seeing a stranger is to sniff him out. They may appraise with their eyes but it is the other senses which reveal more."

"He puts his nose in dog poo."

"Well, I did not say what he sought was always pleasant to us," she laughed. "A seaman can smell that which a landlubber cannot. A change in temperature; or the saline content of the water. The wind being blown from a different direction; the distant odors of land."

"And that's why you weren't lonely?"

"It was one way. And then, of course, there are all the legends of the sea. The spirits which wander; the gods who watch."

"Enough for one night!" Seth decided, slapping his knee. "Or you'll have us all dreaming of Davy Jones."

Right on cue, Paula began to cry. Little fists curled, pink toes kicking skyward, she had had enough of talk. Time for more corporeal concerns.

"The baby is hungry."

"The two of you get ready for bed," Barbara directed. "I shall feed her."

"What of the captain?" Peter teased. "What's he gonna do?"

"First officers do not tell their commanders what to do. But if I were him," Nelander decided, "I would change into my nightshirt and crawl under the covers. The sun is up earlier these days and a farmer has much to do. I would not have him grousing about when Mr. Noise Box brings the dawn."

"And a terrible loud demon he is," Seth teased, remembering her earliest encounter with the formidable rooster.

They made their preparations and by two bells -- nine o'clock -- they were snug as bugs in a rug.

Even if those bugs could only be seen under P.T. Barnum's microscope.

Face flush from exertion, Captain Ward drew in on the reins.

"Whoa, boy. Whoa."

Blaze halted just before the hitching rail, flicked his tail then whinnied in hunger. When no one came out to greet the new arrivals, a look of consternation flittered behind his orbs.

"Nelander! Patricia! Peter!" No point summoning Paula. When Seth found the others, she would be with them.

Unaccustomed to receiving no response, he abandoned his original intent to drive to the barn. Hoping down, he drew off his gloves, grasped the rolled side of his hat and removed it. Running a hand through long hair, he took a step toward the door, raising his voice.

"Nelander?"

No answer. Leaping up onto the porch without benefit of steps, he stuck his head inside. All quiet. Half a dozen paces took him to their bedroom. The baby's cradle lay empty.

Normally not a worrying man, the absence of his family disturbed him. Despite Dr. McTree's assertion that things had returned to normal between himself and the town of Lawrence, he would not put anything past the townspeople. A poor lambing season, an outbreak of chicken pox, or a run on the bank could set tongues wagging. It would not take much for "bad luck" to turn into "bewitchment." And it would start all over again.

"Nelander!"

Returning to the yard, he grabbed the bell cord and pulled. Not to set the time, but in summons.

*Where are you?*

"Patricia! Peter!"

He rang the heavy brass bell again, purposely tolling ten times. Aboard ship, the counting went to eight then started again at one. Any more than that would warn the initiated they were needed.

*All hands on deck.*

The absence of Herman should have been a comfort. Were something amiss, the dog would have raced out to meet him, barking and pawing. The fact he, too, had disappeared pointed to a family outing rather than a danger. Yet dogs were fallible creatures, unable to defend themselves or their charges against a bullet. He might just as likely discover the animal shot out back as gaily leading the parade home.

Following tracks did not present an option. While the ground was moist from recent rainfall, too many, scuffled back and forth, eliminated any possibility of a trail.

Anxiety mounting, he rang the bell another ten times.

"Where are you?" he demanded to the empty sky. "You knew I was coming back this afternoon. I am hungry," he added, as if that would have the effect of creating the family out of nothingness. "I want to eat. Where is my dinner?"

*They have gone into the fields. Nelander has brought a book to read aloud. Or they have walked down to the pond. To check out the best place to launch the dingy I have not yet made.*

Reasonable explanations.

Life was full of reasonable explanations. Even death, the hardest to accept of all life's eventualities, might be explained away as "natural."

Returning to the house, he wandered into the kitchen. If they had been taken by surprise, he would discover the dishes unwashed, perhaps water still in the basin beneath the pump. All appeared as it should. The beds, too, had been made, with Nelander's penchant for "nautical corners." Casting about, he searched for a book she might have selected, then abandoned the effort as hopeless. While most had originally been his, he could not identify, without a thorough examination, if any were missing.

Rubbing his breast where he had suddenly developed an ache, Seth sniffed, wiping his nose with the back of his hand. An act which reeked of poor upbringing, he had no concern for appearances. With no one watching, he might have stripped naked to change from town to work clothes without eliciting a single whistle.

Hesitantly touching his palm to the stove, Seth determined it had not been used since early morning. About the time he left. They had not, then, cooked a noonday meal for themselves. The pain in his chest increased.

*I am being needlessly suspicious. Foolish,"* he chided. *There are no signs of a struggle. All is as it should be.*

Except for the empty house.

His hand shook. What good the seed he had bought in town if he had no one to grow it for? What matter a crop or a harvest without a first officer and crew with whom to share the rewards?

The descriptions brought a tortured smile to his lips. First officer. Crew. How much Barbara Nelander had changed his life. Not only in obvious ways, but in how he thought, which words he used to express himself.

She, the wayward seafarer who had become his friend, then his wife. Mentor to his children; mother to their own. The woman who dressed in men's clothes because those had been what she wore working aboard ship. The sailor who could hold her rum better than he, cuss with vigor and who expected to "pull her weight" when it came to chores and farming.

He loved her and love hurt.

Seth Ward had almost forgotten how much.

# CHAPTER 5

He caught sight of movement out of the corner of his eye. A small head bobbing over the distant hill. Followed by another and then another. A tail poking out among the tall grasses.

He waved because that is what men did when they were relieved. A single, solitary motion of the hand.

*Welcome home. I knew everything was all right, all along.*

Kansas farmers did not weep for joy or otherwise.

That emotion they saved for funerals.

When the mourners had all gone home. Leaving him alone.

"Papa!"

Meeting them half way, he waved again and called, "I'm home and no one was here to meet me."

"We left a note," Nelander explained, laughter in her eyes because she had not read his mind. "On the table. Didn't you see it?"

"Must have blown off," he lied. He had looked everywhere but the table.

"And anyway, we did not expect you until after dark. Why are you home so soon?"

"There wasn't any waitin' at the Feed and Grain. They filled my order right off."

"Why is that?"

"No one's buyin'." Inadvertently dropping the "g's" from the end of words, he expressed a hidden concern. "The farmers don't have any money. At least not much, I guess."

"I am sorry to hear it."

"Where have you been?"

"We went out to the Windsor's farm, Captain," Patricia supplied.

"Our farm, you mean," he grunted with more ire than intended. "What for?"

"To clean it up, some," the adult explained, resting a hand on the boy's shoulder. "If we're going to try and sell or rent it out, I want to show it off to best advantage. Hasn't been anything done there since they left. An inch of dust over everything."

"I weeded the vegetable patch, Captain," Peter importantly advised. Seth's eye twitched.

"If you put that energy into weedin' our own garden, I'd be obliged. We've got beans an' pumpkins an' onions an' cucumbers to put in." He meant the addition of the last two items to smooth over his temper.

"I will, sir. Tomorrow, for sure."

"And what'd you do?" he demanded of his elder daughter.

"Swept the floors and washed the windows. Two of them were broken, sir. From the snow storms. I expect we'll have to replace 'em."

"I expect not."

The gruff tone silenced the conversation and they walked back without further comment. Arriving at the yard, he motioned the boy.

"Come with me and help get the wagon unloaded. Then I want the horse rubbed down and fed. Patricia, check the chickens. And milk the cow."

Not Blaze. Not Bessie. Just, "the horse." And "the cow."

Holding her thoughts, Nelander went into the horse, changed the baby and tucked her to bed. By the time the others returned, dinner had been placed on the stove. Seth retired to his rocking chair and sat glumly by himself until called to table. The meal and clean-up proceeded without comment.

Not until the two youngest had gone to bed did she speak.

"Have I done something wrong? Going to the Windsor's old place? You would have preferred we spend our time here?" He tapped his foot. "Just tell me, Seth. I do not want to displease you. I know there is much to be done, but I thought...." The sentence went unfinished, finally causing him to sigh.

"Of course you did not do anything wrong. And you are exactly right. If we hope to recoup any of the money we wasted on that damn place, we've got to set it to rights." She cringed and turned away. "Where are you going?"

"To get something to read." Carelessly inspecting his stack of periodicals, Nelander selected one at random. "You do not mind?"

"I brought a month's worth of newspapers from town. You may have one of them if you wish."

"And peruse the local gossip? Hector Anson has a new awning outside his store; Tinker Taylor, the blacksmith, has burned himself stoking the fire; his wound is reported to be coming along nicely. All those customers, inconvenienced by the delay in getting their horses shoed may complain to him directly at his residence on Sidewinder Street. Hotel clerk Abel Billup is sporting a new hat these days. A patron of the Tankard's Draft Saloon was discovered under one of the tables yesterday last, having passed out from what Mr. Daft described as an episode of apoplexy."

Without intent, she succeeded in making him guffaw.

"The owner of Tankard's is not 'Mr. Daft.'"

"It sounds like 'draft,'" came the objection. "A slip of the tongue."

Rocking slowly in his chair, he prodded the paper. "What else is in here? It is easier to have you tell me than to read. My eyes are tired."

Taking the *Gazette* with her, Nelander resumed her place and her creative narrative.

"Mrs. Provost, wife of Mr. Christian Provost, president of the Lawrence Bank, recently purchased lace curtains for the windows of their domicile. The fabric came all the way from New York and the design is patterned from draperies described in *Godey's Ladys Book* of July, 1858. The citizens of this city may now boast we have the latest fashion available anywhere west of St. Louis."

"I saw them," he imagined through drooping eye lids. "White. I remember remarking they would be grey by fall. Go on."

"The Right Reverend Ted Ginnis, as he likes to pretend, has taken to offering Bible lessons on Monday and Wednesday nights from 7:00 to 8:00 o'clock. P.M.," she added. "All heathens are welcome. The fee is fifty cents a week, from which two cents is donated to the Women's Charity League."

"Two cents from each student, or two cents out of his combined take?"

Nelander inspected the pretend article, pantomimed turning a page, then shrugged. "It is unclear."

"Two cents a week. What else?"

It did not stretch her mind to conjure other news items.

"As many of you know, the mayor is convening a assemblage of the town's leading men to discuss the matter of waste disposal. The advent of warmer weather has brought to the fore the unsightly -- and odorous -- habit of many town dwellers who dump their chamber pots into the public streets. The first meeting was held on Thursday. In attendance were Mr. Larson, Mr. Timberjohn, Mr. Rockledge and Mr. Wrycomb. Mr. Paulbert was expected, but his flock of pigs escaped and were seen running down Front Street, adding to the general stink found along the boardwalks."

"There is no such thing as a flock of pigs."

"Damn right. It says here Mrs. Hastings caught one, battered it over the head with the flat of an axe and served it for dinner that same evening. Due reparation is to be taken up the next time the circuit judge comes through."

"What is her defense?"

"That it was hers. All porkers look alike when served on white stoneware platters."

"Just so. What else?"

Pleased to have found a subject on which she might amuse, Barbara licked a finger and actually turned a page.

"Guest speaker at the 'Committee on Shit' meeting was Mr. Anson. He advised that privies be limed every six months. A discussion ensued on whether the cost ought to be borne by the private home and business owners, or be assumed by the city. Mr. Anson favored the latter suggestion, as such people were notoriously lax in paying their mercantile bills. Mr. Rockledge saw nothing wrong with the problem and declared Lawrence no more smelly than most cities and a 'sight' better than Topeka. The motion was tabled until the next session."

"I bet he's never been to Topeka. Go on."

"A heavy shipment of crates arrived at the depot last Monday. They were addressed to a 'Mr. Francy.' Such a person is unknown in this city. The crates are being stored until such time as said owner comes to claim them. If no one appears within a reasonable time, they are to be sold at auction. Speculation arose that the crates contained four roulette wheels and were actually purchased by Mr. Daft. Not wanting to be accused of introducing gaming devices to Lawrence, questions swirled on whether this was a nefarious way to justify their presence."

"Prob'ly so." Seth ran a thumbnail against the grain of his stubbled cheek. "But that'd mean *Dick Duggan'd* have to bid on his own merchandise."

"A nominal cost, surely. Who else wants roulette wheels?"

"If they was seasoned wood, I'd make an offer, myself. To burn. Must come with marbles, too." Craning his neck, he stared over at her. "Ever play marbles?"

"I have known sailors who did. But it is difficult aboard ship. Just when you have the shot lined up, she yaws and the pieces roll out of position."

"Never thought of that. What did you play?"

"Cards, mostly. With a deck of fifty-one," she grinned.

"What'd you use for money?"

"Fish bones. By the time a voyage was over, the luckiest had enough to construct a whale. What about you?"

A tinge of red came into his cheeks and his foot moved in rhythm to an unheard melody.

"Oh, I played cards, some, too. Not poker, though."

Anticipating a story, Barbara motioned him on. "Tell me about it."

"There was this fella; name of Billy Bob Bobbin. He was older'n me and Norman. About my brother Rick's age, I'd guess. Lived in town. His father was a merchant of some sort. What was it he called himself? An 'Import/Export Man.' That was it. He brought goods in an' then resold them with a proper markup. Wouldn't have surprised me if he dealt in liquor. Fer the Injuns. Never liked 'im. But Rick was tight with Billy Bob. They hung out together."

Getting up, Seth stretched his legs, wearily rubbing sore muscles. "One night Rick brung somethin' home; hid whatever it was under his mattress. Bein' boys, Norman and I were curious."

"You don't have to be a boy to be curious."

"You woulda been, too," he grinned. "So about a week later when Rick was gone, Norman and I checked. What do you think we found?"

"Tell me."

"A pack of playin' cards, all right. But not the ordinary kind. No, sir. These had pictures on the back. French ladies, I 'spect you'd call 'em."

"I 'spect I'd call them something other than ladies," she guessed.

"Scantily clad, they were." He whistled for effect. "Mighty revealin'. Women dress like that in France?"

"Women all over the world dress like that -- if they're paid for it," she dryly observed.

"Well -- we spent many an hour starin' at them gals. Always puttin' the deck back before Rick came home. Got tired of it after awhile, though."

"Do tell."

"Didn't know how to play poker. My pa didn't take with any immoral games."

"I wonder what he would have said about the cards?"

Seth winked. "Likely would have burned 'em."

"After havin' a gander at your French ladies. So, what did you eventually do with the cards?"

"Used 'em as shooters. You know." He demonstrated by jerking his hand. "Flipped 'em against the wall. The object being to see who could get a leaner."

"I've played that game."

"With cards like those?"

"With better -- or worse, depending on your point of view. Seamen like a bit of titillation, too, you know."

"Seems to me they would have offended you."

She thought and then shrugged. "I didn't think of myself as a woman -- not in that way. So I guess I didn't care. It was just the way it was; part of the world I accepted."

He grunted. "Got to be we played a little rough. Bent some of the edges. That's when Rick found out we'd been under his mattress. He never said anything, then one night, we found a regular pack of playing cards in place of our gals. Took the fun out of shootin'. Never did find out what became of them."

"No doubt Billy Bob's father traded them to the Indians."

He grinned and yawned. "Time for bed."

She went with him and they curled up together. On the whole, Seth decided, he had the best "leaner" of them all.

## CHAPTER 6

She did not convince herself the ship had weathered the storm. No officer worth his salt unbattened the hatches before the sky cleared and the waves subsided. It would have been a fair assumption that Barbara Nelander-Ward had prepared herself for a journey around Cape Hope.

In a figurative sense.

With emphasis on the "hope."

A week after the incident over the Windsor farm, clouds began to gather. This time, her participation in the impending onslaught was more ornamental than functional, in that she bore no direct responsibility for the thunder. No more than Zeus could be blamed for the lightning bolt occasionally dispatched from Olympus.

That god, after all, had minions to do his dirty work.

Arriving home after a long day in the field, Captain Ward heaved his soiled work gloves onto his rocking chair with unusual vigor. One fell to the floor from the force of the blow. He kicked it across the room. Paula began to cry.

Rather than address his pique, Barbara picked up the infant, rocking the babe in her arms.

"Supper will be ready directly. If you will wash up, I will serve you at table."

He grunted and did as told, plopping into his chair, chin resting on elbows. Patricia and Peter assumed their places and the family ate in silence. Afterwards, they gathered in the living room. Nelander lit the lamp. Seth's hand slapped down against the arm rest of his rocker.

"There's an hour's daylight left. If you wish to read, move closer to the window. Or go outside and catch the last rays." Barbara lowered the wick and blew out the flame. Taking a stack of periodicals, she made it half way toward the door before he spoke again. "I didn't mean for you to go. I was addressing the children."

"No. You are right and I do not mind economizing. I will sit on the porch. Come, children. And bring your slates. I want you to practice your letters."

They followed, giving their father a wide berth. No sooner had they settled outside when he flew to the door, standing in the open archway with a scowl of annoyance.

"It is too cold. Come inside at once. We are not so poor that we have to freeze."

Her first inclination was to remain where she had settled, but understanding the underlying problem if not the actual cause, she did not wish to refute his claim on their finances. Motioning inward, the family resumed their original positions in the living room.

"Light-the-lamp."

Striking a second Lucifer and touching it to the wick, the clean globe reflected a cheery flame against the polished metal reflector, augmenting the light. Satisfied that his wishes had finally been realized, Seth picked up the Lawrence *Gazette* and pursued several articles before tiring of the occupation.

"Come," he tried, nodding at his daughter. "Let me see what you have done."

Hesitantly offering her slate, the child balanced on tiptoe, attempting to read his expression.

"These are pictures you have drawn and not letters."

"Yes, sir. I have gotten the alphabet down and I can write sentences."

"Then why draw pictures? Only the ignorant draw shapes in place of words."

"I like to draw, papa. I feel I can express myself better that way. Do you recognize what I have done?"

Taking greater care, then purposely turning the chalkboard upside down, he attempted to identify the scene.

"This is the barn and this --"

Chagrined, she reached out a timorous hand.

"It is the north pasture, sir. There are the new trees, just starting to grow. And the wild flowers. And here... a rabbit, just peering out from behind a rock."

"Ah. So it is. Trees and flowers and a rabbit. Show it to Nelander and see if she can make sense of it. Although I have already given her the answers," he added.

Patricia took the slate and showed the junior officer. Her immediate reaction dispelled Seth's gloom.

"This is excellent! Very well crafted. Right down to the leaves and the rabbit whiskers. How did you develop such skill, Master Patricia?"

"From picture books; but they were never good enough, so I decided to draw my own."

"I am very impressed. You have an artist's eye for detail. And a style of your own. I feel as though I could pick one of the daisies and ruffle the fur of the bunny."

"Try that," Peter offered, "and it will bite you!"

"Indeed, it is lifelike enough to believe so. We will have to buy you a sketch book. And some colored pencils or water paints. All this lacks is some yellow and red and a touch of green here and there to make it a masterpiece. If I buy you those, will you recreate this scene for me on paper?"

"I will be happy to."

"I will make a frame for it," Peter offered. Barbara beamed with pure pleasure.

"Our able-bodied has true talent, Captain. Why did you never tell me?"

He shrugged, then drilled a hand into his pocket.

"There is no money for colored pencils and sketch books."

"But surely they cannot be expensive. I have some 'egg money' saved --"

Rising from her place on the couch, Nelander crossed to the mantel. Prying up the lid of her small red tea chest, designed with a four-masted schooner, she reached inside. Finding nothing, she checked to be certain appearances were not deceiving, then quietly replaced it.

"I see."

Flushing in anger, Seth stomped his foot, hesitated, then stood up. Mouthing words in silence, he choked over them and placed distance from himself and the others as if to mitigate his crime by space.

"The seed. It cost more than expected. And then there are other expenses. I damaged the blade on the plow this afternoon. It will have to be taken to town for repair. The smithy wants his fee just like all the others."

"All right."

Which exonerated the sin but not the hurt of being caught.

"I took your money. Without asking."

"Our money."

"Have it back, then," he cried, tossing out a thin roll of bills. When she refused to take them, he pressed them on Patricia. She sobbed and hid her arms, so the paper fell to the floor.

"Pick them up."

"I do not want a sketch book, papa. Use the money for the plow. And the seed."

"I said pick them up!"

Glancing miserably at Nelander, the child did as directed. When Seth would not give over the tea chest, she replaced the money on the mantel.

"Really. I am happy doing my lessons." Tears glistened at the corners of her eyes. "I should have done the lettering. I will in future."

"Go to bed, damn it," he growled. "You, too, Peter. We must all be up early."

Frightened at his mood, they slunk away, leaving the officers alone. Nelander went back to reading. Shadows in the room lengthened as the lamp wick burned down. Not until one particularly long and mobile shade obscure the print did she take note. The captain, purposely positioning himself in the way, avoided eye contact when he spoke.

"I'm sorry."

"It is not to me you should apologize. But if it will make you feel any better, I accept in the name of the crew. And I am sorry, too, for suggesting we spend money on that which is unnecessary. I thought only to encourage the child. I really was impressed. Her work is excellent; hardly that of a ten-year-old. But we will speak no more of it."

"I didn't want to discourage her. It's just that...." Losing his voice, he rocked back on his heels. "Everything costs money. I am nearly at my wits end. It will be months before I can hope to reap a crop and until then, I don't know what to do."

"We can survive on what we grow in the garden. And fish. I have been to the pond. There is a good, strong stream which flows into it. We can expect catfish. And trout."

"And what of cornmeal to fry it in? Or flour and yeast for bread?" Dropping his head into his hands, Seth's shoulders shook. "I have been through hard times before, but you forget... the sacrifices. And the children. How are they to understand?"

"They are old enough."

"But I cannot endure seeing them suffer. This is a hard life, Nelander."

"Life is meant to be hard. It molds character."

"Do you really believe that?"

"Yes."

He tried, failed, and knit his hands. "This... living from hand to mouth. From season to season. Growing the same crops as everyone else. Dependent, like them, on the same buyers. The first to market sells for the highest price. All the rest receive less, without regard for quality. Do you know what I keep thinking about?"

"Tell me."

"Terrance Windsor's horse, Brandy. He wanted to race him; win a trophy. So he could prove he stood for something. Accomplished more than just eking out a living. And the cattle he wanted to raise. Be more than a farmer, maybe. Sell them for beef. Earn some spendin' money, and then some. Actually put something aside."

"I think about that, too." She rested a hand on the arm of the chair. "But the land is what you love. It is as much a part of you as the sea is to me."

"How do you know that?" he reacted in surprise.

"You told me. But even if you had not, I see it in your face. The way you look when you're out in the field. Bending down to let the soil run through your fingers. Putting in the seed; nurturing it as it grows, as an extension of yourself. Horses and cattle are not your calling. You were born with an affinity for growing things."

"And look where it has gotten me."

"You have a house; a barn --"

"Two mortgages."

"One of which I have burdened you with. But I will make it right. I swear."

"We thought to do good. Enough said. Will you come to bed?"

"In a while. Your scientific journals have me mesmerized. There is so much new to me in their pages. I want to learn, Seth. And perhaps...." She tried a smile. "One day, make a contribution."

"You do not consider little Paula a contribution?"

"I consider her an addition. I speak of something... I will not say substantial. More profitable, perhaps?"

"If the editors take to printing currency, that would be most useful. Perhaps you could write them a letter and suggest it."

"I think that an excellent idea."

He bent over to blow out the lamp but she prevented him with a slight motion. "Leave me to my thoughts."

He shuffled across the floor and when he caught her attention, toothily grinned. "I will miss you beside me."

"You will be asleep in two minutes."

"It will be a long two minutes," and added with a tease, "What part of two minutes is a 'bell'?"

"One fifteenth."

The immediate response took him aback.

"How did you come upon the answer so quickly?"

"A bell is thirty minutes. Ergo, one minute equates to one thirtieth; two minutes twice that, or a fifteenth."

"I can see why your father had you handle the payroll. Not even a sailor worth his salt could best you in an argument over his wages."

"I take that as a high compliment, sir."

He danced a little jig, pulling a comical face while imitating her Canadian accent. "'I see here, Master Peg-Leg you spent two days, seventeen hours and eleven minutes on shore leave. That is seventeen and eleven more than authorized. That, sir, I detracted from your salary. Then, you drew a pair of drawers and five candy sticks from the company store: for which I must dock you $2.20. And then," he pursued, wetting a finger to simulate a pencil point, "I am compelled to subtract three hours and twenty-three minutes for what I generously ascribe as 'loitering.'

"'Loitering?'" he demanded, lowering the timbre of his voice to simulate the crewman, "'I beg your pardon, Mr. Nelander. I ain't never loitered in my life.'

"'Do you know what it means?'

"'Yes, sir. Havin' doin's wid the locals. I swear, whatever that gal tolt you was a bald-face lie.'

"'It was not she who informed, me, sir," he continued in dialect. "It was her father. And he could hardly be considered 'bald-faced,' sporting a full growth of beard. And then there was the time you slept through your watch -- sick, you said. Drunk, says I. Perhaps I ought to subtract double the assessment on that infraction '

"'Wait!' he cries. Befer I'm reduced to payin' you fer my services rendered. I'll take what you offer, an' no denyin'!'

"'Very good, my man. Next!'"

"Just so!" Nelander clapped in approval. Seth bowed.

"Will you come to bed with me now?"

"After listening to a rendition of my prowess as a paymaster, I am tempted to charge you for such company."

As the double entendre struck, he jumped back as though stung.

"That would mean --"

"Charging you for my services. Such a thing is not unheard of?"

"But that would make you -- and me --" He yelped and skedaddled, leaving his wife with a broad grin. Tempted to follow after all, she let the moment pass and resumed her reading. It was not that she felt time press. Rather the opposite. An entire vista of opportunity lay before her.

If only she could find the key to unlock their future. Not of ships and sails as she had once dreamt, but one with lead-lines to land. A pirate treasure buried ashore. Somewhere in the pages of the New England *Journal* lay a map marked with a large, bold "X."

Written in code, the way buccaneers of old constructed diagrams that only the initiated could decipher. Obscure references, dotted lines, arrows drawn like serpent tails, compasses darkly imprinted with N-S-E-W designations. Scowling clouds winking in one direction, sea nymphs in another. Antiquated spellings in Olde English or *Francais* or Barbados slang. Daggers dripping blood-red ink, cauldrons bubbling flesh off recently slain enemies, black scavenger birds perched on the rim, oblivious to the heat. Waiting for the skulls to be removed and the rest discarded. Dinner for them, a waypost for the ocean scoundrels.

Somewhere in her new world, a symbolic death's head and crossed bones marked The Spot. It did not tax credulity to believe Blackbeard and Henry Morgan had crossed the Kansas plains to bury their treasure outside Lawrence, Kansas. If a woman could travel two thousand miles from San Francisco, they could at least be expected to cross half that distance from the opposite direction.

It was, as Seth Ward might point out, simple arithmetic. The adding and subtracting of salient facts.

They arose early the following morning. After breakfast, the captain indicated he would take the plow into town for repair.

"I would go with you," Nelander remarked.

"Are you up to it?"

"Indeed, I feel the need to stretch my legs."

"On a wagon?"

"I might walk beside it. Besides, I may spot a gam of whales which need chasing."

Hearing her site the crew's favorite pastime, he blew air through his cheeks.

"Will you harpoon one, then? For blubber? With all this nighttime reading of late, we are in need of oil for the lamp."

"I am not one for hunting whales."

"Nor of being swallowed by one, I trust. Would you harness one of your dolphins to the wagon and give old Blaze a rest?"

"Harness a wild creature? I would as soon harness you."

He huffed and came after her. Chasing her around the table, he trapped her by the window.

"I have been known to be wild in my day."

"Aye. But the brass ring you wear in your nose has tamed you."

"Not my nose! My finger," he displayed, flashing the wedding ring identical to the one she wore. "And if this has tamed me, shall the same be said for yours?"

One word put an end to his speculation.

"No."

"Well,damn!"

Patricia hefted a chunk of soap from the sink. "That's a cuss word, Captain. Open wide and we will cure you of that habit, right enough!"

He let loose a loud groan. "Surrounded on all sides by dissidents!"

"It was you who complained of my salty language, sir. Shall you not be held accountable to the same standard?"

Seth offered her with an exaggerated pout. "No." Stomping toward the door, he waved a hand, half in dismissal, half in invitation. "Why do you wish to visit Lawrence? Are you planning on joining the Ladies League?"

"I have a letter to post." She meant to belie the significance and failed.

"A letter? Ordering more chilies?" She shook her head. "We have not pizzoned any townsfolk in some while. No doubt there are any number of excess persons in need of Reverent Ginnis' services."

"If it takes the so-called Reverend Ginnis to get them into heaven, then St. Peter is on holiday and they have left the Pearly Gates unattended. We have a stock of chili. This is another matter, entirely."

"You have written to the editor. Asking him to print money."

"To be drawn exclusively on the Lawrence Bank, so as not to have a run in the rest of the country."

Which did not explain the letter. Nor did she mean it to. He shrugged.

"Very well. Come with me. Will you take the baby?"

"To show her off so our neighbors may see she does not have hooves and a tail? Or gills and webbed fingers?"

"To brag on her beauty."

Nelander grinned. "If they are accepting entries for the Most Beautiful Baby at the Fair, then I shall most certainly apply. I will take her."

He swelled with pride. "It may be said, Nelander, you and I do good work."

For a moment too brief to reveal any more than surface thoughts, the officer considered his statement then nodded.

"I trust that will be said of us."

Leaving him without an answer but a headful of questions.

Seth Ward could not know Barbara Nelander had found her treasure map. Nor could it rightfully be said she knew precisely what lay beneath the "X."

Pirates were notorious for leaving false trails.

# CHAPTER 7

The last of the winter snow had finally melted from behind the northern exposures and the fields burst with explosions of color. Ten thousand different shades of green played backdrop for sundial dandelions, purple clover, white-rimmed grasses, blue chicory, heavy-headed sunflower and thistle buds, promising a cacophony of varied hues for months to come. Adding to the profusion were strangers to the prairie: crisp pink and yellow snapdragons, splotches of crimson geranium heads, black-eyed Susans, petunias and lilac.

Tilting her head, Barbara drew in the hues through the mediums of sight and smell.

"If I try hard enough, I can almost hear the tinkling of the Lily the Valley bells."

Rushing off to grab a handful of the spring flowers, Patricia presented them to her mother.

"Captain Papa will like to see these on the table."

"Then pick as many as you can and we shall present him with a bouquet."

Shading her eyes from the early morning rays, Nelander turned away as movement over the edge of the horizon caught her attention. Making out a small wagon, she hailed the stranger out of courtesy, then walked in that direction, closing the gap to make identification easier.

"Hallo!" the driver called, returning her salutation. Thinking she ought to recognize the voice if not the face, Nelander strode nearer. Just as she put a name to the countenance, he identified himself.

"Pete Erlinger. You remember me, Miz Ward. I'm the postmaster in Lawrence."

"Of course."

Hooking one thumb beneath a suspender strap, he politely tipped his hat.

"I'm the one, you might say, who had a hand in helpin' your man win the Eatin' Contest."

"Yes. You were the one who sold me the stamp which went on the letter to Mexico."

"Didn't know what I was doin' at the time, 'courst, but if I had known about that chili powder, I'd a brung it straight out to you when it arrived. Never saw no one put ol' Matthew McConaghie in his place like you did. Not 'till the sheriff arrested him fer tryin' to steal water durin' the drought. But that was different."

"It is a pity Mr. Bochner never got around to hanging him as he promised."

"Don't know as I'd go that far, but he sure made a peculiar sight behind bars. Him an' those boys kept pretty quiet after that, though. Keep to their place, mostly."

"That is because they do not have the potable income to waste at Tankard's Draft."

"Ain't that the truth of it."

Walking alongside the wagon, she offered a hand and they shook.

"What brings you out this way?"

"Got a package fer you. It's marked 'Urgent,' so I didn't dare wait until the captain come into town. Thought you might be waitin' on it."

"I am, indeed. You have done me a great service."

Hardly able to contain herself, Nelander removed the tarp and eagerly appraised the crate. Altogether, it measured three feet by four. Her lips pursed.

"Is this all? No others?"

"No, ma'am. Jest this. 'Spectin' more?"

"I don't know. Didn't rightly know what to expect. How heavy is it?"

"Not very." Observing her heft the contents then try to move it, he quickly intervened. "Long as I've come this far, why don't you let me take it all the way home fer you. Hop in."

He slid aside and she joined him on the wooden seat.

"Patricia, come. We are going home with Mr. Erlinger."

The child joined them, curiously peering into the back.

"What's in the box?"

Assuming Mr. Erlinger had as great a desire to learn the contents as the girl, Nelander did not hesitate to disappoint.

"A surprise."

"Is it a big one?"

"Bigger than it looks, I hope."

Slapping the reins over the back of his horse, the postmaster hurried them along.

"Buy sumthin' fer Seth, did you?"

"It is more in the way of a family gift."

"Oh. Too light to be china. I got a shipment of pure English bone china, once. Don't know why they shipped it by post. Woulda been cheaper to send it by freight wagon. Kinda tinkled when I took it off the stage. Know what I mean?"

"Perfectly."

"The shipper packed it in sawdust well enough, but, you know.... Roads is bumpy. An' I bet it made ten transfers from New York to here."

Too well familiar with coach transfers, Nelander shivered.

"It is hard enough traveling by stage. And no one takes the care to pack passengers in sawdust."

"Guess you didn't buy any china."

"Is it a dingy?" Patricia interrupted. "A ship for us to sail on?"

"No. The captain is going to make one."

"Is it a pirate chest? Filled with gold?"

"You are getting closer."

"Swords and eye patches an' peg legs?"

"Let us say it is treasure of another sort."

Drawing up outside the Ward "ship," Mr. Erlinger hopped down and grabbed the crate. Arms spread wide, he shimmied sideways through the door then looked for directions.

"Put it anywhere, thank you."

"There you go." When she gave no indication of immediately inspecting the contents, he scuffed his shoe. "Want me to pry back the lid? I brought a crowbar."

"That was very kind of you. But I think we shall wait for Captain Ward."

"Oh. Right. Well, I guess I gotta go back, then."

"Allow me to pay you for your trouble."

Handing him a coin, he took the gratuity with a grateful nod.

"Much obliged. Hope to see you at church on Sunday."

"I look forward to it."

Sorely disappointed that he had not learned the contents of the "treasure," Pete Erlinger waved a good-bye. "Give my regards to the captain."

"I will."

Seeing him out, Nelander waited until his wagon had disappeared over the horizon before returning to her purchase. Patricia tugged at her arm.

"Want me to go git papa?"

"No. This can wait. Besides, he would not appreciate being interrupted. The fields are in much disarray from the floods. He and Peter are busy clearing away all the rock deposited by the flash flood waters. He cannot get the seed in before that is done and it weighs on his mind. What I wish for you to do is go outside and work in the garden. The beans beg for planting."

"Are you coming with me?"

"You are old enough to know how it is done. I will be out directly."

Reluctantly obeying orders, the girl left Nelander alone with her crate. Taking a broad-bladed knife from the kitchen drawer, she used it to pry up one corner, then completed the task with brute strength.

Standing back to take stock, she gently removed a thin burlap covering from the interior. Immediately the scent of must and peat assaulted her nose.

Picking up one of many small bundles, she unknotted the twine fastening and laid the contents on the table, counting as she went.

"One, two... five... nine. Ten."

They came, then, in packages of ten.

Ten times five-hundred equaled five thousand. She could not guess whether there were 5,000 or not. In time, she would find out. Or not. At the moment, raw numbers were irrelevant.

Sitting down, Nelander eyed the items from a lower perspective. Expectations to the contrary, they did not appear as she envisioned. Running a shaky hand through her close-cropped seaman's hair, she chided herself.

"All right. I hoped for something spectacular and disappointed myself. That does not mean I was wrong." Inhaling deeply, she held her breath before slowly letting go. "The captain will be in a better position to judge. He understands these things better than I."

Left unspoken but not unthought lurked a terrible guilt.

*What have I done? What have I wasted precious money on? Money that I cannot replace.*

Too early to expect Seth and Peter home, she nevertheless hid her ten small examples of fool's gold with the rest, then replaced the burlap. Still unsatisfied, she laid the top back on the crate and pushed it under the table.

Out of sight but not out of mind.

Not when she had seen firsthand ten decimated corpse-like things, more fit for Reverent Ginnis' obsequies than pirate treasure.

She had found the article in a dusty old farming journal, as if her eyes had been guided there by destiny. Letters of inquiry followed, all to strangers back east. To men she had never met nor ever would. Asking many questions, receiving encouraging answers. Hatching a plan.

A way to elevate the *Pirate Treasure* above all the farms in Kansas. A hedge against corn and wheat crops which were not first to market. And maybe more than that. A chance to make real money. The idea of solid cash jingling in their pockets. Of tea canisters filled with legal tender. "Egg money" for sketch books and plows.

Twenty dollar gold pieces to present to Mr. Provost. To pay down and one day pay off the onerous mortgage owed the bank on the Windsor place. It had been her idea to buy it. Her responsibility to make good the debt.

Images of crowded harbors filled her mind. Of captains who had brought in water-damaged cargo. Arguing with insurance adjustors. Life-and-death struggles, not merely ones of profit, for the officers who came away on the losing side of such encounters faced ruin.

The frenzy of selling a manifest no one wanted. Trying to hawk up the price, accepting what could be salvaged.

*Success in this business is all that matters, Bab'ra,* her father had said, using her shipboard moniker. *A captain may be respected for his ability to survive a nor'easter, but it's his business prowess which keeps him afloat. A man who can't sell what he brings into harbor sinks his ship surer than striking rocks along shore.*

Officer Nelander had knowledge of gales and low tide but she had no experience with outright deception. The men with whom she had communicated by post had strung her along, made promises, offered encouragement. She had their letters. Proof positive she had assessed the risks, considered all outcomes.

Every one but the scenario which now faced her.

Worthless merchandise.

Despite the care taken, she had bought substandard cargo. Worthless goods.

They had sold her a pig in a poke.

The seaman's equivalent of receiving ballast instead of saleable goods.

A world, shot to hell.

Filling the rest of her day with mind-numbing tasks, Nelander assisted Patricia in the garden, planting bean, cucumber, squash and pepper seed. Back aching, she left the onion bulbs for the morrow. Sweat rolling from face and armpits, she washed in the sink then ruined the effect by cleaning out the chicken coup.

"Damn fool. Damn fool. What right did I have to think I could discover a secret no one else had ever attempted? I am a seaman, for Christ's sake. I should never have come here; should never have stayed."

A small voice behind her turned Barbara's blood to ice.

"Why do you say that, sir? Don't you love papa and Peter and me anymore?"

Doubly shamed for she had not meant to be overheard, the landlocked sailor spun around, face a minefield of tortured emotion.

"Patricia, I'm so sorry. I never meant for you to hear...."

Holding out her arms, she summoned the girl, but Patricia refused the solicitation of mercy. Shaking her head as though seeing a stranger in the place of one who had become her mother, lips moving but no sound coming forth, she sniffed back a tear.

"Patricia, please. I only wanted to do good but I fear I have done something terribly wrong."

"Wrong that you have come here!"

Shocked at the accusation and the hurt inflicted, Nelander tried again.

"No, I did not mean that."

"You said it. I heard you."

"In anger, child. A moment of weakness. Of frustration."

"It's that box, isn't it? That damn box." She did not care that she cussed for no punishment meted out could equal the pain of betrayal. "Everything was all right before that came. What is in it?" She gave her own answer to what her breaking heart interpreted. "It is the devil in there."

"No, Patricia. There is no devil; no such thing as a devil. Not the way you mean. Just the devil in our minds. That which made me speak inappropriately."

"I do not understand you." She backed further away. "People believe in the devil. That's why they turned against us -- because they thought Peter was bewitched. You think so, too. That's why you're sorry you came!"

Cold chills nearly caused Barbara to double over. Clutching her side, she staggered forth.

"Dear God, nothing of the sort."

"That's why you're sorry you came here, isn't it? Well, go away, then. And take that devil baby with you. Papa and Peter and I were a family before you came. We don't need you."

Stunned at how thin the veil between past and present hurts truly were, and how easily ripped away, Barbara sank to her knees.

"My unhappiness has nothing to do with Peter. You saw how I defended him. How I made him a pirate."

"He is not a pirate." Her little hand pointed toward the flag staff. "Take down that Jolly Roger. It is a lie. And that bell -- I will never ring it, again!"

Before there could be any thought of catching her, Patricia darted away. Without looking back, she ran into the fields, arms and legs a whirlwind of tangled motion. Nelander sobbed and melted into the earth.

It is said and fairly meant that a man -- or a woman -- does not die of a broken heart. After twenty minutes of solitary confinement in the bowels of her soul, Barbara Nelander-Ward got up and walked slowly toward the bell. Grasping the rope, she rang it eight times. Twelve o'clock. Noon. Lacking any idea of the actual time, it seemed as good a place as any to restart the rest of her life.

Unable to rid herself of the stinging demand, *Take that devil baby with you,* she fed and changed Paula. Normally tasks of pleasure, for they brought her closer to the infant, she took no joy in the work. Unable to sing or hum a lullaby, the baby responded to her mother's silence by kicking and angrily clenching her fists. When those actions had no effect, she wailed, a deep, plaintive, frustrated cry.

"Hush, baby, hush," Nelander pleaded. "You are innocent and no devil's child. I love you. I love you."

To the infant's ear, the gibberish language sounded harsh and unconvincing. Crying louder, her reddish-purple face puckered. Unable to endure the sight, Barbara placed her back in the cradle and returned to the kitchen. Not daring to sit anywhere near the hated box, she hurried into the living room. Catching sight of Seth's magazines, she gave them a vicious kick. One fell out from the rest. Her eye fell on an advertisement, set off by thick, black lines.

"All Sales Final. No Refunds."

*Be sure of what you buy, Bab'ra,* Ned Nelander had once lectured. *But be more certain of the men with who you deal. Men are a slippery lot. They got their own agenda. Some is fair and square but others are two-headed sea serpents, talking out of both mouths.*

Fool me once, shame on you. Fool me twice, shame on me.

A sentiment worthy of people across the globe.

But in her case, the warning did not work. Being fooled once was enough to ruin her. Opportunity did not knock twice.

Gathering the scattered papers in a frenzy, she pushed them toward the fireplace, then sought a match to cremate her mistake.

Finding none and too horrified to seek those by the stove, she ran outside. There, afternoon shadows from the flag and bell poles draped across the ground, serving as prison bars. Unable to cross them, Nelander hung back, finally throwing a hand over her eyes.

The skull and crossbones flapped in the breeze. For all the world, it sounded like a death rattle. At the moment, she did not have strength to kill. The box had gotten to her before she could lift a hand to defend herself.

Leaning back against the house, Bab'ra Nelander dozed. Dreams came, in the form of waves crashing, masts snapping, men shouting. And the heat. Terrible, oppressive, choking heat. The sun seemed to burn a hole in the sky. Despite the tossing and heaving of the ship, not a breath of air stirred. Trying to breath, scalding air burned her lungs. Lack of oxygen made her dizzy until she lost her balance and fell. Into the water, not cool and refreshing but bubbling hot.

Lacking buoyancy, she began to sink, first legs and torso, then arms and head. Madly thrashing, she found herself being borne away in the jaws of a giant white shark. Screaming for help, her cries faded as a piercing, stabbing, pinprick sensation of supreme agony crept up her leg.

*I am dying,* she thought. And then, more firmly, *I am dying!* Slowly, the heat of passion faded away, replaced by the cold of certainty. *I am dying and I do not care.*

Dying, to dream no more. If only the pain in her leg would go away... then peace. The bewitching peace of nothingness.

Seth shook her by the shoulder, rousing consciousness. She sobbed and he guessed only half the reason.

"Nelander, wake up. Your foot has fallen asleep and the blood is returning. The pain will pass."

"No. No.... I made a mistake. A terrible mistake." Repose, as tortured as welcome, abandoned her and she cried anew. "Go away. Leave me alone. Patricia has told you all and now you know. I cannot face you."

He frowned and leaned closer, the warmth of his breath falsely caressing her cheek.

"You have been dreaming. A nightmare. You are awake, now. Everything is all right."

Using his hand to help her up and cursing her own weakness, Nelander spat and shook her head.

"Nothing is all right. Everything is all wrong. You know."

Professing supreme knowledge, Seth extended his hands, palms up.

"I do."

"She has told you everything."

"She did not have to. I figured it out for myself."

The pain returned, this time radiating from her temples.

"There is nothing else to say."

"As captain of this ship, there is a great deal to say. Or rather, an explanation to be made."

"I made a mistake --"

"By forgetting to ring the bell," he happily supplied, the tone of jest maddening her. "All the way home, Peter and I listened for it. The very sound gets our stomach juices flowing. How are a man and a boy supposed to prepare themselves for supper when they do not hear the bell?"

"How are we to know when our shift is over?" Peter demanded, hands akimbo. He dug his foot in the earth, so like his father.

"We are not to... ring the bell... any more."

"What is this? An officer neglect in her duty. And passing it off by some weak excuse that we are not to ring the bell anymore? Of course we will. This is a pirate vessel, and I will tolerate no change in routine. The crew," he winked, "expects no less."

"The crew...? But --"

"And where is Patricia? Shirking her chores? Is this what happens when I am away?"

"Patricia? You have not... seen her?"

"Not hide nor tail."

"She did not come to you; not speak to you?"

Finally grasping some error in his initial judgment, Seth hitched a shoulder.

"She did not. Why? What has happened? Has she upset you?"

"No. No. Something I said... in anger. It is all my fault. A misunderstanding."

Sensing the need for privacy, he turned to the boy.

"Peter, go and find your sister."

He did not argue. Waiting until Peter skipped behind the barn, Seth crossed to the bell and rang it. That omission put to rights, he returned to Nelander, squatting down beside his wife. Unable to face his tender stare, she looked away.

"I have done something terrible."

"Then we will undo it."

"It cannot be undone."

"Then we will live with it." An idea struck and he stared inside, the laugh lines of his face turning graven. "Not the baby? Something has happened to Paula?"

Barbara quickly reassured. "She is all right. No harm has come to her."

He sighed and petted her arm.

"Then it is not so terrible, after all."

"Worse than you think."

"We have each other and our children are safe. Whatever else may have happened, it cannot be worse than that. We will deal with it."

The strength of his conviction should have reassured her but the horror of her act overcame whatever benefit she might have derived.

"I have spent the last of my money. Wasted my savings on a fool's errand."

"What are you saying?"

"That money which I had left in the bank. That, which I had hoped to tide us over until the crops came in." Her throat constricted. "That, which I could have spent on colored pencils for Patricia and a new pair of boots for Peter and to pay the blacksmith and...."

He swallowed and bit the underside of his lip.

"I did not know you had more money. I thought the five hundred dollars you gave me to be the lot."

"There was more."

"But I had not counted on it. So we are no worse off than before."

"I am worse off, because I knew!" she cried, fighting tears. "I wanted to give it to you... to make things right. To make a contribution. You remember?"

"I remember," he whispered.

"I had an idea. It came to me from reading your periodicals. Something so wondrous, it would be as though we discovered pirate treasure coming up out of the earth."

"What do you mean?"

Gently taking his hand, Nelander led Seth into the house. It took all her courage to point under the table.

"There. Blackbeard's chest. Only I have been cheated. It contains nothing but empty promises."

Following her directing, Captain Ward knelt on the floor and pulled out the crate. The magnanimity of it frightened and settled in his bones.

"What is in this?"

"See for yourself."

Working his fingers under the lid, he lifted it off with the superstitious awe of a man about to view the face of one recently deceased.

What he beheld came close.

Five thousand dried and withered twigs, neatly tied into bundles of ten.

After a moment to compose himself, Seth faced her. Slowly and with deliberation.

"What type of plants are these?"

"Strawberries," she said.

## CHAPTER 8

"Strawberries?" he repeated.

"Deader'n a mackerel."

Her expression had an unexpected consequence. Seth burst out laughing. "Around here, we're more likely to say, 'Deader than a door nail."

Nelander stared at him with dull incomprehension.

"Did you hear what I said? The plants are dead. Whether they were put in the box that way or perished along the journey I cannot say. It makes no difference. I bought them without guarantee. They cannot be returned." Her lips curled. "Buyer beware."

He blinked, tugged on a lock of hair then returned to the erstwhile pirate chest.

"You bought strawberries?"

The wondrous tone, the innocent query, constricted her throat.

"For us... for you. To plant in your valley. The one you so loved as a little boy. I remembered the story you told; of how you found wild strawberries and ate your fill, then picked a handful which you carried in your cap. All the way back to town. A man stopped you and asked what you had." The words tumbled out, as vivid to her as if she had been the one to live the adventure. "'Strawberries,' you said. And he bought them. You sold all you had. That money became the start of your treasure. That which enabled you to come back here."

Nelander sniffed and wiped her eyes. "You couldn't buy the valley because the Windsors already owned it. So you took the adjoining property."

"Yes. That is true," Seth avowed.

"A quirk of fate.... My intervention... God's idea of a bad joke... call it what you will. The Windsors abandoned their farm and we bought it. Had they returned as planned, we would have sold it back to them." Her voice strengthened. "But without the valley. That, I would have insisted we keep for ourselves."

"You never said such a thing."

"I did not; but I had it in my mind. Our... profit margin, if you will. A reward for doing the right thing. But as you can see, God punishes the blameless as well as the guilty. Ask Lot," she ended with a sneer.

He shrugged. "I do not know any family named Lot. There is no one in Kansas going by that surname."

"You take my meaning."

"You bought strawberries."

The inflection bespoke of reverence.

"I wasted every penny we had. I tossed in our lifeline."

"Strawberries? To plant in my valley?"

"Yes."

"Because of a story I told?"

Her jaw hardened. "Because the man in town bought your berries. He said he had not tasted strawberries in so long a time. I have never stopped thinking about that. While people may not need strawberries to live, they are a delight, a... treat. Something to eat out-of-hand, like candy. Or serve in a bowl of cream, turning an ordinary breakfast into something special."

Taking her hand, Seth wrapped his fingers around hers.

"Tell me more."

No condemnation; no anger.

"I read all about it; an article on strawberry cultivation. The type of soil required. The use of water and fertilizer. The amount of sun. How the plants reproduce themselves by growing runners. In a sense, they are self-perpetuating."

"I had no idea."

"The fruit comes out in spring. Not usually the first year and possibly not the second. By the third season, when the plants are full and lush, they produce a prodigious crop of hearty, plump berries. I envisioned them growing up and down the sides of your valley. Bright green, spotted everywhere with red." She took in a deep breath and hurried on, the faerie tale once more a reality before her eyes.

"In the beginning, I thought you and I and the crew could pick the fruit ourselves. Take them to town and sell them at the farmer's market. We would be the only ones with strawberries. Sell them by the pound or the half pound. Or the handful." She grinned. "They would not be expensive.

Anyone could afford to buy them. The season is short -- a month; six weeks. We would not wear out our welcome."

Seth's eyes sparkled. "I see it all. Clearly."

"Women would buy them for the table. Men -- like that stranger you met -- would eat them on the spot. Even children. For a few pennies they could satisfy their taste for sweets."

"No one has ever grown strawberries in Lawrence. Or in the state, for all I know."

"With five thousand plants, we could set up our own business."

"That's a lot to pick."

"I thought about that, too. Once we had established a taste in the minds of the townspeople, we invite them out to the valley. Let them wander about the field and pick their own. Then they would bring what they gathered to a stand and have it weighed. They would determine what they paid."

"We would need a scale."

"Of course. I'll write it off as a business expense."

"We could advertise, too; make it an Event, like the Fair. Families would arrive with picnic baskets. After they picked what they wanted, they would eat there on the valley floor. The children could play with one another. Perhaps we could organize games."

"Make it an outing."

"Precisely."

"All the while we are making money. Without the labor," he decided. "I like that."

"It would only be for a month or so, as I said. Still enough time for you to put in corn and wheat and tend those crops. Patricia and Peter and I -- and one day, baby Paula, could tend 'shop' while you farmed. So what we took in would all be extra money." She sighed. "Breathing room."

He whistled. "That is a scope I can hardly fathom."

His use of a seafarers term brought a sad smile to her wan countenance.

"Eventually, if we were successful, we could plant more strawberries. We cannot ship them, of course, because they are too delicate. But that is part of the plan. No one can ship strawberries in. We have a corner on the market. Lawrence is big enough, I believe, to eat all we can grow."

"It is a stunning proposal. And... you read about this in one of my journals?"

"I told you I wanted to contribute. I was not looking for anything specific; just trying to improve my mind. Learn what you already know so I might be a help. I had nothing specific in mind. But when I found the article on strawberry cultivation, I thought I had found an answer."

He ignored the quiver in her voice.

"But how did all this come about?"

"I wrote to the editor." She tried a smile. "One of the many letters I posted."

"Ah, yes. You are the most writing-est woman I have ever known. Quite shocking in Kansas. Everyone in town speaks of it."

"I asked the editor to forward a letter to the author and he did. I received an answer and we established a regular communication. He told me all about strawberries and I asked whether he thought they would flourish in the Midwest. Our winters are not so severe the plants would die in the cold and our springs are ideal for growing. So I asked to purchase plants and he sold them to me."

Overcome by the horror of her fateful decision, Nelander broke free his grasp and drew away.

"I wanted to plant them this spring -- immediately -- so we could get a head start on next year. Reap a small harvest and maybe make up for what we lost in the drought."

"You said nothing of this to me."

"I wanted to surprise you. I was not sure what you would think and I did not want to be put off." Failure settled over her. "I took my money -- I *risked* my money," she underscored, "and sent it to him. And he has cheated me."

If the confession had not been enough, Seth Ward's world turned upside down when Nelander burst into tears. One hand crossed over her breast, the other beating herself on the forehead, she succumbed to the powerful force of heartbreaking disappointment.

When he tried to comfort her, she held him at bay, red orbs glistening with salt water, manufactured from the inner workings of her soul.

"There is nothing you can say to console me. Our money is all gone, the damn bank will foreclose, we will be set adrift and all of us will perish."

She believed what she said and he saw that she did. Seth's own emotions stirred, yet in a different direction and he tried once more to engulf her. Ignoring her protests, arms went around her, holding tight.

"Nelander.... Barbara. I have never seen you weep so. Had I thought about it, I would have prayed to be spared such."

"Hands off, I beg you. Let me go. I will leave this place --" Stiffening her muscles so that she appeared more marble statue than human being, a cold clamminess swept over her flesh, giving him the uncomfortable sensation of impending death.

That, of which, he had had too much experience in his twenty-eight years.

"I will take my 'devil baby' and go."

Her tears had solicited compassion. These words, however, evoked fury.

"Who has said such a thing? Tell me and I will tear him apart with my bare hands. I have had it up to here," he demonstrated by raising a stiffened mock salute to his brow. "There are no bewitchments and no devil babies. My children are born and raised of God and --"

"Stop, Seth, stop! Enough. Do not ask me, for I brought the admonition on myself. It is no one's fault but my own. Say, if you will, *I* called Paula a devil baby --"

"No, Papa Captain. It was not Nelander who said such a terrible thing. It was I."

He gasped and spun around, facing the newcomer to the scene. Color drained from his face and neck, leaving him ghost white.

"You? My daughter?"

"Yes, sir. It was I who called Paula a devil baby. And I am willing to rot in hell for my sin."

Crossing into the room from the doorway, she made a brave, almost hopeless gesture of despair. Barbara backed away as though she were the one bearing the weight of the crime and spoke honestly.

"Patricia, my love. You had every right to say what you did. The description was not meant against Paula but me."

"And yet I said it."

The captain threw back his head in frightened confusion.

"Tell me, for pity's sake, what is going on?"

Not hearing, or unable to respond, Barbara addressed the girl.

"I thought you would go and tell what happened. So that by the time they returned, I would be turned out like a dog. Despised. Held in contempt."

"I ran into the woods." Her body shook as she struggled to come to grips with a very adult world. "I meant to go to papa and repeat what you said. But I did not."

"Why?"

Patricia sniffed back her own tears, then, in a startling revelation of her own parentage, scuffed her foot along the rag throw rug.

"I didn't know what's in that box, Officer Nelander. I just know that it's something terrible; something which had made you sad and upset. A disappointment, bigger than a whale."

Tortured by the confession and the little one's nautical description, which marked Patricia for Barbara's own as much as the scraping of her foot linked her to Seth, she fumbled over a grin and a sob.

"Oh, my child, I am so sorry you had to bear that."

"It is something meant for a surprise. I saw the look on your face when Mr. Erlinger brought it. There was great happiness in you. And then you opened it and it was all wrong. That's what made you wish you had never come. When you said that I was scared -- and mad. So I ran off. But I know better, now."

"What has changed your mind?"

"Mama whispered the truth in my ear."

Nelander let out a cry and would have fallen had not Seth acted quickly to support her. His own head buzzing with words only partially understood, he spread his legs for balance, gently patting his wife on the back.

"Whatever was done or said is over. Now, it is my turn to speak." Guiding Nelander back to the crate, the width and breadth of a child's coffin, he waited until Patricia and Peter had gathered before speaking. "These strawberry plants are not dead. They are dormant."

If Barbara Nelander comprehended, she gave no indication, forcing Peter to ask.

"What does that mean?"

"They are asleep. The grower has prepared them for travel by shipping them 'bare root.' Without soil or green, growing leaves." He shoved his face under Nelander's. "Are you following me?" A slight shake of the head indicated "No." He picked up a bundle.

"If you take a fully mature plant and put it in a dark place without sun or water and leave it there, the plant dies. That is because the leaves require light to sustain them and the roots need liquid for hydration. It keeps trying and trying to thrive and when it cannot, the life goes out of it. But when you take away the soil and cut it back so there are but few, if any leaves, the plant thinks it is winter. It does not try to grow but only preserve itself for spring."

He pointed at his diminutive crew. "There are two type of plants: one which lives but a summer and then dies. Those are called 'annuals,' because their life span is less than a year long."

"Like the pumpkins and the beans, sir?" Patricia inquired.

"Exactly. They make many seeds and in the spring, it is these seeds which grow. Then, there is the other kind; that which returns, year after year."

"Like trees, papa?" Peter asked.

He nodded. "They are called perennials because they come back, year after year. In the fall they lose their leaves because the winter is too cold to sustain them. The trees go dormant until spring, when the warm weather tells them the ground is thawed and they may wake up."

Nelander awoke as if from a trance, pupils distended.

"Good God, Seth, do you mean to tell me these strawberries are really dormant and not dead? You are not just saying that to save my sanity?"

"There is no question of it. Look," he demonstrated, removing one of the top plants. Parting the few tiny dried leaves, he revealed a pale greenness beneath. "This plant is alive, waiting only to be exposed to light and water and soil before it bursts into a rebirth of new life."

"But... nothing was said to me about the strawberries being dormant. I presumed... they would arrive lush and green."

"I suppose the grower thought you knew. After all, a *man,* B. Nelander, willing to risk so much, would be expecting bare-root plants. He had no way of knowing he was dealing with a --"

"Woman."

"With a sailor," he gently corrected.

She laughed and it felt like the first time.

"I have nearly ruined everything."

"But you have not. What you have given me is a great surprise."

"Surprised," she repeated, picking up one of the bundles. "Pleased-surprised or unhappy-surprised?"

He hesitated long before answering. "Why didn't you discuss this grand scheme with me?"

Her back straightened. "Because I was afraid you would say no. You would think I was only suggesting it because of a story you told. For the valley I made you buy." She spoke over his objection. "Because it cost a great deal of money. Money more prudently spent -- or saved. For a rainy day."

His face puckered at the expression; one they had discussed when drought parched the land.

"I might have raised those objections."

"And you would have been right. I could not take the chance you would talk me out of it."

"You were so sure?"

Her teeth gritted and she wiped her brow with a shaky hand.

"I was so determined. Not precisely the same thing. Reading that article, all the letters I exchanged, gave me a new sort of -- I suppose I would call it inspiration." Her face puckered. "Like Terrance's prize horse; or his beef cattle... yet not so... far afield? That is the expression?"

"Yes."

"You referred to the money I set aside from my seaman's wages as mine. I planned on buying my own ship; to captain in my own right. That means taking risks. Sometimes, huge risks."

"But now you can never buy that ship."

"You are wrong, Captain Ward. This land is my ship. The *Pirate Treasure.* What we call her and what she is. Pirates bury treasure, just as farmers plant seeds. I looked at the strawberries as just that: a chest full of doubloons and ruby jewels, coming up out of the ground."

Taking out several tied bundles, Seth stared at them a long beat.

"You asked whether I am pleased or displeased. Being the captain, I shall defer judgment. I have to think on it. There are more variables involved than merely buying the plants and developing a plan." Separating them out on the table, his eye twitched. "What I will say is that it required a great deal of bravery on your part to enact all this. I trust I will have the strength to see it through."

"Thank you. We begin in the morning."

Fortunately for family harmony, Nelander was not looking at Seth's face as she made her declaration. Her attention had been diverted elsewhere.

From outside the house, the bell rang. Four times. 6:00 P.M.

Goose bumps spread across her back. Three of the five occupants were within vision: Seth, Peter and herself. Baby Paula lay in her cradle. That left Patricia as the only one who could be tolling the hour.

The girl who had promised never again to ring it.

Time had a way of healing all hurts.

Barbara Nelander thanked God for Her haste.

# CHAPTER 9

Preparing an early breakfast, Nelander had the coffee brewed and the meal on the table as her sleepy-eyed husband wandered into the kitchen.

"What time is it?"

"Wash up and sit down. We have much to do today." His metamorphosis into a fence post did not dampen her enthusiasm. "I have already been to the barn and selected shovels and trowels."

"What for?"

"So we may plant the strawberries."

He poured a cup of coffee, added fresh cream, then blew over the surface, watching the ripples go from one edge to the other.

"In that, you mistake."

The flat tone caught her off guard and she quickly turned.

"But you said they are alive --"

"I did."

"Then we must hurry and plant them. Now that they have been exposed to light, they will think spring has arrived and start to grow. If we have not put them in the ground...." He made no follow-up. She frowned. "I did understand you? That time is of the essence?"

"It is."

"Then we must plant them. The earlier they are started, the greater the likelihood we may harvest a small crop next season."

"What you mistook was my intent. I have fields to plow. Corn and wheat to put in."

"But what of the strawberries?"

"Later -- when the cash crop is sowed. Perhaps."

"Perhaps?"

"There are a thousand things requiring my attention. I had not planned on time for strawberries."

"Last evening.... I thought we had an agreement."

Wearily sitting at the table, he unfolded the cloth covering the bacon, selected several thick slices and put them on his plate.

"Have you any idea what you are asking?"

Taking her place, she made no move to feed herself.

"No."

"Then let me explain. Ten, even twenty-five plants might be put in the garden." He overruled her immediate protest by raising a hand. "That ground is already tilled. Never mind that you want them for the valley. That is where they would go. But five thousand? The enormity of the task is overwhelming."

"Surely, in a day or two -- with you and I and the crew working together."

He rolled his eyes while drumming his fingers.

"Nelander, you have bought enough plants for an entire field. A commercial enterprise."

"That was my intent."

"No one puts in 5,000 plants at one time. Not unless he has four or five hands working for him. And a field already prepared. You cannot simply dig a hole and drop one in."

"Why not?"

Closing his lids, Seth rolled his eyes.

"The most obvious answer is time. The simple act of digging 5,000 holes by hand is staggering. It would take weeks, not a day or two. Certainly not with only two adults and two children working at it. Secondly, and more significantly, you create a terrible problem by doing that. Without properly turning down the soil, you do nothing to prevent the growth of weeds. Within a month, the wild grasses will be a foot high: choking the strawberry roots and overshadowing the leaves. They simply will not get enough sun."

She colored in shame.

"What are you saying?"

"They must be planted in tilled soil. There is absolutely no way around that."

"You cannot plow the valley?"

He severed a slice of bacon with a savage gesture.

"The sides are sloped. That will be difficult enough. But we are speaking of land which has never been cultivated. It is backbreaking labor to break in virgin ground. The plow must go deep and the clods of earth removed.

The rocks have to be dug up and carted off by hand. For that matter, the area is filled with brush and saplings. All of those have to be removed down past the roots before I can even think of plowing."

Taking a slice of bread, he rolled the meat inside and ate out of his hand. The food had no taste.

"Have you never wondered why I plant on only a small portion of my land?"

"Yes."

"Because I am only one man. It takes months of strenuous effort to prepare a field. Even then, the maintenance of it requires constant attention. Working in organic material; sowing. Weeding. At times staking. Removing weak and sickly plants or those which grow too close to another. From the first thaw until the crops are harvested, I work from sunrise to sunset. I don't have the time or the energy to work more than I have. Eventually, as my son grows, he will help me. With two men, we will eventually open more land. But he is only seven, going on eight. Still a boy."

"I had not fully realized."

"Even now, I am nearly overwhelmed. You have seen me hire hands to help."

"Yes."

"They do not come cheap. When times are good and I have money to spend, we can absorb that cost. Not this year."

"Might they not work for a share of the crop when it is harvested?"

"Their needs are immediate, just like everyone else's. They have room rent to pay; food to buy. A man wants to be paid at the end of the day or the end of a week. Not at some future time."

"Does this mean you will not plow the valley?"

He leaned across the table, resting his elbows near her.

"'Will not' makes it sound as though I have a choice. You saw the damage wrought by the flash floods. All that I have to clear before I can put in seed. We need corn and wheat to sell. This year. Not the year after next when we may or may not see a return on your strawberries."

Nelander stood and walked stiffly toward the window. Looking out, the naiveté of her assumptions nearly overwhelmed her indomitable spirit.

"There is so much of which I am ignorant. I believed I had planned carefully and yet I see now that I made a grievous mistake." Parting the curtain further, she felt the back of her hands begin to sweat the way they did when she faced danger at sea. To have backed down then meant death. Not only her own, but the lives of the crew.

Nowhere in her nature did defeat find a foothold.

"All right. You have put it to me plainly, and for that I am grateful. Finish your breakfast."

"Barbara." She did not respond. "I have thought about it all night. I tossed and turned, trying to find an answer. I want to see your strawberry plants growing in my valley. I want to share your dream. I simply do not know how to make it work." His voice grew strident. "Plant what you can in the garden. Around the barn, perhaps, where the dirt is beaten down."

The hackles on the back of her neck rose.

"No."

"Save some, if not all. Perhaps, as you say, they will put out runners. Make new plants. Eventually, we can transplant them."

"Damned if I will."

He threw his napkin down in disgust.

"Very well, then. I have work to do." Pushing away from the table, he turned toward the bedrooms. "Peter! I am leaving. Get ready."

Mechanically wrapping the uneaten food in a cloth, she added meat, bread and cheese for their noontime meal and handed it to the boy as he hurried out.

"Are we going to plant strawberries?" he asked, stuffing his pockets.

"You are going with your father. To work in the corn field."

Puzzled, he hastened outside, hurrying after the captain. Once Blaze had been hitched the pair departed. Neither waved a good-bye.

Mind numbed, Nelander cleared the table. Angrily priming the pump, she worked her muscles, allowing water to splash over the dishes. Her contribution, if it could be called such, lay in keeping house.

And wasting money which could not be replaced.

The banging of the door finally roused her from black thoughts. Patricia stood there, holding two trowels and a burlap sack.

"We can't tote that damn crate but we can put the strawberries in here," she indicated. "I rummaged around in the barn and found the backpack papa used to carry Peter in when he was small. With mama too sick to care for him, the three of us went out together. We'd set him under a tree but when he cried, papa'd carry him on his back. We can do the same with Paula."

"I do not think papa wants our help." Her lips tightened. "I know nothing of planting corn. Although, I suppose, I could haul out rock."

"We're going to the valley."

"The captain has already explained to me the impossibility of the task."

"Then we better get started, 'cause 'impossible' is mighty hard odds to beat."

Stifling her first impulse to snap, a glint of light caught her eye and she squinted to better identify the source.

"What is that on your shirt?"

"Mama's broach. We're takin' her with us."

Which defused all argument.

After all, few people were more superstitious than a sailor. If Mama wanted to come, Nelander hoped she would bring friends. Lots of them.

A horse and plow would not hurt, either.

With baby Paula strapped to her back, lunch slung over her shoulder and a pick and shovel cradled against the crook of her arm, musket-style, Nelander looked more like a '49'er than a farmer. Smiling ruefully into the western horizon, verbalized thoughts were addressed to a distant friend.

"Well, Dutchy, little did I know that before I ever made it back to Canada, I'd be putting my energy into prospecting."

Detecting none of Barbara's former bitterness when speaking to herself, Patricia felt free to ask, "Who's Dutchy?"

Carefully observing the child's stride, which effectively copied her own, she felt a deep pride stirring. Throwing back her head, then offering a wide grin, she demanded, "In the three years I've been here, you mean to tell me I've never told you about Dutchy?"

"No, sir. Not as I recall."

Which meant, *I want to hear it all again, because now that we're alone, you may say things differently.*

"Well, if you ain't a walleye in a trout stream."

Loosely translated, she said, *You're a smart one and you can use your intuition to advantage.*

"Dutchy is a friend of mine. Aboard the *Bottom Dollar,* he served as cook. I hired him when no one else would."

"Why is that?"

"He was a runaway; a slave from Virginia. His master brought him to New York and he escaped. Made his way north to Nova Scotia. He didn't know anything about the sea, but he learned."

"Just like you're going to teach us."

"The pond is a mite smaller than the ocean but it's close enough."

"Mr. Dutchy wasn't a slave aboard ship, was he?"

"Neither Captain Nelander nor myself believe in human bondage. He was as free as the next man. Although, according to law, he was still a slave. I gave him papers in San Francisco, setting him free. How do you feel about that, Master Patricia?"

"It makes me right proud, First Officer. We have some Negroes around Lawrence. They're mostly free, too. They live outside town, in their own place. They call it Little Lawrence. Papa does, too." Her face grew stern. "I've heard some call it Nigger Hole. Mr. McConaghie and his boys, they do."

"I am grieved to hear it. The captain told me the people of Kansas are mostly against slavery. Around these parts, especially."

"I guess that's right. That's why they've come here. When I was young, papa used to hire some of them to help him in the fields. Whole families would come out and I'd play with the children."

"Did you like them?"

"Yes, sir. I wish they could have stayed. It was nice having playmates. My favorite, though, was Blind Betty. She's a grown lady; older than mama and papa. She couldn't see, but she knew everything that was goin' on."

"How could she tell?"

Patricia's eyes narrowed. "She could hear everything. Even sounds no one else could. An' she said the land talked to her. That was a good thing, too, because her own son -- that's Mute Thomas -- he couldn't talk. But he sure could work hard. I bet Mr. Dutchy was like that."

"He was, indeed. He worked as hard as anyone and he earned his wages. But after I lost the *Bottom Dollar,* no one wanted to hire him. And maybe he didn't want to go back to sea. Needed a change, he said. So he went off to look for gold. The hills, he had heard, were filled with it."

Patricia easily made the connection. "So that's why you're thinking of him, now. With that pick an' shovel, we're sort of prospectors, too."

"We're looking for treasure of a different sort, but it amounts to the same thing."

"You suppose he found any?"

"I hope so."

"Me, too."

Another hour's walk took them to the rim of the valley. Coming in from the north-eastern side, they crossed the open plain, finding themselves in the heart of the secret hiding place. Gratefully lowering her bundles, Nelander rubbed her shoulders, then took stock of the land.

What confronted her was a task of enormity. Although she had forgotten, Seth had been correct in his assessment. The hills sloped upward at an angle, making any type of plowing difficult. Worse, with spring upon them, the area had already begun to green. Snarled, prickered bushes grew in abundance along the sides, while a profusion of saplings thrust upward from the floor. No thought of cultivation could be considered before they were removed.

"Hell's bells!"

Hands on hips, Patricia drew the same conclusion.

"Reckon we got our work cut out for us, right enough."

The adult gave her a peculiar stare. "You are not daunted by the prospect?"

"If that means am I scared of hard work, I 'spect not." Spitting on her hands, she asked, "Where do we start?"

Tempted to take a rest and give the matter serious consideration, which meant to contemplate the possibility of defeat, she could not say so. Not and shatter the mate's resolution.

No officer worth his salt could do otherwise.

"We may as well begin with the obvious: clearing away the brush. The captain says they have to be cut out, roots and all."

Patricia threw back her head, then pointed toward the willow grove.

"We'll put the baby in the shade so's the sun doesn't get in her eyes. We won't be far enough away that if she cries we won't hear."

Spoken like a seasoned veteran, she hoisted Paula onto her own back, picked her way through the tangled underbrush and deposited the infant under a tree. Calling over her shoulder, she added, "When she gets bigger, we'll have to put her in harness so she don't wander off. But for now, she ain't goin' nowhere."

The lapse in proper grammar elicited a smile. Reflecting that the apple did not fall far from the tree, she indicated an area and the pair commenced their labor. The initial effort of digging in the earth proved easy enough for the recently thawed ground provided little resistance. The hard work came when she attempted to extract a bush.

Wrapping her fingers around the base, Nelander tugged. The stem seemed to stretch but would not give. Applying more muscle proved ineffective.

"I guess we'll have to dig deeper around the roots."

Probing the area with the shovel blade, she used her foot, driving it a foot into the soil. Gingerly working it around, she completed the circle then tried again. This time the plant gave way but not enough to be lifted out.

Striving harder, a second and then a third attempt were required before they managed to unearth it. Already sweating under the warm rays, Nelander ran a hand around the back of her neck and heaved the bush away.

"One down an' --"

"Let's make it one hundred to go," the officer suggested, purposely under-counting the number. Removing a piece of paper and a pencil from her pocket, she made a large numeral. An hour later, she drew a cross through four uprights, making the symbolic five.

"Time for a drink," she suggested.

"Rum?" came the hopeful query.

"I had not thought to bring any, but if we are to toil like this, I may bring a flagon tomorrow."

"Good!"

Laughing despite herself, Nelander guided Patricia to the creek. Gratefully removing her shoes and socks, she dropped her swollen feet into the icy water. Allowing them a moment to become acclimated, she scooped up a handful of the bright liquid and drank. The crystal clear taste offered an unsought refreshment.

"Now, this is something to which I am unaccustomed."

Rivulets of water dripping from her chin, Patricia raised an eyebrow.

"What's that?"

"Fresh water."

"But the ocean is full of water."

"You forget: it is saline and cannot be drunk. Aboard ship, the only drinking water we have comes from barrels filled months ago. It tastes of wood and likely has more than its share of creepy-crawlies in it."

"I never thought of that. Did you ever run out?"

"Came close."

"What do you do, then?"

"The easiest thing is to catch rain water. We're always doing that. If it doesn't rain, then we ration. Cut down. No washing."

"And then you drink rum?"

The fixation with alcohol did not surprise the world-wise seaman. When she had been Patricia's age, the idea of being grown-up enough to share an adult's beverage had caused her great self-respect.

"There isn't enough rum on board. And it wasn't issued often. Only on Sundays or after a particularly strenuous job. As a reward."

"Well, hell, we better lay in a good stock!"

The exclamation would have gotten her swatted, but Patricia saw it coming and darted out of the way.

"I'm a bad influence on you."

"Right enough. At this rate, I'll never find myself a husband."

She meant to shock and succeeded. Splashing her with water as punishment, Nelander sighed and reached for her socks.

"Before this is through, neither one of us may have a husband."

They worked another two hours, the task becoming harder and harder as they tired. Patricia gave no indication of wishing to stop, however, prompting Nelander to seek a means of rejuvenating them.

With a wink and a whistle, she began to sing.

"Oh, Tommy's gone, what shall I do?
A-way-y, Hi lo.
Tommy's gone and I'll go too,
Tommy's gone to Hi lo.

"To Hilo town, we'll see her through,
For Tommy's gone with a ruling crew.

"Oh, Tommy's gone from down below,
And up aloft this yard must go.

"Oh, Tommy's gone, we'll ne'er say nay
Until the mate sings out, 'Belay!'

"I think I heard the old man say
We'll get our grog three times a day.

"Oh, one more pull and that we'll do,
So let her roll and let us through.

"She'll ship it green again to-day;
The mate is sore and hell's to pay.

"Oh, Tommy's gone, what shall I do?
The mate is sore and so are you.

"Oh, Tommy's gone and left us, too;

We like the mate -- Like hell we do!"

Patricia clapped her hands and danced to the music, bursting out into a loud "Hurrah!" at the concluding line. Proud that Nelander had shared a song -- and a naughty one at that -- she raced over and embraced the woman.

"That was the best, ever! Do you know more like that?"

"More -- and worse," she grinned in conspiracy.

"Will you teach me the lyrics?" Seeing she would get that wish, the young crewman pushed her luck. "Will you tell me what all the bad words mean?"

Nelander evinced shock.

"If I did that...." Her brows furrowed in imitation of the rows they had not yet dug. "Then your father... would complain... you know more... than he does!" she concluded with a hearty belly laugh.

Patricia made a cartwheel and landed in the grass. Pulling a straight face, she made a final pronouncement.

"Them's good wages you pay, Officer Nelander."

Reducing them both to a fit of hysterics.

What had started out as a bad day reversed course in an instant.

# CHAPTER 10

They came over the hill, trudging slowly, the way men moved when the incentive for haste failed to buoy their spirits. Peering into the shallow valley, the lilting sounds of joy wrapped invisible hobbles around their feet.

Removing his hat, Seth Ward fanned the brim past his face. The act cooled him but offered no explanation for the unexpected merriment.

"What do you make of that?" he demanded of the boy at his side.

Peter removed his own hat and copied the gesture.

"It ain't what I expected."

The droll observation nearly bent his father at the knees.

"Reckon that crick water's got some magical potion in it?"

"Reckon I aim to find out."

Letting loose a wild hoop, he raced down the incline, joining the pair with a rapidity suggesting wings had sprouted at his ankles. Finding his own feet suddenly inspired, the captain followed, loping in an easy gait. Pulling up short of the two females, he scrutinized their faces, seeking an answer. Finding none, he scanned the grassy floor, noting the determined but scant progress achieved. That left him at a loss.

"Didn't expect to find you in such a good mood."

"That, sir, is a lie," Nelander brazenly contradicted. "You did not expect to 'find' us, at all."

He blinked. "Then, what are we doin' here?"

"You have come on an errand of mercy. One you did not expect to complete. But one you felt obligated to begin. And for that, Mr. Ward, I am grateful. Come. Sit down. We are about to partake of comestibles."

"Dinner?"

"The noon-day meal."

He squatted beside her, peeling off his sweat-stained work gloves.

"What you been drinkin'?"

"Rum."

He almost believed her. Peter snickered.

"Tell us the truth."

"Water."

He grasped a handful of grass and pulled it up.

"Sumthin' we outta bottle an' sell?"

"More'n likely. I've seen preachers hawk pure branch water for a dollar a jar. Cures gout."

The grass trickled from his fingers.

"What else it cure?"

"Whatever ails you. Constipation. Diarrhea. Male complaints."

Seth coughed.

"Don't have any."

"Yes, you do. Your 'male complaint,' sir, is that there is too much work and not enough hands."

"Your crick water gonna grow me a third?"

She handed him a piece of bread rolled over cheese.

"No. But Master Patricia and I have been talking."

"That's always cheap. An' about what I kin afford."

She poked him and he dropped the food. Waiting until he had made the appropriate grunt and retrieved it, she continued.

"You were right. There's bushes and trees all over the place. They have to be taken out -- uprooted. Then, the land has to be plowed. The rocks taken out. All that before I can think of planting my strawberries."

He noted the possessive and flinched.

"That's a fact. I see you made a start. Thought I had talked you out of it."

"Patricia talked me back into it. And then she said mentioned something very interesting."

"What would that be?"

"'Little Lawrence.'"

He caught the drift which spoke well for his powers of deduction.

"Gotta pay Negroes the same as regular men."

"You have to pay them. But maybe not the same."

He shrugged. "Mebbe not the exact wages, but --"

"I had something different in mind."

"Gonna tell me?"

"Do you want to know?"

He detected the challenge and considered.

"Yes."

The simple reply relieved her, for she had not been sure.

"We don't have the cash money but I thought we might offer a trade."

"What'd we got to trade?"

"Land."

The enormity of her statement caused him to pull back. Averting his face, he took a bite, chewed it and deliberately swallowed. His tan seemed to fade away and his voice lowered.

"We can't sell any land to Negroes. There'd be a hell of an uproar. You think a bewitched boy was bad. That would be worse." His hands knit. "Maybe men are free on the ocean and maybe that's right. Maybe the townsfolk tolerate them in Nigger Hole, but having them come out here -- owning the Windsor farm? That wouldn't set."

"I didn't say owning. We could rent it to them. How'd that 'set'?"

"They don't have any money."

"But they do have labor. I'm not saying we give them all the acreage; just enough for a garden. And the house to live in. In exchange, they work for us. Not all of them," she hastened to add. "A few. Blind Betty and her son. Some of the others. Can Mute Thomas use a plow?"

"I expect so. But we only have one."

"That's right. But you don't use it every day; and not all the hours of a day. While you and Peter are hauling rock out, he can use it then. Or in the evening, when you're finished."

"In the dark?"

"If he has to."

"Blind Betty won't be much use."

"Patricia tells me she can see with her other senses. Enough to dig out roots, maybe gather up the loose brush. Break up clods. Help with the planting." His knuckles whitened. "We can't do it alone and we can't afford not to do it at all. I didn't think my idea through, and I got us in a pickle. This is a way to save my plan."

"I don't know. Don't even know if they'd be willing. Those people are tight knit. They live together. They have their own community."

"So, we expand it a little. And we won't know unless we ask them. May we?"

"Barbara...."

"Seth."

His cheeks puffed out and he made a low blowing noise.

"Didn't know what I was gettin' into, marryin' you."

"Is that a compliment or an insult?"

"It's a fact."

"Shall I feel sorry for you, or pat you on the back?"

This time, he blew on his fingernails, then polished them against his rough work shirt. The meaning of the gesture escaped her. While Nelander could hardly believe it to be derisive, her experience with mime generally reflected the darker side of a man's personality.

"What does that mean?"

"You don't know?" Peter asked in surprise.

Suspecting the questionable gentleman would not explain, she descended to his level.

"Well, now, I know what this indicates." Using a pointer finger, she wound it in circles around her head. "A crazy person. And this --" Utilizing both hands, she formed a head, neck and stupendous bazooms. "This refers to --"

Before she could finish, his hand shot out, pressing against her lips.

"Never mind!"

Too late. Peter tugged at her arm.

"Tell us."

"A woman with prodigious endowments." His eyes widened, either in wonderment at two obscure ten dollar words or at the idea of a lady, so blessed.

"Wow!"

"Seamen use the expression, 'stacked.' While it may be used to refer to any female, they usually reserve it for one with a plunging neckline. A lady of the evening. A whore."

Seth groaned.

"You know," Patricia whispered loudly to her brother. Like Miss Belle at the Tankard's Draft. She sure is... stacked."

Seth's head tilted at a peculiar angle.

"How do you know Miss Belle?"

"The question might more rightly be," Nelander intervened, "How do *you* know Miss Belle?"

The tip of his nose quivered.

"She used to sing at church service," he blurted.

"Oh?"

"Until the town elders put a stop to it," Patricia elucidated.

"They did not allow her in church?"

The child puffed out, importantly tapping her chest.

"Wasn't her they minded, so much as her costume. They said it distracted men from worship. Sure had a nice voice, though. Sang like a canary."

"How do you remember that?" Seth demanded. "You were no more than a toddler at the time."

"Oh, I remember lots of things. When she heard mama was sick, she brought her out a shawl."

"How kind."

"She is a nice lady. I heard her tell mama that if she got too sick, she'd take me an' Peter into town and watch after us."

"Did she?"

"Yup. But mama said no, she'd keep us. After that, papa started takin' us out in the fields with him when he worked. So we wouldn't get snatched, I guess."

"Would you liked to have gone with her?" Patricia shook her head.

"Oh, no. But it sure woulda been different. She said I could use her face paint to draw. Maybe make some pictures for her room."

"Draw a portrait of 'papa,' perhaps."

"Like as not."

"That's it!" Papa slapped his thigh. "It weren't nuthin' like that," he unconsciously drawled. "In the beginnin', lots of folk brought things out."

"But how many offered to take your children? I would know more of Miss Belle. Perhaps we can do some business together."

"What-kind-of-business?"

"She probably has a good head for figures. And knows a thing or two about salesmanship. Once we get our business up and running, she might be a useful asset."

"Oh, good. I not only married a sailor, now, I got a strawberry farm an' blacks an' a woman of the evening workin' fer me. That'll bring in the crowds."

"Sort of like a troupe," Nelander readily agreed. "'Seth Ward's Red, Black and White Traveling Show. Has a ring to it."

"Are we going to travel?" Peter eagerly inquired.

"No. We ain't."

"Aren't," Patricia officiously corrected.

"Maybe we could go to New York City."

"Yes." Barbara thought that a good idea. "They have all sorts of plays there. We could rent a stage. Miss Belle could sing -- like a canary. Religious songs, to be sure."

"And maybe the one's you're gonna teach me," Patricia suggested.

"Oh, those, too."

Patricia grinned. "'Oh, Tommy's gone and left us, too. We like the mate -- Like hell we do!'"

Seth waivered, swaying like the long grasses. "What's that?"

"A chantey."

"Patricia could paint pictures to draw the crowds."

"With face paint?"

"No, dear. With real water colors. Or oils. And Peter.... Peter could bang the drum while our black minstrels rattled their dried gourds and played the fiddle. Do you think Mute Thomas has that skill?"

"No."

Whether he did not suppose, or knew for a fact Thomas had no musical talent remained open ended.

"I, of course," Nelander continued, "shall sell strawberries."

"What will Captain Papa do?"

"Use his muscle to throw out the thugs, of course."

The crew clapped. It seemed a good plan.

Seth rose unsteadily to his feet.

"All right. Come on, Master Peter. We have work to do. In the corn field. Thank you, ma'am," he stiffly bowed, "for the victuals."

"You hardly ate."

"Enough to fill my head. See you this evening."

Taking the boy by the hand, he started away. She hesitated, then called after.

"You will think about what I said? About asking the Negroes?"

He waved and they trotted off.


That evening over a supper of fried ham, boiled potatoes and onions, Seth addressed the issue.

"I've been givin' what you said considerable thought. About the strawberries... and such."

The tone gave no indication of which way he leaned.

"I would like to hear."

"None of us can look into the future."

"Agreed."

"If I could, I'd maybe change my mind. Times are hard." She let that pass. "You've heard me speak of popular sovereignty."

"That of the states to decide for themselves whether they wish to be free or slave."

He nodded. "This past October, men in Kansas approved an anti-slavery constitution. There was a lot of talk on both sides. Nothing came of it. Before that, there was all this trouble with John Brown at Harper's Ferry."

"You call it trouble and I call it evil."

"No denying. Wish I could say that was an end to it, but it's.... Not a beginning, either. More like a continuation. I was reading in the *Gazette* about some fella called Jefferson Davis. Makin' it illegal to prohibit slavery in the territories."

"But the people in Little Lawrence are all freemen."

His lips twisted into an ugly grimace. "Ask your friend Dutchy what he thinks of that. You reckon because he has a piece of paper sayin' he ain't bound that makes him safe?"

"Safe? No. He will never be safe until slavery is outlawed. No one will," she menacingly added.

"There's a presidential election comin' up. No one knows who's gonna be nominated. There's a lot down South who don't like the Democrat, Stephen Douglas."

"And who is on the other side?"

"I hear a lot of names. Don't none mean much to me. But he'll be an abolitionist."

"That's good. Better than that toothless shark we have now."

"All I'm sayin' is, tempers are hot. I told you how those rascals in Missouri came over the border into Kansas to vote for slavery. They can just as easily cross and burn a few farms... of men known to oppose 'em."

"Men who hire Negroes?"

"Men who not only hire 'em but who offer 'em land. A white man's farm. We have a family to think about."

"And a moral stance to defend. Would you raise Patricia and Peter and Paula believing one thing and defending another?"

"I would not. I just wanted to be sure you saw both sides."

"If you are asking if I am afraid, then the answer is yes. Only a fool sails blindly into a storm with his masts unfurled. But by lowering them and careful navigation, he may yet succeed. And be better off than by standing pat and waiting for the gale to pass."

"You have made up your mind, then?"

"I am waiting to hear what you are of a mind."

Carefully maneuvering his fork and knife so they formed an "X" on his plate, Captain Ward sighed.

"I did not ask what you paid for those plants and I am not about to. It was your money and you did it for me. And the crew. To make a contribution. If we don't get them in soon, they will die. There's no denying. That would be a sin. And I'm not a man to spit in the eye of God."

"Go on."

"Nor am I one to overlook a Grand Scheme. It's a good plan, Nelander. A... damn good one." He swallowed and worked on a grin. "Strawberry Fields. I like it. I say we talk to Blind Betty and Mute Thomas. See what they have to say. There's no guarantee they'll accept. They have a lot to lose, too. But if they're willin', then I'm all for it."

He reached across the table, offering his hand. She took it and they shook.

Patricia and Peter exchanged glances. The utensils on their father's plate reminded them of the crossed bones beneath the skull on their Jolly Roger.

And, of course, an "X."

An "X," also used on pirate maps to mark buried treasure.

In either case, an omen no buccaneer could ignore.

CHAPTER 11

The wagon wheel rolled into a deep crevice, lurching the passengers in the conveyance forward. Jostled against Seth, Nelander righted herself while shooting a disdainful glare at the road.

"If it were any wider, that damn rut would serve as a moat." Gathering herself, she cradled one fist in the other. "It is a wonder no one repairs it."

"I expect the locals know it's here and avoid it."

"Your 'expect' is kinder than mine."

He squinted into the sun. "And that would be?"

"That the 'locals' put it there to keep the inmates in."

Stepping down, he eased Blaze forward, gently guiding the wagon over the sunken obstacle. Searching the road for more and seeing none, he rejoined her and took back the reins.

"Gid-up."

Crawling at a snail's pace, they rounded a crook in the road, passed a stand of long wood and came out into the environs of a small town. Comprised of three parallel streets, it appeared as any other community, with one stark difference. All the inhabitants were dark skinned.

Surveying Little Lawrence from her elevated perspective, Nelander's lips pursed.

Rows of shacks, most temporary structures of poles and blankets met her eye. A common well sat in what might be called the town square. Children, playing tag around the stone circle, turned frightened eyes upon the strangers. Most ran off, leaving only two to hold their ground.

Politely removing his hat, Seth addressed them.

"Howdy. My name is Captain Ward an' this is my wife. We mean you no harm." Without speaking, one pointed back the way they had come. He interpreted. "They're telling us to go back; that we've lost our way." She nodded.

"Child, my name is Nelander. Can you direct us to the home of Blind Betty?"

"What fer yuh wan' her?"

Reaching into the back, she brought up a sack.

"We have brought her a present. Bacon and corn meal."

Hungry, greedy eyes flickered.

"Gimme it."

She would have obliged but Seth prevented.

"No," he said.

"But why? He is hungry."

"They are all hungry. We've come on business, boy," the captain redirected. The child shrugged, losing interest. Seth urged the horse forward. Once they had driven twenty yards down the road, a rock went whizzing by his ear. Another struck him on the back.

Putting a hand on his knee to restrain him, Nelander started to speak but he shook her off.

"I have no quarrel with them. White men have no place here."

Nodding in gratitude, she turned away. The town reeked of poverty. Tendrils of smoke wafted into the air from cooking fires, but the smell held no appeal. Stray dogs, mangy and gnarled, slunk between narrow alleyways, tails tucked between their legs, teeth bared. Several pitifully thin hogs rooted in an open cesspool. Bits of paper and dried leaves blew across open airways.

"If this were a ship," Barbara observed, "I would condemn it."

He shrugged. "And then, what?"

"Who owns the land?"

"I don't know that anybody does."

"If they are so hated, why are they allowed to stay?"

"I can't say. They've been here for as long as I can remember."

"How do they live?"

"Men hire themselves out sometimes. Those that'll have 'em. Women do some washin' in town. Mebbe some domestic work fer them that can afford it. They're tolerated more'n accepted."

"It would not take much to improve their lot. Where are all the Christians in Lawrence? Why doesn't the Ladies Charity League raise a fund for their betterment?"

"There are lots of poor whites in town. They don't help them, either."

"That is not an answer." Drawing arms around herself, she found that position uncomfortable and swatted away a legion of large, black flies. "It reminds me of Snow Bluff. Where I found the Windsors. Squalor and poverty. Hopelessness. No way out."

He bit his lower lip. "You never said."

"Some people are offered hope and reject it. Others have no hope. Between the two, I pity these people more."

"There," he indicated. "On the outskirts, if I remember right."

Urging the horse forward, they traveled past the last of the lean-to huts, arriving at a small dwelling, neater than the rest. A small garden by the side, well-tended, already showed signs of greenery.

Alighting, Seth offered Nelander his hand. Together, they stepped toward the open front.

"Blind Betty? It is I, Seth Ward. I and my wife. May we speak to you?"

A rustling inside, then the head of an old woman appeared. Snow-white hair covered with a red kerchief, she wore a knit shawl and long dress, made of rough cloth. Her feet were bare.

"Mista Ward?"

"Yes, ma'am," he replied, stepping nearer.

Tilting her head sideways, a slow, thoughtful expression crossed her wrinkled face. Her voice was soft and respectful.

"Yuhr wife, yuh say?"

"My name is Barbara, but I am called Nelander."

"Bab'ra," Blind Betty repeated. And then, clearly enunciated, "Nelander. Ah. Yuh have remarried, Mista Seth."

Taken aback and yet not disconcerted by the pronouncement of her former sea name, "Bab'ra" glanced at Seth, whose face expressed the sentiment, *See? I told you so.* Answering the question directed to him, he softly replied, "Yes, ma'am," acknowledging the statement.

"Ah was sorry to hear abo't Miz Ward. But dat a long time 'go. Yuh found yuhrse'f a new woman. She not frum hereabo'ts."

"No, ma'am," Nelander spoke for herself. "I come from a long way off."

The old woman bowed her head. "Dat be good." Her hands worked themselves over the shawl. "How be yuhr two young'uns, Mista Seth?"

"They are fine. Nelander and I just welcomed a daughter into the world."

"What be her name, suh?"

"Paula."

"Paula." And then more quietly, "Paula. She look like yuh, Mista Seth?"

He grinned. "The spitting image, mother."

The term of endearment found favor. "Den she be a pretty woman, suh. Ah'll say a prayer fo' her. So da Lor' a'ways bless an' keep her."

"I would be most grateful."

"Yuh baptize her, Mista Seth?"

"Yes, mother. With my own hand."

"Den da Lor', He be pleased. Der's others, not as holy as yuh be."

Taking the sack from Nelander, he offered it. "We have brought you a present."

Gingerly accepting the gift, her hands swept over the burlap.

"Bacon an' corn meal." At Nelander's gasp, she grinned. Putting a finger to her sunken orbs, she offered a wise smile. "Ah cain't see, but Ah kin smell."

"I never realized corn meal had an odor," the officer offered in puzzlement.

"Doughs widout eyes use odder ways. Da wor'd is full ob scents. Da flowers. Da grou'd. Da sky. Da wind."

"That I can easily agree with. I am a sailor, Miss Betty. Before I came to Kansas, I made my living on the sea. I often found myself... using other senses. The ocean spoke to me. And the breezes blew in many tidings."

"Yuh talk to da fishes?"

"I did."

"Wad they say?"

"They told me of their life below the water. Of swimming in the water. And diving deep below."

"Yuh like wad dey say?"

"So much so that I often wished I were a fish."

The old woman rubbed her hands.

"Ah like dis 'Nelander,' Mista Seth."

"She is the light of my life. And she has something to ask you."

"Den Ah will listen." Making way, she indicated they crawl into her home. Nelander went first, Seth behind. Blind Betty followed.

If they expected her to wait on protocol, the pair were mistaken. Seating herself on a sort of rag chair, she astutely faced her visitors.

"Ah am prepared to listen. Yuh, Miz Ward -- Nelander," for she seemed to like to say the name, "tell meh why yuh cume. Fo' yuh is da one brought him here."

"No, mother, it was the captain who drove the wagon."

An undercurrent of good humor filled the dwelling as Blind Betty chuckled.

"Da captain, is it? Ah like dat. An' what yuh call yuhr ship, Nelander?"

"The *Pirate Treasure.*"

"Yas. Fo' sho'. Da *Pirate Treasure.* Now, tell me yuhr idea. Da one what brought yuh both to mah doorstep, an' what it has to do wid buried secrets."

Realizing her original mistake in thinking the old woman meant she had physically driven the wagon, as opposed to the true interpretation that the visit had been her idea, Nelander matched smile for smile.

"It has to do with a little boy's dream. And strawberries."

Hands to her knees, Blind Betty gently rocked.

"One dream be Captain Seth's an' da odder be yuhrs."

"Yes, mother. When... Captain Seth was very small, he discovered a private valley where wild strawberries grew. He fell in love with it and always dreamed of one day owning that property. But when he grew to manhood, he discovered another had purchased the property. During the terrible drought last year, those neighbors packed up and left."

"Dey be da ones owned Captain Seth's valley?"

"Yes, ma'am. By leaving, they forfeited title to the bank. I asked him to buy it in the hope the Windsors would return. They did not and we were left owing a great deal of money. I wanted an answer as to how we could pay for it. The idea of cultivating strawberries -- of growing many, many plants and selling the fruit occurred to me as a way of fulfilling both our dreams -- and our very practical problem."

"How do yuh think Ah kin he'p?"

"Without consulting the captain, I used money of my own and purchased 5,000 plants. I imagined he and I and the crew could plant them quickly. I was wrong."

"The valley must be plowed, mother. The soil prepared," Seth continued. "We need help. I cannot do it all and still get in my own crops."

"An' so yuh cume to meh?"

"To you and Mute Thomas."

The Negress faced Nelander.

"Who t'ought ob us?"

"It was Patricia, Seth's oldest child. She told me of your goodness. I applied to the captain and he said we might ask you."

Seth began to speak but she waved him silent, addressing Nelander.

"Yuh tell me mo'."

"We cannot pay you, Miss Betty. But we have come to offer a trade."

"Ah am listenin'."

"A house to live in -- the Windsor home -- and two acres for a garden in exchange for your labor. Mr. Thomas to do the plowing and you to help with getting the strawberries in."

"Help?"

"The crew and I -- that is, Patricia and Peter and I -- will work beside you, of course."

"Work in da fields besides niggers?"

"No, ma'am. Work in the field beside friends."

The old woman continued to rock, but her hands had picked up a half-formed reed basket which she wove while considering the proposition.

"Dis sea yuh cume frum, Nelander -- it mus' be a mighty strange place."

"I would say, rather, the land to which I have returned is a strange and frightening place."

"Der mebbe trouble ober this what yuh ask."

"And I am sure someone said that to Jesus when He began His ministry. But He did not let it stop Him."

"Praise da Lor'."

"Praise the Lord."

"To habe mah own house. Ah neber thought ob sech a t'ing. An' a garden. Dat be mos' won'erful. But Ah be an old woman."

"And I am a young one. Together, I believe we can accomplish anything. And if it comes to a fight, Mother Betty, I have already fired

Captain Ward's musket once. I would not hesitate to use it a second -- or third -- time. Aiming at an enemy's midsection."

"Ah won' habe no blood shed, Nelander. But Ah kin plant yuhr strawberries. An' mah boy kin plow yuhr fields."

The awareness that she had come so far to see her hopes fulfilled sent shivers down the former "Bab'ra's" back.

"You tell us when you can be ready and we will come back and take you there."

For a moment she felt her expectations dashed as the old woman stopped her weaving and made a curt gesture.

"No, Miz Ward. Yuh do no sech t'ing. Mute Thomas an' Ah will git our own selfs out dere. Yuh take us 'way, dere be talk an' finger jabbin'. We takes ourse'fs 'way, we jest dis'ppear. No one miss an ol' nigger woman an' her son. No one cums lookin', no one finds us. Dat buy some time."

"I do not want you to be afraid --"

She shook off the objection. "Ah ain't 'fraid. But Ah's libed long e'nuf to be careful."

"It is a long way. And how will you find it?"

"Da Lor' guide our footsteps."

Sensing an end to the conversation, Seth nudged Nelander.

"We must be going. We are very grateful."

They had crawled outside when a voice reached back and touched them.

"Yuh a'ways was a good man, Mista Seth. Now, yuh a better captain."

He mumbled something and they hurried away. Once back in the wagon, Nelander grasped his arm.

"Does she understand the urgency? That the plants must be gotten in immediately?"

"She does."

"We did not say so."

Craning his neck, he quietly observed the sky.

"Tomorrow morning they will be at work."

"How can you be so sure?"

"Because the Lord will guide their footsteps."

She did not speak again until the wagon left Little Lawrence behind. Not until the road wound long and empty before them did she dare breathe her other thoughts.

"Have I set something in motion I had better left undisturbed?"

He tugged at his gloves, letting his eyes wander.

"We have set something in motion. Where it will lead is anyone's guess."

"She said sneaking away will buy time. I wonder who we will have more to fear -- the whites or the blacks?"

"Why do you say that?"

"No white person is likely to miss Blind Betty and Mute Thomas. Whether they live or die is of little consequence, as long as they do it in their proper place," she added in derision. "Only the Negroes will know they have packed up and gone. Will they resent our offer? Could they possibly be jealous?"

He hitched a shoulder and scratched an itch he had not felt a second ago.

"I think you mistake. While no whites go to 'Nigger Hole,' they have their ways of finding out what happens there."

"Then damn them." She poked him. "Then darn them." He did not smile at her tease.

"The world is changing faster than you or I or anyone can guess. Tempers are short and the law does not stand for what it used to. Senators who do not live in the Territories enact legislation which affects them only in the abstract, leaving others to sort it out. Men with no conscience speak of high ideals. People use teachings from the Bible to justify modern concerns, yet they pick and choose. The same ones who use it to justify slavery do not want to pay their taxes to a Federal government they no longer support."

Pulling away, Barbara watched the wagon wheels turn, pacing her thoughts to the slow clockwise motion.

"All my life, I never concerned myself with the opinions of others. I had my place, my work, the ocean. On the sea, I was far removed from... interaction with others opposed to my beliefs. The captain's orders became my duty and I saw no other. I never envisioned myself... summoned to a higher calling. I just want to be left alone to do... what I believed right."

"It's funny, you know -- to think of the distant currents which brought us together. If it were not for adversity, you would never have left the *Bottom Dollar* and we would never have met."

Her eyelids closed and she shivered.

"You are telling me to be brave."

Seth did not speak again until the wagon rolled to a stop on the crest overlooking their home. When he did, his voice sounded distant and reflective.

"Has it ever occurred to you that a strawberry looks like a heart?"

She might have cried.

But such an emotion was foreign to pirates.

Especially those with booty to be buried.

# CHAPTER 12

They sat on the porch watching the sliver of moon move across the sky. Not yet the third week of March, it could not yet be said to be spring. But the wind whispered promises and even in the shadows, branches, heavy-laden with buds, awaited some magic moment to unfurl their leaves.

"How soon do you think they'll come?" Barbara asked, rolling back her shoulders to work out a kink.

"A might sooner than the Windsors."

Instantly offended, her head snapped his way, only to behold an impish grin, which even in starlight held more elf than anger. Tossing a stray piece of grass at her, his eyebrow raised.

"You burn a short fuse, Officer Nelander."

Startled, not at his observation but from the fact he could now tease about their former neighbors, she plucked off the strand and wove it around a finger.

"Aye. That's been said about me. But I'm not one to tolerate injustice."

"Wish there were more like you. Plannin' on sending them a letter? Telling Beth about the baby?"

"No."

"I see. So there's a bit of wounded pride about you, too."

"Since when are you so hot on writing letters? Seems like every time I go to town to post one, you're huffing and puffing like a blow fish."

"Not me. Must be some other Seth Ward."

"I'll tell you what. I'll write to Beth if you write to your brother."

"Don't know where Norman is."

"Send it to the Army. They'll forward it."

"By the time he gets it, Patricia will be married and Peter will have his own farm. Paula'll be ready to leave for Boston."

"Oh?" Curious to know his thoughts, she prodded. "What'll she do there?"

"Ship design, I expect. But it wouldn't surprise me any if she decided on a long voyage, first. So see how things are done, first hand."

"That's an interesting thought. I have never projected that far into the future." Crossing her legs, she used them as a sight line, following the direction far into the fields. "What do you see for the years to come?"

"You and I staying young while the children grow."

"You said Patricia would be married and Peter would have his own place. Is that what you want?"

He dismissed the idea by feigning a yawn.

"For the boy, yes. He was born to this land and he has a feel for it. He's tied to it as much as I am. No," he corrected, "that's not quite right. Not tied. That makes it sound like a prison sentence. He's bound, you might say. Already dug his toes in the soil and put down roots."

"Will you give him this land?"

"You mean, will he inherit it? Of course. If he wants it. But I don't expect to be givin' away title any time soon. He'll be fledged before we've given up the ghost."

"Then what will he do?"

"That depends."

"On what?"

"If he finds a gal he's sweet on."

"How does that alter the situation?"

Hang-dog Herman pushed his way out the door they had left ajar and plopped himself down on a corner of rag rug which had been placed there for him. Nelander scratched him behind the ears as his tail thumped in pleasure.

"Do you see this?" she asked. "Herman has the entire rug to lie on and yet he curls up on the edge. His paws are comfortable but the rest of his mangy body is on the cold boards."

"That's the difference between cats and dogs. A cat, now, is just wakin' up this time of the evening. She'll poke her nose out, dig her claws in the rug, stretch her shoulder muscles, then go out on the prowl. Doesn't matter if she's well fed or not. Cat's always got things to do: mice to chase, new smells to check out. She's gotta see for herself; never takes anyone's word that nothing's changed. A dog, now, he takes a good sniff then flops down to contemplate his full belly. And to get a head rub. He don't mind workin' hard all day, but comes sundown, he's ready to relax."

"Is that how people are? Either a cat or a dog?"

"Pretty much so. You're a cat. Always on the prowl; always thinking. Never satisfied. Always gotta make somethin' better. Lofty ideas. That's you."

"You flatter me."

"Just sayin' that's the way you are. Peter's more like me. An' I'm like Herman. We get up with the sun and we work all day. What we do is important but it isn't earth-shattering, if you take my meaning. We're common folk. We like to stay put, see things grow. Our strength is what's inside us and what's around us. We're slow to rile but we'll fight for a principle. You, on the other hand, just like to fight. Arch your back, give a hiss in warnin' and then out come the claws."

"The next time I hear of a cat having kittens, I will surely bring one home. It will be nice to have the company of one's own kind."

"You do that."

"Now tell me," Barbara continued, running her hand down Herman's spine to scratch at the base. "About Peter -- and his 'gal.'"

"He'll be like I was. Work this place, happy as a -- clam." She grinned.

"When he gets older, will you pay him wages? Like your brother Rick paid you?"

"That was a whole 'nuther case. Rick moved his wife into the house after ma and pa died and I moved to the barn. For doin' that, he owed me. I'll never kick Peter out. So I won't pay him. But comes time he wants to get married, that'd be different."

"We could let them stay here. Maybe build an addition. Or finish the loft."

"I'll finish the loft, a'right. He gets older, he'll need his privacy. He'll go up there an' Paula'll take his room. But move a woman in here? No. They'll need their own place." He began working on the dog's head. The tail thumped harder. "Things go well for us, we'll give him a stake on his wedding day."

"Will they move far?"

"That, I don't know."

"I'll miss him. It would feel like someone pulled a tooth, leaving a big gap in my life."

"That's the natural order. Besides, we'll be ready to see him go. We'll want our own space, too. Like to send him to college, first, though. To an agricultural school. Where he can learn about scientific farming."

"Where? Back east?"

"Have to do some thinkin' on it. There's some good ones there. They teach modern techniques. Crop rotation. Fertilizers. Chemicals in the soil. Maybe even new ways of plowing. Or predicting the weather. Who knows?"

Abandoning the dog to his master, Nelander got up to stretch her legs.

"I suppose if he found a 'gal' in New England, he might want to stay there."

"What'd be harder? A Midwest boy living on the east coast or an east coast girl uprooting to Kansas?"

"Harder for the young woman, no doubt. She'll be leaving civilization behind." Seth huffed. "And Patricia? Is her destiny only to be married?"

"You make that sound bad."

Crisscrossing the lines of shadow, Nelander rang the bell, marking the half hour before rejoining him.

"I didn't mean to. What I meant was, she has talent. Her drawings capture a spirit; the living, breathing feel of what she puts down. I'd like to give her the chance to develop her artistry. That's all."

"Now, you're talking serious money."

Gliding around the hitching rail, Nelander danced with herself a moment, before setting her sights on the distant sky.

"Have you ever thought what might happen if the strawberries really did turn out to be a gold mine? If we have good harvests and sell the fruit? Not just make a small profit to augment the corn and the wheat but really make a lot of money?"

"Maybe a little," came the begrudged reply as he dug his fingers in Herman's coat. To hide the confession, he grumbled, "Someone's got to brush this animal. He's got burrs datin' back to the Great Flood."

Not bothering to differentiate between Noah and the more recent flash flooding that followed the drought, Barbara near nearer, so her face almost touched his.

"It's possible. I've done some calculations. In two or three years when the plants are fully producing. Ten cents a basket doesn't sound like much, but when you multiply it by one thousand you get one hundred dollars. Multiply it by ten thousand and you make one thousand dollars. That's twice what the corn and wheat bring in."

"That's a whole heap of strawberries."

"Yes, it is. But once we establish ourselves, we can buy more plants. Plow more ground. Expand."

"You're talking about every man, woman and child in Lawrence buying from us. People don't need strawberries to live."

"They don't. But if we price them reasonably -- ten cents a basket, like I suggested -- then almost anyone can afford them. And we could ship them short distances -- to nearby towns. Who wouldn't want to spent ten cents, or twenty, or an entire dollar, buying fruit for the breakfast table?"

"I hadn't taken it that far."

"I have. Of course, I realize there are obstacles: dry growing seasons and insects and disease. Some years will be better than others. But think of one thousand dollars, Seth."

"Added to the other crops."

"Or not. I had it in mind you could give up the corn and wheat. It's backbreaking labor. If we could live on the strawberries, you wouldn't have to go out in the fields every day and come home exhausted."

His face twisted and he rubbed the calluses on his hands.

"That's something I'd have to think hard on."

"Not if we had money in the bank." Snuggling beside him, her aura slowly encompassed his. "What would you do with one thousand dollars? Extra, I mean."

His head snapped to attention.

"Pay off the farm. Both of them. So we'd be beholding to no one."

"All right. But I mean, over and above board. What if you couldn't use it to spend on debts. Or on the house. What if it were just for yourself?"

"Now, you're askin me to make up a story."

"All right. Make one up. You have one thousand dollars burning a hole in your pocket and you have to spend it in... one week. Tell me what you'd buy."

His foot shook at the awesome responsibility.

"I'd buy you --"

"No, no. You can't buy anything for other people. Only yourself. Come on. Dream a little with me."

"Why?"

"Because I'm asking you to. Please?"

Slipping an arm over her shoulders, Seth pursed his lips.

"Only on myself?"

"That's right." Knowing what would inspire him, she playfully added, "And if you don't spend it all in one week, you lose it. So, go on a spending spree."

"I'd buy a horse," he declared. "A riding horse. A fine one. Three or four years old. And a new saddle and bridle. That way, ol' Blaze could get a rest and I'd be a fancy fellow."

"Good. That's... one hundred dollars. You have nine hundred to go."

"Oh, no. I said a fine horse. One with good blood lines. Make it a hundred an' fifty, easy. And fifty for the saddle and tack. That's two hundred."

"All right. You now have eight hundred dollars. What else?"

"A new pair of boots. Not the kind you buy in Anson's Dry Goods Store. A pair measured for my feet. With soft leather. Ridin' boots more than working boots. And... a dozen pair of good cotton socks."

"How much?" she demanded, making mental calculations.

"Fifty for the boots and five for the socks."

"Keep going."

"A new hat. No, make it two new hats. One for ridin' and one for church an' dress-up days."

"Good. Twenty-five dollars."

"A new leather jacket." He winked. "One with fringe. And a winter coat. A nice thick one. Warm. With a lamb's wool collar. And gloves."

"Let's be generous and make that one hundred dollars."

Getting into the spirit, he nudged her. "How much have I left?"

"You've spent $380. Keep going."

"This is hard work," he complained. "Who'd a thought?"

Picturing himself walking the streets of Lawrence, he peered into shop windows, observing all the items perhaps wistfully considered but never purchased.

"Books. I want a whole library of books."

"What kind?"

"Every type there is." Suddenly pained, he squeezed her hand. "Some may have to be ordered. They won't get here in a week. Does that count?"

"As long as you submit your list, that is acceptable."

Greatly relieved, he released the pressure.

"All right. I want pleasure books: novels. All the newest ones and those I have to catch up on. Name me some authors," came the sharp, almost frantic demand.

"Dickens. The Brontes. Victor Hugo -- translated, certainly. Do you want poetry, too?" He nodded. "Whitman. Hawthorne. Melville, of course."

"Why, of course?"

"He writes stirring sea tales."

"What's his first name?"

Joyfully slapping a hand against the dog, Nelander elicited a huff. "Herman." Seth guffawed.

"Really?"

"Truly."

"All of what Mr. Herman Melville wrote." His impatience mounted. "Who else?"

"Richard Henry Dana: *Two Years Before the Mast; The Seaman's Friend.*"

"Him, too. Go on."

"Edgar Allan Poe. He wrote tales of suspense and mystery."

"Good. I've read some of his short stories."

"Then we need a complete collection. And then there's Washington Irving. And Shakespeare."

"He was on the tip of my tongue."

"Are you interested in the history of your country?"

"Everything."

"Thomas Paine. He was instrumental in your American Revolution. *Common Sense. The Rights of Man. The Age of Reason.* And I suppose you will have to have the writings of Benjamin Franklin and Thomas Jefferson."

"I suppose I will. I want almanacs, too. Past and present. And subscriptions to *Scientific American* and *The New England Journal.* For life," he added."

She duly noted, "For life."

"How much, now?"

"That depends. Do you want popular prints or those with gilt edges and leather binding?"

"Do you have to ask? I am a wealthy man."

"We will go with presentation copies. Even so, sir, I cannot possibly put you over two hundred for the lot."

The meager sum seemed to deflate him. "So little? It makes me wonder why I have not purchased more of these in my present circumstance. The mass prints, to be sure. But they read just as well."

Feeling sorry for both of them, Barbara hurried him away from gloomy thoughts.

"You are little more than half way to your goal. Keep thinking."

Once again envisioning himself in town, Seth peered through the windows of Lacy's Restaurant. Licking his lips in anticipation, he declared, "I want a fine meal. The best they have. Thick-cut streak, fried chicken, catfish; bacon and eggs. Wheat bread and corn meal; beets and onions and squash. Apple pie. And coffee."

Altering her voice, she politely inquired in a French accent, "And will you have wine with dinner, *messieur?"*

Startled and hurt, he demanded, "What name are you calling me?"

*"Messieur.* That is the word for 'gentleman' in the French language."

"Do tell. And I suppose you speak French, too?"

"Like a native, sir. For, in fact, I am one."

"Of France?"

"Of French-speaking Canada. Canada was colonized by the French and many people still speak French as their only language."

"I thought Canada was owned by the English."

"They came, too."

He sighed. "Better order me some history books, too. Of Canada."

"I shall throw those in with your previous lot. We were speaking of fine dining?"

"Inasmuch as I grow strawberries, I shall forgo ordering any of them. Ice cream. What about that?"

"You may have ice cream, sir. Fresh churned. In what flavors?"

"Strawberry!"

In his excitement, he forgot not to order that flavor.

"Very well. What else?"

"You       mean       I       get       more       than       one?"

"You have five hundred and eighty dollars to spend, sir. That buys you a lot of ice cream."

"Very well. What other flavors have you?"

"Vanilla; with Madagascar vanilla beans. Chocolate; flavored with cacao beans from South America."

"Haven't you any American flavors?"

"Of course, sir. We have a very fine maple-black walnut ice cream. The maple syrup is produced in Canada; the walnuts grown in Missouri."

He looked up sharply. "How do you know that?"

"That black walnuts are grown in Missouri? I read the newspaper."

"I am done with ice cream."

"Then, will you have some champagne, sir?"

"Where does that come from?"

"France."

"No. Don't we grow any champagne in the U-nited States?"

"Grapes, you mean? They grow wine grapes in California."

"I will try some of that."

"It-is-out-of-stock."

"Forget it, then. What else can I have?"

"Escargot."

"What's that?"

"Snails." He wrinkled his nose.

"Something better."

"Truffles? That, sir, is a type of mushroom."

Swishing the imagined flavor in his mouth, Seth decided that might do.

"All right. What else?"

"Caviar."

"I don't like the sound of that. What is it?"

"Fish eggs. The very best comes from Russia."

"No."

"Smoked salmon? From Scotland?"

"What state is Scotland in?"

"It is a country. Bordering England. Where English walnuts grow, by the way."

"I would rather have some New Orleans praline, then." He pouted. "I suppose salt-water taffy comes from... salt water? In your neck of the woods?"

Her expression darkened. "I have seen it made elsewhere."

"I will have some of that. To go. And a bag of peppermint sticks. And some horehound drops. And rock candy."

"That will set you back at least twenty-five cents. I am afraid we are not getting very far, sir."

His voice assumed a little boy quality.

"How much for the meal? All told?"

"Without the escargot, caviar and champagne, I can charge you no more than twenty dollars."

"What does that bring me to?"

"Four hundred dollars left."

A hand flopped over his head. "This spending money is hard business."

"You have my sympathies, sir. What next?"

"Can I not let it go at this?"

"And lose it all? Certainly not."

Seth resumed his mental journey. Bypassing several shops which held no interest -- not even for a man with money to burn -- he finally dawdled outside the tailor's.

"I will have a new suit made. Two suits."

"Surely, for a man in your station, seven? One for each day of the week?"

The extravagance made him shudder.

"Four, then. Fine broadcloth. A black one and a dark blue one and a pin-striped suit. And a vest. A... royal blue satin vest!"

Nelander "wrote" on a piece of paper.

"What about fancy shirts?"

"Good! Two of them."

Amending that to "Twelve shirts; with extra cuffs and collars. White, of course. And ties? Two dozen of them. And pocket linen. A gross will do nicely."

He began to sweat.

"Surely that puts me over the top."

The interrogative went up in smoke. "May I suggest cufflinks? And pearl button covers? Or do you prefer ruby?"

"I'll look like a cigar store Indian!"

Nelander peered at him from over her "list."

"While I may not be native to these parts, I have never heard of a Red Man wearing cufflinks or button covers. For those, you must pay a visit to the jewelers."

"There is no jewelry shop in Lawrence."

"Yes, there is. It opened last week. Just in time for you to spend your hard-earned money."

Suspicions aroused, he inquired, "Where is it?"

"Right beside Mrs. Debasio's dressmaker's shop."

"Can I buy a dress?" he hopefully inquired.

"Only if you intend on wearing it."

"All right. I'll go in the jewelers. Although I don't believe there is one."

The clerk at the "Coming Soon to a Town Near You" Jewelry Store cleared her throat. She sounded suspiciously like Barbara Nelander.

"Good evening, sir. What can I do for you?"

"I need some... cufflinks."

"Very good, sir. We have some lovely ones. These have diamonds. Just mined from... Connecticut. These will suit you nicely. See how they sparkle in the sun."

He worriedly pulled at his collar. "I thought you said it was evening."

"The last rays of the sun."

"Oh. How much do they cost?"

"Two hundred dollars."

This time, he coughed, inadvertently spraying the "clerk." Mightily embarrassed, he attempted to wipe away his mistake.

"Not to worry, Captain Ward. A man of your status need never apologize."

As he considered, his smile turned upside-down.

"Then I don't think I like being rich. It makes men...."

"Selfish, greedy and bad-mannered," she supplied. "But have no fear. When you come home, I will beat those characteristics out of you."

He surprised her by declaring, "Good!"

"So -- you will take them?"

"Guess I better."

"Excellent. Now, may I interest you in an engraved Elgin pocket watch? With a very fine gold chain?"

"I prefer silver."

"How plebeian of you, sir. This one is silver. How do you like it?"

He inspected the engraving but no matter how hard he concentrated, he could not make out the picture.

"What is it?" he finally asked in exasperation.

"Buckingham Palace, sir."

"Where's that?"

She quickly went on to the next watch. "What of this? It has a very fine depiction of... the Topeka Courthouse." He shrugged. "This one? A magnificent stag. Or perhaps you are more the buffalo type?"

He finally grinned and she thought she had a sale.

"Got any with a schooner? In full sail?"

"Just your luck, Mr. Ward. We have one here. Not much call for sailing vessels in this neck of the woods, though."

He envisioned the watch clearly. "It'll take it! And a knife -- a pocket knife and a good, sturdy work knife."

The clerk appeared offended.

"For that, you will have to go to the mercantile."

He appeared crestfallen.

"Oh. How much I owe you?"

"For the diamond cufflinks and the Elgin watch -- with the schooner engraved on it -- and your initials, sir, which I will throw in for no charge -- $250.00."

"Done!"

He paid her and skipped merrily to the general store.

"Mr. Anson, a pocket knife -- the best you have. And a good work knife."

"'Evenin', Captain Ward," Hector Anson announced. His voice sounded higher than usual. "Good to see you out and about. Glad to oblige our leadin' citizen." Handing over the requisite items, he charged his customer "Ten dollars. What else?"

"A fishing pole. And tackle."

"An excellent choice. What else?"

"A new waterproof."

"One yellow rain slicker added to the list. What else?"

Seth ticked off on his fingers. "A barrel of the dillest pickles this side of the Mississippi. Two crates of Georgia onions... and an apple tree!"

"Certainly, sir. And just what size apple tree would you like? Seedling, middling height or one as tall as a four-mast ship?"

"One just high enough for a man with a boy -- or a girl -- on his shoulders to pick the top apple. How much does all that come to?"

A quick calculation brought a smirk to Barbara Nelander's face.

"Nine hundred and ninety-nine dollars. You, sir, have exactly one dollar left to spend. Think carefully."

Scratching his chin in a contemplative manner, he struck on the perfect ending to his shopping spree.

"A deck of cards."

She replied without thinking.

"But they cost only ten cents -- five, if you buy them used at the Tankard's Draft."

Holding up a finger, he suggestively raised and lowered his eyebrows.

"Not the kind I have in mind. You know the ones -- with racy depictions on them -- of sassy French ladies."

Having been caught in his trap, she laughed loudly.

"All this while I have been encouraging you to buy French wine and French comestibles and you top me with a deck of playing cards."

"That, my dear wife, makes the best present of all."

Proving once and for all that a man with money can have fun, but his real wealth lay in those he loved.

## CHAPTER 13

She would not have believed it if she had not seen it with her own eyes.

Signaling to Patricia, the two ran through the wide mouth of the valley, coming to a stop midway between the entrance and the point where the stream disappeared. Out of breath and gasping, Barbara approached the man she had never met but knew as surely as though they had already been introduced. Hand out, she spoke through a smile.

"My name is Nelander. You must be Mute Thomas."

It never once occurred to her that the youthfully middle-aged man with coal black skin, close-cropped hair and a muscular frame might not have the power of speech. She therefore evinced surprise when he gestured a greeting before bowing. Waiting for him to straighten, her hand remained outstretched. He stared at it in some trepidation.

"My father always said you could tell a lot about a man by how he shook." She exhibited improper technique by letting her wrist go limp. "I may not be a 'he,' but Ned Nelander'd turn over in his grave if he ever thought I didn't follow his instruction."

Summoning Patricia, she demonstrated.

"This here is the 'milksop' handshake. Men who shake this way are deceitful. They affect gentlemanly manners without having a clue what a true gentle man is. Never do business with that type. Then there is the 'good old boy.'" Grasping the girl's hand, she simultaneously slapped her on the back, nearly causing her to fall. "He pretends to be your best friend while sharpening the knife to stab you."

Repositioning Patricia, Nelander stooped her shoulders while offering to shake.

"The man who can't hold up his head is what Ned would call 'humble pie.' He is usually anything but that. Either he's trying to sell you inferior goods at a quality price or is so unsure of himself he couldn't tell which way the wind was blowing without a consultation."

Stepping closer to Mute Thomas, she gently took his hand, wrapping it around her own.

Adopting a strong Nova Scotia dialect, she quoted, "'You look a fella straight in the eye when you greet, Bab'ra, an' use a smooth, steady grip. Not hard enough to crush bones, just hard enough so a fella knows you've the strength of your convictions."

Naturally reticent, Thomas glanced over at Blind Betty. Although his mother could not see him, there existed a form of subliminal communication between the pair.

"Go ahead, boy. If Nelander wants yuh to shake, den shake." The man complied. "He been taught all his life, suh, not to touch white folks; 'specially not any white woman."

"Between ourselves, we will have a different law. You cannot speak, Thomas?" He shook his head. "From birth, or caused by an accident which was no accident?"

"He neber did make no noise," Betty explained. "He a'ways been silent as da field mice or da deer."

"I can think of worse company to keep." She relinquished her hand, nodding in acceptance of his shake. "The name, though, I was not so sure of. One would naturally be tempted to draw the conclusion that 'Mute Thomas' held his peace, but where I come from, 'Shorty' is apt to be a six-footer and 'Happy' a poor sod with depressed spirits. I expected a yacker more than a mute."

Unconsciously raising her voice, she evoked a grin in Blind Betty.

"Yas, Nelander, but he can hear right good. Like a mouse or a deer. Peoples a'ways t'ink a man cain't talk den he cain't hear, but yuh tell him sumthin' onest an' he'll do it."

"That I can well observe." Walking further into the narrow flatland, she noted a prodigious amount of brush already cleared. "Captain Ward said you would be here when we arrived but I hardly believed that possible. Did you hitch a ride?"

"No, suh. We walked. Set out right afta yuh lef' an' used da stars fer light."

"Then you must be tired and hungry. Let us eat, first --"

A moving shadow caught her attention and she looked up to see Thomas signaling with his hands. Watching carefully, she easily made the translation.

"I can see that you wish to earn your keep before resting, but I will not have you starve. Aboard ship, it is a seaman's right to be fed before he begins his assignment. If he is not, he becomes surly and disobedient."

Affecting a glum countenance, Nelander stomped around the "deck," grumbling under her breath. Waving one hand, she paused, went to pick up a bucket by the handle and dropped it. A mumbled curse expressed annoyance but hardly contrition. Then, glancing upward she pretended to climb the mast, clearly dogging by taking frequent rest periods.

Thomas clapped in approval, then manipulated his fingers at his mother.

"He says yuh good at makin' signs. An' he won' neber act like dat."

"Not if we give him rum, he won't," Patricia volunteered.

"No. Then he will sleep the day away and wonder where the sun went. We will make a fire and warm the food we brought. If you wish to work until that time, I will note it in the log."

This elicited more hand signals, which she again rightly interpreted.

"A 'log,' Master Thomas, is the record of a ship's progress. The captain or one of the officers charts the course, the weather and the condition of the vessel -- including, when necessary, whatever notations on the crew he may wish to preserve for posterity."

Seeing she had somehow made a mistake, her head went back in question. "I have said something to disturb you?"

"Yuh mus' not call him 'master,' suh." Betty immediately corrected. "Da word 'masta' be one dat refers to a slabe's owner. Or da oberseer. It best yuh not use it, suh."

Annoyed that she had not foreseen the improper usage, Nelander dug her hands in her pockets.

"Damn language, anyway. I am accustomed to using such a word with my crew as a term of respect. Not precisely the way it is employed aboard a naval vessel but more in the accepted form of 'mister.' I would, however, not wish to offend." Winking at the other woman, she added, "In the same vein, I suppose 'mate' is equally unacceptable. I suppose, then, it shall have to be simply 'Thomas' until I can come up with a more acceptable rank."

Briefly observing the pair return to work, Barbara and Patricia made a fire and heated that which they would have eaten for the noon meal. When ready, she signaled them over.

"Come and refresh yourself."

With only one coffee cup, Nelander drank then passed it to Betty. She accepted it with a firm grasp, the equivalent of a handshake, sipped and nudged Thomas. He, too, partook of the hot beverage, then offered it to Patricia. Not normally a coffee drinker, she comprehended the significance and took her turn.

When they had finished, Nelander doled out the food, then grabbed the burlap sack she and Patricia had brought the day before.

Removing one of the bundles, she untired the twine and dealt out the ten small, unpretentious plants.

"These are the strawberries. Captain Ward tells me they are dormant; requiring only sunshine, water and soil to revive. My instructions are that they are to be spaced four to six inches apart, with the entire root covered. If it does not rain within several days of planting, they must be watered by hand. At least," she conceded, "we have a creek and the task will not be overly stressful."

Blind Betty's ever-moving hands made a slight gesture of dissent but she did not speak her thought.

"We do what yuh say, suh."

"Oh, no. Not only what I say but what I do. Patricia and I are here to assist. We will come every day and put in a full eight hour shift. Longer, if necessary."

"Yuh got yuhr on' 'sponsibilities, Nelander. Yuh got da babe an' da house an --"

"Paula has gone with the captain and Peter today. They are watching and feeding her but tomorrow she will come to the valley. And for every day which follows until we have prepared the field and planted the strawberries."

"And watered them," Patricia eagerly supplied.

"How yuh feel 'bout dat, chil'?"

The girl puffed out her chest. "I want to contribute, too."

"We are a crew, working together for the common good. There can be no discussion on that point."

"As Ah libe an' breathe."

Completing the meal, the crew got up, each ready to pull their fair share.

"Thomas, as the expert, kindly assign Patricia and I our duty."

Clearly startled, he hesitated, then took in a deep lungful of air through his nose. Thoughtfully considering, he pointed to the brush already cleared, indicating they remove it.

"Very well. Where shall it go?"

Hesitating a moment, he finally nodded at the checkered tablecloth which had served as their breakfast table. Demonstrating they put the loose grasses, twigs and small branches there, he slung it over his shoulder and took a few steps up the incline. Stopping suddenly, he changed his mind and began dragging it. Nelander cleared her throat, flexing her biceps. His eyes widened.

Taking stock of the woman's muscle, he recommenced his enactment by repeating his original demonstration. Slinging the makeshift sack over his shoulder, he carried it to the crest of the hill where he safely deposited the material in a natural depression. Astutely watching his movements, the seafarer gave a hearty "Ho!"

Patricia stared at her in surprise.

"Hoe?" she asked, adding the silent "e" to her question. "Is that good or bad?"

Nelander made the distinction. "It is a sailor's call. H-o, exclamation point. Tell me what cleverness he has displayed."

Not to be outdone by all the play acting, the child hooked her thumbs in her shirt pockets the way a man would slip them around his suspenders.

"Whall, I reckon the cleverness comes frum him traipsin' the load up that darned hill fer us. Cleverness," she added with spit, "fer us, that is. Don't see no benefit fer 'im."

Clapping in reward for the thespian performance, Nelander tousled her hair.

"No argument there; but not what I had in mind. Try again."

More seriously, Patricia stalked the hill, trying to discover the meaning.

"He got the brush outta the way so we can plant."

"Correct. What else?"

Scrambling up the incline, she called back, "He put them in a place we can compost?"

"An idea which had not occurred to me. Good. What else? Use your sailors' skills."

"But Mute Thomas ain't a sailor."

"No, but he understands the natural elements. That makes him a good observer."

In the sentence came a clue. Pacing back and forth across the lip of the land, hair blowing in the breeze, she suddenly snapped her fingers.

"The wind, Officer Nelander! He piled it outta the wind so it don't blow back into the valley!"

"Ho!" And then a second rousing "Ho!"

Swelling with pride, Patricia took the cloth and raced back down.

"Yes, sir, I'm learning! Let's git started! At the farm, Captain Papa's got a tarpaulin we kin use. It's bigger an' tougher than this. And we kin save the tablecloth fer eatin' on!"

"A mate after my own heart."

Giving Thomas, the new recruit, a thumbs-up, the crew went to work. Using a pick, Thomas dug away at the brush, moving quickly from one to the other. Blind Betty followed, removing the wild plants from the ground and shaking off dirt from the roots. Patricia gathered them onto the cloth and Nelander toted them up the hill. By the time the sun reached its zenith, they had made considerable progress.

Betty made coffee, then fried victuals she had brought with her, making hotcakes in the bubbling fat. They had just settled down to eat when two new faces appeared over the horizon.

Peter waved a greeting and raced down the hill while Seth took his time, walking carefully, the way a man did when he did not wish to outrun his shadow, which played, like a puppy, at his feet. Finally reaching the party, his sunburned face glowed.

"I'd have thought you all'd been working a week. Hardly recognized the place. Afternoon, Miss Betty."

"Good aftanoon, suh."

Squatting on his haunches, he took a cup of coffee, sipped the hot brew, then sighed.

"'Nother day or so and you'll be ready to plow. How'd your four get so much done?"

"Teamwork," Patricia supplied. "Later on, Nelander'n me are gonna start a compost heap."

"Are you?"

"She is cut from your jib, Captain."

"As self-serving as that may be, I'll take it for a compliment, Officer." Rolling a chunk of bacon into his hotcake, he ate with his fingers, wiped his mouth on his sleeve, then suddenly raised his nose and sniffed.

"Darned, if I don't smell sumthin' bad," he drolled. All eyes turned to him. "Might be Injuns. Or a bear an' her cub draggin' a carcass back to their den. Then, ag'in, it might be a mess o' range cattle passin' by. Come to graze on them grasses you been cuttin' down. They kin leave a powerful stink behind."

He might have gotten away with it had not a tiny pink hand reached out of the backpack he wore and grabbed a strand of hair. Giving it a powerful tug, he jumped as if a bee had stung him. The source of his "smell" became readily apparent.

Everyone laughed.

"Give her to me, wicked man, and I'll take care of your problem." Lifting Paula out of her carry-all, Nelander kissed the child. "Is your papa being mean to you? Poor baby. You and I," she continued, hugging the infant, "never complain when he's about his business, an' that can be powerful odorsome!"

Ignoring her husband's red face, not lost on even the unsighted, she took the child to the creek, washed her off and changed the diaper. Returning with the precious bundle, Barbara presented her to the elder.

"This is Paula, Miss Betty."

Accepting the charge, the old Negress ran her fingers over the child's face in pure delight. Paula grasped one and held fast.

"Dis be a won'erful chil', Nelander. She full ob spirit."

"Comes by it naturally," papa bragged.

Motioning the parents forward, Betty examined each of their faces, running her sighted hands over their noses, lips, cheeks, brow, before making a final determination.

"She got yuhr blood, no doubt. She be a pretty gal." Raising a little leg, she gently swung it. "Tall, like da captain. An' strong, like da mudder. What color yer hair, Nelander?"

"Brown."

"An' yuh, Capt'n?"

"Brown. Like the earth."

"Oh, dis chil', she be ob da earth, a'right. But she got da water in her, too. She gonna be a woman ob both worl's. Yas, suh. Dere no be puttin' dis little one down."

"She will, Miss Betty, be raised as blind as you, for she will be taught that all Men are created equal. She will never see color."

"No, Nelander," the old woman sternly rebuked. "Ah see color. Don' need no eyes. Be all 'round me. Da green ob da trees, the blue ob da sky." Her voice turned ominous. "Da blackness in men's souls. Don' need no eyes to see dat." She turned to Seth. "Yuh tease 'bout smellin' sumthin' bad on da wind. Yuh be right, but it ain't no bears nor range cattle. It be in da hearts an' minds ob dem what walks on two legs."

"I am concerned about the tan of wheat heads and the yellow kernels of corn. The spring red of ripening berries. The blue of my children's eyes."

"We all be puttin' new names to dem colors befo' our days is done."

He grunted and did not want to pursue the prediction.

"I can take a day or two off from plowing, Mute Thomas. The boy and I will be clearing out rocks and then puttin' in seed. You come by the house early day after tomorrow and I'll let you have the horse. You won't have time to get everything cleared but I want the land furrowed and the strawberries planted. Those you can."

"Five thousand," Nelander stated. "We will get them all in."

He shrugged, still disturbed by the previous conversation. "Come on, Peter."

The boy jumped to his feet, turning to his other parent. "We going to take Paula back with us?"

"She can stay here." Barbara did not have to add that she feared contagion from her husband's ill mood. It could not be rightly be said hers fared any better but Seth did not argue.

"See you at suppertime."

Leaving the backpack, he and Peter hurried away, heads bent from the weight they carried. In this case, figurative being heavier than actual.

The crew in the valley toiled until a close approximation of four bells, then Nelander straightened from the arduous work, ruefully rubbing her aching back.

"I am not one to complain of manual labor, but this is hard!" Running a hand through her short, sweat-stained hair, she wiped the moisture on her trousers, then summoned the others in. "Let us call it a day. I want to show you the Windsor house before we lose the light."

Mute Thomas touched his mother, making some letters or symbols on her palm.

"He says we jest fine here, Nelander. Da night not so chill we cain't sleep out. Later," she softly added, "we kin throw up a lean-to. Not in da valley, here, but mebbe in da trees up yonder. Be nice fo' us. Real nice, habin' space to sit out an' be away frum odders. Listen to da sounds ob nature. A rem'ber dat frum when Ah was a little'n. Jes' about da size ob Miss Paula."

"No, ma'am. There is a perfectly fine house which needs keeping. I will not have you sleep in the open when you might be doing me a service." Emphasizing the last, Nelander leaned forward to bring home her point. "I have done my best to straighten things out, but there is simply too much for me to accomplish. Floors to sweep; windows to wash. What do you call them -- dust bunnies -- to be trapped and escorted out."

Patricia tried to correct the assumption "dust bunnies" were not living creatures, but a wink quickly silenced her.

"Then, of course, there is the roof to repair." Exaggerating the locals, she moaned, "Lord only knows when my man'll have time to see to that. He's so busy, you know, what with the plowin' and sowin' an' all."

Mute Thomas chuckled behind his hand.

"Then there's the whitewashin'. No fe-male in her right mind would ever put her hand to that! I know my place. It's in the kitchen, makin' bread an' in the bedroom, pleasin' my man an' makin' babies."

The stunningly shocking statement finally carried the day.

"Oh, Lor', Nelander, where yuh say yuh cume frum?"

"Nova Scotia. It is a province of Canada, your neighbor to the north."

"Dey's plain talkin' folk."

"More than that. We do not have slavery. In fact, if what I hear be true, many of your people are taken there for safety."

"Ah kin see why Mista Seth fell in love wid yuh, Nelander. He be a good man an' yuh be a good woman, suh."

"I take that most kindly. Now: you will stay in the house? For wages, of course. I do not know how we will pay you, but I will think of something."

She tried to pass, but Blind Betty's hand shot out, accurately grasping her arm.

"Yuh kin say what yuh wan' -- Ah 'spect yuh and da captain'll habe some 'splaining to do when folks finds out what yuh gone an' done. But betwix yuh an' meh an' mah boy, Ah don' wan' no foolishness. Yuh brung us out here an' gibe us work to do -- honorable work. Now, yuh give us a place to stay. Ah ain't neber had a house befo' -- not a right fine place. Or eben a garden to call mah own. We'll gets along fine widout no 'wages.'"

Her grip tightened.

"An' no promises made, Off'cer Nelander. Dere be a time cume we need to git out an' we'll go."

The officer's back stiffened and her eyes narrowed.

"I made a vow to one family that I would cherish their friendship and defend them to the last. They swore the same. We took a pirate's oath. I did everything I could to uphold my end. By so doing, I put my own family in harm's way. A danger we are not yet clear of. And will not be for many years. For that, and for the Windsors' repudiation, I grieve. It was a hard lesson."

Feeling herself released, Nelander stepped aside. But she did not go far.

"Perhaps a different person would learn from their... I hesitate to call it a mistake, but I shall: learn from their mistake. I am not the same person I was. But experience has tempered my resolve. Miss Betty, you and

Thomas are my friends. I welcome you into my family as equals. I do not expect you to run on me, nor do I expect us to run on you."

Picking up her baby, then resting a hand on Patricia, she faced the pair with cold, steely orbs.

"My father taught me that you judge someone by his heart. He also said you live by your beliefs. I may say with pride that he died defending his. I expect no less of myself, for I could not live a coward's life. I have fought for everything I achieved and I pray God I am never in the position where I must back down. I have no idea what the future holds. You say it bodes ill. So be it. We will face that when it comes. But I swear by all I hold holy I will be with you, beside you -- in front of you, if needs be -- when trouble comes."

"And she's not the only one." Patricia's avowal came out of nowhere. Balling a fist, the child held it to the sky. "I am right beside her."

Blind Betty wept.

God only knew know long it had been since tears of praise leaked through her dead eyes.

# CHAPTER 14

They walked together, one seafarer from Canada carrying a babe born in Kansas, one daughter of a dead woman reputed to haunt the prairie, one sightless old woman and one man, silenced from birth.

They formed a formidable pirate crew.

Coming through a stand of trees from the east side of the property, they arrived at a house. Deserted, by the looks of it. In need of floors swept, windows washed, shingles replaced. Early spring weeds grew in the garden. The remnants of a burned barn resembled a gaping hole left by an explosion.

"Oh, surely, Lor' dis be heaben on earth," Blind Betty declared.

To which Mute Thomas lipped, "Amen."

Setting down the tools he carried over his shoulder, the Negro fell to his knees and kissed the ground.

Whether he had any awareness, that act served as an "X."

"X" for treasure.

"X" for a name on a deed.

"Go in," Nelander urged, nearly as excited as they. "Have a look around."

Taking his mother's hand, Thomas guided her up the porch step, then glanced around, just to be sure. Patricia motioned them forward. Reverently turning the knob, he gave the door a gentle shove. Hinges squeaking, it slid inward.

"Welcome home, Mrs. --" Barbara stopped, puzzled. "I beg your pardon. I do not know your last name."

Blind Betty had an answer.

"It be Nelander, suh. Miz Betty Nelander an' her son, Thomas Nelander."

The seaman swayed in the storm which swelled in her breast.

"So be it. Mother." Waiting for the gale to pass, she wiped her face with a shaky hand. "I hardly knew my birth mother. I can count on my fingers the number of times I have seen her since I was five years old. She has always been a stranger to me. And I never had a brother. Which served me well, for if I had, I might never have been taken to sea. It is high time I had both."

Following them inside, she heaved a deep breath at the amount of work to be done.

"I did my best to prepare it for a new owner --"

"No, ma'am. Dis be fine. Mighty fine. No better'n all da worl'."

The present occupant seemed to agree, for a large orange cat appeared out of the hall, tail waving above her head. Letting out a loud "Meow!" she appraised the newcomers, then made a slow rotation around Betty's ankles, rubbing her cheeks against the flesh.

"Look!" Patricia cried in delight. "A big, fat cat."

"Cat, yes. Big, yes," Barbara agreed. "Fat -- perhaps only temporary."

Bending down, Betty petted the animal's sides.

"Yuh be right, suh. She be in da fambly way."

"Kittens! Can we have one? We need a good mouser, and --"

"Yes," Nelander decided. "Captain Ward needs a good mouser. And I," she added, sliding her tongue across her canines, "need the company of my own kind. Your father accused me of being feline. Now, it will be two against one."

"If you are going to keep one, can I have another for myself?"

"I think you should."

"Oh, ho!" she shouted. "When, Miss Betty? When is she to have kittens?"

"Mos' inny time, chil'. She musta cume in here to make a nest fo' da litter."

"Cats are seamen's friends," the officer advised. "They are good luck; and hard workers."

"Do they get rum? Like the crew?"

"No, their tastes are somewhat more simple. Tomorrow, I will bring her some food, so she need not go hungry before her delivery."

As if to belie the statement, a mouse recklessly scurried from one corner to the other. The cat, otherwise reluctant to abandon the fingers scratching her head, dashed after. Just seconds too late, her paw immediately disappeared through a narrow crack and she pressed against the wall, utterly intent on the task.

Although unable to see, Betty correctly interpreted the sounds.

"Dis cat don' need no food, suh. She able to he'p herse'f. We won' be spoilin' her, now. 'Spect mebbe fo' a little pettin' here an' dere."

Thomas grinned and clapped his hands. With attention on him, he tapped his thighs, mimicking an invitation. With the "cat" safely on his lap, he lavished kisses while stroking its head.

"I see. She will work for her keep and in return, your mother will lavish affection."

He enthusiastically nodded.

Acutely embarrassed, Betty shooed Thomas away.

"Won' be nuthin' like dat. Ah got no time fo' wastin' on critters."

Patricia went over to the cat. Before she could be told not to touch it for fear the animal might bite, she held out her hand. The cat sniffed it, flicked an ear and meowed.

"I was going to warn you, Patricia, but I see you more correctly sized up the situation."

"She already welcomed Miss Betty, so I figured she'd do the same for me. I know all about handling 'critters.'" Her face crinkled. "But that's what I wanted to say. I don't think this here cat would appreciate being called a critter. Isn't critter a word used for any kind of creature? Like a cow or a dog or a snake?"

"I suppose so. Why?"

"Cats aren't like others. They're independent. A cat's a cat. It isn't a dog or a cow or a snake. Now," she declared, rubbing behind the ears, "you can call a dog most anything. As long as you say it nice, it'll love you. Take ol' Herman. I wouldn't want to be called Herman. You wouldn't want to. But Herman -- he don't mind."

"I suppose that means you wouldn't want to be called 'Bessie,' either."

"I would not."

"All right, Master Patricia. You have carried your point. We shall henceforth never again refer to a cat as a critter." Directing her voice to Betty, she asked, "What will you call it? I can see I will have no peace until the -- *chatte* -- that is French for 'cat' -- is well and duly named."

"Dat's it, Nelander. Chatte, she is."

"Now that we have got that settled, why don't you have a look around before Patricia and I must leave."

Receiving his parent's permission, Thomas went directly to the kitchen. Priming the pump handle, he gave it half a dozen downward motions before a gush of water came up the pipes. Clucking his tongue in delight, he fairly did a dance around the room. Hurrying back, he signed in Betty's hand.

"Dat fine, boy. Dat fine. Oh, Lor' we ain't neber had no pump befo'. A'ways had to go to da well in da square to draw water. When da line be long, dat meant a walk through da wood to da stream. 'magine habin' our bery own pump!"

Nelander and Patricia watched as Thomas curiously opened the cupboards, peered into the lower cabinets, then raced through the living room to the bedrooms. The basic plan closely resembled the Ward's house, with the exception Terrance had never constructed a loft.

Hurrying back, he tapped three times on Betty's arm to signify the number of bedrooms, then dashed outside. Stopping before the burned outline of where the barn once stood, he shot the officer a quizzical look.

"Lightning," she explained. "It happened during the drought. Without water to put it out, it just burned to the ground. The roof of the house may have been damaged. You'll have to see when it rains."

"We fix it up right fine fo' yuh, Nelander. Thomas kin do mos' innythin' an' Ah'm good wid mah hands."

"Well, bless you, then. Enjoy your home," she offered. "Enjoy your first meal. We will see you tomorrow."

Before she could slip away, Betty approached. Even without sight, she moved quickly and with certainty. Grasping her new neighbor, she reverently bestowed upon it a devotional kiss.

"Yuh be a saint, Nelander. Da Lor' bless an' keep yuh, an' protect yuh an' yuhrs in da times to come."

"My God bless and keep us all from the folly of men," she added, waving good-bye.

Gathering up Paula and Patricia, the trio made their way quickly through the fields.

"It'll be good to see a lamp burning in the Windsor's farm," the girl declared. "It's nice doing a good deed. Especially when we're getting two cats out of it." Skipping ahead, she reconsidered and turned back. "It's still a good deed, isn't it, if we get something back in return?"

"It is."

"I'm glad. From my way of thinking, we got the better of the deal."

Barbara would have been tempted to agree, but reserved her unconditional accord. Much depended on the success of her venture. If the strawberries failed to thrive, if they did not produce the crop she anticipated, or by some odd chance they could not sell what they harvested, the bargain would be a bad one, indeed.

Without a supply of money coming in, not only would she and Seth lose the former Windsor property, they stood more than an unequal chance of losing their own farm, as well.

One plan, gone awry, and disaster lurked around the corner.

Which not even a pair of litter mates could balance.


The following morning found Nelander, Patricia and Paula at the valley. Blind Betty and Thomas were already there, knee deep in digging and chopping. Shouting a welcoming "Hello!" they set about their tasks, eagerly gathering the uprooted brush and carting it away in Captain Ward's tarpaulin.

Seth and Peter did not come for lunch, so they dispensed with the meal quickly before going back to work. Resting only when near total exhaustion or to tend to the baby, Barbara groaned as her aching muscles protested the unaccustomed labor. Back aching and calf muscles cramping, she finally gave way, flopping under the budding willow trees near the stream.

Wearily massaging arms and legs, she slowly caught her breath, yet her heart would not stop pounding. As much as they progressed, so much more lay ahead. Every hour they took preparing the field meant that much longer a delay before planting. And without willing thoughts of gloom, Seth's absence frightened her. While it was reasonable to assume he had decided to finish in the corn field so Thomas could have the horse and plow on the morrow, she could not shake the idea he knew more than he said.

Perhaps he had inspected the plants and determined they were dying. Or already dead. Not wanting to waste time with that which could not be salvaged, he had stayed away rather than have to explain the true state of affairs.

Or, perhaps, like her, their grim finances burdened his soul. Without any certainties in life, the corn and the wheat represented their only chance for survival. Without a good harvest, they could not meet their obligations.

Flushed from the rapid heart rate which would not slow, she wondered if she had not compounded her error a thousand-fold. While chances were slim they could have found a buyer for the property, they had discussed the possibility of renting the land. Seth had indicated there were laborers in town who might be interested. Men who had no down payment, but good, hard-working fellows seeking a chance to establish themselves. No matter how little they paid, cash in the hand spent easier than good deeds.

While the Wards needed people to help with the strawberries, it might have been more prudent to cut a deal with tenants. In exchange for letting them grow their own corn and wheat, she and Seth might first have required them to help clear the valley. Once the strawberries were in, she supposed nature would take its course. What weeding might be required she and Patricia could handle.

Instead, she had jumped at the idea of inviting two penniless Negroes to help. Their work ethic was beyond question, but she could debate her own decision. Ignoring the warning that some, if not many in Lawrence would disapprove the choice, she willfully put the family in danger. Ignoring men's prejudices, a command decision had been made without first weighing the consequences.

If the temper of the times grew worse, which Seth, among others, believed to be the case, trouble would hang over their heads like a noose, waiting to be tightened. If John Brown were an example of the lengths men would go to prove a point, others would stop at nothing. Even bloodshed did not seem to frighten these zealots. In truth, they seemed to bring it on, as though that were an answer in itself.

Men had no business warring over principles which ought to be self-evident. One human being was no better than another, no matter the color of their skin. An individual might be good or he might be bad, but those were judgments established by ethics and set in law. No one deserved to be chattel because of the caste into which he or she had been born.

Yet those were ideas born of a free country. In one torn apart by slavery, law became secondary to greed and perverted morals. People justified opinions based on a book written two thousand years before. Holding their own interpretations to be sacred and the only true Way, they strove to enforce their beliefs on a world they saw as only black and white.

Barbara Nelander's world was green and blue. It smelled of salt water rather than sweat of bondage. It rocked to the undulations of waves instead of emotion. Separations were by hard-earned rank, not inherited by birthright.

She had tried to bring the ocean to Kansas, only to be reminded the Midwest was a long way from either coast. Seth had tried to warn her but she had not listened.

Shame burned in her soul, for it had been she who named him captain. She had placed him above her because he knew the land and the people. She had promised to learn its ways, just as she had once promised Ned Nelander she would adopt the sea as her own. She had never crossed her father but she had forced Captain Ward into an untenable situation.

Barbara had paid 5 cents apiece for 5,000 strawberry plants, no more native to Lawrence than she. To make them adapt, she had recruited a crew of misfits, flying in the face of conventionality. Rather than assimilate, she had set herself apart. And by doing so, had cast the Wards adrift.

Had that been what he had tried to tell her by not coming for the noon day meal? She did not have an answer.

Worse, she had no way, short of direct confrontation, of eliciting a response.

Nelander suddenly felt unequal to that contest.

Rousing herself with forced effort, she returned to work, no longer able to take delight in their progress. Because of this, the rest of the day dragged. By evening, she felt unnaturally tired.

If her new neighbors noticed the silence of the intervening hours, or sensed her flagging spirit, they made no comment. Perhaps they guessed the reason. It would not have taken a gifted mind reader, for troubles, like political tempers, were often worn on the sleeves.

"See you in the morning," Patricia sang in childlike innocence. "Are you coming by for the plow? Papa Captain said we might have it tomorrow. Or shall we have him lift it into the buckboard and bring it out, ourselves? That would be fine." Grinning broadly, she explained her enthusiasm. "That way, I get to drive. Nelander can do it, but I have more experience."

Assuming a lightness of his own, Mute Thomas made a walking motion with the second and third fingers of his left hand. Not content to convey his message, he rolled his shoulders, using both arms to affect a swimming motion, inferring the parting of low-hanging branches as he made his way across the field.

The girl shrugged. "All right."

Determined to carry a brightness for all of them, she skipped ahead, ranging so far in advance she had to stop and wait for Barbara and the baby to catch up. Almost out of sight on one occasion, she compelled the adult to call her back. When she appeared, a bunch of wild flowers protruded from her digits.

"Look! It seems just yesterday everything was brown and withered and today, spring has sprung! I bet if we stopped right here and stared at the grass we could see it grow. And the trees -- already sporting a cover of green. I bet in a week you won't be able to see through the branches, anymore."

Refusing the bouquet, Barbara tiredly said, "Carry them for me. I am so dry, I fear they will wither in my hands."

Not put off by the denial, Patricia continued to bound about like a frolicsome deer.

"I missed the spring last season. I feel cheated out of a whole year. Without any rain and all that heat, nothing started growing until almost fall. But the captain was right. He said seeds carried by the flood would take root in all sorts of strange places and that in a few years the woods would take on an entirely different appearance. You can see it, already. The parts which died away are barren, but along the edges, new life is creeping out."

Ashamed for not having noticed, Nelander forced herself to look. The sight caused a reaction of shock, for Patricia's observations were prophetic. The landscape she had come to know so well in the three years of her new life had mysteriously altered. Entire chunks of wood had disappeared, creating different lines of vision.

Even the hills seemed strange, re-sculptured by the mighty force of raging waters. Those landmarks she had used to navigate through the pastures were gone, leaving her with a sensation of loss and isolation. Without being aware, her ocean had altered. It no longer appeared friendly and familiar but alien, as if the great hand of God were warning her away.

*This would have been what the earth looked like to Noah,* she mused, *when the waters receded.* First, he would have witnessed the tops of mountains, then the higher elevations and finally the plains. New lakes would have asserted themselves into valleys, streams changed course, towers of rock reduced to dirt-covered floors.

Had Noah simply been grateful for the chance to once again step on dry land, or had the revamped face of the planet frightened him, too? How long had it taken to adjust? Months? Years? What season had it been when the waves receded? Had he faced the same problems as she: hurry to get in the crops before it was too late? Had his extended family gone hungry that first year? Had they worked together for the good of all, or had this unexpected adversity brought out their differences?

Perhaps God had washed away the original corruption, but it had not taken long to re-root. First, quarrels over who maintained rights over the cattle and chickens. Then, those fortunate survivors, forgetting their close brush with death, would have begun to draw lines.

*This is my farm. I am taking these fields for myself. You must till the ground somewhere else.*

*I have more land than you. Therefore, I will make the rules and you obey.*

*I will trade you this for that, but not that for this.*

*I am better because I am taller or stronger or have more gold.*

*You are different because your skin is darker or you do not speak the same language as I.*

How many decades passed before the New became the Old?

And what had God thought of it all, His grand experiment in starting fresh? Had He been tempted to quash it all and begin with a new Adam and Eve?

Why hadn't He?

Tugging at the sleeve of her shirt which had pulled up from repeated re-shifting of the baby's weight, Nelander speculated on those unanswerable questions.

Perhaps God had set a time limit. Two thousand years. Three thousand: however long it had been since the Flood.

*If I see no improvement, I will put the wheels in motion. Instead of destroying everything myself, I will permit you to destroy one another.*

Had He a mighty conflagration in mind? Not a fire, but a war?

*If you cannot settle your differences peacefully, I will look the other way while you legislate hateful laws, draw your lines, segregate your people. Instead of rain for forty days and forty nights, I will let you use rifles and cannon.*

*And lo, the land will be bathed in a new Flood. This one of blood and gore and shattered bones.*

Patricia Ward saw hope and vigor in the altered landscape. Barbara Nelander saw a bubbling cauldron of mistrust and hate.

Ignoring the lessons of the past, the servants of God had blissfully destroyed a second Eden. This time, however, no one had been forewarned. No Ark existed which the chosen could board and save themselves.

In a manner of months or years it would, again, in French, *pleuvor a seaux.*

Rain cats and dogs.

Barbara Nelander had come to a foreign land.

And now feared she alone comprehended the language.

## CHAPTER 15

"You are late," Seth said, greeting his wife and daughter at the door. "I had begun to think you fell in."

The expression caused a spark in Nelander's brain.

"What?" she asked, feeling adrift in an unknown sea.

"Got lost," he explained.

"No. No...." And again, "No. We... worked late. To get as much accomplished as possible. For the strawberries."

No one in Sodom and Gomorrah had lived to eat strawberries.

"How's it coming?"

The lightness of his tone confused her.

"We're going to start plowing tomorrow, Captain Papa," Patricia reminded him.

He appeared to consider. "'We?' Are you going to stand behind the traces? You know," he continued, "one of the first discussions Nelander and I ever had concerned that very thing. She saw no reason why I should not teach my daughter how to plow. She says you are as strong as any boy your age. What do you think of that?"

"May I, papa? May I?"

"Then what will Mute Thomas do?"

"He can stand behind and break up the clods."

Stroking his chin, he gave the idea credence. "Plowing is a tiring chore. One even I do not anticipate with much pleasure. I think I would leave him do the hard work, but if he allows you to hold the reins, or, better yet, lead the horse, I have no objection. That much Peter does and he is a great help to me."

Her eyes rounded in anticipation.

"Then I will do it."

"Leaving Nelander and Blind Betty to follow. You will need a wheelbarrow, too," he decided. "Remind me in the morning to put one in the wagon."

Seeing Barbara pale, he quickly took the baby, relieving her of the burden.

"Here, go sit down. You have taxed yourself beyond endurance." His tone grew serious. "I feared this. The effort is too much, and you, only recently given birth."

"I am all right."

"All right, pray God, with a good night's rest."

His sudden invocation of the Lord drew a low moan from her breast. While a god-fearing man, he seldom evoked the name in casual speech.

"What made you say that?" she demanded, trying hard to penetrate his thoughts.

"Say what?"

"Pray God."

He shrugged and moved away, Paula squirming in his arms.

"We have had enough tragedy in this house. I am trying to protect us." Seth worked on a smile as he disappeared into their bedroom. "Seaman's superstition."

Nelander's temper did not improve during the evening meal, nor did she have any more to say than a "Good night," when Patricia and Peter slipped off to bed. Waiting until Seth disappeared to complete his daily business in the outhouse, she crept noiselessly toward the crate where most of the strawberry plants yet resided. With an awe far greater than his teasing seaman's superstitions, she lifted the lid.

Too dark to see more than shadowed outlines, she stared at the plants. From what she could ascertain, none of them had been disturbed since she had removed a quantity to take to the valley in the burlap sack. Had one, or two or even a dozen been removed, she would not have been able to tell. He might have selectively removed the deadest of the dead, but the rest remained.

Had he left them as a lesson? Something Ned would have done.

*Prepare well, Bab'ra. Examine all sides of a problem before you act. Never respond in haste. There's always time to get it right, but never enough to repair the damage you in error.*

She had been thinking about her father a great deal lately. Wondering what he would think of her new life in Kansas. Ruminating over his expressions; the way he sounded when delivering good advice. Hardly a preacher sort, Captain Nelander was one to keep his own council, speaking only to issue orders, or occasionally to dispense wisdom.

Had she loved him? For the first twenty-three years of her life, Bab'ra had seldom given the matter any consideration. Until age five, he had been a mystery figure, flittering in and out of her mother's home after a separation of long months. She anticipated his visits because he habitually brought home small gifts: a whale's tooth, carved with the figure of a mermaid. A box of French chocolates. A ship in a glass bottle.

Three presents in five years. Not counting her earliest days of which she had no remembrance, that meant the seafarer touched foot in Nova Scotia no more often than once a twelve month. Probably less often than that.

Her mind caressed the memory. The scrimshaw she had carried around in her pocket, not so much as a remembrance of him but as a relic of the sea and the creatures which lurked beneath the waves. Unlike other girls who dreamed of being a mermaid and luring seaman to their sides, she fantasized exploring the depths of the ocean bottom with them as guide.

Beneath the waves she would discover secrets of the sea. Sunken boats, half covered in sand and silt, starkly naked masts reaching upward toward the sun it would see no more. Shrouded mounds of hull, cracked from impact. Twisting turns through green-covered corridors, home to schools of tiny fishes, bizarre crustaceans, wide-eyed eels.

Beyond the wrecks, she would explore the geysers, putting a hand near, but not too close, to the scalding flow, super-heated by the interior fires of the earth's tumultuous soul. Using her inquiring mind as a notebook, she might catalogue an entire array of creatures unknown to Man; those which hid along the undulating bottom, living and dying and perpetuating their species undisturbed by the affairs of larger, more intrusive creatures who fancied themselves molded in the image of God.

Sometime between her fourth and fifth birthdays she had asked an old salt to drill a hole through the top of the scrimshaw so that she might put a cord through. Wearing the tooth around her neck, she felt the power of the sea.

She had meant to save the confections, as well, but her mother told her they would melt in the summer heat. Late one night, perched atop a rock outside the harbor, Barbara had opened the box and inspected the contents.

Twelve "bonbons," small lumps, like coal, nestled side-by-side, tops decorated with sugar roses. Some of the chocolate had melted and reformed, leaving irregular shapes with yellowish globs of butter fat along the sides.

Taking one in her hand, she had hefted the weight then nibbled at a corner. The filling had granulated and tasted of some fruit she could not identify. Raspberries, she finally decided. As good a guess as any.

She speculated now if the taste had actually been strawberry and decided it had not. Just as well.

Dutifully eating all twelve candies because they had been bought with the best intentions, she had flung the small wooden box into the sea. Her mother had thought it might be used for storing keepsakes, but a seaman's daughter had little need of that. What little she possessed: a scaling knife, a handful of hooks and a spare fishing line, were stored in a tin can which fit easily into her pocket. Putting them into a box would not be convenient.

The ship in a bottle she had taken with her when recruited to serve aboard the *Bottom Dollar*. Shoving it in the bottom of her duffel, she had forgotten about it until cleaning up her belongings after the crew's quarters had filled with water from a particularly bad storm. The glass had broken, leaving only the tiny ship worth saving. She asked around whether any of the crew knew how to put it back in another bottle, but none did. Applying to the captain, Ned informed her the craft had been constructed piece-by-piece and that, fully constructed, could never be replaced.

Not one for "keepsakes," Bab'ra had tossed it overboard. Not surprisingly, Ned did not remember having given it to her, so there were none to mourn its loss.

The scrimshaw she kept longest, but one evening, while monkeying along the crossbeams, the cord had snapped. She had not realized until too late and by that time, the heavy tooth had slipped off and disappeared. She thought it might have been caught in the folds of her seaman's blouse or dropped into a pocket of her flowing trousers and paid the loss no heed. Subsequent investigation revealed no such thing had happened.

Briefly disturbed, Nelander had shaken it off. The weight around her neck had been annoying and the medallion flopped when she climbed or stooped to perform routine tasks. In any event, the tooth had been returned to its proper place. Back to the sea.

She wondered, indeed, if that was where she belonged. Riding the waves and not drowning in an ocean of waving wheat.

A hand rested on her shoulder and would have startled her, had her nerves not been honed by tragedy. She had not heard him come up.

"Looks as though you're lining up the corpses for burial," Seth observed of the strawberry plants, set out in a row. To another, the statement would have shocked. Receiving no reaction, he continued. "Norman wrote to me, once. He's not much of a letter writer, so I tend to remember what he said. Described a time when the dragoons came upon a war party. Five or six were killed. They lined up the soldiers, just like that. Had a service, then dumped 'em in a mass grave."

"What did they do with the dead Indians?"

"He didn't say."

Scooping up the plants, Nelander returned them to the box. Like the keepsakes her mother thought she should have.

"Why didn't you come out to the valley for your noon day meal?" she blurted.

He affected surprise.

"Had some work I wanted to start."

"Start?"

He shrugged. "'Spect you'll figure it out sooner than later."

She let it go.

"Is there any point plowing tomorrow?"

"Unless you're plannin' on diggin' little holes fer every plant, I don't see any way around it."

Again, the casual attitude. It evoked ire.

"You comin' out to help?"

"Wasn't plannin' to. Peter an' I got our own work to tend to."

"I see. I thought...." Her jaw tightened. "You might want to give us the benefit of your expertise."

"You'll do fine."

"That so?"

"You read me the letter. From that fella in -- where was he from?"

"Virginia."

"Plant 'em four to six inches apart. Cover the root. Water 'em if it don't rain. Seems pretty straight forward to me. If you can't figure that out, Blind Betty will. I reckon she's got a green thumb."

"I thought," Nelander sarcastically noted, "she had a brown thumb. Which is another reason I'm in trouble."

He leaned against the counter. "Who said you were in trouble?"

"Ask me that again when we're all shot in our beds by 'nigger haters.' Kansas is full of 'em, as I've been told."

Sidling closer, he whispered, breathing into her face.

"That what's been bothering you all evening? I saw you chewin' on sumthin' and it weren't supper."

She ignored the tender familiarity of his speech.

"What does 'green thumb' mean?"

"Someone who's good with growing things. A person who can raise a crop from a rock garden."

"What makes you think Betty has that talent?"

"Black folks have a way with the land. They understand it; they're close to it. Talk to it. Coax it along like it was a friend an' not an enemy."

"Seems you've described yourself that way."

Seth withdrew, dropping a hand into his pocket.

"Mebbe that's why I don't look at Negroes as others do. I judge 'em a different way."

"How?"

"By what's behind their eyes. A man's got a light behind his eyes or he's got a fire. He wants to do good an' be left alone, or he wants trouble. He takes what he's been given or he lets that fire burn through his insides. Might be a reason he has a hurt; might be he don't. But if he can't settle and put that energy to a constructive purpose, then he's... a bad apple."

"It only takes one to spoil a barrel."

"Not if you find the rotten one and take it out. Thought being a seaman, you'd like that."

"You can remove a bad apple but taking out a man is a lot harder."

He scuffed his foot. "That's where the gunsmoke comes in."

"Bringing us back to being shot in our beds."

This time, he surprised her by grinning.

"No one'll shoot us in our beds. Likely we'll be woke up, furst. Probably hear 'em comin'. Be up an' standin' outside."

"Who are they, Seth? The ones who will come? Will we know them?"

"Might be. Might be not. Could be McConaghie an' his boys. Or outside agitators from across the border."

"How do we stand against them?"

"Talk reason."

"And if they don't listen? All because of my strawberries --"

Seth turned on her so fast she would not have had time to protect herself, had he intended violence.

"Barbara, your strawberries are only a small part of this larger picture we're facin'. My feelings are well known. I'm a free-soiler. I voted against slavery and I'll do it again. The fact we brought brown-skinned's onto our land might be a burr on their backside, but when a man's lookin' fer trouble, he reaches out fer anythin'."

Crossing the kitchen, he stared out the window. The peace he saw there: the gentle movement of the breeze, the sway of newly budded tree branches, the smell of earth, the rustle of a rabbit. All cloaked the impending conflict.

"If trouble comes, it won't be because of anything we did or didn't do. It'll come because of how we've lived our lives. One thing or another may set deeds in motion, but only because you and I are who we are."

"Good people," she declared, moving to join him. Touching the curtain, her hand lingered on the cloth. "What do you see out there?"

"Crops growing; corn and wheat and strawberries being harvested. Patricia with a sketch book, drawing a portrait of Peter, who squirms and can't stop fussin' with those three hairs he's got sprouting outta his upper lip. Paula kicking up her heels and hollerin' until they chase her away. You and I sittin' on the porch and I'm asking you how you'd spent one thousand dollars. Only this time, it'll be real and not pretend."

"Is that really what you see?"

"If you look for good things, you see good things." Resting a hand on the back of her neck, he lightly massaged her muscles. "Bet ol' Ned told you that a time or two." He felt her body quiver as she silently laughed.

"Sounds like something he'd say. But I sure as hell never heard anyone call him 'ol' Ned.'"

"First time for everything. Come on. Let's go to bed. Now that I've worked the kinks out of your neck, it's my turn to get rubbed."

This time, Nelander laughed out loud.

"Twenty seconds is what I owe you. Think you can fall asleep that fast?"

"Nope."

He took her hand and they retired for the night. Neither of them were asleep in anything like twenty seconds.

## CHAPTER 16

Mute Thomas plowed one sloping side of the valley, Patricia held the reins of the horse and Nelander and Blind Betty broke clods and toted rock. Paula assisted by catching the Zzz's her parents had missed.

By noon, all five broke for lunch, too exhausted to do any more than shovel cold bread and cheese into their mouths. Washing it down with icy creek water, they allowed themselves thirty minutes before getting up and having another "go." Seth and Peter did not come, nor had Barbara expected them. Her fears of the day before might have been exaggerated, but for whatever reason, the captain opted to stay away. Offering a vague excuse for his absence.

*Had some work I wanted to start. 'Spect you'll figure it out sooner or later.*

She had not, but no longer cared. One thing "ol' Ned" did say was that hard work kept a man's thoughts in check. His cure for the world's ills was a job. Anyone who toiled from sun up to sun down had no time for fretting. Bab'ra had believed him then and did so, now. However simplistic, it served as a universal truth.

Right behind "Do onto others."


The next morning, Thomas resumed the plowing while the three capable of crawling around in the dirt to useful purpose started planting. With a solemnity suitable for the occasion, Nelander took out the topmost strawberry, cradled it in her hand a moment, then passed it to Patricia. She kissed it and gave it to Blind Betty. The Negress reverently repeated a prayer.

"Bless yuh, mah chil' ob leabes an' roots an' little baby berries. Sweet Jesus an' His serbents lookin' out fo' yuh."

"Amen."

Beginning at the top of the dale, they soon discovered six arms and legs tangled quicker than butter melted on a hot day. Shoving her seaman's cap back, the officer came to a decision.

"We shall each work our own row. That way, we won't be trampling one another."

"But Miss Betty can't see, Nelander. How will she go in a straight line?"

The cap came off, waving as an ineffectual fan.

"Well, I'll be 'darned.' I plum forgot!" Which, by George, she had, for the old woman had adapted so completely to her affliction it was easy to overlook. A solution came without undo consideration. "Wait here."

Scrambling down the slope, she went to the wagon where Seth habitually kept a small tool bag. Prying open the neck of the stiff leather, she peered inside and found exactly what she sought. Carrying it with her, she made a detour up the opposite side, stopping at the pile of brush they had cleared away. Selecting a handful of twigs, she stripped them so they would serve as stakes, then made her way back.

"Patricia, help me."

Handing the girl a ball of string, she kept the end for herself, then directed the girl to the end of Betty's row. Straightening it out, she tired her piece to a stake, then crawled on hands and knees along the line, further securing it with additional support as she went.

"There, Miss Betty. All you have to do is follow the string. That'll keep you in place."

Getting down, Betty tested the line then clapped in joy.

"Dis be fine. We keep da string in place, Nelander. Mark ebery row da same. Dat way, Ah kin follow it when Ah'm weedin', too."

"Ah, yes. The farmers' bane. Good idea."

By nightfall, they had planted all the strawberries which had come in the burlap sack. Wiping her hands free of encrusted soil, Barbara grunted in satisfaction.

"Tomorrow, we bring the crate. Two or three more days like this and we'll have them in!" Gently stooping to kiss the old lady, she left her head bowed as she spoke. "I can't thank you and Mr. Thomas enough. You have worked twice as hard as I. Without you, I could hardly have hoped to see my dream come true."

Extending a trembling hand, Betty touched her friend: an act no Negro would ever contemplate unless utterly sure such an overture would be welcome.

"Yuh speak ob a dream, Off'cer Nelander. Ah wonder if yuh kin know how long Ah dreamed ob a home ob mah own. Ah neber thought to libe dat long. Put mah faith in heaben, an' here Ah habe it on earth. A roof ober mah head, an' a garden."

"And a cat," Patricia reminded her.

"Dat's right. A cat. Chatte. An Lor'," she exclaimed, putting a hand to her mouth. "Ah sho fergot to tell yuh. She done had her kittens!"

"How many?" the girl cried, filled with excitement.

"Eight. Eight young 'uns small as a cotton bole."

"What colors are they?"

Betty pretended to consider. "Why, dere's a purple one an' a blue one. He got a big white spot on his back. Den dere's a yeller tabby; wid da longest fur yuh eber did see. 'Nother one's black, all black, not a spot o' nuthin' else. Dat one a yowler. Den dere's an orange kitten. Looks jest like a ripe gourd. A'ready got claws as sharp as needles. A good hisser, too. Don' take no guff. An den --"

"Purple? Who ever heard of a purple kitten?" The child finally caught on. "Wait a minute! What am I asking? You can't see."

"No, chil', Ah cain't. Mah fingers tells me a whole lot, but dey don't tell meh da color ob kittens. But Ah do beliebe Thomas tolt me dere was a purple one, sho."

Nelander caught her breath. For the first time in her hearing, Miss Betty had not affixed the "Mute" to her son's name. That made her proud, for respect was a hard-earned commodity in any person's world.

Patricia stomped her foot.

"How could Thomas tell you when he can't talk?"

"Sho he can. Ain't yuh neber seed him writin' on mah palm?" She displayed the underside of her hand. "Ah taught him how to read an' write. When dere sumthin' he needs to tell meh, he writes here. Jes' like Ah was a book."

"You can read and write, Miss Betty?" Nelander inquired, hardly covering her surprise. "Who taught you?"

This appeared more than the old woman was willing to convey and she brushed it off.

"A gran' lady taught meh. But dat be a long time ago an' Ah like to put it outta mah head. No sense speakin' ob da pas'."

"But is there really a purple kitten?"

"Yuh habe to cume an' see when dey git a mite bigger. Mama cat's right protective now. But it won' be long fo' dey out an' about. Den you pick two fer yuhrse'f."

"You said, didn't you, Nelander? That we could have two kittens?"

"I did, indeed. Especially," she added with a huff, "for your father. To keep him company."

Patricia considered. "Then, we may need more than two. One for me and one for Peter and one for you -- and one for Captain Papa. That's four."

"And one for Paula and one as a mouser in the barn. That's six. Which leaves only two kittens for Thomas and Miss Betty."

"Are we really going to take six?"

"No. But we can tell 'Captain Papa' we are, just to see his hair stand on end."

"Let's do it!"

They parted for the night and true to form, Seth's hair shot out like a Chinese rocket when informed his wife and daughter would be bringing home six cats.

Left speechless for the good part of a minute, the only comment he could summon went something like, "Then I guess we'll have to start growing cattle in the pasture to feed all these hungry mouths."

Which was taken as disapproval by Barbara and approval by Patricia, Peter and Paula.

Herman, the dog, had no comment. It was supposed he contented himself contemplating growing beef steak in the fields.

When Mister Thomas came for the horse and plow before dawn the following morning, Seth took him aside and held private consultation. Whatever the one-sided dialogue, both men emerged looking serious but not grim.

Being excluded from the "pow-wow," an Indian word Nelander had come to associate with anything from Sunday-go-to-church-meetings to hens clustered in a group noisily appraising Mr. Noise Box's latest dance, she felt naturally suspicious. Sauntering into the yard, she settled into a chair on the porch, sipping freshly brewed coffee. As they approached, she blew over the top of the cup, ostensively to cool the hot beverage. Seth sniffed appreciatively.

"Something sure smells good."

"Whal," his first officer slowly articulated, stringing out the syllables, "it sure as Heck ain't comin' frum the south western portion o' the property."

Captain Ward did not need a compass to determine precisely where he and Thomas stood.

"Make a full pot, did ya?" he asked, matching his drawl with hers.

"Mebbe I did an' mebbe I didn't. Reckon you'll have to mosey on in and have a gander."

"We are, sir," he grinned at Thomas, "in the dog house."

To which she took exception.

"No, sir, you are not. But at this moment, the Dog is more likely to sleep in your bed tonight as you."

The threat did not loosen his tongue concerning the Private and Confidential meeting. Motioning his able-bodied, the two men went in the house in search of coffee. Their grins upon returning with brimming mugs made Nelander sorry she had not washed the rest down the pipe.

She did not offer to help them hitch Blaze, nor lift a finger as they struggled to get the heavy, awkward plow onto the back of the wagon. Only when they carted out the wooden crate of strawberries did she offer advice, and that, in a tone of command.

"Be careful."

"Yes, sir."

The superior spoke with just enough respect to save his life.

Less grateful for the reprieve than he should have been, Seth slapped the horse's rump and waved the driver off.

"Take care, now." Thomas raised a hand in acknowledgment and slowly urged Blaze forward. Watching a moment, Seth cradled both mugs to his chest as he sat beside Nelander. "He said he'll be done plowin' this morning."

"That's not what you talked about."

His lips twisted in protest. "Course it was."

"Then why did you go out back? Unless one of you had to take a piss and the other wanted to watch."

The captain's furious blushing forced him to clear his throat before continuing.

"Wasn't anything like that. And I suppose if it were, we'd have been a mite more discreet about it."

"I see. What you had to do was private but not prudent." She clucked her tongue. "Don't seem to be able to get away from those rascally 'p's.'"

He grunted. "Just wanted to ask him how it was going."

She shot him a look of pure annoyance.

"If you don't want to say, keep your trap shut. But don't lie to me."

He started to reply, wisely thought better of it, and clamped his teeth together.

After ten minutes of uncomfortable silence, she got up and went back into the house. Washing her cup, she set it upside down to dry, then summoned Patricia.

"Time we got a move on."

"Yes, sir!"

Reaching into the back pocket of the trousers which Barbara had bought her at Anson's General Store, Patricia extracted a pair of work gloves. Wiggling her fingers into the leather, she held them up for display.

"A sight big, but papa won't miss 'em. These are his spare pair. I thought we could share them."

"That's a good idea. My fingers are splitting around the cuticles. I don't mind the blisters or the calluses but I have a bad habit of biting off the hangnails." Trying on a glove, she found the fit adequate. "Next time we're in town, we'll have to get some of our own. For weedin'," she added. "An' gardenin'. What about Peter? Does he have a pair? Maybe his would fit you better."

Daring to intervene, Seth approached, hands in his pockets.

"They don't come in his size. Probably no one figures a boy -- or a girl -- cares about protecting his hands."

"I never heard anything so ridiculous." Nelander's eyes darkened. "And I suppose men don't use lotion, either, not giving a thought to comfort."

"I've a balm out in the barn. Use it to rub on Bessie's teats when they're sore or reddened. I've had occasion to use it, myself."

"Do tell. What's it called? Farmer John's Beastie Salve? Considering all I've learned about Midwesterners, I am surprised it does not come with a warning stating it is not for human use. Granting males are human, which I am occasionally loath to do."

He hunched a shoulder and drifted away.

Packing a meal for herself, Patricia and the "Nelanders," Barbara slipped Paula into her harness and the group set out across the field. The bright, yellow rays of the rising sun guided their path and they made good time. Arriving before full light, they applied themselves to the job of planting the strawberries taken from the crate.

With three working in tandem, the females had one side of the valley planted before noon. Telling Patricia to prepare dinner, Barbara set out by herself. Although possessing no distinct awareness, she felt a keen desire to stand back and inspect what they had accomplished.

Mounting the crest, she walked along the edge, assimilating the cumulative effort of six hard days. Her eyes beheld a marvel.

The wildness had disappeared. Gone were the profusion of bushes and brambles, prickers and saplings, replaced by twenty perfectly straight rows, separated by an equal number of walkways to facilitate weeding, watering and eventual harvesting. Although the plants were not yet green and showed no signs of waking from their dormancy, she felt a sense of life, of latent potential.

A week ago, such a sight had seemed an impossibility; a fool's desire. Seth had not believed it could be done and yet, with determination, effort and risk, half her aim had been achieved. Tomorrow or the following day, the strawberries would all be in, ready to begin their new life. She wondered what they felt. Grown in Virginia and transported by rail and stage to Kansas, their awakening in such a strange place must be an occasion of wonder.

"I know how you are going to feel," she spoke, addressing the slumbering crop. "I, too, have come from a long way away, and when I look around myself, I can hardly believe what has happened. It is all so... peculiar. No ocean on which to escape. No cool winds, whispering of foreign lands. A different way of judging. Strange speech patterns. Twisted perspectives. A dependence on the land instead of one another. A segregation by color rather than ability."

Hands on hips, she traversed her new domain.

"Will you wake up and wonder what has happened? Could this all be a dream?" Her head slowly shook. "No, my friends. And I pray it is not a nightmare for you, either, for I am counting on your cooperation. More than I dare let myself ponder."

Picking her way slowly down the side, she cut across one of the paths.

"Instead of black and white, you represent red. That, at least, I hope is common ground."

She might had added, *And yellow, for gold, or green for folding cash,* but did not. At the moment, it seemed too selfish.

Reaching the end of a row, Barbara walked down the edge, coming out near the "V" shaped end of the little valley. Jumping over the creek before the waterfall, she arrived at the stand of willow trees. Kneeling down, she used her hands to search the green velvet grass they had left intact. A moment's quest revealed a tiny wild strawberry plant. Lowing her face, she inhaled the gentle fragrance.

"You," she whispered, "and those which came before, were the genesis of my dream: imagined once by a little boy who filled his stomach on your sweet berries and sold the rest for what was to him, a pirate treasure." Her lips semi-circled upward. "Of course, he did not know he was a pirate, then. I had to tell him."

Tracing an "X" in the earth, her expression grew contemplative.

"'X', my love, marks the spot on our private treasure map. You saw it once, without realizing. Now, I have well and properly laid out the spot. For you and I and our crew and our crew's crew. The Wards and the Nelanders -- and the Nelanders. And for all who will follow in our stead."

Shivering in anticipation, she mused, "What shall we call our enterprise?"

But she had already given herself the answer.

*Nelander's Red Treasure.*

"Nelander" covering a multitude of "sins."

And the valley?

*Strawberry Field.*

## CHAPTER 17

By evening, Barbara Nelander had an inkling. Perhaps more. But she said nothing.

They worked all afternoon on the opposite side. Finished with the plowing, Mute Thomas assumed the more physically intensive labor of breaking clods and hauling away the unearthed rocks. His mother and the two Wards crawled over the upturned soil, separating a single plant from their bundle, jamming the point of a hand spade into the ground, then propping the strawberry with one hand while scooping loosened dirt around the roots with the other.

Between the toting and the digging, none of the three females could attest Thomas actually had the harder job.

Patricia abandoned her glove early on, giving it to Betty. It did not take long for the tips of her fingers to bleed, yet she said nothing. An able-bodied seaman never complained. Certainly not a buccaneer.

At least not out loud.

And absolutely never on a job for which she had volunteered.

Her first officer felt the same, but in a slightly more vocal manner.

"Damn! These plants are hard to separate!"

"Dey tangled up in demselbes, right 'nuf," Miss Betty agreed. "But da mo' we git out, da more we habe to put in."

"Yesss." The admission being a guarded one.

"I can tell you one thing," the girl added. "I'm never going to eat another mouthful of food without being grateful where it came from -- and for the farmer who grew it."

"Amen to that," Barbara agreed. Rubbing her aching back, then taking a swig of sun-heated water from their common jar, she swished it around her mouth then spit. The greedy soil immediately absorbed it. "And this blue sky -- not a cloud in sight. I was hoping it would rain but I can see now we're going to have to water once we get done. Tomorrow... or the next day."

The prospect held more dread than she cared to admit although not for obvious reasons.

Finishing up just as the shadows threatened to engulf them, she bit on a fingernail, discovered it had been split and drew back her upper lip. It no longer surprised her that one of the first things Seth had asked for in his fantasy spending spree had been a pair of gloves. That he had not ordered a large porcelain-covered tub the size of New Hampshire remained a mystery.

Had he presented the same challenge to her at this moment, a tub would have been her first purchase. And her second. And third.

With hot and cold running faucets, although at the moment, she could not fathom why she would ever need heated water.

Winter seemed an age away.

"We'll wrap it up for today."

Walking with stooped back, Nelander hobbled her way down to the valley floor. Draping a damp cloth over the crate to keep the remaining plants damp, she gave her best impression of a sailor traversing a slippery deck on her way to the wagon. Patricia followed with the benefit of youth, an annoying spring to her step.

"See you tomorrow."

Mute Thomas waved and the pair set off, the girl holding the reins. Grateful she did not have to walk home, Barbara closed her eyes, head drooping. She did not bother fighting off sleep. If she slept, she would not have to face that idea which had earlier occurred. Better to address it tomorrow, after a meal and a long night's repose.

Seth and Peter were sitting on the porch as they rolled into the yard. Without being asked, the boy led Blaze toward the barn, while Patricia smacked her lips.

"What's for supper?"

Nelander groaned.

"Something soft. I am too tired to chew."

"I suppose," the captain observed, "that means you want me to fix it."

"I'll make a deal. You feed the crew and yourself and I'll nurse the baby. Once she's down for the night, I'm going to follow."

Placing a concerned hand on her arm, Seth used the other to wipe the sweat stains from her brow.

"I'm worried about you."

"No need. I've worked harder in my life. Although not much," she grimly acknowledged.

"I don't doubt that. But never before after delivering a baby and tending to her needs. Like it or not, that takes a toll. One I don't overlook."

She stared at him in amazement. "You know, I'd forgotten. Not that we have Paula," she hastily countered, "but how short a time it's actually been. It seems like she's been with us forever."

"Go sit down. Take off your shoes and socks. I don't mind --"

"-- rustling grub."

Accepting his proposition, she dragged herself into the living room and sunk into a chair. Uncovering the protective hood from the baby's face, two huge eyes the size of watermelons met her stare. Thin pink lips puckered and little gurgling noises arose from her throat.

"Yup. You're due. It's your turn, now."

Dropping her head close to the child's, Barbara inhaled through her nose, heart swelling at the scent of infant. No one had ever told her that a baby smelled differently than an adult and the phenomenon surprised her. At first she thought it an aberration, a distortion of her own senses, but as the days passed and it persisted, she had come to realize its verity.

Pausing now to enjoy this pleasure, she smiled.

"Hard work, little one. For me and papa and Patricia and Peter. And for you, too. You don't know it, yet, but one day you may stand at the top of the valley and see a field of green, decorated with a profusion of white blossoms. There's gold in them thar hills, Paula -- red gold. Promising a better life for all of us."

By the time Seth came to get her, he found his wife and daughter asleep. Loath to wake either, he debated getting Nelander up to eat, then decided against it. Leaving them together, the picture of beloved harmony, he fed the remainder of his crew, then left the children to clean up while he went back into the living room. Moving his rocker closer to Barbara, he let his own eyes flutter shut.

Awaken toward midnight by the strident cries of a once-again hungry infant, the mother fed her while the father retired to the kitchen. When his wife joined him twenty minutes later, he offered a bowl of bread steeped in evening milk.

"Eat it," he directed. "To keep up your strength, then it's off to bed."

Without argument, she ate, he sitting quietly at the table beside her. Once or twice it appeared he wished to speak, but ultimately did not. Nor did she press him. If a secret were on the tip of his tongue, it would have to wait until morning. Or some morning in the future.

When the strawberries were all planted.

Which would be another story, entirely.


Nelander, Patricia, Miss Betty and Mute Thomas worked all the next day planting strawberries. By six bells -- three o'clock to a landlubber -- they completed the last row. With all four finally united on the valley floor, the task behind them seemed an astonishing achievement.

"It be good," Betty declared, head titled upward, observing their accomplishment through the medium of sense. "Now, we had bes' git to waterin'."

"No. No. Tomorrow."

"Ah don' mind, Nelander."

"Please. I want you to go home and start your own garden." Suddenly remembering something, she crossed to the wagon, pulling back a tarpaulin. Taking a sack from the flatbed, she hurriedly returned. "Here: for you. Seeds. I wasn't sure what you wanted, but these are what we grow in our own garden. Pumpkins. Onions. Cucumbers. And beans -- three different variety."

Dipping a hand into the bag, Betty withdrew a bulb, running it over in her fingers.

"Onions. What color it be?"

"Yellow."

"Good. Dat be right. But yuh need dese fo' yuhrse'f."

"We have enough to share. And there are some tomato seeds, too. And corn, of course. Not enough for you to sell, but to eat. Plenty to tide you through the winter. Captain Ward has potatoes, too, he wants to give you. He said he would ride over in the next day or two when the ground is tilled. He wasn't sure you knew how to plant them and wanted to explain."

"Oh, Lor', yuh do too much, Nelander."

"We do what we do because you are friends." Kissing the old woman on the cheek, she turned away, not from a welling of tender emotion, but another, less tender feeling. "Mr. Thomas, will you put the crate in the wagon for me?"

She stiffened herself for a glare, a look of rebuke or ridicule. He never looked in her direction. Lifting the wooden box as though it were empty, he slid it along the bottom until one end touched the back of the seat. Securing it with rope to prevent sliding, he crossed around front and affectionately patted Blaze's neck.

Still, Barbara could not believe he would let her off the hook so easily. Eyes narrowed in weary offense, she baited him.

"So: our work is done and we may congratulate ourselves." She might have been speaking in French. "Five thousand plants -- well and truly laid."

If he rightly interpreted the double entendre which had less than a lady-like significance, he gave no indication. Instead, he busied himself lifting Patricia up and placing her astride the back of the horse. Eagerly grasping the mane, she looked back over her shoulder.

"May I ride like this all the way home? It's almost like having my own pony."

The unintended reprieve loosened Nelander's tight grip on herself and she nodded.

"You may. But don't forget you have a buckboard attached to your rear. No fancy racing over hill and dale."

"Yes, sir!"

Placing the baby aboard, Nelander pulled herself up, taking the reins from Thomas. Trying to catch his eyes a second time proved no more successful than the first.

"Good-bye, then, neighbors. Tomorrow, we form a bucket brigade. Work with which I have a great deal more familiarity. Although, not, I confess, in hauling water up. My task has always been bailing it out."

Motioning Patricia, the girl kicked her heels.

"Gee up!"

The animal responded to the nautical translation of "Giddy-up!" and obligingly pressed itself against the harness. The wheels rolled and the wagon easily slid forward.

Discovering little need for guidance, Nelander's mind wandered. Letting her eyes rove across the prairie, she absorbed sights still new to her perceptions. Rather than a limitless horizon, hills merged into one another, sometimes disappearing into dips but always coming up the other end. Rounded tops of trees marked the beginnings of wood; snaking sides of the creek marked man-made territories. Patches of daises and bluebells grew in odd places, the seeds having taken root where topsoil, washed from cultivated ground, had settled.

Rocks of all sizes littered the area, dropped in random patterns as the flood receded. It reminded her, somehow, of the moon, dark craters carved out of shale or limestone splashed between hills created from impact by wandering meteors. Craning her neck higher, she tried to make out faces, just as she had as a child when staring upward at the celestial body.

Even then, she had not imagined the expressions all happy ones. Many seemed stoical or grim, as if aware of a duty to balance out the fanciful image of a distant paradise.

Caught speculating one night, Barbara's mother had inquired what she saw. She expected a girl's reply of faerie caves or dragon tracks and instead received a rendering of a barren planet, devoid of water.

"The moon," the four-year-old had said, "must be very old. See how it is wrinkled."

"But child, lovers look upon it and feel the warmth of its shine."

"It is not hot," Barbara had decided, although she had no educated reason for saying so. Nor did she have the least regard for lovers, whoever they might be. "There are no oceans. What good to anyone?"

"You do not find the glow beautiful?"

"I find it lonely."

Mrs. Nelander had gone away, sorry she had bothered her daughter. The woman had no love of the sea and as little regard for the livelihood which deprived her of Ned. She was not even sure her husband loved the sea.

On occasion, she could not decide whether he loved her. He might have re-named his ship the *Bernice* but he had opted to keep it the *Bottom*

*Dollar. Bottom Dollar,* indeed, for as much as he earned from its ownership, that much more he put back in. Where other captains took their profit and lived in luxury ashore, he turned his over.

"There is always insurance to buy," he had explained once, when confronted by her pique. "The hull to replace. Wood does not last forever, you know. Even the stoutest oak wears away from exposure and salt. Then there is the mast. A good one will set me back two hundred pounds."

He had an entire laundry list of things to buy.

"I want to purchase a cargo of shoes and boots; leather saddles. Harness and tack. Take them to the west coast. Before that, I have my eye on a manifest of cotton. Take it to England. I can always get a good price for it there. Bring back tea." He had grinned. She remembered it, yet. Stored away in memory, alongside moonlit nights and shooting stars.

"Would you like me to bring you back a tin of fancy black tea? No reason Mrs. Nelander shouldn't drink the best."

And he had. And she drank the best alone, brewing it in an English teapot decorated with red and white roses. Using a sterling silver tea ball, manufactured in Boston, by some famous silversmith. Not so odd, for Boston was renowned for metalworking. But he had bought it in London.

She would have preferred the money.

All things considered, she would have preferred he retire. But men from Nova Scotia never retired. They kept going back to the ocean until they came home one day, crippled from a fall off the yardarm. Or missing a limb, lost to a shark or a whale. Or they did not come home at all, and the captain had to make a call on the widow, offering her hollow tales of heroism a woman believed or not, depending on her nature.

Once in a blue moon, a ship never returned and no one ever knew what happened. *Lost at sea* covered all speculation. An unexpected hurricane. A ruptured rib below the waterline. Died of thirst. Perished from hunger. Mutiny.

And then came the mournful tolling of the bell. One time for every seaman. Bernice Nelander had an antipathy for bells. She never knew a sailor's wife who did not.

When news of her husband's death came, she had not been surprised. Jacques Falon walked up the broken clamshell walk to her door, wearing his dark blue officer's jacket. The one with gold buttons. Even a rawboned bride knew a man did not play dress-up in warm weather unless he bore important news.

In a community where men made their living on the sea, "important" meant only one thing.

Death.

Why the letter had come to Captain Falon remained a mystery. One she only probed when the nights grew long and her bed cold. To outright ask would have been demeaning.

It might have been that a missive arrived in care of General Delivery and one of the men opened it by accident. More likely, the postmaster guessed its contents. Wishing to spare Mrs. Nelander the horror of reading bad news, he had given it to the only captain then in harbor. Once or twice that responsibility had fallen to Ned. He had never appreciated it, nor had he ever shirked his duty.

Removing his cap, Jacques had knocked. In a sequence of threes: rap, rap, rap. Pause. Rap, rap, rap. She did not hurry to answer the summons. The precious moments she stole represented her final seconds as a married woman. After that came widowhood.

*"Bonjour, Madame Nelander."*

"Good afternoon, Captain Falon."

They must have their formalities.

"There has been a letter, *Madame*. Shall I come in?"

Stiffly nodding, she stepped aside. He did not sit.

"Would you like some tea?"

Just a question to delay the inevitable.

"No. Thank you."

"Is it bad news?"

"I am afraid so." He had not brought the paper with him. "An accident. In San Francisco. That is a city on the western coast of the United States. California."

"Yes. I know."

"Captain Nelander has been killed. Some sort of altercation."

Jacques Falon had known Ned Nelander since they were boys. They had shipped out together on their first voyage. She recalled the name of the vessel. The *Cracked Claw*. A reference to lobsters.

Jacques might have called the deceased by his first name. But not on such a mission.

To the dead belonged all honor and glory.

"I see. And his ship?"

"Sold at auction. That sum has been placed in trust. The authorities there are awaiting final disposition. Proof of next-of-kin. I suggest you seek the advice of a maritime attorney. He will help you prepare whatever is necessary."

That meant she would have to journey to Halifax. Wearing widow's weeds. She would have to ask one of the local men to go with her. Lawyers did not like dealing with women.

She would have to offer restitution for his time. The legal man, too, would require a fee. If she did not pay up front, he would charge her double. Or perhaps he would, anyway. Seamen and their families knew lawyers as worse than sharks. They swarmed around the smell of blood. No matter how cold.

"I will do that." A hand went to her mouth. "What other details?"

"That is all I know." He shifted weight from one leg to the other. "There was no mention of Nelander."

*Nelander.* She had forgotten about that other. Her daughter.

"I suppose she will return here eventually." Her heart hardened. "Expecting her 'cut.'" Whatever Bernice received from the settlement would have to last the remainder of her days. Seaman's widows seldom remarried. Men would only come courting if they heard her judgment had been a substantial one. She would have to weigh the benefits against the risks of such an alignment.

In her sea of bereavement, that was all she had left.

That, and a grown child. Her consolation lay in the fact it made no difference to her future whether that offspring be a boy or a girl. A boy had no obligation to his mother. He would marry and have his own family to support. A girl would be married away, the concern of her husband. The elderly were cast aside.

Like cracked claws.

Destined to save and scrimp their bottom dollar.

"Thank you for coming."

"The men will hold service in the chapel. Tomorrow. I will come for you at ten o'clock." He did not use naval time. Not for a woman suddenly dissociated from the sea.

Bernice Nelander had been to many services. She could recite the prayers by heart. This one would not include, *and we commit his body to the deep.* Captain Nelander had not perished at sea. He had died "in some sort of an altercation."

The pastor would say, *In the midst of life we are in death.* And, *Thou knowest, Lord, the secrets of our hearts.*

She had never been a religious woman and she kept her secrets close.


Shifting her attention back to the present and away from a recent past of which she played no part, Bab'ra Nelander clenched her fist. She never had gone back. It was just as well. Until this moment, she had forgotten. Her "kingdom" was not of this earth. At least, not the portion called Nova Scotia.

She expected her mother would have received her settlement by now. Possibly even collected whatever insurance money might have been owing. Once, she had expected her fair share. But that had been another Bab'ra Nelander. With a different perspective. Her inheritance, such as it was, lay in the skill which Ned Nelander had instilled in her.

That, and her wages.

Those coins saved while other seamen frequented whore houses and taverns.

Half she had given to Seth to tide them over after the drought. A portion had gone to put a down-payment on the Windsor property.

What remained she had spent on strawberries.

"Spent" seemed a euphemism. "Squandered" might have been a better word. Tempered, perhaps with "misjudged."

For a secret lurked within her, waiting to be confessed.

## CHAPTER 18

She saw him walking through the pasture, hands swinging by his side. She thought at first something had gone wrong, seeing no other explanation for his appearance. Patricia saw him too, and waved.

"Hallo, Captain! Look at me!"

Seth waved back, a friendly, careless sort of gesture. Increasing his gait into a trot, he came alongside, hardly out of breath. Brushing his daughter's leg with an easy greeting, he winked, silently granting permission for her to maintain the place of glory. Grumbled words went along with the approval.

"I can see after this there'll be no stopping you. Next, it'll be, 'Papa, can I go for a ride?' and then, 'Can I have a pony of my own?'"

Hopping into the wagon, he took the reins from Nelander, assuming control of the wagon.

"Don't mind if I drive, do you?"

"No point asking me. Crewman Patricia was doing all the work."

The girl returned her hands to the horse's neck and Seth re-directed their course on a roundabout route east of the farmhouse.

"What are you doing out this way?" Barbara asked because she could think of nothing else to say.

"I figured you'd have all the strawberries in by now and thought I'd have a look. But as you beat me home, we might as well go on a trip. Haven't had time to check out most of the land since the weather got warm. Thought I'd have a look-see. Unless you had other plans?"

"No. I had nothing else in mind."

They traveled in silence for half an hour, pausing occasionally to stare at the changes wrought by the receding floodwaters. Some of the scars had already been covered. Grass grew around fallen logs, weeds and wildflowers bloomed under the shade of crookedly jutting roof shingles, fence rails and barn slats. Responding to the glint of afternoon sun on a metallic object, they drew closer, revealing the reflective material to be an upturned cook pot.

Tugging on an earlobe, he quietly observed, "Out of destruction comes rebirth. Look at how the rainwater has pooled in there. Our little neighbor friends -- the rabbits and the groundhogs -- have found themselves a watering hole. Might even be the robins and sparrows use it as a bird bath."

"You said they would come back and they have."

"Tragedy for some, benefit for others. That's the natural cycle."

Avoiding the larger issue, Nelander observed, "Still, when I think of all the creatures which died of thirst, or drowned... or lost their homes, it makes me sad."

"Me, too."

Noticing how her leg shook, he slowly turned around, freeing him to broach the subject which had brought him out.

"How'd it go in the valley? I see you brought the crate back with you. Good. It's a nice, sturdy one. I can use it in the barn. Store some tools in it, maybe."

She swallowed and wished for the power of invisibility.

"It is not empty."

"How's that, again?"

"It-is-not-empty."

Seth mulled over the statement, running a fingernail under the thin leather rein as an aid to comprehension. It seemed not to have helped.

"Want to tell me what that means?"

"I'm a damned jackass."

"I hope that's your description of yourself and not what anybody else said, 'cause if it is I'll have to whup 'em. That nosy postmaster, Pete Erlinger, been out snoopin' around? On another errand of mercy? Askin' what you're doin'?"

"Nothing like that."

"Oh."

The farmhouse came into view. Looking down, Barbara did not see it.

"Only a blowfish of the worst kind would have made the mistake I did."

"I've known a few 'blowhards,' but I never met a blowfish. What kind of critter is that?"

"One which believes that by filling itself with hot air it can deceive... a predator." She flicked her hand in dismissal. "More rightly I should say, I am a tuna trying to take on a shark."

"I suppose there is a size discrepancy there, a'right."

"You know what I mean."

"I'm listening to what you have to say."

"I thought I had it all worked out. Seems my calculations were slightly awry. I... bought cargo to fit the hold of a schooner when I didn't have a ship bigger than a rowboat."

"You telling me you couldn't fit 5,000 strawberry plants into one small valley?"

This brought her head up.

"You don't seem surprised."

"I'd be a mighty poor farmer if I were."

Goose bumps ran down the back of her spine.

"You... knew?"

"I may not have the ability to navigate from Nova Scotia to Boston and I can't read a sextant, but I can do simple arithmetic. Don't require any fancy instrumentation to judge the width and breadth of a piece of land. I sat down with a pencil and paper and calculated acreage, giving you an average of five inches between plants. Came up with a total of roughly three-thousand. How'd I do?"

"I didn't count them, but I'll take your word for it."

"That means you've got two-thousand left. What do you reckon we ought to do with 'em?"

"Put them on the compost heap."

"You're talkin' mighty expensive fertilizer."

With a cry of despair, Nelander threw up her hands.

"Seth, don't play games with me! I know what I've done. I've wasted a hell of a lot of money. What I paid for those extra 2,000 could have gone for --" She did not have the heart to finish.

"But all your calculations of us gettin' rich are based on 5,000 producing plants."

Pushing him aside, she tried to get out of the wagon. He restrained her.

"For God's sake, let me go."

"I will, for it's a heavy weight you're bearing. Just first, answer me one question."

She glared at him, eyes flashing.

"What one question?"

Taking off his hat, he used it to point toward the rear of the house.

"If you don't want it, what am I gonna do with that field Peter and I tilled? A 'bitch' of a time we had, too. Never been plowed. Darn near broke my back gettin' it ready."

Crying in surprise, Barbara stared ahead in stark wonder. Behind the building she beheld acres of freshly upturned land. Her mouth went dry.

"What the --? When did you do that? Where did you find the time? I thought... the corn and the wheat --"

"Right you are. Peter and I worked like dogs. I told you I couldn't take time from the cash crops to put in those strawberries and I meant it. But once I figured out you'd never get more than 3,000 in my valley, he and I gave up our rest periods. We worked straight through an' then dragged ourselves home to plow here. Never bothered before because the soil wasn't good. But I did some checking and found the waters had deposited a thin layer of topsoil over the land. The drainage isn't what I'd want but it's better than letting 2,000 plants go to waste."

Realization came slowly.

"That's why you didn't come at noontime?"

He nodded. "Had other work to do."

"But -- you didn't tell me."

"Wanted to surprise you. Did I?"

Throwing her arms around him, Barbara gave him a bear hug.

"But Seth.... Captain...."

"Had to live up to my name, didn't I? Besides, let's not count our chickens before they're hatched. It's late. We only just finished and those plants have been in the crate a long time. We've lost some of 'em, sure. But I'm hoping we can save most."

Overwhelmed, she clung to him for support.

"Plant the strawberries here? Have two patches?" He nodded. She bit her lower lip. "That's what you were talking to Mute Thomas about; telling him what you had in mind. Warning him not to say anything."

"It was our secret, a'right. He figured the same thing I did. Didn't want him spoilin' anything 'cause sure he woulda told you."

"Then... we didn't need the valley, after all?"

"That's not what I said. The soil there is ten times better'n what we have here. It'll hold water better. Besides, the whole Plan was predicated around that valley. I wanted it to work. It meant more to me than... I can say."

Kissing him on the cheek, she trembled.

"When can we start? Today?"

"Tomorrow. Tom and Miss Betty will spend the day in the valley watering those you put in and the four of us will plant what's left. Take stock: get the healthiest in first. Then the rest along the edges. I can't promise anything, but we'll see."

"Jesus. Will I ever learn?"

"Takes a while to convert a sailor to a landlubber. But you've come a long way. And I'm telling you right now," he warned. "The strawberries are your affair. You water 'em, you weed 'em. I've done what I can -- more than I thought I could," he thoughtfully added. "Once the rest are in, I've got to turn my full attention to the crops. Until you can prove to me there's serious money to be made selling fruit."

"I will," she promised. This time, a vow made with informed consent.

They began in the morning, Patricia and Peter setting out the string lines while Seth and Nelander inspected the plants. Impatient to begin, she chaffed at his diligence. Finally annoyed as she hovered too close, he backed her off.

"Go into the house. You know where my ledger is kept?" She nodded. "Beside it is another. A new one. Fetch it, if you please. And bring a pencil and some scrap paper."

Glad for the opportunity to move, Nelander did as directed, returning almost immediately with the requisite items. Sensing her curiosity and mounting enthusiasm, he bade the book be opened.

"I want you to keep a -- log book. Put a title on the first page. Call it anything you like. Mine says 'Crops' and then the year."

"All right."

"If you're going to do this right -- be a scientific farmer -- then you have to maintain a record of everything."

"I am keen on that."

"Good. You'll have to backdate the work you did in the valley but you can start today with this field. First," he ticked off on his fingers, "the date and the growing conditions."

"Which mean?"

"Weather; atmosphere. Clear sky; cloudy. And a description of the temperature: hot; warm, cool. Rainfall. I developed a measure of precipitation: we can share that data."

"What you suggest is similar to what I maintained in the *Bottom Dollar's* log, so I have experience. What else?"

"You've got two plots of land, so I suggest you divide the ledger in half. One section for the valley, the other for this field. How many plants did you actually put in over there?"

Nelander's tongue probed the inside of her cheek before answering. "I do not know."

"You will, because you're going to count them. One-by-one. And you're going to do the same here. That's your second task. I suggest you make a diagram, a sketch of each row and the exact count per row. They're probably going to vary somewhat."

"And the purpose?"

"To identify patterns. They'll make themselves pretty apparent. Some rows will get more drainage; others more sunlight. The ones toward the middle may have better soil. When you start thinning out the dead and the weak, you may discover something in the charts your eyes didn't tell you. We'll test different fertilizers, too, to see which work better. I've never grown strawberries, so we'll have to test several types. That's when your notes really come in handy."

"I can see that."

"Third, you observe when the first blossoms come. Which sections bloom more than others. Same thing with the berries. Be interesting to know in a general way what's the percentage of success."

"Meaning --?"

"How many blossoms actually produce fruit."

"You mean some won't?"

"Correct. Lot of factors effect pollination. Wind currents. Bees. Moisture. The same goes for ripening. How long from flower to red fruit? How many days will they stay fresh on the plant before they start getting soft? We've got two years before we can expect a full harvest. This information will enable us to make an accurate determination of when to start picking, which areas ripen faster, how much we're going to get."

"This," Barbara declared, "is exciting."

Her eagerness pleased him.

"I find it that. Never expected anyone else to."

"We're a good pair."

Seth winked and went back to inspecting the plants. Kneeling beside him, Nelander separated those which passed muster into piles of ten to facilitate counting. In an hour, he finished and looked to her for answers.

"One thousand, five hundred and thirty-one to plant. Two hundred eighty-eight discarded." She pouted. "That's a lot."

"Some of the 288 are dead, for sure. That's to be expected."

"I-did-not-expect-it," she replied in a chipped officer's tone.

He snorted. "No. You expected all 5,000 to be dead."

"Looking past that, I anticipated all 5,000 to be alive."

"When you order such a large amount, there's always some that don't make it. The weak, the diseased. Some crushed; some maybe not viable when they were packed. That, sir, is business."

"It would be better business if Mr. Bentell had sold me 5,000 healthy plants. Since I am keeping an accounting, sir, I shall surely write him with the salient details. And demand a refund for those judged 'damaged in transit.'"

He choked in a fashion similar to that of a man swallowing a bug.

"You do that. But wait awhile. If we have space, we'll try planting a hundred or so of those I discarded. They may yet have some life. That leaves 188 which may have died from our negligence."

"I paid for 5,000. I will grant Mr. Bentell the one hundred and eighty-eight. He may reimburse me for the rest."

Getting up from his knees, farmer Ward brushed off the encrustation of dirt.

"You still have to count those in the valley."

Making a notation, she elucidated, "Fifteen thirty-one here. So I should have 3,181 in the first field."

"For all we know, you may have more than that. A good grower who hopes for repeat business often adds extra."

"We shall see."

Realizing that he had created a partner if not a monster, Seth summoned in the crew and dispensed assignments. Carrying ten piles of ten, they settled into their private rows and began digging holes. By sundown, a considerable portion of the task had been completed.

Gathering at the well to wash, Patricia shoved her hands into the water and made a hissing sound, equating her burning flesh to a horseshoe being cooled from the anvil.

"If I ever git born again as a strawberry, remind me to position myself so's I'm one of the first planted. I'm afeared them last ones just got tucked up right quick."

Laughing at the joke and in sympathy with her plight, the family traipsed into the house, collapsing into chairs.

"Ain't we done a peck o' work," Peter declared, fanning his sunburned face with the flat of his hand.

"And then some," Barbara agreed, positioning her neck behind the headrest to massage aching muscles. 'I wonder what the ship's doctor has prepared for supper?"

"I dunno." Eyes closed, Captain Ward hollered, "What's to eat, cook?" He listened, lips slightly parted. "He says he's got fried spuds an' some bone marrow soup."

"I was thinking more of beef steak," the first officer protested.

"The barrel's got nothing left in it but pork rind and grizzle."

"What about those green bananas we brought aboard? And the figs?"

"He says you ete them last week. And a sorry sight you were, running to the lee side of the ship to do your business."

"What does that mean, Papa Captain?"

"Figs gives you loose bowels."

Nelander eyed him from under half closed lids.

"How do you know? When's the last time you ate a fig?"

"Read it in a book. About this sailor who got abandoned on a tropical island. That's all he had to eat and he learned right quick not to overdo. Figs and coconuts. Ever are a coconut?"

"Sure. You pound a nail through the shell to make a couple holes, then drink the milk. Afterward, you take a rock and break it open."

"Milk comes from coconuts, too?"

"It's called milk because it's a watery-white. Tastes sweet. The meat -- that's what the eatable part is called -- comes off in chunks. It grows around the inside perimeter. The rest is hollow."

"You mean, like a squash?"

"Like enough."

"Reckon when we git rich, we'll be etin' coconuts fer breakfast."

Smiling at the pleasing idea, Nelander forced herself up and trudged toward the stove. Wearily stoking the ash, she added wood, blew on it until flames licked around the edges, then took stock of the pantry. The idea of preparing a meal held no attraction. As an officer, she had been used to being served, not wearing the hat of both commander and cook. Yet she could hardly deny the crew their food.

Resigned to the task, Barbara removed a protective cotton cloth from a kid of beef and sliced off a section. Trimming the meat into strips, she set it aside while peeling and boiling potatoes. Listening to the merry bubbling, she hummed while pummeling hard biscuit into crumbs. The ingredients ready, most of the water was drained from the potatoes, then the other ingredients added to form a sort of porridge. Ten turns of the pepper grinder and a generous dose of salt completed the seasoning.

The odor of the commingling ingredients raised her spirits. Discovering new energy, she set the table, poured milk into glasses for the crew and set out a pitcher of water for the adults. Peter wandered in from the barn, nose twitching.

"Smells good. What are you making?"

"Scouse."

"What's 'skoose'?"

"A delicacy; a sort of seaman's pudding." She gave him a nudge. "A treat." His eyes rounded.

"What for?"

"Oh, I don't know. Because it's Friday. Because you and the captain surprised me by plowing the field. Because we worked hard and I've caught a glimpse of the lighthouse."

He bounced on his toes. "That means we're near land."

"And coming into safe harbor. Do all those things merit a treat?"

Puckering his face, he shrugged while lowering his voice. "I'll let you know after I've tasted it."

Giving him a swat on the backside, Nelander directed the boy to the table.

"Sit down, Doubting Thomas. Captain Ward; Master Patricia. Attend."

They came, slipping into their accustomed chairs. Seth unknowingly copied his son by sniffing and inquiring, "What are you making?" Peter supplied the answer.

"A treat."

"What's the occasion?"

"It's Friday."

He did not offer his father the rest of the list. "Friday" seemed good.

"Oh."

Wrapping a towel over the cast iron handle, Nelander brought the meal to the table.

"Dig in."

He did, using a large wooden spoon. Steam spiraled upward, filling the room with a stimulating aroma.

"What is this?"

"Skoose."

"Scouse," the seaman reiterated, putting a slightly different dialect to the foreign word.

"Got pizzon in it?"

"No pizzon."

Seth grunted, displaying no opinion on whether he considered that a good or a bad development. Nevertheless, he let the cook taste the concoction first. She did, with obvious delight.

"Good. It's been a long time since I've eaten this."

Patricia went next, chewing carefully.

"Tastes like a sort of hash."

"I suppose it is. Aboard ship it's more of a Sunday meal. A great change from plain boiled potatoes and tough meat."

Still unconvinced and wary of a possible threat, Seth sampled a small portion off the end of his fork.

"A bit heavy on the pepper."

A glare from the cook would have seared his food had it not already been hot.

"Pepper is a spice. A flavor treasured by men used to bland dishes. I suppose next you'll say it's too salty."

"No. Never that."

Reaching for the grinder, he added another four turns, loading his dish. The act prompted Nelander to remark, "While you're eating, you can put your mind to what you're going to make tomorrow. It's your turn."

"I thought captains were exempt."

"Normally, they would be. But with a crew of five, and one hardly expected to participate, you pull your weight with the rest."

"Who says?"

"The *Pirate Handbook.*"

The response caught him off guard.

"Have I read that?"

"I'd be surprised if you hadn't. The crew has."

"That's right, Captain," Patricia volunteered. "Peter and I got it memorized. And when Paula gets older, we'll read it aloud to her."

"I've already begun," her brother interjected. "Read her the first chapter last evening."

"I see." His eyes narrowed as he considered the statement. "What, exactly, did that cover?"

"All about how pirates chip in to do their duty. No one's above swabbin' the deck."

Seth choked and not from pepper.

"I am quite certain it said nothing of the sort." Unconcerned, Peter rattled on.

"Puttin' down the sand and sweepin' it up. Paintin' the gun rails. Polishin' the brass. Usin' a needle an' thread to mend the sails."

"It had all that, this book?"

"Yup. 'Course, I skipped over the parts about sharpenin' the cutlasses an' washin' the blood from the hand spikes. Paula's a mite young to hear sech."

"I am sure she appreciates your discretion." Shoving in a heaping forkful, the senior officer spoke with his mouth full. "Just where did this book come from?"

"It's been around."

"I see." Meaning, of course, he did not see. Patricia chimed in.

"First printed in 1589. During the reign of Elizabeth."

Barbara followed the thread. "And carried on board Drake's ship. It is rumored he tore out the pages dealing with the fair and equitable sharing of booty with his monarch."

"But we have them in our copy."

"I am relieved to hear it. Otherwise, I might be done out."

"You are not, sir," Officer Nelander officiously informed, "a queen."

"But I'm the king of my own castle."

"When we find a castle you may bring up that argument again."

He huffed and returned his attention to eating. No further remarks were made about spices or fortified manors.

That evening, the crew retired early. Making his excuses, Seth stayed up. He did not come to bed until after ringing the bell six times for eleven o'clock. Slipping quietly under the sheet, he closed his eyes and immediately effected snoring.

Proof positive Captain Ward had not uncovered the hiding place of the *Pirate Handbook.*

Or determined to his satisfaction whether or not it actually existed.

## CHAPTER 19

Dipping the pen in ink, Nelander used a straight edge to draw a line. Blowing on the last of her columns to dry it, she pulled back to admire her handiwork.

"I think I am going to enjoy this ledger. I had forgotten how much keeping a meticulous log meant to me. While I never imagined myself being a scientific farmer, I can readily see the merit."

Examining the book Seth kept for his own purposes, she marveled at the detail. Divided into sections, the first part dealt with dates, weather and observations on the corn and wheat. The second part contained both bar and line graphs comparing present data from the previous five years. Except for 1859 when lack of rainfall and unusually high temperatures stood out in stark contrast, most of the indicators were remarkably similar. Times of planting, first sprouting, height of mature crops and dates of harvesting ran true to form, varying by days instead of weeks.

The last section dealt with finances. Carefully entering the price paid for seed and fertilizer, it also contained wages paid to hired hands and the purchase or repair of farm implements, as well as feed and the rare husbandry services for the animals. Separately, he jotted down prices received from the harvest sale and whatever other incidentals had garnered extra income. Red numbers marked loss; black indicated profit. Numbers carried over from past seasons gave a penny-for-penny accounting of income spent and earned.

While she had seen him work on his books she had never before asked to review the figures. Seeing them spread out before her proved almost as awe inspiring as frightening. After the bills were paid, very little remained.

Seeing a shadow fall over her work, Barbara looked up. Seth stood over her.

"No one ever said farming was an easy life."

"I did not have to be told, but the margin for error is so slim."

"I never denied money was ever far from my mind."

Picking up the cork used as a stopper in the ink pot, Barbara ran it around her hands, studying the lower end which had been stained from contact with the indelible writing fluid. She invited him to observe the object.

"Look at this. What a remarkably steady hand you have."

"How so?"

"The ink line; completely straight, all the way around. A hasty man shoves it in at whatever angle, causing an irregular pattern of stains. Almost like the rings of a tree. They vary by year, depending on rainfall."

"You have a good memory. I showed you that phenomenon two years ago."

She nodded in remembrance. "I found it fascinating. No more so because someone actually deduced the reason. I wondered what drew them to that conclusion, and how it became -- I won't say folklore. Oral history. How did it pass from one man to the next and from generation to generation?"

"You have an inquiring mind."

"No more so than you. Reading about advancements in farming. And implementing them, when none of your neighbors bother. Even when they see the positive results you achieve."

"I guess because they're used to doing things one way."

"That is the temperate interpretation. I would say, rather, they do not believe in what they cannot see."

Turning around his chair so he could face her, Seth shrugged.

"But you just said my improved crops were proof of scientific methods."

"Did I? From where I'm sittin'," she remarked in a deep Midwestern dialect, "I don't 'see' nuthin' of the kind. That Seth Ward -- he's got a fair piece o' property. The sun shines better there than on mine. An' he's got a crick -- high water table. Might even work a tad harder, pullin' weeds. That's what I know, son. What I kin observe wid my own two eyeballs. Don't prove nuthin' else. Them 'methods' he's always spoutin' about -- readin' up on fancy New England 'techniques.' Layin' down 'chemicals.' Yappin' about crop rotation; plants usin' up the soil. My pappy never took no stock in that an' neither do I."

He guffawed, pulled up his chair and stretched out his legs.

"You got the twang but I'm not so certain of the words. 'Spouting'? 'New England'? Didn't we fight a War fer Independence wid them redcoats?"

"You got the gist." She glanced over at him. "So why is it they can believe tree rings are the result of a water table and not in scientific farming?"

The back of his ankle itched and he scratched it with his toes.

"You gettin' at they're lazy? Or just pigheaded?"

"I suppose I am thinking they are resistant to change. You can believe something that's been handed down from pappy to pappy but not a new concept developed in your own lifetime."

Uncertain where she was taking the discussion, he pointed toward the cork.

"How's yours look? Straight across or slanted?"

This time, he elicited a smile.

"Oh, you cannot judge me by that test. Aboard ship, nothing is ever straight. The vessel always lists to one side, whether from cargo shifting or the force and direction of the wind." She moved the bottle in demonstration. "A small object like this is always tossed around."

Now that they gotten where they were going, Seth busied himself rolling up his shirt sleeve.

"I'm listening."

"Have you ever read the Bible?"

"Parts of it. The Psalms. Some of the New Testament. I find it a hard go."

"There's a lot in there about slavery. Justifying it, you might say."

"That don't seem right."

"Yet it is the word of God. If you believe that."

"Don't you?"

"I believe it is the story of the Savior, written for the temper of the times. Like advances in agriculture, the new must be incorporated into the old."

He whistled and began work on his other sleeve.

"I'm right glad you came here with ideas about strawberries and not about preaching."

"I came here with ideas about neither and developed them as I went. May I ask you a question?"

"Go ahead."

"Knowing what you do, if I offered you five hundred dollars cash money, would you rather have that than the strawberries? Or let me put it another way," she hastened. "If someone came up right now and held out $500 to buy any and all strawberries that ever grow from our patches, would you take it?"

"Assuming that's a break-even proposition for me? You see," he added, pushing back in the chair, "I never asked what you paid."

"Yes. Say a stranger wishes to make good your loss."

"What about my labor?"

The question annoyed her and she shrugged it off.

"He's only speaking of a tangible exchange: money for money. You spent $500 on the plants and he's willing to give you $500 to buy them back." Then, quickly, "Not the land and not actually the plants but the fruit."

"In other words, I have to make a decision on the future: whether I reckon I can ever recoup my investment -- and then some. Or sell out now and have security in the bank."

"That is well put."

"Got a buyer in mind?"

"That is not the issue. We are discussing a hypothetical question."

"You're never gonna prove to anyone you're from Kansas using words like 'hypothetical.'"

Pleased with himself at the joke, he tapped his chest to indicate superiority, then used the arms of the chair to hoist himself up. Crossing to Barbara, Seth took her hand. Guiding her to her feet, they walked to the door. Turning the knob with his free hand, they went outside.

A warm, humid breeze blew in from the southwest, uncomfortably laden with moisture. Taking time to mark the half hour by ringing the bell, he then wandered off toward the back where the strawberry field stretched beyond the darkening horizon.

"Five hundred dollars is a hell of a lot of money. A fortune. It's a year's hedge against bad crops. It's new boots for a boy with growing feet and maybe some put away for his education. It's two new wheels for that lopsided wagon and shingles for the roof. It's a sketch book and pencils for Patricia and a whole jar of peppermint sticks. Money takes the rough edge off a man's insides."

Reaching down, he grabbed a handful of dirt and rubbed it against his fingers.

"Having $500 means going to town an' being able to look any man square in the eye; never having to look down 'cause you owe him what you can't pay. It raises you above the other farmers. You take on new respect. A man with $500 doesn't have a bewitched boy; he's got a p-culiar child." He let the dirt go and wiped his hands. "But there's one thing he doesn't have, Officer Nelander. Hope in the future. That cash money spends mighty fast. Oh, he thinks it'll last a lifetime. Earning interest. Being spent here and there but never making a dent in his savings. It'll be there for the hard times. Funny thing, though. It won't be. A year or two from now, after the wagon wheels get replaced and his boy's grown outta his new boots, he'll be right back where he started. Just a dirt farmer living hand to mouth."

Using the illuminated white string as a guide, Seth walked down one of the paths in the strawberry field, Nelander following.

"Pretty soon, that fear in his gut comes back. He starts worrying about the weather; how the corn'll come in. Whether the ears'll be full and yellow or shriveled and no good for anything but fodder. He starts gnawing at his fingernails when the horse needs to be re-shod. Or the cow gets too old to give milk." Air puffed out from between his lips. "Everything starts getting to 'im. Bills pile up. He looks at his life and wonders what it was all about. Whether it was worth it."

Reaching the end of the row, he sightlessly picked his way around the path and down another. She followed in his footsteps.

"If you really want to know if I woulda taken the chance you did -- spending a life's saving on a dream -- a wild, crazy scheme -- I'm ashamed to tell you I woulda found seven hundred different ways to talk you outta it. It's never been done. No one ever planted strawberries in Kansas. We don't know about disease; might be some mold grows over the leaves and spread it through the field like wild fire. Maybe it's too hot; too little rain.

The winter's too cold. They freeze up and die. Maybe they'll all turn green in spring but won't make fruit. What then?"

Dragging his feet, he stumbled over a rock and cursed, expressing, without intent, the inner conflict tearing him apart. Groping in the dark, he found it, or perhaps a cousin, snatched it up and heaved it away. The sound of the rock falling lent a muffled period to his exclamation.

"And that's not the half of it. Maybe they do bear fruit. Next year or the year after, the valley's full of red. We've got to hurry and pick 'em. Six of us, if you count Blind Betty and Mute Thomas and acres of fruit spoilin' on the ground. So -- we got bushels full. Bring the crop to town and sell it. Five cents -- ten cents a handful. Takes ten handfuls to make a dollar. How many handfuls to a bushel? Twenty? That's two dollars. Two dollars won't even get the plow sharpened."

An owl hooted. He paused to listen. A low noise in the distance. The nearly inaudible sound of a mouse squealing as pincer-sharp talons penetrated the skin on its neck. A death cry.

"Jesus Christ, Barbara, I woulda been right to talk you out of it."

Her throat constricted and she wanted to cry. But she could not. She would go down with her ship with the sound of defeat. Even knowing her own decisions had sunk it. That was not the way she had planned on meeting her Maker.

With bitterness and gall.

Saint Peter would have no mercy.

Nor would she expect any.

Seth Ward was not privy to her thoughts. He had his own to choke on.

"I won't answer your question about a fella offering me $500 for the strawberries because there is no such man. And I'm glad there isn't."

"Why -- why do you say that?"

"Because we've come back to that hope I spoke of. Of course, I had it rammed down my throat, but no matter. Sometimes, that's the way it is. Not my plan or your plan but God's plan. He knows best. 'Here it is, Seth Ward. I've thrown you a bone. Let's see what you can do with it. Fret over what might have been or learn to hold your head up without that damn five hundred dollars in the bank. So, Seth, you make two dollars on a bushel of strawberries. That's two more dollars than you had. And God knows," he shivered, "maybe there's twenty bushels of strawberries in the field. Maybe fifty. Maybe a hundred."

He stopped cold and Barbara ran into him. Frightened, she quickly made an apology, but he was quicker. Spinning around, Seth grabbed her by the arms. Even in the wan starlight she saw his flushed face, the sweat gleaming on his brow. Felt the heat of his breath, the clamminess of his flesh.

"I'm the one who preaches new ways but I didn't have the balls to put my money where my mouth was. You did and you don't even have any."

She did not know whether or not he meant to joke and so did not smile.

"You're God's hand, Nelander. It cost five hundred goddamn dollars to buy hope. I'm scared crapless. But I'll grab that chance by the teeth and shake it for all I'm worth."

This time he laughed and the spittle flew over her face. A moment before, it would have felt like a slap.

"Selling out now is the coward's way. I wouldn't sell for a thousand dollars."

Without meaning to, he had answered her question.

"Think carefully," she said.

"I have. Thought of what could go wrong and what could go right. I never saw the balance to it until now. Maybe I'm a fool." He put a hand to her head and tightened his grip around her neck. "You tell that mythical man that Seth Ward isn't interested. He and Barbara Nelander have themselves a strawberry field. Strawberry fields," he corrected. "They're gonna make a go of it. Ten cents at a time."

She had no idea how she found herself hugging him or when the tears started. One thing was perfectly clear, however. When the mysterious but not mythical man returned to the *Pirate Treasure,* their dry-docked farm ship in the wilderness of Kansas, she would reject his offer.

Five hundred dollars in exchange for hope was a bad bargain.

## CHAPTER 20

Baby Paula bounced on Barbara's knee and laughed. Others might have considered it more a gurgling or a bubbling but her mother knew better. The joyous sound was definitely a laugh. Not only that, the child highlighted her happiness by shoving fat little fingers in the air. Having learned the hard way that infant fingernails were the sharpest substance known to Man, she ducked back, wary that a wayward thrust might find its way into her eye.

Eight equally frisky kittens explored their new universe, sticking inquisitive noses into clumps of grass, batting down pesky shadows and declaring war on hapless litter mates.

The watchful mother cat, not unlike her human counterpart, distanced herself from her offspring, lying outstretched in a patch of sunlight by the porch. Eyes half closed, she pretended to sleep. Only the occasional flicker of a tail, or the twitch of an ear gave her away.

"Two orange kittens, two long-haired grey tabbies, a dusky black, a white-and-black spotted kitten, a pure white one and an all-black kitten. She's the runt," Patricia described. "When can we have them, Miss Betty?"

"Two mo' weeks. Miz Chatte'll let us know. By dat time she be tired ob feedin' 'em an' she'll push 'em outta da nest. Jes' like a mudder bird does to her young when it's time to fly."

Grabbing a pair of kittens, the girl frolicked with them in the grass, incurring instant baby ire. One arched its back and spat while the other flexed new-found claws.

"Careful, Patricia. They'll scratch."

"I know." Which meant, *I do not care.* Putting the animals down, she crept around on hands and knees, bumping noses with the babies and occasionally knocking them off wobbly legs. "Which are we to adopt? Have you chosen?"

"I have never had any particular favorite color in cats. You pick."

"How many can we have?"

"Two."

"Two?" Her lower lip protruded. "I thought we decided on six."

"The 'we' is a liberal interpretation."

"One for me, one for Peter, one for you, one for the captain...." She scratched her head, trying to remember the other reasons they must absolutely have six. "That's it! One for a mouser and one for the barn."

"I strongly suspect Captain Ward will tell you that whichever you bring home will be mousers, so that eliminates two off the top of your list. He will also say he doesn't want one of his own."

"You have whittled me down to three." Seeing Nelander hesitate, she drove home her point. "I must have my own and if I do, Peter will want his. And you said you needed companionship of your own kind. So, may we have three?"

"You are putting me in an awkward position, for it is I who must break the news to the captain. He will grunt and groan and pace around the room like a fish on a line. He will have all sorts of reasons why we only need two -- and if I reel him in too hard, he will break free and declare we do not need a cat, at all."

"Yes. He will do all that. But you are a better fisherman than he is a fish."

"Meaning?" she sighed, rolling her eyes with tried patience, "All right; three it is; a great compromise. But I must say, you are growing too wise for me. Perhaps it is you who should present our case."

The use of the word "our" was not lost on the listener.

"Oh, no. I am only a child and he is used to giving orders to me. But you are an adult and I have never yet heard him give you an order."

"Lor'! How old dis chil'?" Blind Betty inquired in admiration.

"I am soon to be eleven years old," Patricia answered for herself.

"What yuh t'ink, Nelander?"

"That I had better carry the day or lose status."

"Good. Then ask him for six," the child suggested.

"We have already had that discussion."

Unperturbed, for not to try meant failure, Patricia went back to playing. Nelander yawned and put the baby on the grass.

"Yuh tired?" Betty asked, sensing the change of position.

"Paula is at the stage where she wakes up every five minutes and wants to be fed. Or changed. Or entertained. She is at her loudest when I drift off."

"Dat be da way ob it. Da captain -- he don' mind?"

"I think he has more patience than I."

"Ah t'ink he habe a different patience den yuh."

Plucking a blade of grass with care so that the white inner portion came out intact, Nelander sucked on the sweetness.

"When I was a child much younger than Patricia, I had no idea of patience. One day was like another and I accepted it because my life was on a straight course. When my father took me to sea, I learned impatience right enough. So much to assimilate – new sights, new smells, new language, new responsibilities. I wanted to absorb it all at once and when I found I could not, I developed a temper." Nelander pursed her lips in an expression her listener divined without sight. "I can still remember my father lecturing me that patience was a virtue – to which I replied that I would rather be without virtue."

Blind Betty laughed because her mind's eye was sharp and Nelander's imagery vivid.

"Oh, Lor', dat got yuh nowheres."

"On the contrary. It got me swabbin' the deck and emptyin' out the slop buckets for the next two weeks. During that time, I had many private conversations with myself because as you can imagine, the rest of the crew shunned me. They didn't like the idea of a girl aboard, anyway, and watching me do the most menial labor, their opinion sunk even lower. The Captain had 'put me in my place,' and they were satisfied."

Stretching her feet, the girl who had grown into a woman, started off into the sky as being the closest thing to an unbroken expanse of blue-green ocean. "Knowing that I had lost every shred of respectability, I had to start over. I did so by studying the waves and the weather; I taught myself the night sky – got to be so I could identify the stars by brightness and position – the names came later. I learned to temper my - impatience - with the weather, for it would do what it would, regardless of Man's intervention. But knowing there was a rhyme and reason to it, the sense of it came to me so it was no longer an enemy. I spent hours staring into the depths, just letting my mind wander through the currents to the sea bed. That conveyed to me an awareness of great age and of the slowly moving pages of history."

Ba'bra Nelander nodded to herself in slow comprehension. "Knowledge is power and eventually, I even developed the knack of handling the crew, which could, on occasion, require the patience of a saint." Her voice hardened. "What I had -- and have little patience for -- is the inexplicable passage of time on land."

Discarding the stalk she selected another, this time tugging too quickly and breaking it at the stem. Snarling in annoyance, she flung it away.

"You plant a seed. It takes forever to grow. You wait for rain. It does not come. A ride to town consumes hours. Then everything becomes a rush: yesterday the crops were not ripe. Today they are. Tomorrow will be too late. After a frenzy of activity, they are harvested, they are sold and the waiting begins again. Winter months drag, then one day, it is imperative to begin plowing. Not a moment too soon, not a second tardy, or else this maniacal timetable is thrown off and the world descends into chaos."

"Seems to me yuh unnerstan, right 'nuf."

"All right, then. Let me say I do not appreciate it." Grabbing the baby, Nelander brought her cheeks close. Like an annoyed kitten, Paula fussed and began to cry. "I want my child to walk. I want to see blossoms on the strawberries. I want to pick them and make money. I want a savings account wider than that damned Kansas River."

Blind Betty took Paula, cooed in her ear. She stopped crying and the old woman put her down, where she had been content to play in the grass.

"Den, one day yuh look around yuhrse'f an' see yuh got all dat -- an' yuh wonder where da time went. Yuh wish yuh could habe it all back ag'in. Yuh old an' don' know how it happened."

Barbara gave her a long look, head tilted to one side in contemplation.

"Words of wisdom, mother. Thank you."

"Ah libed longer den yuh an' Ah know."

"You, sir, are a blessed spirit."

"Ah take dat mos' kindly an' Ah pray yuh a'ways t'ink so."

"I cannot think of a reason why it would change."

"Dere we are ag'in, talkin' 'bout time." Getting to her feet, she waved the other from following. "Ah git us sumtin' cold to drink."

In her absence, which seemed to cast a pall over the sun and shroud the world in gloom, Barbara crawled over and picked up one of the kittens. Petting the tiny head, she tried to look into the future and see it as a cat.

And found she could not.

The frantic barking of a dog brought Seth to consciousness with the immediateness of a fire bell. Feeling Nelander shift positions, he knew the sound had awoken her, too. All sleep gone from her voice, she demanded, "What is it?"

"Herman. From the yapping, I suspect he's got a coon treed. You wait here and I'll go out and see. Might be I'll have to bring him inside or we'll never get any peace."

The explanation was reasonable but she heard the lie behind the words.

"I'm coming with you."

Noting the fact he did not bother dressing, she followed suit, doing no more than slipping on a pair of shoes. By the time she reached the yard, however, he had disappeared.

"Seth? Seth, where are you?"

The only likely tree where Herman might have trapped a raccoon was the one where Belinda's swing hung. Neither man, dog, nor beast was to be seen anywhere near. Her interpretation had been right.

Trouble.

The sudden resumption of barking, this time further away, gave her the direction. Hurrying toward the back of the house, she came upon the strawberry field. Even in the darkness she could see something was wrong.

The white twine, used to mark rows, no longer reflected starlight. Their absence left a gap and her tongue went instinctively around her teeth, seeking a hole. She found none but it did not lessen her anxiety.

"Seth? Captain?"

"Over here," he called.

Cursing the convolutions of the land which made a sound appear as though it came from one direction when it originated in another, she picked her way through the rows, dilated pupils desperately searching for the tangible. Hearing her missteps, he called again.

"I'm portside of you."

Following the nautical direction for left, she came upon him a hundred yards distant.

"What is it? What's happened? Where are the --?"

He answered the first two interrogatives with one word.

"Deer."

A sickening chill exploded in her gut and she bent at the waist, hoping to dispel the pain. It eased the cramp but not the concern.

"What does that mean? Deer?"

"They've found the strawberry patch."

Revelation came with a second round of agony. "You mean -- to eat the plants?" She could not tell whether he nodded. "Have they eaten my strawberries?"

Instead of denying or confirming, he grunted.

"Can't tell how much damage they've done. Made a mess of the rows. Have to wait until light."

"Hell's bells! Who invited the damn deer?"

Out of the darkness a noise shattered her ear drums. Even in shock she identified it as laughter.

"Hell's bells if you didn't, Nelander," he gasped around his peels of sudden amusement.

"I did nothing of the sort. I may speak French but I have never been accused of communing with wild, four-legged terrestrial creatures."

"You sent out your invite soon as you put in the first plant. Damn me, I shoulda known." Putting two fingers to his mouth, he issued a shrill whistle. "Herman! Herman, back, boy!"

Mad dog paws trampled earth as the canine hustled to respond. For all of Nelander, it might have been a herd of buffalo descending upon them. Only one animal arrived, however, but that one full of energy, wet nose and dripping saliva.

"Atta boy! Good dog!" Roughhousing with the guardian, Seth dropped to one knee. "Saved our bacon, didn't you, you old rascal. Scared them critters off. Good boy."

Finally grasping the true horror of the situation, she frowned.

"You mean, the deer would have eaten my strawberries? The plants, themselves? Without waiting for the fruit?"

"Right to the ground. I was so worried about them chompin' the corn it didn't occur to me they'd come so close to the house. Had the dog guarding the west field. He musta heard 'em and come up."

She derived little relief from the explanation.

"Get the rifle and go after them. Shoot as many deer as you can before they do any more damage."

The command surprised him. Abandoning the dog, he stood, staring queerly into the shadows comprising her facial features.

"Never heard you talk like that before."

"For God's sake, they could have ruined us."

With an angry stomp he leaned closer.

"Listen to me. If they ate the corn, or trampled the wheat, that would be bad. Dire. That's how we make a living. Right now, the strawberries are a hope, nothing more. They're a...." He fumbled for the word. "An adjunct. Some future consideration. I can't go shooting all the deer in the wood to save one crop."

She remained resolute. "Why not?"

"There's too many of 'em, for one thing. Second thing is that deer are a natural part of nature; part of the checks and balances. They have just as much right to live as anything else. And," he added, clenching his fist, "they're beautiful creatures."

"Fine sentiment for a farmer." She relented because she understood what he was saying. "But they're not going to fine dine on my strawberries."

"All right. I know."

"We'll have to put up a fence --"

He arched an eyebrow.

"*We* will?"

"Show me how and I'll do it."

"That's not the answer. A deer can jump any fence. They can leap higher'n a man."

Biting her lip, Barbara spun around in despair.

"Are you telling me there's nothing we can do? That I have to stand around and watch while those -- damn beautiful deer -- rob me of all this?"

"I'm not saying that. Easy, now," he warned, choosing the wrong tack to elicit comfort.

"Don't tell me to be easy when I see five hundred dollars' worth of my life's savings go down with the ship."

"Sorry. Sorry. We'll handle it."

"How, Mr. Cavalier?"

"Whoa. Slow down."

The moment the denigrating appellation came out of her mouth, Nelander realized she crossed an unspoken barrier. Ashamed, she stepped away, inadvertently trampling a strawberry plant.

"Forgive me, sir. I... misspoke myself. In the heat of battle."

The anger in his eyes did not cover the hurt.

"All right, then. I forgive you, but I've never talked to you like that and I expect the same respect from... my first mate."

He made her smile and she "darned" him for it.

"You are right, Captain. But...."

"We'll have to get another dog. One to watch out here. Chase off the deer."

"How long will that take? We can't let another night go by --"

"No. We can't. A small herd of deer can wipe us out in six hours." Stooping down to pick up a plant, Seth shuddered. "I should have realized. My fault."

He turned away but she grabbed him as further grim realization struck.

"What about the valley? Dear God, tell me deer do not go there." Before he could reply, she attempted to rationalize. "Surely the 'critters' which supped here would be too full to make the journey --"

Resting a hand on her shoulder, he forced a crooked grin.

"Kansas has more than enough deer -- and raccoons and other varmints -- to eat the crops of every farmer in the territory. The ones we stuffed tonight undoubtedly have cousins over the hill."

"Then we are ruined!"

"We don't know what damage has been inflicted. Whatever it is can be dealt with. We will go in the morning and take stock. All right?"

"But Seth, I wanted this to be perfect."

"We have a perfect baby. And two perfect crew. We have each other; a perfect love. For that, we bend the knee and give thanks. For the rest, God expects us to cope as best we may. I have said: we will get a dog. Two dogs. One to stay here and another to protect the valley. In the meantime, we shall guard the land ourselves."

"But, now?"

"We take turns staying up. Banging pots and pans to scare off the invaders. Not exactly pirate weapons, but in this case, more than effective. Does that suit your buccaneer's hot blood?"

"I believe it does."

"Very good. I will stand first watch --."

"No, sir. My job. Besides," she tried, evoking an unfelt pleasantness, "I have a desire to watch the sun come up. I miss that; the sight of a new day dawning. The wind in my face. It helps put things in perspective. But you go. Sleep. I will watch the ship."

"Do you need a jacket? Some coffee?"

"No. But if you've a mind, send out some cutlasses and war shields -- known in your parlance as wooden spoons and frying pans."

"I will do that, Officer Nelander."

He left. Half an hour later, Patricia emerged out of the shadows with a handful of kitchen utensils. Handing them over with grim solemnity, she bowed.

"Master Patricia reporting for duty, sir."

The officer might have rejected the child's offer for she preferred handling the night and the enemies alone. But she had learned never to reject help when given from the heart. Best intentions were better gratified than refused, lest they be withheld in the future.

"Thank you."

"We'll get them buggars, Nelander."

"You bet we will. Never let it be said the crew of the *Pirate Treasure* were defeated by voracious 'darlings.'"

"We won't be satisfied until we see the whites of their tails!"

"A lesson, Master Patricia, learned from your forbearers."

Commander and crewman kept watch until the sun broke over the crest of the horizon then retired below decks, or in this case, back to the farm house. Seth had already prepared breakfast.

"And a hard time I had, too," he groused, serving the coffee. "Wasn't anything left to cook with but a rusty old pan I found in the rear of the cabinet and a stick I picked up from the yard. Good thing you left the coffee pot, girl, or I'd have had to cashier you."

Round eyes preceded, "Pay me off?"

"To cashier means to punish. It's a military expression."

Whether she knew the meaning or not, Patricia played the idea for all it was worth.

"Oh. I figured you was gonna open the drawer like in Mr. Anson's store and pay me a bonus. If I'd a taken the coffee pot, that'd a spared you the trouble a brewin' up some pizzon."

"Pizzon? How would you know? You don't drink coffee."

"Scrubbin' out the burned pot is enuf fer me. Don't have to look a swayback in the mouth to know it ain't got no teeth."

Captain Ward lunged at her and missed.

A fact he regretted. But only slightly.

# CHAPTER 21

The deer had been to the valley. They could see that before the wagon rolled to a stop inside the mouth of the cut-out.

Hoof prints marked their progression from the edge of the depression down across the rows. The white string had been snapped and the remnants of nibbled green-tipped plants lay everywhere.

"Damn."

The true extent of the damage had been mitigated, however, by industrious work. Mute Thomas and Blind Betty were already present, replanting and straightening the carefully arranged piles of dirt. Although they had surely heard the wagon coming, neither met the family, opting to continue their labor.

Hoping down from the seat, Seth let the horse graze as he approached.

"We had the same visitors last night at the farm." Before Thomas could start hand signals, he waved him off. "My fault. I should have realized."

"We stay here da night frum now on, Captain Ward," Betty offered. "Won' be no mo' ob dis. An' we put back what we kin. It ain't so bad as yuh t'ink, suh."

"Of course it's not. Just a setback. We'll recover."

Ignoring the intake of breath he heard as Nelander walked among the rows, he shoved a hand in his pocket.

"I'm going into town to buy a dog."

This elicited a new set of hand gestures which Betty translated without benefit of having seen them.

"We ain't got no 'sperience wid dogs, suh. Least ways not wid ownin' em."

The statement caused his lip to curl. Barbara addressed the pair.

"What does that mean?"

He chose not to answer.

"I'll be back this afternoon. Do what you can here."

The baby in Barbara's backpack began to cry. Reaching a hand over her shoulder, she tried to still it.

"We'll see you later, then." And added, "Be careful."

The warning came from inference rather than knowledge. She did not know why he should be careful. Only that some danger lurked.

"I will."

"Do you want my cutlass?" Peter offered, hefting the weapon from its leather scabbard. Seldom without it, the wooden sword served as a badge of status as well as protection from worldly adversaries.

"No, son. I won't be needing that." He might have added, *You keep it,* but that would have sounded paranoid, interjecting a concern he did not wish to acknowledge.

Resuming his place on the wagon seat, Seth waved good-bye. Already tense from having overlooked the threat of four-legged predators, he chafed at the idea of another day away from his own work. Yet he had to prevent further marauding or risk losing Nelander's crop.

Typically, farmers knew when their neighbors dogs went into heat from the reaction of their own. That meant a litter in two months. If a man needed a dog, he waited the appropriate time, then applied at the porch, carrying a basket of eggs, a loaf of fresh baked bread or some other barter. Puppies not being an uncommon occurrence, he was generally given his pick.

After the Windsors packed up and left, however, the Wards had no near neighbors. That meant Seth would have to ride all the way to town and make inquiry. The idea did not appeal to him on any number of levels.

With a resolution he did not feel, he slapped the long, lose end of the reins over Blaze's back and set his mind. He had promised to come back with two dogs and that he intended to keep.

The old clock perched atop the undertaker's establishment tolled ten as he approached Main Street. Stopping before the mercantile, he stretched his legs, secured the horse, then approached the store, keenly scanning the billboard outside for notices advising "Pups to good home." He counted seven offering "Mousers, top quality," and ten more, advertising sundry service from "Sewing done in my home, cheap," to "Nives sharpined wile yuh wait."

On another day he might have smiled at the misspellings.

Only one notice piqued interest, promising "Hunting dogs for sale. Good bloodlines," but the price put him off. "Twenty dollars each." He had come for mongrels, not to mortgage the farm.

Removing his hat to wipe off the early spring sweat, Seth entered the store, nodding familiarly to Hector Anson, the proprietor.

"Morning."

"Mornin', Capt'n. What can I do you for?"

"Lookin' for a dog. Maybe two. Anyone mention they have a litter they're eager to be shed of?"

"Something happen to Herman?"

A man might not remember the names of an acquaintance's children but he never forgot the name of his horse or his dog.

"No, he's just fine. But I've plowed some new land and we had deer trouble last night. Need some more help around the place."

"Plowed more land, did you? What'd you put in? Corn? Didn't see you buying extra seed."

"No. Not corn."

Anson slapped his hand on the counter and grinned.

"Chilies is it, then? Gonna pizzon the whole countryside?"

He grinned back. "If I thought it would work, I might." Spoken lightly, the statement could be taken for a joke. "No. Something else."

"Not more scientific farmin' of yours, is it? Some fancy crop you read about in one of them periodicals?"

"You've guessed it."

Which meant, *None of your business* and sounded like *That's exactly what I've gone and done.*

"They don't have deer back east? Didn't warn you about them tasty green leaves bringin' in a herd?" He shrugged. "How much damage they do? The deer, I mean." He thought himself clever and Seth did not dissuade him.

"Nothing we can't recover from."

"'We,' is it? That wife of yours, Nelander, helping you out? That why you plowed new land? Got two extra hands workin' for you? Better'n a boy, she is, I bet."

He might have said yes, but the question had been meant as an insult.

"Peter's big enough to help me."

"Lot of folks here been wonderin' if you was gonna plant in Terrance's fields. That's what you bought his place for, wasn't it?"

"The flood left a good foot of topsoil in the acres behind the house. Made it worth my while to see what would grow there." Leaning across the counter, he shoved his face toward the shopkeeper's. "I was asking about dogs."

Hector Anson wisely withdrew. Grabbing a rag from beneath the counter, he ran it over the age-polished wooden top as an excuse for his withdrawal.

"McConaghie's sellin' hunting dogs. But I don't suppose you want to do business with him."

"Not lookin' to buy. Trade, maybe. Nothing special. Just a pup or an old cur or two that'll get along with Herman and doesn't mind working three hundred and sixty-five days a year."

"You might ask Doc McTree. He was in the other day an' mentioned his bitch had pups."

"I'll do that. Obliged."

Shuffling out to appear in no hurry, Seth left the wagon where it was and walked, crisscrossing three streets and down a fourth before coming out at the physician's home. Set neatly on a corner lot, the well-maintained dwelling served as both residence and office. A large sign with letters burned into the wood advised, "Hank McTree, M.D."

Hoping to find the doctor at home and unencumbered with a waiting room full of patients, Seth tread lightly on the gravel sidewalk, taking off his hat before knocking on the door. While another sign warned, "Come In," he had never felt comfortable barging into another man's house. He would wait for an invitation or leave.

A voice from within called, "Greetings, Captain Ward. Door's open. Let yourself in."

Obeying orders, he first stuck his head in, saw McTree over by the window watering a plant, then slipped through.

"How'd you know it was me?"

"You're the only man in Lawrence who knocks."

"Reckon that makes me the only one who can't read."

"Never apologize for good manners. You do your mother proud. And your stiff-necked father, no doubt, who drilled them into you." Putting down his tin watering can, the doctor wiped his hands on a towel to dry them from the leaky spout. "What can I do for you? Not sick, I trust."

"No, sir. Anson told me your bitch had puppies and I'm looking for a couple."

"Oh." McTree groaned, then gave a sharp whistle. A medium-sized dog with shaggy hair and an overlarge black wet nose bounded in. Affectionately rubbing the animal behind the ears, he then gave it a swat on the backside. "I've already given away the pick of the litter. Didn't know you were in the market or I'd have saved them for you."

"What you have left?"

"The runt and a crooked tail beastie. Full of life, though. Wanna see them?"

"You bet."

Following McTree, they crossed two rooms before coming out at the back door. Nudging it with his elbow, the rusty hinges squeaked as they went through. Two puppies, one the size and color of a setting sun and the other a rambunctious black and white mottled pup tumbled over one another in their eagerness to greet the newcomer. Both yipped in high, loud puppy chatter.

Seth grabbed the little one, bringing it close for inspection. For his trouble the dog rewarded him with a frantic licking of his face.

"Full of life is right. Weaned, are they?"

"Yup. Ready to strike out on their own. I was hoping for a good home. Wasn't sure I'd find one. They're not exactly looksome."

"Judging a dog by his appearance is as foolish as looking at a man's beauty and thinking that makes him a pure soul. Never knew the two to go hand-in-hand."

"Can't say I'd disagree."

Picking up the other puppy, the doctor displayed its tail. "He was born this way. Come into the world marked. I'd like to think that meant God wanted to keep a special eye on the pup."

"What you call him?"

"Haven't named them, yet. Hate to get a dog used to one name and then have the new owner change it. My taste seems to run counter to most in town. Hermes; that's the god of physicians. Copernicus. Galileo. Hippocrates. All scientists; great men."

"Then what about Minerva, here?" Seth asked, indicating the female dog which had joined them to oversee her offspring.

"Her actual name is Pallas Athena, but I shortened it to Minerva."

"Sounds easier."

"Found her one night when I was coming home. Abandoned in the woods. I never knew her parentage. That's like Athena; she was born of Zeus without a mother."

"Good trick. I suppose most women would appreciate knowing the secret."

McTree laughed and set down the puppy. "I've always said if it were up to males to bear the children, we'd see the end of the human race in one generation. How's Nelander, by the way? And little Paula?"

"Both doing fine."

"Glad to hear it. What do you think about the puppies?"

"Take 'em both and thank you for it."

"Good. I sort of wanted them to go together. You know: you get attached and then when you realize a pack of howling mutts in the backyard isn't much of an invitation to patients, you get it in your mind they can stay together, somehow. Like brothers and sisters. Keeping in touch, you might say."

"Never knew you for the sentimental type."

"Oh, there's lots people don't know about me. Come on back in. Have time for a cup of coffee?"

"No. But I don't mind dawdling with you. We never have much of a chance to talk. Whenever you're around, there's usually blood."

Minerva led the way inside. When assured her master was not going anywhere, she circled the area around his favorite chair then plopped to the floor, waiting his eventual arrival.

McTree made a fresh pot of coffee and while the two men waited, Seth dug into his pocket, extracting a small farmer's purse.

"What do I owe you?"

The doctor scratched his chin in mock concentration.

"Now, if I coulda passed them off as blue-blooded hunting dogs --"

"I know. Matthew McConaghie an' his hounds. Twenty dollars or half your next crop."

While he tried to lighten the first sentence by making a joke with the second, McTree caught the inflection.

"Is it the money or the master you don't like?"

"Neither" came out too quickly.

"Got something against hunting dogs?"

"Depends on what they hunt." McTree waved away the purse and Seth returned it to his pocket. "Wouldn't mind if you gave me a bill of sale, though."

"Think I'll renege on my word and take 'em back? After they win first prize at the Fair?"

"Times bein' what they are...." He left the thought unfinished. "Like to give you something for 'em, though. Just to make it legal."

The physician might have remarked that between friends, a handshake customarily sealed a deal. But "times being what they were," he did not.

"Glad to give you a piece of paper."

Moving into his study, he pulled up the top of a roll-top desk. The interior presented as neat an appearance as the house. Pigeonholes were filled with correspondence or unpaid bills, while the writing surface had paper, a steel-tipped pen and inkwells set for easy use.

Expertly dipping the writing instrument into a pot of ink, McTree wrote a statement, transferring ownership of "Two puppies, one burnt-orange runt female and one crooked-tailed black and white male to Seth Ward." Dating the document, he signed it, drizzled sand over the lettering to dry the ink, then handed it over.

"This do?"

"Right fine."

"Have a seat and I'll get the coffee."

Taking a chair near the doctor's, he waited, hands on knees, until presented with the steaming beverage. Blowing over the top, he sipped and leaned back. While making small talk was not one of his better talents, he tried to cover the silence his companion seemed content to let stand.

"How's business?"

"I don't see many patients here, anymore. No one has the money to pay, what with the drought destroying last year's crops. Times like this, people resort to treating all those boils and broken bones they wouldn't have hesitated to have me look at before." Crossing his legs, he gave the visitor a hard stare. "Course, there are always a few who don't mind running up a bill and then conveniently forgetting about it. I bet I could walk down Main Street and not catch a single eye."

"Bet you could. Had that experience myself."

The veiled reference to bewitchment prompted the doctor to ask, "How's Peter getting on?"

"He's a pirate, now, and those are sturdy fellas. Pirates aren't afraid of what people say. And, of course, he's got his cutlass. Be a brave boy who challenged another carryin' such a weapon."

"Was just wondering. Thought maybe Peter needed a dog. Sort of like for friendly protection."

"No. Nothing like that. We've had deer trouble. Nelander bought some strawberry plants from back east an' the deer thought they tasted right fine."

"Strawberries? Do tell. Never heard of anyone growing strawberries hereabouts. Be nice on flapjacks; or in a bowl of cream."

"Five thousand plants."

The enormity caught McTree off guard.

"Five thousand? What for?"

"To cultivate; and eventually sell. Commercially. Something like ten cents a basket. Sell 'em in town at the Farmer's Market."

"Do you think you can make money on it?" Uncrossing his legs, he leaned forward. "Won't have any competition, that's for sure. And ten cents a basket sounds reasonable. Maybe too much so. What kind of a crop are you expecting?"

"Don't know. We'll have to wait and see. Might be a nice income. I don't know," he repeated.

"Where in tarnation did you get the time to put in five thousand plants? And where'd you put 'em? Not in the corn field?"

"Always had my eye on a piece of land at the far corner of the Windsor property. A shallow valley. Found wild strawberries there when I was a boy. That's what gave her the idea."

McTree went into the kitchen and brought back the coffee pot. Topping off both mugs, he set it down on the floor and resumed his seat.

"Lot of people wondered about that. Why you bought it."

"You mean how, don't you?" Seth demanded, eyes narrowing. "Where'd I come up with money when no one else had a dime. The down-payment was Nelander's, if you must know. Her savings, from when she worked on her father's ship. But we didn't buy the place for that reason. She wanted them to come back. Went all the way into the Nebraska Territory lookin' for 'em."

"Did she?"

"Found 'em, too. In a bad way. Made them an offer but they wouldn't come back. I told her they wouldn't. She felt bad about the whole thing. That's where the idea for the strawberries came in, I guess. To make something out of nothing."

"I like it, Seth. It works out, it's brilliant." He fiddled with his cup. "Godawful lot of work, though. A wonder how you managed with just you and Peter."

"Nelander and Patricia took over the strawberries."

"Plowed the fields, too, did they?"

Ward's jaw worked while he fashioned the sentence.

"Had some help."

"Did you, now?" When the captain gave no indication of prolonging the conversation, the doctor pushed it. "Wonder who that might have been? Not Tiny Deagle? He's still looking for work. Him and his brother. Then, there's Paul Baxter. He's been out to your farm a time or two helpin' harvest, hasn't he? But I saw him only last week and he didn't mention he'd seen you."

Seth stared at his hands. "Nothing like that."

On a silent command from her master, Minerva got up and trotted outside. Her ears hung low as if she had resigned herself to the inevitable. Giving each pup a stern lick across the snout with her sinuous pink tongue, she guided them back inside. Hardly ever allowed the luxury of exploring

Mother's Terrain, they yipped, bit one another's tails, then bounded across and around the furniture, sniffing out new and exciting trails.

This exercise gave the men an excuse not to make eye contact.

"Thought what you're going to call 'em?"

"Not me. That'll be up to Nelander and the crew. Something nautical, I expect. Not as fancy as 'Pallas Athena' or 'Copernicus.'" He forced a grin. "Dardanelles. Mizzenmast. You know."

"Always said a good name sets a man or a beast out on the right foot." Reaching into his pocket, the doctor withdrew a leather pouch. Dipping in his fingers, he produced a generous amount of shredded tobacco. Shoving it into his cheek, he plucked away several stray bits, then offered some to Seth.

"Don't chew."

"Habit I got into when I was a student. Started out using it as a reward to myself when I got a good grade. Or to keep me awake nights when I was on duty at the hospital. Put in long hours. Coffee and tobacco. Kept me going."

"Where was that, then?"

The question was meant to put off the inevitable. As a military tactic, it came too late.

"Philadelphia." McTree chewed the wad, then aimed a stream of black liquid toward a small, recently cleaned spittoon. "You're crossing a grey area, you know -- giving a dog to a black man. In some parts, it's illegal. Might be here, too. If I don't check the law, someone else will."

The detail they had danced around hung in the living room like an accusation, which it was not.

"Who said I was givin' a dog to anyone?"

"I get around, Captain. I'm probably the only white man goes into Little Laurence. The only one who's welcome. Besides you, that is."

Taking exception, Seth gripped his hands until the knuckles turned white.

"There's lots of men in Kansas feel the way I do. Men who don't like slavery."

"I would agree with you. That doesn't mean they want a 'Nigger Hole' outside their town. Doesn't mean they'd hire 'em, either -- pay 'em a decent wage. Not when there's white men without jobs."

A pinkish-red color crept up Seth's neck.

"I'm not payin' 'em anything! There never was any talk of money." Which amounted to an admission. He struck the arm of the chair. "They're workin' on the barter system. What white would do that? Besides," he lamely added, "What makes you think I've got Negroes at my place?"

"I told you. I go out to Little Laurence. I'm allowed; treat the children and the old folk. Sometimes suture a wound or set a bad break. I, too, work on the barter system."

"So?"

"I know them all by name, or at least by face. Strike up conversations. Seems Blind Betty and her son, Mute Thomas, have up and left." He snapped his fingers. "Just like that. Didn't tell anyone where they were going."

"You'd expect someone would go lookin' fer 'em."

"Maybe they did. Or maybe, like white folk, they just decided to let sleeping dogs lie. They went out to your farm, didn't they? To plant strawberries." Seth shrugged. "Might be, they're even staying at the Windsor's old place. Need a dog to keep watch in that valley of yours."

"What if I do? There ain't no law against me ownin' three dogs."

"You can own as many as you want. But when you give one to a Negro, that raises eyebrows. When you let dark-skinned people stay at the former home of a Caucasian family, that does more. Raises ire. Gets men to thinking what side you're on."

"Never made a secret of it."

"The way things are, it's sometimes wiser to keep your own council."

Angry at the turn of subject, the captain rose and turned his back on the physician.

"What about you? You tend their hurts."

"I'm a doctor. I've sworn an oath."

"To treat people. There are those don't consider blacks people."

"You and I both know they're wrong. But it doesn't stop talk." Rubbing thumb and forefinger, he summoned Minerva. She came over and he scratched behind her ears. "You and I are held by different standards. Why didn't you hire the Deagle boys? Or Baxter?"

"Can't afford to pay a decent wage. That explain it?"

"Yeah. But it mighta been smarter to have offered them the same deal you gave Miss Betty and the boy. Give them a chance to turn you down. Man mighta thought twice, being given the opportunity to homestead a farm."

"They're just staying there. Looking after the buildings. Can't afford to have it empty. The rats take over. Birds roost in the rafters. Well goes foul. They've fixed it up nice," he said. As an excuse, it fell flat.

"Ever thought what happens, someone rides out that way? Sees Negroes planting a garden? Putting a cow in the barn."

"There is no barn. It burned down."

"Ah. Yes. Don't expect anyone to come out and help you rebuild it."

Finally at the end of his rope, Seth spun, teeth bared.

"If you don't want to give me them pups, then say so. I've wasted enough time."

"Didn't say so. We have a contract. I just wondered if you'd thought about it, that's all. Not the dogs," he dismissed, startling Minerva with a violent hand gesture. She got up and wandered toward her water bowl. A few desultory licks satisfied her thirst. "I didn't know where Blind Betty and Mute Thomas went, but I should have guessed. No one in Lawrence even knows they're gone. But eventually, some boy out shooting rabbits or that old gossip, Pete Erlinger, will be out your way. And they'll see. Next thing you know, you'll have a delegation at your door."

"And you'll be with them, too, I suppose. Carrying righteous indignation."

"Nope. I'll be standing beside you. And Nelander. And Patricia and Peter and Paula. We make a mighty small army."

"There are others -- decent folk --"

"For God's sake, Seth, where's your mind? Voting to keep Kansas a free state is one thing. Inviting niggers into your back yard is another."

Sweat leaked from the captain's brow and armpits. The tickling sensation exacerbated his temper.

"They have to stay somewhere. They have to work for a living. They're human beings, for Christ's sake. Take dignity away from a man and he becomes an animal."

Realizing he had taken the subject further than intended, Dr. McTree rose from his chair and scooped up the orange puppy.

"I hope those strawberries take root and grow. I hope they produce fruit and you sell them for a good profit. I hope we have another vote on a state constitution and Kansas comes in free. I hope to God people see reason and that somehow we can avoid violence. But I'm afraid there's a lot of innocent people going to get hurt before this is over."

Holding over the puppy, he depositing the squirming mass of paws and ears into the other's arms.

"I'll get you a rope. Can't expect 'Dardanelles' and 'Mizzenmast' to stay put in a moving wagon."

Seth went outside and waited for the other to bring the rope. The puppy pressed its wet nose against the uncovered area of his neck. It felt cold and sent a shiver down his spine.

"Here you go."

McTree fastened one end around its neck and another to a metal hook in the back. Grabbing the black and white, he did the same. Minerva hopped in after them. The doctor shooed her down.

"You're not going, girl. You're staying here. With me."

*Where it's safe.*

He held out his hand and the men shook.

Both hoped it would not be for the last time.

All things considered, Laurence, Kansas, was short on great expectations.

# CHAPTER 22

"Get up! Captain, open your eyes. It is urgent!"

He would have shot up like an Independence Day firecracker but for the hand pressed to his chest.

"What is it?" he whispered, supposing the pressure was meant for silence. Nelander dispelled that first impression by speaking in a normal, albeit slightly higher voice.

"Put on your trousers and come with me."

It could only mean one thing.

Adventure afoot.

As though to confirm this determination he slid off the bed and raced for his pants, hung over the back of a chair. Bare toes came in contact with chair leg. He howled. Multicolored stars exploded behind his eyeballs.

Nearly launching him through the ceiling.

Less grandiose than a Chinese rocket but more spectacular than a Fourth of July celebration.

"Rats!"

He heard her chortle. His lips pursed.

His first officer would have used the expression *Damn!* And felt no guilt.

On the whole, he would rather have had her parents than his own. Even if it meant going to sea at the tender age of five years.

Shoving his limbs through the legs, he yanked the loose braces over his shoulders and followed her into the living room. Eyes not yet accustomed to the darkness, he entangled himself around a small beast eagerly nipping at his pant cuffs. Larger than a rodent and smaller than a grown dog, the collision prompted a second exclamation inadvertently paying homage to the first.

"Darn vermin!"

The puppy exploded into a paroxysm of tail wagging.

"What's keeping you?" Nelander called.

Awkwardly regaining his balance, the captain shot a rueful expression toward the open front door.

"I nearly fell below the Dardanelles."

Although he had meant his two choices to be examples rather than actual names, once he told his story about the trip to Dr. McTree's in slightly amended language, the crew had immediately adopted them. Keeping the orange runt for themselves, they had ceremoniously bestowed "Mizzenmast" to Blind Betty and Mute Thomas.

At the moment, Seth deeply regretted not giving them charge of both and *damn* the consequences.

Hopping one-footed to the entranceway, a burst of unexpectedly bright moonlight nearly blinded him. The yard, barn and fields stood out in stark detail, the most minute details augmented by the celestial light source.

His wife and three children stood by the well, frantically motioning him forward. Nearly having to shade his eyes against the glare he hurried forward.

"Hurry up, Papa Captain!"

The puppy burst through the door. Tail at attention, legs flying, nose alternately pressed to the ground and shoved into the night air, the ball of energy soon directed its attention toward poor Herman. The elder statesman of the Canine Contingent puffed in sad contemplation, expanding his cheeks with a mournful "Huff!" as though to say, *If four kittens weren't bad enough. Why am I to suffer this abomination?*

Seth sympathized and wondered if he and Herman might not be better hiding out in the doghouse for the next six months.

Following their lead, Seth limped out back behind the house. Although the fantastic moon glow had prepared him for some spectacle, when he beheld nearly took his breath away. As far as his eyes could see lay a field of surrealistic green, bedecked with a mad sprinkling of white. Stopping dead in his tracks, his mouth gaped.

"Sweet Jesus." Bringing a hand to his temple, he stared in awe. "When did this happen?"

He had seen the strawberries come alive. Like one thousand tiny miracles, the dried and withered plants had slowly turned from brown to green. At first, there had been nothing more than a hint, a shadow, a tease of what might be, followed by a pale, almost whitish green. Next had followed small, tenuous shoots, straight up, reminiscent of nature's lancets.

From them had issued other stems and finally small pointed leaves, covering the landscape with little pea-colored strangers.

The valley, too, had been transformed from brush and weeds into a two-sided unveiling of deep verdure, soft, like velvet. That, he had anticipated.

No, Seth reminded himself. That, he had prayed for. What he expected had been much less: the survival of two thousand or perhaps fewer, woefully attempting to dig stunted roots into unproven soil. A handful of leaves on each plant, withered by the Kansas sun, confused by the change of latitude and longitude. Aliens in a foreign land, silently communing in a language known only to themselves, trying to decide whether they wished to accept their new situation and grow, or to send their plant spirits onto a further journey.

There were those who tried and failed, but the vast majority thrived.

Green. They had turned green and he had rejoiced. But this he had not expected.

White. The white of blossoms.

Seth Ward's throat constricted and he swore off returning the kittens and the puppies to whence they had come, suddenly feeling more generous toward life in all its myriad forms.

"Do you see?"

The question was rhetorical. Nelander knew from his expression he did see. But she had to ask because she wanted to hear.

"I see. But I do not believe. I thought -- you said -- we should not expect blossoms the first year. Nor many the second. Not until the third year could we anticipate a significant harvest."

"I did."

His farmer's common sense took hold, like mushrooms, burrowing in the dark.

"We must not be hasty."

"Of course not." He looked at her sharply. "I do not deceive myself. The plants are young. Perhaps the blossoms will die. We cannot expect fruit. It is too soon. But Seth, it is a glorious sight. It means," she finished, readjusting Paula so she, too, could assimilate the sight, "they are trying. Fulfilling their role in nature."

Stepping forward, carefully, as if fearful of treading upon the moonlight, which danced upon the earth like jewels, he took in a deep breath.

"This phenomenon... the glow. I have never seen anything like it."

"It's faerie dust, papa. The elves have sprinkled it over the field for us to see."

"I believe you are right, child. There can be no other exclamation."

Taking his hand, Barbara walked with him.

"A confirmation of our faith."

"Your faith."

"All of ours. If I close my eyes I can almost feel as though I were at sea. The way the wind caresses my cheek. The whispery sound of leaves, almost like waves lapping against the bow. My head filled with wonder so that I list from side-to-side. The twinkling of stars so near it seems you can reach out and pluck one for your pocket. The silvery color, almost a sea blue."

"Our *Pirate Treasure,* my love."

"Yes," she intoned into his face. "We have brought the ocean to Laurence."

"Or perhaps we have transported Kansas to the Atlantic."

"That, too."

"Strawberries. Who knew strawberries would be the link?"

"*Mama* knew," Peter emphasized, separating his birth mother from his adopted parent. He passed by them, his boy's form ethereal in the supernatural lightness of the night. "She breathed upon them and she told me. Ain't no more bewitchment, she said. And then she said something different."

"What did she say, Peter?"

"Turn your cutlasses into plowshares."

He drew his wooden sword and made a swishing sound with his lips. His back thus turned, he did not see the gems of tears glistening in his parents' eyes.

"A wise woman."

"A gift from God."

They walked the length of the field, then along the perimeter, having said enough. Time, now, to absorb the wonder.

Finally tiring, they sat in the grass, legs crossed, Indian style, their baby between them. Those with younger legs continued their trek up and down the rows, occasionally stopping for a closer examination or to smell the subtle, wondrous perfume.

Under the mystic spell, Seth felt his eyelids droop. He fought the numbing comfort, fearing that when he opened them again the scene would be lost. Finally unable to keep awake, he rested his head against Barbara's shoulder and drifted away.

She woke him later with a tap on his arm.

"Captain? The sun is rising."

Stifling a moan of disappointment, he lifted his head. The night aura had faded, giving way to the first rays of dawn, prying themselves loose from the constraints of the distant horizon.

"It is gone," he whispered. She nodded. "Did you see it go?"

"No. My eyes were shut. I was dreaming."

"Of what?"

"I do not remember. Something... comforting."

"I am glad."

She might have added, *It could not have been anything but comforting,* but that might have opened the door for confrontation. That she did not desire.

A light coverlet of dew had settled over the land. In first light, the water crystals sparkled.

"Shall we go home?" he asked.

"We are home," she replied.

A better answer he could not have received from one of God's angels.

"Do you mean that? Home? You, a seafarer, born of water and wind?"

"Home is where the heart resides." She touched her chest. "You have made a landlubber out of me, sir."

"Is that a good thing or a bad thing?"

"It is an unexpected development."

"I used to worry that one day I would wake up and you would be gone. A note on the pillow would say that you had heard the call and gone back to where you belonged. May I stop worrying?"

"No. But if one day I do go, you will come with me. Is that fair enough?"

"More than fair." He yawned. "Shall we go whaling?"

"I would not be adverse to a trip to the northwest, but only as sightseers. Not to hunt. I have found... other ways to light my lamp."

She kissed him and he kissed her back.

"I am glad."

"So am I."

The bright, clear ring of a bell reminded them of other duties. They paused to count.

"Four bells: five-thirty. The crew is restless."

"The crew," he snorted, rolling his eyes, "is hungry." Baby Paula's fist into the air gave approval to the sentiment. Seth gave Nelander his hand and helped her up. "Shall we go and feed them?"

Feeling just giddy enough to tease, she asked, "Who first? The baby or the barnyard animals or the kittens or the puppies or Herman or the two older children?"

The answer came, not surprisingly, from the category, *None of the above.*

"Me."

Proving to Nelander's satisfaction, at least, he qualified as the more selfish of the lot.

Or the hungriest.

Which, in this case, happened to be both.


Daylight proved their nighttime ramble to have been something of an aberration. There were blossoms on the strawberries, but not the vast quantity suggested. The rich green of the leaves, however, remained, giving cause for optimism.

Ledger in hand, Nelander walked between the cultivated rows, jotting notes on her diagram. Returning early from the corn field, Seth joined her.

"How's it going?"

If he worried about her suffering disappointment, she put his mind at ease.

"Excellently. As you suggested, I am indicating those specific areas where the flowers occur. And you were right. There does seem to be a pattern. When I'm through, perhaps you can help me find an explanation."

"Be proud to."

"I will do the same if we harvest any berries this spring. I find it fascinating, really. And not very different from commercial fishing."

"How so?"

"A seasoned fisherman charts in his log where he has had the greatest success. Not only that, he writes about currents, weather and water temperature. After several seasons he has a good idea where to set his nets. See?" she indicated, handing over the book. "I have columns for rainfall and hours of sunlight."

"And this space?"

"To gauge the effects of fertilizer. I haven't the money to buy commercial chemicals but I have started my own compost heap. Egg shells; chicken droppings taken from the coup. That which Master Peter removes from the barn."

"Why not just take from my compost?"

"That is for the garden. As you rightly say, we must not short our food crops. But I am also writing down the composition of what we hoe into that soil, as well. The crew is of the opinion sour milk does well as a fertilizer. I am curious to prove their observations. Half the beans have received some while the rest have gotten the regular mixture. Or, it may be a combination works best. We shall see."

"I approve. I've never had time to study the garden."

"The scientific method appeals to me. Since you first brought it to my attention, I have given the matter considerable thought. And I am not without my own motives."

"You like beans that much?"

She grinned and took the book back.

"Pumpkins."

"Pumpkins? You have a hankering for pie? Not a bad idea, considering that expensive cinnamon I bought."

"The Fair."

His eyes disappeared into the top of his head. "I might have known. You, sir, are a competitor at heart."

"I believe I am." Leading him back to the porch, they settled into the chairs, made more comfortable by the addition of feathered cushions. He glanced at them in some surprise.

"Where did these come from? Not you."

"I should say not. Needlework above and beyond repairing my own clothing surpasses my skills. Patricia made them. She gathered the softest down she could find from the chickens and sewed them for us. I am inclined to think marsh grasses a better substitute, but no matter."

Settling down, Seth stretched his legs.

"This, from a woman who did not know the difference between a hen and a rooster. Or even why we kept Mr. Noise Box."

"Yes, well, he is decorative."

He chuckled. "But we were speaking of competition."

"At sea, it is always a matter of pride who has the fastest ship. My father was never much for racing, but the crew loved it and from them I developed a taste for winning."

"Were you ever involved in a race?"

Resting her head back against the wall, Barbara used a free hand to pluck an annoying pin feather out from underneath her bottom.

"'The Old Man,' as captains are invariably referred, was hard to press into doing anything which did not make a profit. While I saw his point, I was more closely allied with the crew. What they wanted, I wanted. We were in port, once -- God knows where it was, I've forgotten -- but there was this ship, newly commissioned. All spit and polish and so freshly painted it hurt your eyes to look at it. And the crew -- hand-picked," she demonstrated, lowering her voice to signify importance.

"It happened we were both taking on cargo and those tars kept yapping about how they had the fastest vessel on the Seven Seas. No self-respecting fellow could tolerate that."

"Sort of like saying your cow gives more milk than mine."

"Precisely. Ol' Ned ignored the issue, even when some of our boys got in a fracas with those from the other ship. He just wagged his finger and told them to mind their own business."

"Them?"

She ignored the implication she might somehow have been involved.

"It turned out the captain was hiring so we sent over Mr. Baxter, our mate."

"As a spy."

"Yup. He came back quite impressed. That was bad, for 'Bax' wasn't easily impressed and he had been with Ned since the dawn of time. But he did return with some interesting news. Captain Smartass was haulin' heavy machinery to Charleston. We were takin' aboard bolts of cotton cloth. That gave me an idea." She flicked an eyebrow at him. "An edge, you might say."

"Cotton is lighter than iron."

"You catch on fast. So we made a friendly wager. We'd both leave port at the same time and whichever of us made it to Charleston first would be declared the winner. We all put in our money and came up with two hundred dollars. The crew of the *Sassy Mae* matched our bet."

"What did 'Old Ned' have to say about all this?"

"Oh," she dismissed, shrugging a shoulder. "We neglected to tell him. "But he sure was amazed at how eager we were to set off; and how we all clambered to obey orders when the sails needed adjusting. Not a grumble or a complaint. Now, the *Sassy Mae* was a steamer so she had the added advantage of bein' able to run the engines at night. Normally, a sailing ship doesn't try to make much time when it's dark. But this trip, we begged and pleaded and kept a man on lookout around the clock. And that's how it went: one of us always dogging the other and the Old Man not knowing why we were so gung-ho to make it to Charleston."

"He didn't ask."

She appeared offended. "That, sir, would have been beneath his dignity. But we did let it slip that Mr. Baxter had a girl in Charleston he was sweet on and let Ned draw his own conclusions."

"How did Mr. Baxter feel about that?"

"There was a race at stake. And four hundred dollars. He woulda swore he was gonna marry a mermaid if it woulda gotten us there any sooner. Last night out we hit a storm. Lord, wind and rain and waves as high as the deck. And none of us wanted to trim sail. That had the captain chewing his -- cud."

Seth winked. "Glad you finally know what that expression means."

"Six tons of rain fell from the sky. Waterlogged the sails but did worse to those damned steam engines." Her face shone with inner radiance. "And all that cotton-pickin' machinery Smartass was carrying. Set him down in the water some. Him, orderin' the fires stoked and us catching the wind. Nip and tuck, sir. By dawn, Charleston was on the horizon and we were ahead by ten leagues."

"How far is that?"

"Close enough to spit in one another's faces, near about. And there was Smartass, hanging over the bow, screaming at his crew. All covered in soot from the black smoke so that he looked like he was changing sides."

"Not recommended, putting in at a Southern port." Nelander gave him a thumbs up. "And what did the 'Old Man' make of all this?"

"We told him Mr. Baxter had a rival on the *Sassy Mae* and the first man into harbor won the lady's hand."

"He believed that?"

"Of course not. By this time he had put two and two together, but he couldn't say so."

"His dignity."

"Right."

"Like father, like daughter." She ignored him.

"It came down to the stretch. Them finally gaining, and us willing the *Bottom Dollar* on. We had some discussion about tossin' the cotton bolts overboard but nothing came of it."

"That would have been undignified."

She bared teeth. "The wind died. We slowed to a crawl. And here comes that steamer. Closer and closer. It was bad. Real bad."

"Honor was at stake."

"There was only one thing we could do."

"Short of tossin' over the cargo." She hissed. He snapped his fingers. "You tossed Ol' Ned overboard to lighten the load."

"Close! We waited until the *'Sassy Ass'* got within hailing distance, then tossed Mr. Baxter over."

"You didn't! What would his fiancée say?"

"He was the mate and it was his duty to see we won. At any cost."

"He weighed that much? Must have been a whale of a man."

"There's a law at sea: if you find a man in the water, you have to pick him up. *We* couldn't turn around and go after him. Not with the wind blowin' the way it was. That meant the boat behind us had to stop and rescue him. Oh, the cursing!"

"They knew what you had perpetrated."

"An accident, sir, I assure you. Slippery deck. Can't be helped. These things happen." She pulled such a long face Seth almost believed her. "So on we sailed, reaching port just ahead of them --"

"And the rescued Mr. Baxter."

"There you have it. There was a row, let me tell you. All sorts of accusations. Even talk of a maritime inquest. The harbor master had some head scratching to do, but in the end, what could he say? We won our bet, collected our two hundred dollars and earned our bragging rights as the fastest ship on the Seven Seas."

Seth whistled. "Don't that beat all. But what of Captain Nelander? Surely there must have been an accounting."

"There was, to be sure. He has fit to be tired: us agreeing to a race and not telling him. But I think what bothered him most was that we tossed the mate into the drink, as it were."

"He thought that foolhardy."

"He did, indeed."

"Risking a man's life --"

"When it were hardly necessary," 'Bab'ra concluded in her captain's voice, lacing it with stern reprimand. "Every jack among us -- and officers, too -- knows the *Bottom Dollar* is the fastest ship afloat. It did not require any highjinks to prove that. Henceforth, we will follow Queen's Rules when engaged in the honorable sport of racing." Her chest shoot in a hearty rumble as she resumed her normal tone. "It did not prevent him from bragging about his accomplishment and for the next year, at least, he took every opportunity to inquiry about the health of 'Mister Baxter's Charleston belle.'"

Thwarted in his effort to guess the outcome, Seth curled his toes, enjoying the stimulation it afforded.

"I see the apple don't fall far from the tree."

Which was taken, and perhaps meant, as a compliment.

# CHAPTER 23

Dr. Hank McTree got down off his buggy, wiped the sweat from his brow, then approached the door. He did not have to knock for his arrival had been heralded by a chorus of yips, barks, howls and growls.

"Come on in," Nelander's voice invited.

He obliged and was immediately set upon by a frantic puppy. Stooping to pet the animal, he offered a wave to the human occupant, then commenced a scratching of the dusky orange beast.

"You don't look like a runt, anymore, Dardanelles," he sagely observed. "Gained five pounds and grown six inches since the last time I saw you. Life must be pretty good out here. Is it?" The puppy nearly convulsed in eagerness at the unknowable but easily inferred words. "What you been feeding this beast?"

"He gets table scraps like Herman. Likes to worry a bone now and again. Sit down. Breakfast's almost ready."

He grinned and tossed his hat onto the couch. Too late he realized his mistake, for within the blink of an eye, Dardanelles had confiscated it for herself. A mad chase around the room proved futile as the dog easily escaped out the door he had erringly left ajar.

Barbara came out, quickly assessed the tragedy then hurried outside.

"Dardanelles, come back here immediately!" She might have been talking to herself. "I'm sorry, doctor. He'll tire of it in a minute and forget about it."

"But will he remember where he left it?"

"No. But the crew are pretty good at locating missing objects. He'll have nipped the brim some, but no permanent damage. I hope."

"No matter. Can't say it's loss would be any great harm." Appraising her more skeptically, he added, "Finding the pup hard to train?"

"No more so than a baby shark. But the captain is 'just delighted' with the way she scares off the deer and the coons, so I guess I have no complaints. She is not, by the way, a house pet. I just wanted you to know that."

"Captain says that, too, does he?"

"He does. She is not allowed inside under any circumstances. He's built her her own doghouse. Which Mr. Noise Box and the chickens finds convenient when he wants to get in out of the sun."

"I see. Handy."

"I thought so. Coffee?"

"Please." He joined her in the kitchen and accepted a cup. "So: what is this special meal that I have been invited to all about? You found a new recipe for chili?"

"More dramatic than that. How is your stomach?"

He patted his midsection. "Just fine. But I brought a dose of bicarbonate of soda, just in case."

"That, sir, misses being a compliment by fifty fathoms."

Motioning him to sit, she went outside and rang the bell. Not as a mark of time but in summons. The barn door slammed and the Ward contingent rushed up to the porch.

"Wash your hands and come in. Before the food gets cold."

The three obeyed and quickly joined their honored guest at the table. Dardanelles followed, assuming her place underneath. Seth greeted him with a handshake.

"Morning, doctor. Glad you could come."

"It's not often I'm asked somewhere for a social visit. Sure someone isn't sick?"

The puppy barked. The captain glowered at the floor.

"Who let that cur in here? If I've said it once, I've said it a thousand times: she's to stay outside."

No one bothered to point out he had been the culprit.

Barbara went back to the stove and poured thick, yellowish liquid onto a hot griddle. Innumerable bubbles popped up around the roughly circular circumference as the mixture sizzled in melted butter. Peering cautiously at the edges, she waited a moment, then flipped it. Roughly thirty seconds afterward, the finished product was unceremoniously dumped on the counter.

"'One for the cat.' You know that Midwestern expression, Hank? It means exactly the opposite of what it states, for I never knew a cat to eat a griddle cake."

"I'm familiar with it," he acknowledged, winking at Seth.

"Sort of on the order of 'working dogs stay outside.'"

"Right. And that's the last I'm going to say on the subject."

Adeptly making another pancake, this one large enough to fit the pan, Barbara slid it onto a dish and offered it to their guest.

"I am afraid we have no maple syrup to offer, that delicacy being as unknown in these parts as straight talk, but perhaps we can provide an adequate substitute."

"Sorghum?"

Patricia and Peter exchanged eager glances.

"No, sir. Try this."

Lifting an Irish green-checkered cotton napkin from the top of a crock bowl, she revealed a quantity of tiny red berries. His intake of breath conveyed astonished pleasure.

"Strawberries!"

"Just picked this morning," Patricia supplied.

"I can't believe it."

"We didn't get many," Seth explained. "But enough to share with a friend."

"You grew these? Really? From your strawberry field?"

"Weren't expecting any," the Originator of the Plan continued for her husband. "Not this year, anyway. But the plants took root and surprised us. These came from the plot out back. We picked more from the valley --"

"But we ate those," Peter finished.

"Had just enough left for one more breakfast. Thought you might like to be included in the family feast."

"Sweet as honey," Seth demonstrated by popping one in his mouth. "Put 'em over your flapjacks or in a bowl with cream?"

"Both."

Helping himself, the physician dropped a dozen small berries onto his plate, then scooped as many more into a bowl. Peter passed the cream which he liberally used to dose the treat, then opted for fingers rather than utensils to sample the fruit. Before swallowing, his taste buds delivered a favorable result.

"Delicious." Realizing too late his eating habits were a source of merriment, he demurely wiped a cloth across wet lips. "When a man eats alone he generally abandons manners for practicality."

"The same may be said for sailors, and men who spend too much time around children."

To demonstrate, Seth copied their guest's style. Patricia presumed on the liberty granted and lifted her bowl to her mouth while Peter tossed a strawberry to Dardanelles. Too late, his father tried to protest.

"Don't waste that on the dog."

"But she likes them."

"She likes everything from meat bones to work boots. And everything in between, including socks, toes and the edges of the furniture. And she is especially fond of newspapers -- particularly those which are unread."

"Which reminds me; I brought out your mail. Don't let me leave without giving it to you."

They ate quickly after these preliminaries, devouring the pancakes, cream, strawberries and coffee in under twenty minutes. When all had declared themselves "Satisfied," they pushed back from the table, allowing stomachs to expand.

"That is the best breakfast I have had in forever," McTree decided. "I can't tell you how much I appreciate being invited to share this special meal."

"You are more than welcome."

"What kind of strawberry crop are you anticipating next season?"

"Difficult to determine. But if what we've seen here is any indication, more than enough to bring to market."

"The prospect is exciting. You must put me down for several pounds worth. With any luck you ought to clear fifty or one hundred dollars. A staggering sum, Officer Nelander, for a crop untried on our prairies and valleys. Congratulations."

"You may save that for when the fact is accomplished. No captain cashes in his manifest without first delivering the cargo."

Reluctantly disengaging the napkin from his neck, the doctor inquired, "Will you show me around? I'd like to see the plants."

"Certainly."

Trooping out the door, the Wards made their way to the back where the long, rectangular field stretched out before them. The amount of green acreage proved staggering.

"Amazing. The resemble row upon row of emeralds. And just as valuable. Who would have thought?"

Seth readily concurred. "Not I. But it does make a farmer's heart glad."

"And those in the valley?"

"Even farther along. Our... hands harvested two quarts. Of course, there are more plants there; a little over three thousand."

Staring at his toes, McTree rubbed his hands.

"Then I hate to wish you ill, but for a man who lives by selling his services, I would be pleased to make regular calls out your way. Paying customers are hard to find."

"By next year I hope most of the farmers will have recovered from the drought."

"They've got their crops in but the harvest will be smaller than usual. Not many had money for seed. Most used corn kernels salvaged from that which would have gone for fodder. From what I hear, the topsoil was all shifted around from the flood, too."

"We had the same problem. But in this instance, it worked to my benefit. Never used this field until now, but the waters deposited a thick layer of silt and it proved good for growing."

Returning to the house after a brisk walk along the perimeter, McTree reached behind the seat of his buggy and brought out a small parcel wrapped in twine.

"Here's your mail. I took the liberty of adding the most recent editions of the *Gazette.*"

"Thanks. Let me pay you for them."

"No need. I read them, first, so they're used copies." Tapping the top, he brought their attention to a notice on the first page. "Seems there's an abolitionist coming to Lawrence to speak about the Negro issue. A preacher from Boston. He's on a speaking tour and Mr. Daly invited him here. I'm not sure that was such a good thing."

Curious, Nelander rested a hand on the buggy.

"Why not?"

"Gets people riled up."

"But maybe they need to hear what he has to say."

"Don't doubt that. He's making his way through Missouri. Everywhere he's stopped there's been trouble."

"What kind of trouble?"

"Fistfights in the streets. A lot of shouting and name-calling. Even some fires and looting."

Drumming her fingers against the wood, she glanced at Seth.

"Seems to me most people already know who's for and who's against the issue."

He shrugged. "I'm not so sure. Mostly, people keep their opinions to themselves. It's safer that way."

"But there's going to be a vote, you said. On a state constitution."

"Whether Kansas comes in as a slave or a free state. Wish it were as easy as a show of hands, but a lot of politics are involved. And the Federal government will have its say. There's a lot riding on what's eventually decided. That, and the presidential election. Don't know much about that fellow, Abraham Lincoln. The Republican platform says it's for prohibiting slavery in the territories, though. That's got to be a good thing. What do you think, Hank?"

"Hard for me to vote for Stephen Douglas. Vice-President Breckinridge will split the ticket, I think. We'll see -- and pray for peace."

"Amen to that."

"Let's hope that next year at this time we're talking about strawberry crops and not war."

"You reckon it'll come to that?"

"Not if cool heads prevail. But there's a lot of hot tempers out there." He held out a hand. "See you soon."

"You bet."

They shook and the doctor offered his hand to Nelander. She took it and firmly squeezed.

"Take care."

He nodded and hoisted himself in the buggy. With a wave and a full stomach he drove off.

That evening after supper, Nelander returned to her ledger while Seth pursued the newspaper. Reading spectacles perched on the end of his nose, he wet his finger, turned a page and finished the article before looking up.

"There's a story in here about what Hank was saying: that preacher fella from Boston. Says seven men in St. Louis were arrested for disturbing the peace outside the lecture hall. One man -- Sebastian Duncan -- was badly hurt in an altercation. Some shops were broken into and effigies were burned in protest. The preacher had to be escorted out of town before he got tarred and feathered."

"That's a sin."

"Maybe. But that's how it goes."

Using a latigo lace to mark her place, Barbara slowly closed her book and wiped the tip of the pen clean.

"Brave men with revolutionary ideas are always held out to ridicule and beatings. He must be very courageous."

"To say nothing of the people who dared attend his lecture. Several of them had their wagons upturned and their horses stolen."

"Seems to me more of an excuse to steal than to express contrary opinions."

"That, too."

"What will the townspeople in Lawrence do?"

"More of the same, I reckon. It only takes a handful to incite a riot. Learned that the hard way."

"You mean about... the bewitching?"

Shaking his head, his foot shook. "Before Will Bochner, we had a sheriff in town; evil bastard." The curse word caught Nelander off guard and she leaned closer. "A pro-slavery man. Used to lead around a gang of 'deputies,' trying to influence people with violence. They burned the Free-State Hotel and tore up the office of the *Gazette* an' two other newspapers. Tossed the type in the Kansas River."

"The sheriff did this?"

"He and his posse."

"Local men?"

"I always thought Matthew McConaghie was part of it. His boys, for sure. Turned ugly fast. What you call the 'Wakarusa War' broke out: those supporting Sheriff Jones an' the damned governor besieged the city defended by the free-state men. Only lasted a week, but got everyone riled. Mighta been bad."

"What finally happened to this Jones character?"

He spat on the floor. "Resigned in January, '57."

"I was hoping you'd say they hanged him." Seth shrugged. "That was only a few months before I arrived." Her fists clenched. "What drove him out?"

"Governor Shannon refused his request to use balls and chains on incarcerated Free-State men at Lecompton. Without harsh corporal punishment, I guess the fun went outta his job."

"You are not serious."

"Damned if I'm not."

"Sweet Jesus." Clutching the pen as a poor substitute for a weapon, Nelander considered before remarking, "I think we should go to this Abolitionist Meeting."

"I had a feeling that's what you were gettin' at."

"It's important. Besides, I'd like to hear what he has to say. What's his name -- the preacher?"

"Thomas Pickering. Why? You know him?"

"No. Just wondering. When's he coming?"

"Next Tuesday." Seth curled the edge of the paper. "I suppose Jim Daly will be there, front and center. Pickering might even be staying with him for all I know. I doubt he's staying at the Winding Trail. Too dangerous."

"Personally, I wouldn't let a dog stay at that hotel. Not with Abel Billup clerking there. He's enough to scare off a pod of whales. If anyone gets caught up in the melee, I'll throw him in for good measure. Along with your friend, Matthew McConaghie."

"He's not my friend."

"That's what I meant."

The captain went back to reading. Or pretended to. "Thought we might wait it out -- read all about it in the *Gazette.*"

"No, you didn't."

"Might be smarter to."

"Might be."

"Won't be many women there, I suppose."

"I'll be wearing trousers. Pull a cap down low."

"You won't pass."

"Neither will you -- nigger lover." He started, grunted, then turned a page. Finding nothing more of interest, Seth threw the paper down and picked up one of his periodicals. She noted the change. "For all your soft talk, Mr. Ward, you're a radical. Any Kansas man who subscribes to the *New England Journal* has got to be a dissident. Can't let things stand the way they are."

When the comment elicited no rebuttal, she reopened her book and went back to writing. The lamp flickered and she adjusted the wick. Barbara had almost finished her notations for the day when he emitted a low, startled whistle.

"Well, hang me high!"

"I wouldn't say that too loudly."

"Turn up the lamp -- quick!" She did as requested and he leaned closer to the print, eyes squinting over the lens of his glasses. "If this doesn't beat all! Why didn't you tell me?"

"Tell you what?"

The question had more eagerness than detachment, however, and a flush came into her cheeks.

"Look here!" Leaving her chair, Barbara came to stand behind him. A finger pointed to the place of interest. "There's an entire article written on the cultivation of strawberries."

"What's it say?"

"It's not what it says: it's who wrote it." He craned back his neck, eyes shining. "You did! Your name, right here in print!"

She looked and saw the words: "A New Crop for a New Land." And underneath, "By B. Nelander-Ward." The subheading read, "Growing strawberries in Kansas. Strategies after a drought." Her breath came in short gasps and she reeled backward.

"I never thought they'd print it. I only sent it because I thought farmers ought to know what we were doing." Then, more proudly, "I wanted to share your ideas about soil and fertilizer --"

"And your idea about expanding horizons. Trying something different. Keeping an open mind. I cannot believe it. I never dreamed of seeing anyone's name I know in print. Yet, here you are -- my own wife -- a published author." Teasingly, he added, "Now I know what you have been working on instead of your ledger."

"That is an untruth, sir. I have maintained strict vigilance in logging the most minute details." Taking the periodical from him, she turned the pages, looking for more specifics. Finding what she sought, Nelander indicated it with stern pride. "Here, Captain Ward, is proof of my assertion."

Beside the continuation of her article the editors had separated text with a bold, 12-point line.

"It is called a 'side bar.'"

"Sand bar?"

"Side-bar; an addendum or additional text supplementing the main theme. What is the heading?"

He pushed his glasses up his nose.

"Sample from an Agrarian's Log. Well, I'll be damned."

"Let us pray not. See? I have copied your style: weather, fertilizer, rainfall, dates of planting, sprouting and harvesting. Comments on sunshine; general appearance. And at the bottom I have included expectations and results. Of course, that is an ongoing subject, carried over from week-to-week.

"For example, this column indicates the first sign of green; the second includes the development of leaves; the third has data on further growth. This entry covers cost: I began it with my initial investment of $500. Any other expenses are written here and carried over from month-to-month. When we eventually make money, that shall be included in the final column, permitting a profit-loss tally at the end of the growing season."

He swallowed and found his mouth dry.

"Barbara, this is fine."

"Thank you, sir." When his eye caught the final paragraph, however, both his salivary glands and tear ducts opened. "She gently prodded him. "Read it aloud."

"'This study is gratefully dedicated to Captain Seth Ward of Lawrence, Kansas, for it was he who taught me all I know and encouraged the development of this system. What I have presented here is an expansion of his own carefully maintained farm records. Without his skill and patience, this experiment would not have been possible.'"

"Truly meant and joyfully acknowledged."

"You... did not have to add that. The strawberries were your idea."

"And only became reality from your persistence."

He sniffed and went back to the front cover.

"I will read it from the beginning."

Nelander left him and went back to her work. An hour later when he showed no sign of getting up, she kissed him on the forehead and went to bed. She did not awake when he joined her later that night.

In the morning, Officer-Farmer Barbara Nelander Ward discovered a framed document hanging over their mantel. Her article had been meticulously clipped from the magazine and mounted in two sections behind a sheet of window glass.

On the dining table she discovered a letter, addressed to the editor of the *New England Journal.* He did not explain and she did not ask. The answer became apparent when she went to chronicle her day's entries. Under the column marked "Expenses," a hand different than her own had added, "$1.00 -- for additional copies of most enlightening article on strawberry farming."

Money well spent.

## CHAPTER 24

The town of Lawrence, Kansas buzzed with activity. Carriages, buggies and wagons lined the streets, horses hitched to every available post. Men tarried on street corners and sauntered the dirt roads, in groups or by themselves. Some had hands in pockets; others glared furtively at passersby, judging motives from drawn faces, or wan countenances.

Unlike Fair Week when the atmosphere rang with gaiety and excitement, a cloud of suspicion seemed to hang over the buildings like an invisible miasma, tainting everything it touched. Men never known to wear sidearms carried pistols in gun belts or sported long Bowie knives in leather sheaths. Hats were pulled low and work boots scuffed along the boardwalk, dragging rather than high-stepping. If anticipation were the order of the evening, then it boded ill for the air crackled with nervous energy.

The Boston preacher, Thomas Pickering, had come and the subject rested on pursed lips and behind hooded eyes.

Slavery.

Emancipation.

Or, more commonly put, "The Negro Question."

Barbara Nelander had lived in Lawrence three years and had come to recognize, if not know by name, most of the inhabitants. Sitting beside her husband as Blaze treaded his way carefully through the crowded avenues, she saw some men she knew but most were strangers, come to listen to the famous man. Or perhaps more rightly interlopers, who already knew what he had to say and were dead set against it.

"Who are they?"

Seth flicked the reins and hesitated for she knew the answer as well as he.

"Missourians, most likely. From across the border. Maybe some have come from Topeka and Burlingame and Olathe. Or crossed the Kansas River from St. Mary's." She had heard that litany before. This time, the list lacked enthusiasm.

Few women were to be seen and most of those easily identifiable from Tankard's Draft. Their clothes sparkled from shiny ornaments and they wore black cotton stockings to show off their legs. The wives, mothers and daughters of Lawrence had gone into hiding.

To protect them from violence.

Ironically, those inadvertently the subject of the debate, the dark-skinned people, were nowhere in evidence. Lacking prior knowledge, a visitor might have surmised that the subject for debate existed only in the abstract, on a distant shore or safely tucked away between the invisible lines of "slave" and "free" states.

Small boys ran between groups, darted out from between conveyances. They held flyers in their hands and offered the printed pages to any who would take a copy.

"Big meetin' tonight! Come one, come all!"

"Reverent Pickering's gonna speak at Meetin' Hall. Eight o'clock sharp!"

Others, older and of a more enterprising nature, hawked comestibles.

"Hot peanuts fer sale! Ten cents!"

"Drink a water! Cold water! Git it here."

"Buns! Fresh buns. Right outta the oven."

Few paid them any heed. It seemed men preferred to quarrel on an empty stomach.

Which did not prohibit them from taking liquid refreshment of a more stimulating nature. Droves hung out in front of the saloon, leaning against the walls in an attitude suggesting their presence held up the walls. Others loitered in chairs set out for the occasion. The batwing doors, in constant sway, admitted and disgorged others. Music from a piano, banged out on worn keys, added a discordant melody to the scene.

"Nice to know someone's going to make a profit from this."

"Dick Duggan, for certain. Him and Reverend Pickering."

She had meant the owner of Tankard's Draft but not the minister. The combination he chose to name and the bitterness in his voice occasioned surprise.

"What do you mean?"

"Someone's payin' him to come here."

"Explain yourself; paying him? Who?"

"Jim Daly of the *Gazette,* most likely. He's the one issued the 'invitation.'"

"All right: the speaking engagement." Seth would not let it go.

"Don't suppose Pickering talks fer nothin', do you?"

"I had never considered it. Yes, I suppose I did." He snorted.

"Doesn't matter who you are or what your cause. Men are always on the lookout to make a dime."

Had her experience with Seth Ward been less thorough, Nelander would have wondered at his anger. Unable to ascribe a cause other than the obvious threat of violence the abolitionist's presence had brought to town, she stored his unexpected remarks away for later discussion.

"I, for one, am glad he is here. I am eager to listen to what he says. And perhaps hopeful he may sway some uncommitted minds."

"He is preaching to the converted."

Putting a hand back to reassure herself the children were safe, Barbara urged him down a side street.

"Let us leave the crew and the buckboard at Dr. McTree's house as we agreed and walk back."

Without additional conversation, he tugged in the reins and directed the horse toward the edge of town. Ten minutes later, they arrived at their destination. Sitting on the porch in anticipation of their arrival, the physician came down to greet them.

"Good evening. Hello there, youngsters. Mrs. Applebee is waiting for you. She has all sorts of amusements for you and a good supper set on the table." He grinned at Nelander. "As a housekeeper, she is an admirable employee. But her less than subtle fussing is a bit disconcerting. Too many observations on how offspring fulfill a man's life."

"In that case, I trust she has an intended selected for you?"

"Any number of them. She believes it is the natural condition of a man to be married."

"And what do you think?"

"Doctors and lawmen should not be attached. One is never at home and the other in constant danger of being shot."

"Perhaps there are those women who would accept such conditions."

"Scarce as hen's teeth." Holding out his arms, he took Paula from her sister. "My goodness, she has grown since last I saw her. Must be the strawberries."

"She doesn't eat strawberries," Peter protested, swinging down with a prodigious leap.

"No. But her mother does."

Being seven years old, the adults forgave him his lack of comprehension.

"Into the house, young man. And Patricia -- as pretty as a picture. If I am not mistaken, Mrs. Applebee has some coloring pencils for you."

"What's she got for me?" the brother demanded.

"Chores."

He groaned and stamped his foot.

"Ain't that a crapper."

Seth grabbed him by the ear and held fast.

"Isn't that a what?"

"A darn good thing, sir!"

Nelander quickly intervened.

"Grammatically, you should say, 'Isn't that a darned good thing."

"And politely," Seth groused, "he may lose the 'darned' altogether."

"Yes, sir." Releasing the boy, he waved them up the sidewalk. "Remember what we agreed: you three are to stay put. No matter what happens, I don't want you outside."

"Yes, sir."

Getting down, he led Blaze around back where he unhitched the horse and set him lose in the yard. Returning, the three began their walk back toward the town proper.

"I have tickets for all of us," McTree commented, reaching into an inner pocket and extracting three passes. "I got them from Daly. They entitle us to sit up front."

Inspecting hers, Nelander cast him a glance.

"What did they cost?"

"No charge to get in. Those with tickets enter first and get their choice of seating. At seven-thirty they open the doors to the general public."

"Is that before or after they pass the collection plate?" Seth asked.

"I suppose they will but I don't know when."

Barbara tucked hers safely away. "Did Mr. Daly say how much he paid Mr. Pickering to speak?"

"Didn't think to ask."

The farmer grunted and they continued without further comment. At the door of the lecture hall, also used on occasion for a gathering of the city council, meetings of the Feed and Grain Association and the Ladies Charity League, Sheriff Bochner and two of his deputies stood guard. He tipped his hat to Barbara.

"Evening gents, Officer Nelander. No firearms allowed inside. If you're carrying any, I'll ask you to leave them with me."

Neither man had a gun and the group passed through. Three cowboys behind them, also in possession of tickets, were given the same warning and then searched.

"Nice to know Bochner trusts us," McTree observed.

"And nicer to know he didn't trust the rest."

Perturbed by Seth's unease, Nelander led them down the center aisle. Twenty or thirty people had already gathered. Most sat along the outer edges, obligingly drawing in their legs as the walkers passed. The air, warm from the summer air, smelled of perspiration, tobacco, musty dirt and sour exhalations. Seth ran a hand under his collar.

"I hope they leave the door open. It's mighty close in here."

The comment, like the pending topic of discussion, carried duel implications. Leaving the door open permitted some flow of air. On the other hand, more than wind currents could slip through the egress. Men, perhaps, who had not been searched for weapons. Men who had not come to debate with words but with fists.

Since all three drew the same conclusions, Nelander let it pass, instead asking the others where they wanted to sit. Receiving no answer, she chose seats in the second row center, close to the podium. Once they had settled, Jim Daly scooted over from his place of honor in the front.

"Good to see you, Captain. And you, too, doctor. Officer Nelander, always a pleasure. How's the little one getting on?"

"She is well and growing like a fish."

"Glad to hear it. Why don't you move up? Sit in the front?" Seth shuffled his feet.

"Why would that be?"

"Like the Reverend to see some friendly faces. Those who know the proper times to applaud. Don't want him to take away a bad impression of our city."

"I expect he's used to bad impressions."

"I am sorry to say he is. You read about what happened in St. Louis? The sheriff is here to make certain the same thing doesn't happen here."

Seeing other newcomers, he dipped his head and hurried off. Left to themselves, Nelander turned back to assess those already seated. True to McTree's word, the early arrivals were local men, dressed in Sunday suits. Many sat stiff-necked, fingers spread across thighs. A handful used their hats for fans, trying to stir a breeze.

Whatever conversations may have occurred had died out and few addressed their neighbors. A feeling of guarded expectation seemed the order of the night, as if none cared to identify any of their friends as "Nigger Men," or of coming out on the side of the anti-slavery movement.

The scene changed dramatically at 7:30 when those without prior approval were admitted. A loud buzz preceded the event, followed by an increase in activity as men pushed and shoved their way inside. Mr. Daly had succeeded in filling most of the seats in the first ten rows but those left unoccupied were rapidly filled, men roughly pushing their way past those in the aisle seats without a word of apology. One settled next to McTree, who flanked Nelander in the middle and Seth on the outside.

Slipping a chaw of tobacco from one cheek to the other, the stranger worked up a mouthful of juice then spat, the thin brown liquid landing near the doctor's foot. Compounding his bad manners, he showed a fresh wad into his mouth and chewed noisily, frequently shifting from side to side the way someone did when restless or finding his seat too small to accommodate his bulk.

In twenty minutes the sitting portion swelled to capacity; by 8:00, the assemblage filled the building, latecomers standing in the aisles and pressed against the walls. Occasionally one would get too close to another, causing brief shouting matches or hotly exchanged words. At ten minutes after the hour when the speaker failed to make a timely appearance, the mood further soured.

"Bring him out! What's holdin' him up?"

"Get the show on the road."

Patrons who had come to see a good performance if not a scripted play, stomped their feet or derisively clapped their hands. Catcalls and whistles swept across the room like wildfire.

"If Pickering's got a case of the ague, I say we get our money back and spend it on some cold refreshment."

The statement elicited chuckles. Not the good-humored type, but that amusement with an edge. No one had paid to enter and beer served in the local watering holes was closer in temperature to a July night than a December morning.

"Where is he?"

"Don't they know how to keep time in Boss-ton?"

Jim Daly nervously wrung his hands, then arose and scurried behind a makeshift curtain partition. Emerging five minutes later, he shoved his way down the center row, beckoning Sheriff Bochner. After a heated exchange, the lawman reluctantly moved forward. Eschewing the podium, he raised a hand over his head and called for silence.

"A'right, gents. You all know me; I'm Will Bochner and I'm the law in Lawrence. I've been asked to speak a few words before the pro-gramme begins." He pronounced the word peculiarly and a tittering arose over his attempted sophistication. "I won't tolerate no violence. You're all to stay put. No throwin' things. Mind yer manners. They'll be a chance to ask questions after the reverend's got through. No shoutin' up until given the signal."

"I heard there was gonna be a slave auction after the talkin', Sheriff. That true?"

Bochner should have let it go but did not.

"No, it ain't true. We don't allow such things in Kansas."

"Mebbe you should. There ain't two ways on the question. Wouldn't be having no trouble if some fellas kept their noses to themselves."

A murmur, less of denial than support, ran along the perimeter.

"I'm here to uphold the peace. Any man gits in a fight, he's taken out and clapped in jail. That ought to be plain enough. Circuit judge won't be through fer another month. That'll be a long time to feed you at public expense. Think about it."

"How many kin fit in yer jail, Sheriff?"

"As many as sardines in a tin. I'm warning you all, and that's it."

Having said his piece, Bochner moved back toward the door, serenaded by derisive stomping. Reluctantly taking that as his cue, Mr. Daly assumed center stage. Clearing his throat, he awkwardly wiped his brow with a starched handkerchief before starting.

"All right, gentlemen. Quiet down. My name is James Daly and I'm the editor of the Lawrence *Gazette*. It is my privilege to introduce you to Mr. Thomas Pickering, a distinguished man of God, orator and published author. I invited him here to speak on the Negro Question."

Hisses and hoots drowned his speech. He waited for them to subside before continuing.

"The main issue of the day is centered around slavery: whether we ought to permit the continuance of human bondage, and in what states and territories slavery ought to exist. There's a lot of debate going on in Congress. Some want to outlaw it, some want to limit it. Others think a man ought to be able to bring his property wheresoever he wishes."

He paused to glance at a scrap of paper. "The Supreme Court's gotten involved. We all know about the Dred Scott decision. Some think it was right; others consider it an abomination. Pretty soon Kansas is gonna be admitted as a State. How she comes in depends on a lot of factors, including the temper in Washington. I thought before any decisions come down, we ought to be exposed to the prevailing sentiment of those back east."

"Back east ain't out west, Jim," a man called.

Learning from Bochner's experience, Daly ignored the challenge.

"It is therefore my privilege to introduce to you Mr. Thomas Pickering."

Bowing out, he ducked as if expecting items to be thrown, and resumed his seat. After some initial fumbling, the curtain parted and the guest speaker appeared.

If the gathering expected a slight, bespeckled man with greying hair and stooped shoulders, awash in an air of scholarship and book learning, they were in for a surprise for Mr. Pickering presented an entirely different picture. Standing well over six feet, he sported a full head of indelible black hair and wild, almost untamed muttonchops, tapering into a clean shaven countenance. Broad shouldered, with hands the size of mallets, he wore a long, black broadcloth coat with split tails reaching his lower calves. A prominent hooked nose set off wide, piercing eyes and a face marked with the scars of acne.

Sturdy-heeled boots rang on the floor as he crossed to the speaker's platform. Whether god or devil, the deities had chosen well their messenger of discord.

Arranging a sheaf of notes on the podium, the wide-lipped minister glowered out at his audience from under bushy eyebrows. When he spoke, the words reverberated against the walls, sharp and disquietingly delivered in a dialect at once familiar and foreign.

"Good evening." he boomed, leaving little doubt he spoke from conviction and a propensity for defending every statement from common to incendiary. "I am Thomas Pickering. From Bhas-ton. The heart of the Revolution. I am from stock used to fighting unpopular causes. My grandfathers fought against the British and I've their crossed swords on my mantel to remind me that words alone don't always carry a point."

"Then why'd you have us leave our arms at the door, preacher?"

The preacher proved deaf to any but his own voice.

"On the last census of 1850, I was listed as a minister. A minister. You here, no doubt, listed yourselves as farmers, clerks, shop owners. Newspaper editors. Lawmen. Honorable professions. Then we have the others. Not so honorable. Men who used euphemisms to describe their work. Speculator. Negro trader. Investment counselor. Merchant. Broker. In reality, meaning *slaver.*"

Leaning forward, he made the crowd feel small in comparison to his prodigious size.

"Why not just come out and list yourself as what you are -- a man who buys and sells human flesh? Why, you ask? Are they ashamed? Why not pound themselves on the chest and write what they mean?" His fist thundered against the wooden stand. "'I'm a Georgia slaver -- a nigger buyer. I'm the man the colored people whisper about.' *Be good, or you'll be sold to a Georgia man.* Meaning, of course, sold to the lowest of the low; the cruel, the violent, the deranged. The man who knows God from a distance, never close up."

A thin man waved his hat at the reverend.

"The Bible says 'Masters, treat your slaves justly and fairly, knowing that you also have a Master in heaven.' That's a recognition of slavery, preacher. Read your own book."

Pickering smiled. The flash of teeth evoked an image of wolves.

"There is a prevailing theory about slavery often mentioned by my Southern brethren. It evokes the concept of Paternalism." His face puckered, assuming a camaraderie, a shared secret with his audience. "You are all familiar with the argument. And a blessed one it is, too... to hear it preached. One of care and concern for the oppressed."

Moving away from the stand, he paced the apron, at times coming precariously close to the edge, so that men sat on the edge of their chairs, wondering if he might fall.

"Paternalism." His voice rose. "We all know -- it is a given fact that black family attachment is easily forgotten. Dogs have litters and the pups are given away. Cows bring forth calves which are slaughtered for meat. Negroes give birth to babies who are sold and taken away to neighboring plantations or distant states. What of that? The Negro people are perpetual children; they are an inferior race. Not un-similar to dogs and cows."

The audience grew restive, uncertain where these facts would lead. Those who had come to hear fire and brimstone and holy condemnation gripped the back of chairs in front of them. Individuals of opposing persuasions shook their feet or elbowed their friends, finding approval in the sentiments, yet not trusting the messenger.

This is not what they had come to hear, the divided and derisive of Kansas. Thomas Pickering had succeeded in alienating all his listeners.

"This is where the superiority of the Master Race comes in. It is our kindness, our understanding which promotes beneficial and long-term advancement of the Africans. For what owner who has followed the admonitions of the Good Book and treated his slaves fairly and justly has not seen love in the eyes of his charges? Yes, fellow Christians, I speak of love. The love of a slave for his master. And who here will argue that that love for the master is greater than that which the brown man has for his own kith and kin?"

He waited but no one dared venture an opinion. Men shifted, shook their legs. Looked down, across, to right or left. But no one spoke. Pickering sucked on his cheek. It might have been a diversion; the way four-legged predators seemed to mimic human facial expressions when circling helpless prey.

"The question, my friends, is not one of slavery versus emancipation, but of welfare for our fellow creatures. The question," he reiterated, "is whether the brown man is better off with his own kind, isolated from the Master Race, or brought into the bosom of the Caucasian family."

Finishing his tour around the stage, he resumed his place behind the podium. His eyes, however, never wavered from the audience. The notes he brought no more than an actor's props.

"I tell you, slavery is a comfortable and natural institution. A slave family -- which is to say a male and a female and offspring, not necessarily of that pairing -- is a source of excessive challenge to constancy. The African race has no moral fiber with which to bind their family union. They are naturally immoral and sexually promiscuous. Left to themselves, males fight over females and females display their charms to men, prohibiting -- nay, eliminating -- any sense of the white man's Godly adherence to right and wrong."

Pickering paused to pour a drink of water from a pitcher placed on a shelf within the stand. Filling it to the brim, he brought the glass to his mouth and drank. Not a genteel sip to "wet the whistle," but a gargantuan swallowing. Adam's apple bobbing, he finished half, then went beyond without taking breath. The audience pressed forward, watching the performance, spellbound. For the moment, and the moment lasted, the burning issue became whether he could drink it all without drawing air.

Closer to the bottom of the glass, then closer still, slower, now, then finally one giant gulp as he drained the liquid, absorbing it into his body, one huge, bottomless pit. As the last went down, he snorted and held out the glass. Men rumbled, breathed for him, wiped their brows.

Enjoying the reaction, the minister nodded in awareness of his feat and returned the vessel to the shelf.

Without breaking stride, he continued.

"Who here have any familiarity with Negroes? Raise your hands." One hand shot up, then another and another. Neither Seth nor Nelander moved. "Good. I take that to be most of you. As for the rest," he leered, lips sparkling with wetness from the water, so recently consumed, "you are liars. Or, at best, unwilling to admit your associations. So be it. I forgive you your lack of courage."

He daubed at his lips as though used to wearing a mustache and accustomed to tugging at facial hairs.

"I address myself to those who raised their hands. I put to you another question: how does a slave mourn? If there be a death of a brother or a spouse or a child: does he moan and wail and weep? Does he cry like a sentient man? He does not. He dances. Yes, gentlefolk. That is the way a Negro grieves. By dancing and playing music and chanting in the Old Tongue. Blasphemy, you call it. Have charity, say I. They know no better. They are children, after all."

Once again he began walking, this time hands behind his back. Striding like a lion, majestic, compelling, a latent threat to the ideas men held holy.

"Slave children grow rapidly to adulthood. By the age of twelve, boys are fully mature. Their voices have deepened; they have the beginnings of beards. They are capable of a full day's labor in the field. Girls develop womanly characteristics and are ready for reproduction. Yes, my friends, they grow but they are not adults. Intellectually, they remain boys and girls forever, incapable of rational decisions. For those, they must look to the white man."

A man sitting in the third row stomped his foot. Another scraped the leg of his chair across the floor. A low mumbling, like a current of bees arose. Pickering did not hear.

"While not a Southerner, I have toured extensively through the South. Reports coming from those who visit those stately plantations exaggerate. They cry that families are often broken up; that fathers are sold to the cane fields in Louisiana; mothers to the cotton fields of Georgia. Children of any age sent away for domestic work." He clucked his tongue. "Lies. Bald face lies. Family separations are scarce; extremely rare. More rare, in fact, than among the lower orders of England, who virtually sell their offspring to the factories."

Tarrying by the curtain, Pickering turned his back on the crowd to adjust a corner which had improperly fallen. Several in the audience hissed. Turning back, he did not appear fazed.

"In Africa, there is a predominant fear of one's parents but no love for the children. Tribal leaders, who maintain control of their subjects by an iron hand, continually wage war against their neighbors. Those unfortunates captured are themselves made slaves to the conquerors; or are actually sold to traders for transportation to America. There is no harm -- or moral dilemma there. Pay a man in beads or trinkets and he will sell his first born son.

"The white plantation owner cares more for his charges than do the fathers and mothers of little black boys and little black girls. The institution of slavery is for the benefit of the brown race. It is ordained by the Most High to promote stability; to instruct in Jesus' teaching; to conquer innate laziness and natural promiscuity." Wiping his hands on his pocket linen, he gracefully dipped his head.

"That, gentleman, is the argument and the justification for slavery. Those reasons given by learned men. Compelling, are they not? Persuasive. Christian. Those, gentleman, are the lies; the naked, perverted histrionics of the so-called Master Race. *Now, I will tell you the truth.*"

Seven words, shot from a cannon, could not have had greater effect.

# CHAPTER 25

"Truth, gentlemen. Standing shoulder-to-shoulder with faith, hope and charity. I began my lecture this evening with the statement that I am a minister. That is truth. I was ordained at the age of twenty-six years after graduating from the seminary. Before that, I obtained a four-year degree in theology." His voice rose in indignation. "So do not quote the Bible to me and expect to catch me unawares. I am only too cognizant of the perversions thrown at abolitionists by... slavery men."

Stepping front and center, Pickering unfastened the buttons of his flowing black coat and spread his legs. This stance, his attitude suggested, was the one he assumed when preparing to fight the devil.

"We were speaking of Truth, gentlemen -- and ladies," he amended, staring at Nelander. Had the intenseness of her posture not betrayed her as a true believer, her position in the second row would have adequately conveyed the fact. Briefly nodding in recognition of her gender, he transmitted an unspoken thought.

*It is as well to know one's friends as well as one's enemies.*

"Let me truly begin my talk with another Fact: and I address myself specifically to that worthy who shouted up a quotation from Colossians 4:1. The Antislavery Movement, generally held to be the sole province of the North, is led by men of the cloth. Men with nothing to gain but the emancipation of human beings, created in the image of our Creator. The prominent defenders of that "peculiar institution" are Southerners; plantation owners with great pecuniary interest in the perpetuation of cheap labor."

"Without slaves, you can't grow cotton!"

Pickering hitched his thumbs beneath his belt.

"Ah. I see we have a plantation owner in the crowd. Welcome, master. I trust your journey from Augusta was pleasant?" Winking at the crowd, he added, "How elucidating to know he has time to spend away from his fields, knowing they are well tended by his overseers. How many Kansas farmers can say the same?"

The question brought an angry murmur and a round of foot stomping. The reverend held up his hands for silence but the dissident was not to be quieted.

"You were so clever, Pickering, to give all the reasons we support slavery. Yet I did not hear you contradict them. That, sir, you cannot do -- not when your own hands are bloodied."

The minister held up his hands and pretended to inspect them.

"Alas, no blood. My hands, sir, are stainless. Can you say the same? Or will you argue that the 'flopping paddle' breaks no skin?"

"Bloodied by association, you hypocrite. I put to you that Northern factories break up families; employ child labor. Pay slave wages."

An eyebrow arched. "You pay your slaves a wage?"

"I keep them, sir, which is more than I can say for you and your kind. I supply food and drink. I provide housing and new clothes twice a year. As well as shoes. I bear their medical costs when one falls ill. If one escapes, I pay their jail fees."

"How 'white' of you, sir. You have adequately described the care and feeding a Kansas farmer provides his horse. Hay and oats; a barn. A trip to the blacksmith for 'shoes.' Care by a veterinary to tend cuts and bruises and a bout of the colic. And if that horse... wanders off... no doubt a finder's fee to his neighbor for returning it."

"I permit time on Sundays for religious services. My people are indoctrinated in the words of Jesus Christ. What factory owner or farmer does as much?"

"You have got me there, sir. A show of hands, please. Who among you reads the Gospel to your plow horse? Or recites Psalms to the chickens?"

"I might, if it'd git 'em to lay more eggs," another called. Men chuckled.

Returning to the podium, Pickering took up his papers, once a prop and now an encyclopedia of facts.

"Let me 'indoctrinate' you good people on the business of slavery. So that we may put it in perspective. For slavery is, after all, part and parcel of the business of farming. Human beings, reduced to the equation of profit and loss."

Riffling the pages, he spoke from memory.

"The technical term for what I am about to describe is called 'Crude Profit': the difference between that for which a slave was bought and that for which he is ultimately sold. If I err, sir -- what is your name?" he inquired of the slave holder.

"Albert Conklin."

"Mr. Conklin, kindly correct me. Now: Net profit is determined by deducting expenses. Food and clothing constitute 4.7 percent of expenditures. Assistants: $21.13 per week for temporary or hired slaves; $550 per year for permanent. That equates to 1.2 percent of 'our' cost. Then, there is interest charged on loans to buy slaves; 6-8 percent is considered reasonable. Factoring in death or the unfortunate escape of a slave adds 1.2 percent to our loss sheet.

"Including incidentals such as the commission and brokerage, bad debt and promissory notes, we come to a rough figure of 15%. Therefore, a slave must be sold at greater than fifteen percent to make a profit." He wiped his hands. "All neat and tidy. When something may be explained in dollars and cents and written in a ledger, that adds the air of legitimacy, does it not? Pity the poor plantation owner. Always worrying about the bottom line."

A crumpled paper went whizzing past Pickering's head. He went and picked it up. Carefully smoothing down the corners, he held it up for inspection.

"An advert for a place called the Tankard's Draft. It seems beer sells for five cents and there are 'fancy girls aplenty' to entertain the customers. Begging your pardon if I offend, but 'fancy girls' is a euphemism for prostitutes. I wonder how any of them are 'light-skinned,' or brown-skinned'? Or if it matters, for the Unchristian act of debasing yourself with any female with whom you are not married demeans all womanhood."

He sought confirmation from the men before ending his search with Nelander. She offered a nod of approval.

An acknowledgment not shared among all.

"You pretend your hands are clean, Reverend, but slavery began in this country by Northern sea captains bringing them in from Africa. If you know your history so well, and you Northern allies are all so 'pure,' explain that profit-and-loss."

Pickering beamed with a pleasing aura of satisfaction.

"You ask of history? I shall be glad to oblige. Although I trust my rendition will not bore those already familiar with the story."

Returning his notes to the podium, he took another drink of water. This time he merely sipped.

"The earliest known instance of Negro slavery began in the year 1442 when explorer Antam Gonsalvez brought ten 'blackamoors' to Lisbon. His stated purpose was to 'save their souls.' How well he succeeded, we can only speculate. What he did to his own shames God."

Several more in the audience threw eggs on the stage. Landing with a hard crack, the shells broke, leaking pale yellow puss over the floorboards. Pickering clucked his tongue.

"I trust those were not eggs laid by Christian chickens."

Laughter occurred in pockets around the front rows. The back of the meeting hall remained strangely quiet.

"We now progress in time to a name most have some familiarity with: Christopher Columbus. That worthy explorer opened up two continents to slavery, shipping home 500 Indians and suggesting they be sold in the markets of Seville. So you can see it did not take very long for our ancestors to go from ostensively 'saving souls' to unabashed profit."

Gliding across the stage, the minister stooped down and cleared up one of the broken eggs by sweeping the dripping mass into his handkerchief. Depositing it by the water pitcher, he cast a look around the room before continuing.

"Sir John Hawkins made three slaving voyages from Guinea to the West Indies. Sir Francis Drake and our own John Paul Jones helped transport black... cargo. Many sovereigns -- those believing they sat upon their thrones by Divine Right -- were involved in this new and lucrative trade. Henry the Navigator; Ferdinand the Catholic; Emperor Charles V; Queen Elizabeth; Philip II of Spain. Charles II of England, who, incidentally, first coined guineas to celebrate the Trade. Philip V, another Spaniard. Queen Anne. A lofty assemblage."

A young man stood up and waved his hand.

"How can they be right and you wrong?"

"Sit down, sir, I beg you. I would not have you tire your feet for I am long-winded."

"Answer the question."

"Gladly, although I find it an odd one."

"Why is that? Because you can't speak against Christian lieges?"

"Odd, because our American Revolution was fought against such a... Christian monarch. King George III, of England. The Mad king. We hardly considered his religious affiliation or his mandate from God when taking up arms against unjust laws. Or do I mistake?"

The young man sat, face reddened by the catcalls and whistles of those in the front rows. Again, Pickering called for quiet.

"Do not ridicule our Southern friend. While our brains have been steeped in tea, his, I fear, has been soaked in julep. Or local brew, sold for the princely sum of five cents a glass."

Contrary to his plea, a round of hand-clapping rent the room.

"You tell 'im, Reverend!"

"That's the way to put it!"

"Go home, you slave owner. Kansas don't want your kind here."

"Come across our border an' we'll show you some western hospitality."

"What percent of his profit will that be when Doc McTree charges him a 'guinea' to patch his nose?"

Mr. Daly finally struggled to his feet and waved down the shouts.

"Please. Let us go on."

He might not have had any influence, but the night belonged to Thomas Pickering. Throwing back the long tails of his broadcloth coat, he strode forward.

"Enough! Do not send our friend packing before he has finished his history lesson. He asked about Christian monarchs and Christian countries. In 1802, the once extensive Danish commerce in slave trading was declared illegal. In 1813, the Swedes followed suit. In 1814 the Dutch outlawed commerce in human flesh. Two months after both Houses of Congress passed a bill outlawing the importation of slaves, the British washed their hands of that nefarious practice. That was 1807. A watershed event in the history of both nations."

"But our Founding Fathers did not outlaw slavery! Slavery is legal. They saw the good of it."

"The saw, sir, the political ramifications and did not have the courage to act further. That, fellow countrymen, they left to us!"

A spontaneous applause exploded from the front rows of the meeting hall. Men cheered and waved their hats. More eggs and rotten fruit were thrown toward the stage. Several, better aimed, struck the preacher. In disgust, he removed his coat and flipped it out in fair imitation of a bullfighter inciting his doomed, horned foe.

An individual who had not spoken before rose to his feet. Face reddened from anger, he emitted a shrill whistle, demanding to be heard.

"You and your pious Northern brethren -- and those fools here you believe your claptrap -- are nothing but clogs in a wheel, spouting Northern dogma. You blind yourselves to the facts. To the good we do. The Negro race will never be self-sufficient; they need guidance and supervision. Set them free and they will starve to death. What then, Reverend? Will you and your Christian Societies take them in? Will you house and feed them? Will you teach them how to read and write? Or will you put them in your factories and sweat houses? I say you are hypocrites and liars."

Several fights broke out as men elbowed neighbors, pushed and shoved, knocking off hats, pulling hair.

"Calm! I enjoin you to calm!" Daly cried. "No violence or the lecture is at an end."

"Let-him-speak." Fighting suspended, all eyes turned upward. Pickering bowed. "You, sir -- your name."

"What does it matter? Channing, if you must. From South Carolina."

"Your face, sir, is familiar to me."

"I have been following you from city to city. Not, I confess, from the start, for your journey has been a long one. I happened to be in Philadelphia on business when you spoke at Independence Hall. Like the rest, I, too, was taken in by your speech -- professing to understand our beliefs, then shattering them in a moment. Very embittering. But then, you were not directing your comments to me or my kind."

"On the contrary, Mr. Channing -- it is to the unconverted I wish my sentiments to reach. While Jesus surrounded Himself with disciples, He addressed Himself to the unbelievers."

"There are many honorable among us who are men of the cloth, Mr. Pickering -- those who defend slavery as an institution sanctioned by God. As a ways and means of preserving our... less gifted brethren. Would you call them liars?"

Abandoning civility for the moment, the minister spoke with contempt.

"I call them misguided."

The crowd reacted along partisan lines, growing restive and impatient for some sort of physical confrontation. Channing remained calm.

"A phrase equally applicable to you, sir. You start your lecture by enumerating the titles men use by which to identify themselves, implying there is some shame to their calling. I dispute that most vehemently. Such individuals are most useful citizens, carrying out the law of the land. You, sir, are an incendiary: one who preaches not God's commandments but sedition."

"In the great tradition of our Colonial ancestors. Those worthies who placed a higher value on Principle than Parliament."

"But not above God's Law. Our Savior walked among slaves, yet spoke not one word against slavery as an institution. Many were His chances -- many, the times He said nothing. A confirmation, sir, of a just and useful system where both parties benefit for the betterment of all. The white men are the keepers of the brown, sir. We have adopted them as our own."

"With equal opportunities, sir?"

"With those equal to their talents. A blacksmith is not a senator; a field hand not a banker."

"Yet, with education either may aspire to higher roles."

"You speak of higher aspirations. Would you have your daughter marry a brown man, Reverend?"

Mr. Channing posed the one question so many asked and so few answered. Heads spun from one speaker to the other, waiting to hear how far either would go in this debate. For the moment, silence assumed dominance over the meeting hall.

Pickering's eyes narrowed and his shoulders rounded as if encompassing the gathering to his will.

"I would have them separate but equal. Just as the Lord decreed by placing the Negro on one continent and the Caucasian on another. We are meant to commune as brothers and sisters, sir. As partners on this one great planet, endowed with life and liberty as those molded in the Creator's own image."

The crowd responded with restive activity, some shifting positions, others gripping hat brims or clenching fists. The minister had provided one answer, yet it hardly seemed a solution. Cocking an ear, Channing listened and understood.

"You suppose too much, sir. There are more brown-skinned men in the city of Charleston than white-skinned. The Negro is an integral work force in this country. The Founding Fathers acknowledged such when they drew up the Constitution."

"'We hold these truths to be self-evident, that all men are created equal."

"All white men, sir. They were slave holders, themselves."

The words shot through the thick air, inciting burning tempers. Many stood, bitterly pointing at one another.

"Damn nigger lovers!"

"Dirty slavers with your whips and chains!"

Before Sheriff Bochner could intervene, if such were his intent, the man called Channing strode down the center aisle, arms upraised. The sudden action temporarily returned men to their chairs. *Our time will come,* they conveyed. *Finish your dialogue before we take matters into our own hands. No one believes this will be settled by words.*

"You profess to know so much about our Southern culture, Mr. Pickering, yet you do not. Unlike your cold-clime associates who derive their wealth from smoke-belching factories and noisy, crowded cities, we seek a peaceful way of life. Through agriculture -- a plowing of the land as it were in Christ's time -- we create wealth without succumbing to the corrupt materialism of Boston and New York and Philadelphia. The South is not the North, Reverend Pickering. We have our peculiar climate, our peculiar crops, our peculiar institutions. We share a Southern identity, grown out of the soil."

Halting his progress at the second row, the tails of his coat brushed against Seth, who sat on the outside. Feeling dirtied, he jerked back and rubbed his leg where the material had touched.

"We -- the men of the South," Channing pursued, oblivious to his *faux pas,* "are not all plantation owners or men of wealth." He swept a hand to indicate the back rows. "But we know our God. We have a social stability unknown in the North, were workers toil in submission for pennies a day. The Irish, the Germans, the immigrants: ask them if they are free! Is a man who owes his soul to the company store any more free than a bonded man? No, sir, he is not!"

"But which would you rather be, sir?"

"I cannot answer that, Reverend, because I cannot change the color of my skin. God made me white. He made me of the superior race so that I might care for those in my charge. Ask the Astors, the Stewarts, the Knickerbockers, the Macys, Grinnells, Kings and the Whitneys how they regard their -- immigrant servants. Where, sir, is your separate but equal? And we are talking here of white men! You have your slavery and we have ours. Pose your question to the Irish laborer, sir, and see what answer you receive!"

Leaping from the stage, Pickering hopped the few steps to Channing, pushing his nose in the other's face. The Southerner withdrew, curling his lips in anger. The action caused the preacher to change his mind. Moving back toward the front, he strode across the open space.

"I will ask the men of Kansas. Who among you would rather be a free man than a slave? Who among you would rather own his farm, than work it for another? Who among you would marry of your own free will, under the blessing of the Almighty, rather than be deprived -- by law -- of that Christian sacrament? Who among you desire to see your children grow to manhood, rather than have them sold away from your loving bosom? Who among you would sell your crops for your own benefit rather than that of another? Who owns a rifle or a dog or would rather be shot by one and hunted by the other?"

His voice rose to fever pitch, cracking at the end as he finished the impassioned plea. Without bothering to hold back those who stood and moved forward, he jabbed a finger at the Southerner.

"You have heard his argument and it falls short, brothers! He paints a false picture. I have seen the whips and chains and flopping paddles. I have attended slave auctions. I have seen children ripped from the breasts of their mothers. I have heard the weeping, the pleas, the begging. I have witnessed the ears severed from unruly brown men."

Tears finally clouding his eyes, he sniffed and tore at his coat.

"I know his methods. I have stood on courthouse steps and listened to the lies. I have attended church and choked on sulphur and brimstone. Here, men of Kansas, is the issue they use to divide us. And it is an evil one, indeed."

Removing a pocket Bible, he kissed the cover before concluding.

"By insisting that slavery is indispensable to all Southerners, the ruling class of plantation owners and politicians draw even non-slave holders to their wicked cause through identification with their slave-holding land." His voice cracked a second time and he roared to clear it. "Listen to me, men of Kansas and Missoura and Arkansas and Carolina and Georgia. I implore you. Do not join their ranks! You are not of their class. Do not fight their battles for them. Do not listen to their call for it comes from Satan and not from God. This country belongs to the free as our forefathers meant. Do not be deceived. This is a political issue, not one of 'benefactors' and 'adopted fathers.' I choose freedom! Are you with me?"

Two hundred and fifty men in a crowded meeting hall in Lawrence, Kansas, leaped to their feet. Teeth bared, arms stiffened, mouths screaming, eyes flashing, they moved *en mass*. In echelon.

Pushing, shoving, punching, screaming in blind rage. Not as a well-trained force, but two sides, angry and inconsolable, opposing one another.

Brother against brother.

Not the beginning and not the end of the Uncivil War.

# CHAPTER 26

Sheriff Bochner supposed the trouble would originate within the meeting hall. Toward that expectation, he had posted his deputies inside, one at every corner. He personally guarded the entranceway, which also happened to be the only exit. Earlier in the day he had given orders not to shoot unless directly fired upon. Failing to control the mob with verbal warnings, the deputies had been supplied with clubs.

"Use these as a first line of defense. Crack a few skulls and the rest will come into line."

Sensible and well-intended, Bochner's preparations displayed remarkable forethought. He had learned well the lessons of the drought. Desperate people often made foolish threats. Responding to loose talk with force achieved tragedy rather than compliance. A dead farmer might no longer be a danger, but he left behind a wife and children for whom rain would bring no release.

Unfortunately, his tactics applied only to those inside the hall. He had not anticipated an assault from without.

Whether on prearranged signal or responding to the level of noise inside the Meeting Hall, no one learned. Witnesses later reported they heard glass breaking and that much was confirmed. The explosive came through the window: a whisky bottle, filled with kerosene and ignited by a lit fuse. The missile blew up in midair, spewing glass chards and flaming liquid over the assemblage. Panic ensued.

Screams of pain rent the overcharged atmosphere. Those nearest the explosion clutched their faces from wounds inflicted by shrapnel. Others, half blinded, blood gushing from head injuries, plunged in every direction, knocking over any in their path. They, in turn, toppled others, until dozens lay on the floor, arms and legs horrifically intertwined.

The snap of a long bone, firecracker sharp, temporarily belayed the pandemonium as men froze, contemplating the significance. The cry which followed, shrill, piercing, agonized, reignited their mobility, however, and those still on their feet pushed forward, desperately seeking egress.

Regardless of the few desperately attempting to extinguish flames fed on flammable drops of liquid, the mob surged ahead, trampling the unfortunate. Heads bumped shoulders, elbows jarred ribs, fingers tore eye sockets. Curtains covering the broken window burst into flame, spreading the fire upward and across the sill, casting an eerie, hellish orange glow over the pandemonium. Creeping greedily to the ceiling, the snapping blue-tipped fingers raced toward the double-layered sheet used to separate the rear of the stage from the audience. In seconds it, too, caught fire.

Heat intensified. Smoke, billowing from the dyed cotton material, added a deadly, acrid poison to the air. Oxygen in the enclosed space diminished. Panting lungs, scorched by unnatural clouds, rebelled, refusing to admit more tainted breath. Men grew faint, some vomiting over themselves and others close. The floor, already obscured with hats, articles of clothing and discarded flyers, became treacherous.

Those nearest the exit -- those uninvited latecomers without a ticket -- were the first to escape. Once outside, they screamed, shouting with what strength they possessed.

"Fire! Fire! The Meeting Hall's on fire!"

"The preacher man done this!"

"God's laid His hand on Lawrence!"

Whatever else they might have cried was lost in translation as they merged with a throng of onlookers. Townsmen who had lacked the courage to attend the lecture suddenly discovered their verve and surged forward, filling their hats with water from the troughs to fling on the expanding conflagration. In the distance, a bell clanged, summoning volunteers to the fire wagon. Horses, frightened by the melee, broke loose, tearing into the street, rearing, kicking, ears pressed back, nostrils flailing. Those who could, ducked out of the way. Those who could not fell victim to the stampede.

Because he had been standing by the door, Sheriff Bochner had been one of the first to escape. Nerves shattered, mind a swirl, he attempted to take stock of the swelling panic, found he could not cope with the scene and leveled his rifle into a mob gathering by the building.

"Back!" he spat. "Back, or I'll shoot, you damn bastards."

One man he did not recognize raised a fist.

"It's the Lord's --"

What was or was not "the Lord's" remained unknown, for he pulled the trigger. Impact from the bullet sent the interloper flying backward. Blood lust sated only temporarily, Bochner waved the weapon at the crowd.

"Make way for the fire wagon," he snarled, "or the damn Lord'll have more entrants knockin' on His gate than He knows what to do with."

They believed him and withdrew, merging into smaller groups, allied along political viewpoints.

"Get out. Get away. Stand back."

Those not directly in Bochner's sights fired handguns in the air. A few on horseback rode the congested streets, waving their hats, shouting, cursing. The mob spread outward. Hitching posts were torn from sockets like rotten teeth; lamp posts uprooted. Rocks thrown through windows. Lawrence, Kansas, devolved into riot. Immune from conscience, looters filled their pockets. From the saloon, a man played "Dixie."

Barbara Nelander had never witnessed a riot, but she had seen panic before and understood its consequences. Grabbing Seth's arm for fear of being separated, she drew her face close to his.

"Stay back. We cannot escape that way."

Behind them, the long curtain, eaten by flame, collapsed to the floor. A whoosh of sparks accompanied a searing wave of heat. They instinctively ducked, protecting their heads.

"Cover your mouth," he grunted, falling to one knee as a foot caught him from behind. Pain shot in all directions, temporarily numbing his toes while knifing his hip. McTree on one side, Nelander on the other, they helped him up. With Seth between them, they inched toward the side, finally reaching the wall. Leaning against it, though heat from the burning wood raked his back, he shook his head.

"Gotta get out."

A stench, this time of roasted flesh, made him gag. Removing his coat, he flung it over his head and shoulders for protection.

"We'll never get past the mob at the door," McTree spat. "Too many, all bunched up."

Hand covered by his sleeve, Seth banged it against the planking. The wood shook under the blow.

"I saw this building go up. Think!" he screamed to himself. "Where are the braces?" Feeling along the wall, fighting his fear, he reached a spot several feet away. "Here! Help me! Knock the wall down. It's our only chance."

The seaman and the doctor responded as one, first pummeling then kicking the side. Already weakened at the ceiling from the path of fire, the upright trembled.

"Harder! Harder! It went up in one piece and it'll come down that way."

A man brushed past them, face blackened from soot, eyes wide in terror. Without sight, he ran into the wall, cried and bounced back.

"Daly. Jim Daly."

Responding to his name, although slowly, the way a drunken man reacted to words only vaguely understood, he nodded.

"Yes. I am Jim Daly."

"It is Seth Ward, Jim. We're gonna knock the wall down. You are going to help."

Daly tried to respond but fell into a fit of coughing. Nearly overcome, his knees buckled. A hand on his back held him up.

"Come on, Daly. Pull yourself together, man. Once you get out of here, you've got a story to write."

"Oh, God," he moaned, eyes rolling toward the back of his skull. "Where's Reverend Pickering?"

Three heads turned, each in the direction that particular individual had last seen the preacher. The shared perspective gave them a fair view of the four points. Tall enough to have been seen, were he standing, their sweep of the compass failed to net one of Jesus' fishermen.

"Never mind," the captain urged, shoving the newspaperman up against the wall. "No sense searching in this murk." He jumped suddenly as a streak of fire nipped at his heels. "We won't have a place to stand, soon. Push!"

Responding to the command voice, the four began a concerted effort to knock down the wall. After several blows, they heard the splintering of timber as wood cracked.

"Harder!"

Working with a frenzy fed by the intense heat and creeping fire behind them, they hit it again. An upper corner of the flat tore loose. Nelander cupped her hands over her lips to augment her voice.

"Look out! Stand back!"

Unable to tell whether any heard and for the moment unconcerned, the crew shoved, feeling the boundary tear free. A blast of outside air stung their faces, feeding the fire at the rear. Flames surged.

One final effort and the wall gave way. It swayed, nearly toppled back, then burst free of the final moorings, falling outward. Amid screams of panic from those on the opposite side, Seth and Nelander grabbed Daly and shoved him through the opening just as the wall struck earth. Ten billion sparks exploded from the force, hurtling debris up and across a hundred yard plain. New fires erupted, spreading along the grass, consuming it with shocking rapidity.

Only dimly aware of the fire bell tolling, Nelander blindly headed in that direction. Alien fingers clad in rubber gloves grabbed her, flung her to the ground. She fought, arms flailing, legs kicking until a heavy wet blanket descended over her slim frame. Desisting all activity, she fought an attack of vertigo as those same hands rolled her along the ground.

She might have traveled a mile in that way, for time, distorted by lack of perception, wrinkled in her brain. Only when another pair of hands removed the binding did she understand what had happened. A wide-eyed, sweat-soaked face peered down at her.

"You all right? You was burnin' like a torch." Helping her up, the stranger drew back in surprise to see he had saved a woman. Slack-jawed, he worked up an apology. "Sorry, miss. Didn't know there was any females inside."

Unsteady on her feet, she wavered, the flesh on her face in agony from deep, slithering pain.

"Thanks."

The fireman quickly abandoned her to help others. Nelander staggered across a line of charred earth, stumbled, then gripped her fists in fury. Feeding anger as a means of sustaining energy, she scanned the scene, so new to her eyes. Around her stood an arc of spectators, frightened by the horror and too numb to move. Behind her, twelve or fifteen fighters fought the blaze, some throwing buckets of water on the outside conflagration, while a second team hefted a hose, spraying water from the tank aboard the fire wagon at the newly created opening.

Without thinking, she spotted a trough, limped to it and ducked her head into the water. The cold almost sent her into shock but as quickly revived her jaded senses. Allowing the slimy liquid to sooth the seared nerves in cheeks and neck, she slowly withdrew, now viewing the world through a shimmering lens of water. Experiencing extremes of color and a keenness of vision which allowed her to distinguish individual blades of grass fifty yards away, she sucked in clean air as though tasting it for the first time.

Awed by this distorted perception, she stared a body on the ground, absently counting the fibers in the blanket covering it before making the connection. With a cry of anguish, she raced forward, gripping the ends and tearing them away.

Tormented by a flashback not her own, she envisioned Peter, a little boy, not his present age, but far younger, digging tiny hands into newly dug ground and screaming, "Mama! Mama!"

Unbeknownst, the same words spilled from her mouth.

Flinging away clumps of moist earth, spitting as bits of dirt covered her mouth, she worked as one possessed, uncovering an arm, then a shoulder and finally a head. Grabbing the locks, she yanked upward, forcing the face toward hers.

Not "mama," but "papa" stared up at her, flesh smeared with blood from a cut near his lip.

He called her a name and for a moment, it did not register.

"Nelander. Nelander, my darling."

Sobbing, she engulfed him, kissing his brow, wiping away his blood with crimson from her own lips.

"My God, my God, you're alive!"

Sobbing, kissing, hugging, they embraced, holding fast. Around them the world disappeared and they became the sole inhabitants of a receding hell which had spewed them forth.

"Seth.... Seth."

"Seth," he repeated as if to confirm his identity. "And Barbara."

He did not ask why she had called him "mama." He did not have to.

Seth Ward was the town authority on bewitchments.

## CHAPTER 27

Dr. Hank McTree joined them by the water trough. A large hole had been burned in his coat and his hair showed charred ends. Clearly beholding his friends in the same condition, he tried a weak grin. His voice shook when he spoke.

"I've heard of bringing down the house, but that was some performance, Captain."

"My pleasure," Seth nodded without consciously performing the act. "Wasn't sure we could do it. Where's Daly?"

The doctor pointed toward an area set aside as a makeshift hospital. "Over there. He's gonna be all right."

"What about the others? How many --?"

He could not bring himself to say the word "dead."

"Don't know. Haven't had time to check. I'm going, now. Just wanted to be sure you two were sucking air."

His use of slang finally elicited a pair of grins.

"What about Pickering? Have you seen him?"

"No."

"Hope to God he got out."

"Haven't seen that other fella, either: Channing."

More begrudging but equally sincere, "Don't wish him any harm, either."

Hank agreed. "You two able to walk?"

"We'll help --"

"That's not what I mean. I'll do what I can here. You ought to get back to my place. See to the children. Then tend your wounds. Smear some grease over your face and hands. Wash up some, first, so keep away infection. Will you do that? Then cover the larger blisters with gauze."

"You're sure? We can stay --"

"I want you out of here. No telling which way the wind's blowing. I spoke to one of the deputies and he told me the whole town's gone crazy. Men ridin' up and down the streets shootin' at anything that moves. Some looting. Others doing God-knows-what. Everyone's riled up. Be careful. Keep to the shadows. Don't accost anyone. That's my advice."

"What about -- Jesus! What about Little Lawrence? There's bound to be trouble there."

"Can't say. But you've got young'uns to look after. I mean it. You're not even armed -- neither of you. Talking's not going to do any good. Get to my place and lock the door. Close the shutters. Don't answer if anyone comes. They'll be lookin' for me, most likely. When they don't get any response, I hope they'll figure I'm out and come looking for me at the Meeting Hall." A fleeting expression of sadness emerged from behind his professional demeanor. "Or, what once was the Meeting Hall."

"You're going to stay here? And treat..." Seth floundered for a euphemism and gave up with a helpless shrug.

"I'll be all right. No one knows where I stand. Besides," McTree tried, working on the effort, "when you're bleeding, you don't ask a doctor his politics."

"Thanks."

Pressing a hand to his, Seth hurriedly shoved away, Nelander at his side. Crossing the street at an awkward lope, they reached the darkened sidewalk. Broken windows and torn boardwalk attested to the fact that looters had come this way before them.

"Look."

Following his direction, Nelander saw that the Tankard's Draft had been closed, the double doors shuddered behind the swinging batwings. No light crept out from behind drawn shades.

"At least they won't be fueling the flames with that damned red eye of theirs."

"I hope someone put his foot through that miserable piano before they locked up."

Only too ready to agree, Nelander checked their route, then marched ahead. Keeping low, they made it to a side alley. She started to duck in but he stopped her.

"Dead end. There's a side street further up. We'll go that way; get off the main route."

Moving quickly, they came to Branch Street, took a right and kept moving. Traversing three more avenues, each smaller than the last, they finally emerged at the end of town. Houses along the road were also closed, no lamps lit. The implication was clear: no one was welcome. Not even a stray dog or a feral cat lurked by deserted porches.

Pausing a moment to catch his breath, Seth rubbed at a blister on his arm, making a face as he popped the skin. The warm trickle of murky fluid set his teeth on edge.

"I feel as though I've been catapulted back in time to the Wakarusa War -- but this is worse. I wasn't directly involved in that -- it was townspeople, mostly. Then, the trouble after John Brown's raid -- they say it was the fighting in Lawrence which inspired him." His entire frame trembled. "But we've got law on our side this time. And it didn't make a fig of difference."

He turned to her, sweat streaming down tear tracts. "What's wrong with people? Nobody's gonna settle anything here."

"No," Barbara whispered. "There's going to be a lot of 'here's.' And what gets settled won't be in a way anyone anticipates."

Trudging ahead, they made it to Doctor McTree's house. The sight of it, so incongruous from the rest, sent shock waves through the pair. Although the door was shut, a lamp burned cheerily in the window and Minerva stood by the gate, tail tucked between her legs. Not as an act of cowardice but in an attitude of misgiving and distrust. Seth offered a hand.

"Easy, girl. You know me. Captain Ward. I'm the one who gave two of your puppies a good home. You saw us this evening."

The friendly voice allayed the fear but not the doubt. Growling low in her throat, the dog padded stiff-legged away from the fence, ready to admit them but not without further consideration.

A whistle from inside brought a wag and then a pink extension of the tongue.

"Minerva. It's papa and Nelander."

Not daring to linger too long for fear their actions might be observed, Seth pushed Barbara through the swinging gate then searched for a fastening. Other than the metal clasp, he saw no way of locking it.

"Never mind. If we barricade ourselves in, that will rouse suspicion. People are sure to come -- looking for the doctor. They won't expect to be stopped at the gate. We don't want to make them any more agitated than they already are."

"But Doc said to barricade the house."

"So he did."

"Meaning we're going to disobey?"

"You're the captain. He's only the... ship's cook," she added, referencing the fact that at sea the cook doubled as the doctor.

He grimaced and they hurried up the cobbled path. Behind the door they heard the scrape of a dead bolt, then observed a shaft of light as the door pulled back. Slipping in, Nelander reapplied the lock as Seth grabbed his children.

"Papa, sir, what happened?" Patricia cried, staring at his face and soiled clothing. "Was there a fire? We heard the bell -- and shooting."

He consoled the crew while Barbara removed the lamp and drew in the shutters.

"Yes. There was a fire. The Meeting Hall burned down."

"Why?"

"Someone wanted to hurt the people inside."

"You're all blistered, papa," Peter observed, pulling away as though his touch had somehow occasioned the hurts. Seth took his hands in his and kissed them.

"We got out all right. With Dr. McTree. Maybe others weren't so lucky." Nelander cleared her throat but he brushed aside the warning. "Remember the Pirate Creed. We tell each other the truth. They're old enough and, by God, they'll see and hear worse. Might as well begin with us."

"You're right. I'm sorry."

Finished with the immediate task of securing the house, Barbara went in search of ointment and bandages while he quickly finished the story.

"There were men in town -- strangers. I don't know where they came from. Some have been following the preacher -- Mr. Pickering. Others just lookin' for trouble. They didn't like what he had to say."

"About the Negroes, papa?"

"Yes."

"Why don't they like them? They're just like us."

"Yes, daughter. They are. But some don't see it that way. They can't get beyond the color of their skin."

Peter squirmed from under his grasp and stood apart.

"What about Blind Betty and Mute Thomas, sir? Are they in trouble, too?"

"No one knows they're out in the valley. I think they're safe for now."

"Will people try and hurt them?" He drew his cutlass and brandished the weapon. "They're part of our crew, too, ain't they? We have to stick together. I'll slay the first bastard what comes near them."

"There won't be any slaying. And no cursing, either."

Nelander saved him the trouble of an apology by entering, arms full of jars and bandages.

"Wash up then come over to the table. Let me treat your wounds."

He obliged, pumping water from the kitchen into a basin, then gingerly applying soap and water to hands, arms and face. When he had removed as much soot and sweat as possible without tearing away tender flesh, Seth dried himself, then perched on the edge of a dining room chair. With neat efficiency, the former seaman uncorked a blue bottle, peered at the contents, then dug some out with a tongue depressor.

"This isn't labeled but it's greasy." Tilting back her head to adjust for the light, she critically appraised his face. "You're a beautiful man, Seth Ward. Somewhat worse for wear, but as pretty as a four-mast against the wind."

"And you, Barbara Nelander, are enough to take a man's breath away. Somewhat worse for wear, but as pretty as a horse pulling a plow through a field of God's green grass."

Touching the opaque lotion to a swollen red welt across his forehead, she hesitated, waiting for a reaction. Receiving none, she rapidly completed the labor, smearing the gel across his cheeks and chin, then down his neck.

"Take off your coat and roll up your sleeves."

The sight of several deep purple bruises and one long, ugly red gash lowered her eyebrows.

"That cut probably needs stitches."

"Bind it tight. It'll heal."

"Leave a scar."

"You won't hear me complainin'. Make me less pretty, though?"

"Nothing a new coat of paint won't fix." Subliminally aware the children had crept up behind her, she included them in the patch work. "Peter, you hold the captain's hand. Patricia, you roll the bandage around his arm. Nice and tight. Leave me enough at the end to tear and knot."

"Yes, sir."

The girl worked with finesse, keeping one eye on her brother to see he prevented the patient from moving. When the roll had gone around half a dozen times, she ripped the end herself, then moved aside so Barbara could tie the strands.

"Feels some better, already."

"Are you hurting? I don't know where McTree keeps the laudanum, but I'm sure we can scrounge up a dram of rum."

"Don't want anything to cloud my mind."

"Some hot tea, then," she decided. "We could all use some." Patricia went to carry out the order while Nelander examined her own body. Tweaking her nose, she made a vain effort to straighten it. "Don't know if I broke it or not when I fell. Nothing for it, though. What do you think, Master Peter? If it turns crooked, will that make me look more like a buccaneer?"

"Don't know as how you could look more like one than you do a'ready," he declared with childlike wisdom. "'Sept mebbe an eye patch."

"Never mind eye patches," his father barked. "And we're not 'recruiting' any peg legs or hooked arms, either."

Hardly put off, the boy withdrew a red bandana.

"Here, sir. Tie this around your head. That'll do it."

Taking the material, she gave it a critical appraisal then set it on the table. After washing up in the same water Seth had used, she applied grease to several large boils and a deep cut over her left eyebrow, then wrapped the kerchief over the sticky mass to prevent it from dripping.

"Tea's ready."

Before they had a chance to drink, a shout from outside demanded their attention. Hand shaking from the unexpected fright, Nelander growled and laid down the cup.

"Nobody move. Don't answer."

"McTree! Dr. McTree! You in there?" The man banged the gate, then sprinted to the porch. Pounding on the door with both fists, he appeared determined to elicit an answer. "McTree! Where the hell are you?" He tried the knob and found it secure. "McTree!"

Pressing a finger to his lips, Seth got up and tiptoed around the room, seeking any sort of weapon. Finding no firearm, he grabbed a poker. Holding it across his body, he stole to the door, standing just behind so that if the intruder broke in, he would be in position to bash him over the head.

"McTree! I need help."

Either detecting a lie in the tone or some latent danger, Minerva flattened her ears and growled. Creeping low, head toward the floor, the dog moved forward, sniffed, then broke out into raucous barking. Not content, she howled, scratching at the wood in mad canine fury. The stranger, ill prepared to face such a welcome, swore, then backed away, footsteps hollow on the wood.

"Goddamn mutt."

Stomping around the side, he might have gotten into the rear, but Minerva raced through the living room to the back. Throwing her weight against that door, she shoved it open and rushed through, too quickly for any of the inhabitants to stop her. Clutching the poker, Seth went to follow but Nelander issued a harsh whisper.

"Let her go. I don't want him finding Blaze back there. If he's come to steal, he'll take him, sure."

"He may have a gun -- shoot the dog."

"Then, sir, we will bury her with honors."

The coldness stopped him in his tracks as the horror of their situation registered.

"Son of a bitch."

Peter pressed close, eyes wide.

"Papa, will he hurt Minerva?"

"I don't know, son. I hope not."

They listened as the barking increased, then silence a moment, stopping their breathing.

"Please, God, don't let him hurt Minerva."

Without making acknowledgment, the adults added a wordless "Amen" to Patricia's prayer. A second later the dog barked again, restarting their hearts.

A crashing sound, a grunt, then more footsteps as the unknown assailant fled, banging the gate behind. Unable to witness the scene, the family could only guess that the dog followed him up the street by the sound of her baying. Nor did any of them move the full five minutes which elapsed before the animal returned, coming in the way she had left.

Falling on his knees, Peter petted the brave guardian.

"Good dog! Good dog."

"Is she hurt?"

"Don't think so. Brave dog! I love you, Minerva. You're a pirate, too."

Choking back a parent's sentiment, Seth sniffed and patted his boy's head before glancing at Nelander.

"You're right. It isn't safe here. That man wasn't hurt. He was looking for trouble." His voice sobered. "Hank was wrong about politics."

"I think we've all been wrong tonight. None of us saw what was coming. Should we have? You knew," she contradicted, relieving him of her assessment of "all."

"No."

"You did. You've been behaving differently for days. Ever since you heard Reverend Pickering was coming."

"There's things a man knows here," he demonstrated, pointing to his head, "and things he senses in his gut." Lifting his arm, the bandage unscrolled, coming loose in wide circles. He grimaced as his child cried.

"Oh, Papa Captain, I didn't do a good job."

"You did fine," Nelander quickly reassured. "The knot came loose. We'll reapply it." One look at the blood-stained gauze changed her mind. "Get another. Quickly."

Patricia and Peter both went for the bandages, coming back with a handful. Barbara selected the proper size then bade Patricia re-do her work.

"Nice and tight."

"I don't want to hurt him."

"It will hurt him more if you leave it loose. We've got to see the sides of the cut touch so they will heal faster." Glancing at her husband's hard-controlled orbs, she added, "We really ought to wait for the doctor and have him suture this. It's deep. Deeper than I thought; might get infected."

"Do what you can. We must leave. Soon."

Recognizing an inner communication between brain and instinct, she dropped the protest. Again ripping the end but this time using her strength to tie the ends with a firm seaman's knot, she inspected the handiwork.

"When we get home I'll give you a thorough going-over; see what else I overlooked."

He expressed doubt by grunting, exerting pressure on his limb to ease the throbbing.

"Peter, go and hitch the horse. Patricia, go with him and stand guard. Take Minerva. If she growls, get back inside. I mean it. You're both brave. You don't need to prove it by fighting off crazed men."

"Yes, sir."

The pair dashed off, leaving the adults alone.

"How much trouble is there going to be?"

"Can't say."

"Are we going to be able to get out of town?"

"Not by the roads. And not by going anywhere near Little Lawrence. We'll cut through the fields. It'll be slower going, but I don't think anyone will be wandering around out there. Once we reach the hills, we can angle back. See if McTree's got a lantern. We'll need some light. Moon's not full enough to give us much help."

In fifteen minutes they had finalized arrangements and piled into the wagon. Minerva stood by the front wheel, wagging her tail in a slow, uneasy manner.

"What about the dog? Shall we take her?"

"She won't come. Better leave her; she's got her place."

"I'm afraid someone will come back; with a gun."

"This house is her ship, Nelander. It's her right to defend it."

"Dumb beats do not understand bullets."

"No more than a captain can control the sea that's dragging him down. But he doesn't complain about it."

"I would hardly compare a man-made disaster to a natural one."

He detected her bitterness and slapped the reins over Blaze's back.

"Maybe not. But the result is the same. Don't know that St. Peter makes any distinction between them who die in just causes and those who bring it on themselves."

"That, sir, we can debate another day."

The wagon rolled over the uneven ground, the horse straining over unfamiliar terrain.

"Shall I light the lamp, papa?"

"Not until we're away from here. Boy, get out and lead."

"No. I will go," the first officer protested. "Let Peter drive. Patricia, you walk ahead. Keep your eyes peeled for rocks or brush. Captain Ward, you sit back and conserve your strength. Give that arm a chance to rest. We'll need it later."

Staring into the dark night sky, Seth found the few stars swimming into one another, more a series of blurs than individual points of light. Suddenly dizzy and unaccountably weary, he sagged back and said nothing. The orders were carried out with alacrity and the wagon progressed, moving slowly but surely toward home.

If, in fact, they still had a home in which to return.

Security, as they knew it, had died an ugly death.

One as hideous as that suffered by two combatants who perished in the Great Conflagration at the Lawrence, Kansas Meeting Hall.

Whether St. Peter made a distinction between the two remained a private matter.

## CHAPTER 28

The wagon carrying the Ward crew struck the paved road shortly after four bells: 2:00 A.M. Heaving a sigh of relief, Nelander motioned Patricia back inside. She took the reins from Peter.

"Good job, both of you. Commendations for all."

Sleepily curling into his father's arms, the boy inquired, "Does that mean rum?"

"Better than that. Medals."

This peeked interest, but Seth tucked the child's head down.

"Go to sleep."

"But I'm getting a metal, papa. What will it look like?"

"Ask the Sandman."

An hour later, Nelander pulled up and shoved her nose into the breeze.

"Do you smell smoke?"

Groggily reawaking his senses, Seth sniffed. "No." It might have been a lie.

Ten minutes later, however, he threw his legs over the side and hopped down. His knees buckled and he caught himself against the side.

"I'm going ahead. Keep moving."

She might have argued for it made no sense to split up. But his reminder of a captain's inability to control the sea restrained her. He would do what had to be done. She could expect no less.

Disappearing into the pre-dawn stillness, Barbara stared after the hole which had swallowed him. Detecting neither ingress nor egress, she might easily imagine him never having existed at all, a mere figment of her imagination. She had experienced that sensation before: the commingling of fact and fantasy. Standing alone at the bow of the *Bottom Dollar,* drenched in a pitch blacker than ink, dark clouds burying the sky, ship's fog lights drowned by mist and all sound absorbed by the vastness of a watery eternity, reality warped.

Just as sailors of another century held their places on deck and wondered whether their craft would sail off the face of the flat earth, she wondered if there really were a farm called Pirate *Treasure*, or if she had dreamed it.

Had she actually come across two thousand miles of land to find herself in a strange, foreign place, or were she really back in San Francisco, standing over the yawning hole meant to consume her father's remains?

Or, had that that pale, wan countenance, shrunken and distorted by death, really been Ned Nelander? It seemed impossible to reconcile. He had always been a dark tanned, hearty man, full of life and energy. Even in repose he had exhibited a vitality promising latent force. He might have lost his life at sea, battling an angry nature which dwarfed even his intrepid will. He might have been tossed from the deck by a broken spar, swinging from well-tarred ropes in a gale of unimaginable power. He might have been swamped in a rescue boat, attempting to save a crewman fallen overboard. He might even have been swallowed by a whale or torn by sharks. But not perishing on land, at the hands of drunken brawlers.

None of it made any sense. She did not belong on the prairie; her heart had never been given to a tall, broad-shouldered man who spoke with a soft Midwestern dialect and used perfect grammar learned from reading Victorian novels and agricultural journals. She had never meant to marry. Her life had been dedicated to the sea and her ship. Her goals had not been to raise strawberries but to transport cargo from one alien shore to another.

In truth, she had never been a pirate. Those were stories shared around a cramped mess table or extemporized in bated breath by brothers possessing no more firsthand knowledge than she. Cutlasses, peg legs, eye patches, skull and crossbones standards and treasure chests were tall tales, whispered by able-bodies who had heard them from other jacks, who got them from friends aboard vessels long gone to their reward in the unfathomable depths.

Seamen were a superstitions lot, wearing silver crucifixes and carrying roundish golden coins to pay the Ferryman. Attending services on a Sunday morn with all the faith of an altar boy, lipping the words, repeating the inscrutable texts in Latin and the King's English, they gave their hearts but not their souls. Those they reserved for the individual more comprehensible to their limited experiences than that ancient mystic who rode the streets of Bethlehem on the back of an ass.

Davy Jones. The collector of seaman's souls; guardian of a deep sea heaven filled with wrecks of lost ships and wayward crews.

Captain Jones, ever patient, ever present.

*When I die, I'm casting in my lot wid Davy.*

*I'm tired, now, an' ol' Davy's waitin'.*

*Put it off as long as possible, son, but in the end, ol' Davy'll git you.*

*Wrap me in canvas an' drop my bones in the deep blue sea, sir, for there ain't nowhere else fer a salt water tar to go.*

Jesus and Davy Jones. One above, one below. Each with a claim on a seaman's soul.

Barbara Nelander did not question where Captain Ned's spirit sailed. What saddened her was the fact such a ghost would be hard put to find his only child's spirit so far from sea.

She hoped he had a map. One with a large "X" to mark the spot.

The baby cried and she looked back, into the inky rear of the wagon. Paula was hungry. She knew neither land not sea. She bore no prejudice. She harbored no hatreds. She had no means of defending herself.

Paula Nelander Ward was an innocent.

She had no way of comprehending that evil had come into her world.

Barbara Nelander-Ward prayed. It did not matter to whom.

She only cared about the result.

And did not know she combined a seaman's superstition with a farmer's faith.

Nor would it have mattered.

The baby stopped crying. She did not have to look back to see Ned Nelander cradling his grandchild in his rough, burly arms. Nor did she wonder how his face had resumed its ruddy glow or why his eyes sparkled like sea jewels.

Some things required no explanation.

A light pressure on her arm brought her head up. She had dozed at the reins, the horse picking its own path on the familiar road home.

"It's all right," Seth said. "No smoke. No fire. I have been to the hill above the house. All quiet."

"Thank God for that." And then, less reassured, "Brought in on the wind? From the Windsor place?"

He made a noncommittal gesture. "I don't think so. Wafted in from hell, more likely. I'll go later and see."

Resuming his place beside her, he took the reins and drove the rest of the way. Letting the passengers off at the door, he wearily descended and walked Blaze toward the barn.

"Get the children to bed."

"You're coming in, aren't you?"

"Chores. I've got to rub Blaze down and feed him. Milk the cow. See to the chickens."

"Surely that can wait."

"Surely not."

Reluctantly agreeing, Barbara carried Paula into the house and set the babe in her bed before returning. Lifting Peter in her arms, her heart caught as a limp arm flopped by his side. Had she not see him breath, he might have been dead.

Patricia dragged herself and without ceremony mumbled a "Good night" and crawled beneath the covers. Assured the girl would be all right, Nelander deposited Peter in hers and Seth's bed. Although their young pirate had come a long way since his days of "bewitchment," she dared take no chances. One nightmare stemming from his experience might set his feet wandering. The last thing they needed was to have him regress back into his days of shock and morning.

"Not the *last* thing," she whispered over his head as she tucked him in. But near enough to cause concern.

Assured he would not stir for the moment, she traipsed into the kitchen and put on water to boil. By the time Seth returned a pot of tea and cold biscuits had been set out for him.

"Not hungry," he protested.

"You will be surprised. Sit."

Taking some of the fresh milk, still warm from the cow, she added that to his cup and joined him at the table. True to expectations, one he began eating, food and drink quickly disappeared.

"What will happen next?"

"In town?" He wiped his lips and poured a second cup of tea. "The first thing, I suppose, is to restore law and order. Then, there will have to be an investigation. Sheriff Bochner will have to try and determine who threw the explosive and make an arrest."

"He won't find the right man."

"No. But he'll jail some poor bastard. Maybe a handful of them. Strangers. Charge them with looting, if nothing else. He has to make it look good. Otherwise, townspeople will be afraid the same thing will happen again."

"They'll be right."

"I suppose they will. But things will die down and life will go back to normal. Like it did after Sheriff Smith's rebellion."

"If I believed that I'd feel better."

"What do you think will happen?"

"Mutiny." He raised an eyebrow. "After civil disobedience, men get a taste for breaking the law. They assume new rights onto themselves. Start thinking they make the rules." She chewed on a hard roll. "That happens aboard ship, the best thing to do is sail to the nearest port and discharge the crew. Start anew."

"Can't do that with a town."

"Too bad." Outside, Mr. Noise Box crowed. Oddly, the sound of normalcy appeared out of place in the new world being recreated around them. "I keep thinking about Hank McTree."

"He'll be all right."

"Will anybody?" Her hand tightened on the butter knife. "I'm thinking about what he said: about patients not asking about a doctor's politics. Everyone's going to be asked their politics. No one's going to be excused. Sooner or later, you're all going to have to take sides."

"You're not including yourself?"

"Why should I? I'm only a woman. Females don't have the vote. They don't generally take up arms and fight. Only men do that. And you're a man."

"All right. I expect I expressed my opinion last night by sitting in the second row. Couldn't have come as much of a surprise. But I'm not ashamed. Someone has to take a stand."

"And do what with it, is the question."

He cut his biscuit in half, then left it on the plate.

"Vote."

"If it were only that, I wouldn't worry so much. But it won't end with a vote. Not on a state constitution and not for president."

"Anyone's better than who we got now." Seth leaned across the table, resting his chin on his elbows. "Besides, once Kansas comes in as a free state, that'll end the discussion. Those fire-eaters will move on to more fertile territory."

"No. Not after the Dred Scott decision. Men will still bring their slaves into Kansas and they'll still be bondsmen. Others will take exception. It won't work, Seth, this concept of slave and free. You saw Pickering and that man, Channing. Neither were prepared to give an inch. They weren't talking to one another, they were just arguing their side."

"Don't suppose after what happened either made any converts."

"Then that's too bad because no one is going to be left alone. They'll have to come out on one side or the other; join a camp. Just like in a mutiny. There is no middle ground. You're either with the captain or against him."

He went back to buttering the biscuit he had no intention of eating.

"Which side is the captain on in this debate?"

"You're the captain."

Pushing away the plate, he grasped his arm, pressed the bandage to keep it in place, then got up.

"There are crops to tend to."

"You've been up all night."

"The weeds know that, too. They'll try to take advantage."

"I'm going with you."

"Where? Out into the fields?"

"Over to check on Blind Betty and Mute Thomas."

"Who said I was going there?"

"You did."

He scratched his head, then yawned.

"Got to change my clothes, first. My Sunday coat's ruined."

"Guess that means we can't go to church any more."

He stopped, tried to determine whether she was joking, then abandoned the effort.

"You're not going."

"To services?"

"To the Windsor's."

"The hell I'm not."

"One of us has to stay here. To keep an eye on the crew. They're too little, Barbara, to be left alone. This isn't some lightning fire where they can warn us by ringing the bell. If someone comes, they won't have that chance."

"Then you think someone is coming."

He unbuttoned his coat and tossed it over the chair back.

"I'll take the deer rifle. If I fire it from Terrance's place you can hear it. Lock yourselves in. Don't try and talk to anyone. Remember: you're the one who said they won't listen." He bent over to kiss her. "I won't be long."

She wondered what he meant by "long," and if those were the last words she would ever hear him say.

"Long," in that case, would be an eternity.

Seth walked over the fields, rifle slung over his shoulder. He wondered if this was how his brother marched, flanked on either side by blue-coated soldiers. They would be stalking Indians, ridding the land of renegades. Clearing it for the homesteaders.

Odd, he mused, how their world revolved around color. Black slaves. Red Indians. White colonists. And how those hues overshadowed the green of the land and the blue of the ocean.

He did not often think of Norman; had not seen his younger brother in a dog's age. In many ways, Norman had always been a stranger. Less so than their older brother Rick, who dwarfed them both in years, but still an outsider to his world of plowing and raising crops. Norman had never been attracted to the land; his had been wandering feet. Even so, when Seth had received the letter stating that Norman had joined the army, he had been surprised. Guns and horses had never been their way of life.

Norman as a dragoon, a dismounted cavalryman. Norman, the tow-headed, sassy, barefoot boy of memory, dressed in a uniform, saluting his superiors and taking orders. Giving them, too, perhaps. Seth had never thought of him as an officer, but there was no saying he had not achieved some rank. He tried to remember how it went. Private. Sergeant. Corporal. Something like that.

Norman, out west. Names of states and territories only dimly visualized, crowded his mind. Texas. The Cimarron. Colorado. Utah. What were they like? Were they worth dying for? Or in? For all he knew, Norman might be buried along some nameless trail, an arrow piercing his heart. Or convalescing in a hospital, with a broken leg from falling off a horse. If that were the case, would he write? Just to tell his brother how he was getting on? Perhaps he would show up at the doorstep one day with a wooden leg. Peter would like that.

Seth shook his head. Norman would make a poor pirate.

Perhaps he had married. Left the service. Started a family. The fact he might have nieces and nephews evoked no tender feelings. Seth knew no more of Norman Ward than he did of Terrance Windsor. Less, in fact. The only detail they shared was that both men had entered and left his life with a feeling of unease.

In their own ways, each had been a failure. They had let circumstances dictate their actions. When life took an unexpected turn, they bolted. He supposed the army was a better occupation than a worker in a hide tanning factory, but neither presented what he held to be an honorable profession. One involved killing, the other hopelessness.

He would not change places with either one. He doubted Norman would trade places with him. As for his friend Terrance, he did not know why he had suddenly thought of him and wished he had not. Let sleeping memories lie.

He wished Nelander had not gone after Beth. He had said no good would come of it and he had been right.

Damn the Pirate's Creed.

A blasphemy which made him cold inside.

They had sworn an oath on Blind Betty and Mute Thomas, as well. To his way of thinking, too much avowal. It got a man in trouble.

Even if he were always the kind to take a side.

And damn Dr. McTree while he was at it. Being wrong about politics. Nelander would not forget that one. He had heard it twice, already. He would hear it again.

He did not want to go to the Windsor place. Not alone. He wished she had come.

And damned himself for his weakness.

The odor of smoke hung heavily in the air. He had not lied to her when he said he had not smelled smoke; that he presumed the stench to have come up from hell. That had been true, enough. But he smelled it now, and it turned his stomach. Wood burning. And something else. Blood.

A farmer knew the scent of blood. Not as well as he recognized the warm, turned earth or the bouquet of growing plants, but he recognized it. Blood from a chicken meant for Sunday supper. Blood from the birthing of a calf or a foal. Or a baby. Blood on the coat of a dog, come in from the fields after it had been out chasing coons or squirrels. Blood on the breath of a mouser. Blood from the cuts of a child, stumbling over a rock; blood on the fingers of a wound gotten while sharpening a blade.

Smoke and blood. Blood and smoke. A combination boding ill in any order.

Despite misgivings, Seth sprinted the last hundred yards toward the clearing, coming to a halt only after being confronted by telltale signs of warning. Innumerable hoof prints marred the otherwise smooth road leading toward the house. Stopping too suddenly, forward motion nearly caused him to trip. He fought to regain balance, then slipped into the brush growing in profusion along the rim of the yard.

Although not a tracker by profession or inclination, he easily identified six different prints, marked by distinct patterns of wear in the iron horse shoes. Six. One deaf man and one blind woman would have no chance against six men riding horses.

A farmer with a deer rifle would not increase their chances.

*Go back!* his mind screamed. *Get out of here and go home. Once they finished with Betty and Thomas they will head for my place.*

*My home.*

Hatred welled in his breast. Hatred for blind prejudice. Hatred for those who would make their own laws. Hatred for the Windsors who had abandoned their farm and left it for him to buy.

Disgust at himself for ever having gotten involved.

Regret at his cowardice. Although he had taken the gun, he had never meant to shoot anyone. He did not know if he could.

*Steady. Steady. Get a hold of yourself.*

He counted, although not in the orthodox fashion.

*One. Two. Five. Ten.*

A little boy who had not quite learned his lesson and hurried through the numbers, hoping speed would cover his mistakes.

Dropping to one knee, Seth forced himself to inspect the tracks. New but not fresh. Hours old.

His nose twitched and he felt like sneezing. Stifling the urge, he crept forward, watching where he placed his feet so as not to break a twig or snap a branch.

Quietly. On tiptoe. To the edge of the yard. Squatting low, peering out. No one there. No horses.

No puppy, either. No signs of life.

Straightening, for he did not believe the assassins -- if assassins they were -- were lying in wait, for the tracks had gone both ways, he stepped into the courtyard.

"Hello? Miz Betty? Thomas?"

*Mizzenmast?*

No answer. Hurrying, now, with dread filling out his sails, he jumped the porch, kicked open the door.

Rude, hand-hewn furniture, unmolested. Several rag rugs on the floor. More reed baskets than he could count, in every imaginable shape and size, serving as everything from sewing basket to herb jar to cat bed. Baked clay dishes sat on the table. A pot and frying pan hung from leather strips threaded through holes in the handles.

He debated whether to check the back rooms when a plaintive meow from that direction caught his attention. Chatte ambled out, tail straight up, like a flag pole. She rubbed against his legs, weaving between them. Another meow.

Spoken in the universal language of all four-legged beasts.

*I am hungry. Feed me.*

Less of a plea than a demand. Dropping a hand, he scratched the feline behind the ears, then crossed into the kitchen, reasoning that if atrocities had been perpetrated in the back, Chatte would not behave so casually. The odor of smoke and blood was stronger there but he saw nothing to explain it. Through the window he could observe the side yard. A hut had been constructed. One he had not seen before. The smell came from there.

Moving out the back he warily approached, cat at his heels. She seemed just as interested as he, but perhaps for different reasons. Sweat dripped from beneath his hat band.

He did not wish to pry. Not of the living.

"Miz Betty? Thomas? It is Captain Ward."

The farmer with the exulted rank. Your landlord. Employer. Neighbor.

Friend.

Fellow pirate.

*I mean you no harm.*

*I am not one of them.*

*Not a man on a horse with hatred in his eyes.*

*At least, not with hatred against you.*

The door to the hut had no latch. He pried it open with the barrel of the gun, for some reason not wanting to touch it with his hand. Inside, a fire smoldered. The smell nearly overwhelmed him. There were no windows.

They had made a smoke house.

He almost laughed.

But not quite.

Strips of meat were suspended over the smoke. Left to dry. He could not guess what it was and did not try.

Backing out, he shut the door, then reassessed the scene. A glance at the sky gave him the hour: ten o'clock. The tracks were hours old. That set the time. Seven or eight o'clock when the riders had arrived. Miss Betty and Thomas had likely left for the day; gone to the valley to weed or water or just to oversee.

Bad choice of words.

To inspect. To protect. To nurture.

He returned to the yard. One set of boot prints. Finding no one at the house, only one rider had dismounted. He had gone inside, looked around but disturbed nothing. Why not? Likely, he had inspected the hut, seen what Seth saw. Drew his own conclusions. What had they been? Getting back in the saddle, the group had ridden off.

Where?

Captain Ward had not passed them on his way. They had not gone to the *Pirate* Treasure. Not across the fields. If that had been their destination, there would have been no point taking the road. That would have put them half a mile out of their way.

Who came ten miles out of town to look at a deserted property? A farm they rightly believed to be deserted.

Seth Ward had no answers.

He would have to dig some.

Not nearly as much fun as looking for buried gold.

# CHAPTER 29

Walking quickly at a pace his brother Norman, the dragoon, would have called "quick step," Seth Ward, the farmer, crossed the field in the opposite direction from his home. Already, in the few months Blind Betty and Mute Thomas had lived at the Windsor place, they had begun to wear a trail toward the valley. Bent grasses, patches of dirt showed through. Once out, once back, two pair of feet treading the ground every day, including Sunday.

A bit of white caught his eye and he retrieved a stick, gnawed at the ends. It caused him to revise his totals upward.

Two Negroes and one puppy; an animal they were, by law, not allowed to own.

For fear it might be trained vicious and set upon the white masters.

They must have their security.

He thought of Channing, the plantation owner from South Carolina. He would have been the first to agree. Perhaps his father had helped pass a local resolution.

No men of color permitted to keep a dog.

Not even for companionship. What brown-skinned man needed companionship when he had a woman he could not legally marry for a concubine and children who might be sold to the cane fields of New Orleans or the cotton fields of Georgia at the snap of a finger?

What was it Reverend Pickering said when mouthing the defenses of slave holders?

*Slave children grow rapidly to adulthood. By the age of twelve, boys are fully mature.*

Words from Mr. Channing's bible.

Seth wondered if he knew better, now.

Or if he ever would.

Trotting, at times breaking into a run, he traveled fast, arriving at Strawberry Field before the sun had reached its zenith. He saw them there, the old woman and the tall, quiet man and the puppy.

Alive.

He would not have ascribed "and well" to the sentence.

"Hello!"

They looked up and waved. A friendly, joyous salutation. Mizzenmast wagged his tail.

Hurrying through the valley's flat mouth, Seth came upon them as they worked their way down the slopes to meet him.

"Mornin' Capt'n Ward."

"Good morning, ma'am." She sensed something had happened and waited to be told. No point wasting words. "I've been by your place. There's been visitors. Did you see them?"

An odd choice of words. Not the "see" to a blind lady but "visitors" to a black mother and son.

"No, suh."

"They didn't come out here?"

"Been no one here, suh."

"I... wondered."

She understood he meant, *I just wanted to be sure.*

Betty turned away, pointing to the rows of plants.

"Dey cumin' fine, Capt'n. All full a leafs an' healthy. Dey make plenty berries next spring."

No sense belaboring a point. She wished to make his trip worthwhile.

"I see that. Amazing."

"Dat da Lor's plan. He make da green t'ings grow. 'Tis a beautiful sight."

"Yes, ma'am. But the Lord had help. You have a green thumb."

A common expression. She smiled.

"Ah got a black thumb, Mista Ward." He understood the distinction. "Yuh an' da Nelander got white ones. Yuhr strawberries grow, too. Da plants, dey know when dey's lobed. An' tended to by good folk."

*We all right, suh. Don't go worryin' 'bout us. Whatever happens is fo' da best.*

He did not have her faith.

"You come and spend the night with us."

"Dat mos' kind. But we got meat smokin'. Don' wanna leabe it. Dat cat." She dismissed his fear with a gentle sway at an invisible feline. "She git in dere, no tellin' what she'll do. Cats," she declared with good humor, "are good eaters. An' smoked meat is better'n a mouse."

The reassurance did not prevent him from trying again.

"Mizzenmast, here, might like to see his litter mate. Dardanelles has been pinin' after her brother. And Herman -- he always likes company."

"He a good dog."

"And the crew. They're always on the lookout for sympathetic ears. They'll talk you to -- sleep -- with their stories about pirates."

"Dat be a fine thing, Capt'n." Placing her hands at the folds of her skirt, Blind Betty made a sort of curtsy. "Yuh gibe dem all mah lobe an' tell dem dat sumday soon meh an' Thomas'll see dem ag'in. An' we be mo' 'en glad to hear all da stories about dem pirates."

Picking on the short hairs around his jaw bone, Seth eyed her with quiet admiration.

"You have heard. Of what happened in town. How?"

She raised a hand, stopped too suddenly, then adeptly pretended to be fixing a loose strand of hair. She was good at hiding her reaction. He supposed she had much practice.

"Ah knows mos' ob what goes on 'round here, Capt'n Ward."

"Someone came?"

Once again Betty started to deny by obfuscation, then ultimately thought better of it.

"No, suh. No one knows weh out here. When Thomas an' Ah lef', we went on da wind." Although her lids were permanently semi-closed, he thought he detected some emotion in the dull film which covered her eyes. "Yuh might say, we didn't leabe no forwardin' address."

Seth waited, tacitly allowing her to finish the explanation. Bending down, her skilled fingers located bits of dried leaves and grass and plucked them from the hem of her ankle-length dress.

"Ah might say a little bird told meh."

"You might. And if you said it, I would believe you. But I suspect our feathered friends have better things to occupy them, then spying on my... white brothers."

"No, suh. Dose people not yuhr kin. Da Lor' judges fambilies by what's in da heart, not by da color ob no skin. Jesus, dey say," she cautiously added, "were a dark man."

"A Hebrew." And then he grinned, divining the second meaning to her statement. "A brooding man."

Pleased to see he had gotten the dual meaning, Betty nodded. "It were mah boy who tolt meh. He read on dem posters dey put up 'round town dat dere was a preacher man cumin' frum Boston. Gonna speak on slabery an' 'mancipation."

The smaller detail piqued his curiosity more than the larger.

"I had forgotten he could read. And you taught him."

"Ah did."

"And who taught you?"

"Ah knows many t'ings. An' taught many chil'ren. But dat be a long time ago, Mista Seth."

He frowned. "When times were different, mother?"

"Times neber be diff'rent. Ah learned it in a household." She enunciated the word with perfect clarity, making him believe she could speak the "white man's tongue" as well as he. He did not wonder why she chose not to. "When Ah was a slabe."

"I did not know you were ever a... slave."

"Bef'o yuh eber cume out dis way. When Thomas was a babe. But Ah got mah papers; so do he. We be as free as inny Negro in dis Land ob da Slabe."

Biting the inside of his cheek, Seth took a step back from the magnificent woman who had known such hardship in what he had been taught as the "Land of the Free."

"Was Thomas there last night?"

"He seed some ob it. Da anger. Da lootin'. Dat fire. Burned to the ground, dat meetin' hall."

"I was there. Nelander and I and Dr. McTree. Up front. We were trapped inside." He pointed to his bandaged arm. "We only just made it out."

That, he observed, was news to her. Her fingers rubbed together in anxiety.

"Yuh a'right? An Nelander an da doctor?"

"Some cuts and burns. Nothing serious. We got back this morning. I was worried about you."

"Yuh bes' be worried 'bout yerse'f. Who was dose men what cume to da house?"

"I don't know. I counted six pair of horse tracks."

"Why dey ride all da way out, jes' to cume to dat place?"

"I don't know that, either. I didn't pass them in the field. They couldn't have been looking for me."

"No one," she repeated with emphasis, "knows Thomas an' Ah libin' out dis way." The creases in her lined face deepened. "But dey will, now."

"You said they didn't come to the field."

Planting her feet firmly in the earth, Blind Betty made her stand.

"Captain Ward, suh, what yuh t'ink when yuh went in? Yuh t'ink a white fambly libed dere?"

"What do you mean?" He flushed, almost before the words died on his lips. Woven baskets; clay cups and plates. A smoke house. Not the way a white family would set up housekeeping.

"Yuh bes' go home now, suh."

"I'm worried about you. Both of you."

"Da Lor' watch out fo' us."

"Yes.... I have heard that, before. No doubt Reverend Pickering thought the same thing. Even Mr. Channing," he added with contempt. "It is peculiar among men that we all believe God has a special interest in our personal safety. But I have never found such to be the case. While He may be all powerful, it seems He takes little interest in the day-to-day affairs of His children."

"Yuh been hurt, Capt'n. Men been cruel to yuh an' yuhrs. But da Lor' knows bes'."

"I have heard that, too. I cannot say I am a firm believer. Come back with me. For the next few days; a week. Until tempers die down."

"Ah am not afraid."

"I am afraid for you." He faltered, kneading his hands. "Nelander says you are part of our family; the Family of Pirate," he explained. "And pirates have a creed. They stand up for one another."

"Ah be mos' proud to be a pirate, suh. Yuh tell Nelander dat. An' da chil'run. Dey fine young'uns. Dey got yuhr mark on dem. But Thomas an' Ah stay out here. We hear trouble cumin', suh, we git out. Hide in da woods."

"They may bring dogs."

"Ah knows about dogs."

"And guns,"

"Ah know 'bout guns, too."

"You cannot run from bullets."

Moving away from him, Blind Betty threw back her head.

"Captain Ward, yuh gabe us sumthin' precious. A house an' land. A garden. An' a purpose, suh. Des strawberries. Dey mah new chil'run; da chil'run ob mah old age. Ah done runnin."

"What about Thomas?"

"He done runnin', too."

"Then I have done you an ill."

"No, suh. Yuh done fo' meh da Lor's work. Yuh gibe meh dignity."

"Rather alive then --"

Her foot stomped, making an indentation in the earth.

"No, suh! Now, Ah said all Ah'm gonna say. Yuh git yuhrse'f home an' don' be worryin' about us."

"I could pick you up and put you over my back and carry you home."

A light finally lit her countenance.

"No, suh. Yuh could not do dat."

He shrugged and grinned. It took an effort, as though the muscles in his face had hardened and he had not smiled in a long time. Out of practice.

"All right. But I reserve the right to... check on the strawberries from time to time."

"Ah 'spect yuh to do dat, suh."

Two strides positioned himself in front of her. Stooping low, Seth kissed her wrinkled cheek.

"You are a pirate of the first order, mother."

"An' yuh a captain, son. May da Lor' bless yuh an' keep an eye on dat hard heart ob yuhrs. Fo' it ain't no hard heart a'tall but da heart ob a true man." She waved him away. "Git out, yuh hear, boy?"

"Yes, ma'am. I hear."

He removed his hat and bowed before waving at Thomas, who had kept his distance.

"Remember: the crew are expecting you. One of these nights. I'll tell them you're coming."

"Dat be good, suh," she answered for him. "Real good."

Seth Ward trudged away, wondering at his light heart.

And thinking himself a fool.


They came three days later, announced by the thunder of hoof beats and the barking of two dogs, Herman and Dardanelles. They came in the night, under cover of darkness, wearing hoods over their heads to hide their identities.

They bore torches, lighting the way.

"Put the dogs up," Seth warned, shielding Nelander with his arm. "Take the children and go in the back room."

In the flickering of the kerosene lamp, she saw the wanness of his face and did as ordered.

"Patricia: get the dogs. Take them with you."

Patricia grabbed Herman by the scruff of his neck and dragged him after her while Nelander took Peter by the hand. The puppy followed, not in play at this new game, but with ears bent down, ruff stiffened, teeth bared. It was a time when youth lost its innocence.

Bringing the crew into her bedroom, Barbara checked the baby, debated taking her along, then changed her mind and wrapped the infant in a blanket, arms and legs covered. Only the little head remained visible, turfs of newly grown hair sticking out at all angles. The blue eyes peered at her in sleepy contemplation.

Turning away with a reluctance which tore her insides, she put a hand on each of the other two children's shoulders.

"Be very quiet. Do not make a sound. Stay here unless papa or I tell you otherwise. Do not, on any account, come out on your own."

"Who's there?" Patricia demanded, lower lip protruding in a display of childlike bravery. "What do they want?"

"We shall soon find out." Moving quickly to the door, her hand rested on the knob when the girl spoke again.

"Captain Papa said for you to stay here."

"My place is beside him."

Nelander stepped out and shut the door, for the first time regretting there was no lock. Treading softly, she made her way back to the living room. Seth stood by the entranceway. Their eyes met and he minutely jerked his head. Not as an order to leave.

*Get the gun.*

She took it down from the wall and checked to see whether it had been reloaded. She had learned much in her brief sojourn in Kansas.

Hearing the riders pull up outside, Seth stepped under the archway and confronted them. She lingered in the shadows. Dragoon Norman Ward would have called that "military tactics."

Instead of open confrontation as perhaps they all expected, Seth shaded his eyes from the glare of the burning incendiaries and nodded pleasantly as if they were strangers lost their way.

"Good evening."

The salutation confounded the group and they looked toward the man in front to address the situation.

"It bein' a good evenin' or a bad one depends on you, Ward," the leader announced. He tried to disguise his voice, speaking in a gruff, gravely tone.

"I will oblige you if I can. What brings you out this way?"

A second momentary indecision.

"There's some in town say you're a nigger-lover."

"Who says?"

A second man spoke. Nudging his mount forward, he drew abreast of the first.

"You were seen at the meeting."

"Along with two hundred and fifty others. And more besides. Watching from the wings."

"Why were you there?"

"To hear a man of God speak on the troubles which plague this nation."

"Yer a free-soiler."

"That I am."

"A nigger lover."

"I am a married man. I love my wife. I love my children. I love my country. I love my God."

"The Bible approves of slavery, Ward."

"Christ mentions a pre-existing condition, adjoining all of us to look to our master who is in heaven. That is hardly an approval."

"There are those of us who want to bring the state in slave. How you gonna vote?"

"You will not alter the outcome by burning me out."

"I asked you a question."

Seth balanced his feet with precipitous care.

"For slavery, to be sure."

The second man hurtled a fist in the air.

"Liar!"

One word against Seth's five.

The loud accusation startled the accuser's mount. Ears flattened, it reared, lashing out its two back legs. The rider struggled for control and would not have succeeded but for the intervention of his companions. Moving to either side, they grabbed his arms, stabilizing his position while a third took the reins. In their moment of anxiety, Nelander could have shot them with impunity.

Great the temptation.

Her finger remained on the trigger as her insides churned. Things were not as they seemed, but she had no justification for the appraisal.

Realigning himself on the skitterish horse, the odd-man-out, for so she judged him to be, adeptly assumed control. While prior effort suggested otherwise, he was an adept horseman. The difficulty came not from a lack of skill but stemmed from an unfamiliarity with the animal.

More carefully modulating his voice, for the interloper had adroitly divined the new rules of the game, he addressed the farmer.

"You've renting out your property to Negroes. Hardly the actions of someone who supports slavery."

"You speak an untruth, sir."

"We have been to the house -- that other you own. It was occupied by a black family."

"Hired by me as servants. I would not have them live here and so ordered them to stay there."

"That must have been quite a sacrifice for your 'servants.'" He turned the others. "I told you." The confirmation rekindled the smoldering tempers of the rest. One in the rear spoke, words muffled by the hood but clear enough.

"What right do you have hiring freedmen when there's plenty of whites in town beggin' fer work?"

"What business is it of yours to ask?"

"Some of them is my friends; good men who lost their land to the damn bank. Men, lookin' to make a new start. There's plenty of others who'd hire themselves out for seed money."

Seth rocked on his heels.

"But there you have it."

"Have what?" he sneered.

"Money. I have no money to pay for -- white -- help. I cannot afford wages. What I can do is trade a house and a garden for labor. Would any of your white friends accept such an agreement? I think not."

"You've got money."

"What makes you think so?"

The leader spoke. "You got it from your wife. As a dowry."

Despite himself, Ward snorted. "A dowry? Damned sure not. It was hers and she spent it the way she wanted."

"That's a coward's answer."

"Spoken by men wearin' masks?" From inside, a dog barked, followed by the higher pitch of a puppy. One of the torches carried by the riders began to smoke, then fizzled out. He threw it away in disgust. Seth spat on the ground. "You need not have bothered, for I recognize your horses. Or do you think I am blind enough not to have noticed, Matthew?"

McConaghie swore and slapped a hand to his side. Seth peered past him. "The other three are your boys. That dapple you're ridin' Douglas is known throughout the county. An' yours, Bill -- I may not be a blacksmith but your buckskin throws out its hind foot when it walks. That built-up shoe leaves a distinctive print; one Sheriff Bochner'd identify in a flash.

"And you, Dick. That pretty mare of yours has the smallest hooves I ever did see. I shoulda picked that up at the Windsor place but I wasn't lookin' that close." He squinted at the last of the riders but had no name to pin on him. Shrugging in casual dismissal, he stepped off the porch.

"You got a beef with me, fight fair. Get down off them horses, any one of you, and put up your fists. Don't come here in the middle of the night all riled up over who I've got working out at the Windsor place. You wanta talk about Negroes, I'll listen. But not like this."

Matthew rose in the stirrups, one hand resting alongside the horse's neck.

"Come on, then, Captain Ward."

The sarcasm broke whatever restraint Seth may have had and with a shriek of fury, he charged the elder of the clan. Fingers searing through vest material, the attacker pulled downward, drawing McConaghie toward him. One foot caught in the saddle iron, and as he struggled to extricate himself, Seth landed a punch to the face. Howling in rage, both boot and body came free, propelled outward by a force greater than the sum of their parts.

Both men fell to the ground, arms tangled. Without bothering to choreograph their blows, they flailed at one another, knees into groins, elbows into eyes. McConaghie held a twenty pound advantage but Seth had agility on his side. Squirming out from beneath the behemoth, he chopped at the back of his neck, then slipped an arm under the chin, locking him in a strangle hold.

Choking for air, Matthew grabbed behind himself, finding a fistful of hair. Tugging for all he was worth, he managed to break the vice-like grip and they rolled a second time, fists pounding into one another's midriffs.

They tussled, head-to-head, at once grabbing the other's shirt with one hand and striking with the other. Noses exploded, cascading red spray across the darkened yard. One boot stomped another; fingers gouged.

Seth fell, got up, swung a blow. Matthew ducked, lashed out a foot. Seth caught it, tugged and dragged him down. Arms raised in madness, the farmer dove into his adversary, thrashing at face, chest, torso. Douglas flew off the saddle, tore at Seth's vest, pulling him up. Furious, the farmer firmed his back, grabbed the youth, then hurtled him over his shoulder.

Douglas landed hard, screeching as the crack of bone bore witness to dire injury.

"You, too!" Ward bellowed, beckoning the other two McConaghies. "I'll take you all on, you sons of bitches. You condemn a little boy you don't even know, then you come out here with faggots to burn my house. You're not men but sidewinders. Nothin' but dirty, rotten snakes. Come outta the grass and face me! I've been spoilin' to take you on for years!"

Dick McConaghie shifted and Seth charged him, hitting man and horse before they knew what happened. Seth bounced off and fell as Dick slid off the rear. Fists up, he charged, delivering a vicious blow to Seth's burned arm. He swore and fell to one knee, ears ringing from shooting pain. Half crazed, he took a kick to the jaw and collapsed, blinded by a swirling dizziness.

Erratically swatting away the irregular splotches of light which burst behind his lids, he curled into a ball. Mistaking the gesture, Dick reached down to deliver one final blow. Catching him by surprise, Seth sunk teeth into flesh and bore down with all his might. The man screamed and drew away in panic.

Bill, the last of the McConaghies, might have taken the opportunity to join his father and brothers, but a tone of authority cut him short.

"Stay where you are."

Nelander stepped out from behind the door, pointing the rifle at his head. The youth's hands went up.

"Don't shoot."

Had she been in a different mood, she might have laughed.

Grasping the trunk of the swing tree, Seth used it to haul himself up. Shaken, bloodied and battered, he worked his jaw to feel whether it had broken, then prodded Matthew with his foot.

"Get up."

The man did so without help and limped to his horse. Bill handed him the reins but he made no attempt to mount. Douglas and Dick joined him, making cursory efforts to assess their personal damage.

Joining Nelander at the porch, Captain Ward pushed in a loose tooth, then spat. The effort temporarily cleared his head and he wagged a fist at the group.

"I can't say this evens the score, Matthew, 'cause I've owed you one since Belinda died. Don't know why you made it your business to interfere then, and I don't know now. But I've a mind this other hooded raider saw some profit in it for himself. What's your name, mister, and what's your game?"

The man's eyes seemed to glow through the slits in his mask but he said nothing. Seth turned to McConaghie.

"There's always been bad blood between us, Matthew, but I spoke for you when Bochner had you locked up. That was a bad thing you did, trying to steal water from the well. Maybe me and the others shoulda let him hang you. But I reckoned I understood. What I can't figure is you joining forces with some damned outsider."

Barbara touched him lightly on the arm.

"Damned, he is. But an outsider? Only in a manner of speaking. Say, rather, a man from out of town."

Still panting heavily, Seth cradled his injured arm to his chest.

"You know who he is?"

"I know who he *was.*" The emphasis on past tense raised the stakes.

Seth frowned in astonishment.

"Who?"

Bile bubbled over her lips.

"A coward." Leveling the weapon, she pointed the muzzle at the horseman. "Give me an excuse."

Neglecting to mention that seamen held landlubbers conception of fair play in disdain, Barbara Nelander depressed the trigger. Orange flame spat from the barrel. A boom of thunder ascended upward.

In their upside-down world, no one thought to question the contradiction.

## CHAPTER 30

Clutching his chest, the man "from out of town" plummeted to earth, falling awkwardly. He howled, moaned, then remained still.

"Jesus Christ, Seth, she shot him!" Matthew swore. Nelander spoke for he who had been addressed.

"Is that any more evil than what you planned to do here? Burn us out? An unarmed man, a woman and three children?"

"We wasn't gonna...." He did not finish for shame. Out of fear for his life, one of the boys pointed to the ground.

"It was his idea. To make you run off them niggers. We didn't even know they was out there. He come to us. He was the one talkin' up that you shoulda hired white men."

Seth shook a fist at those still mounted.

"You McConaghies are no friends of mine but I thought better of you than this. Damn bastards," he spat. "And I almost bought a dog from you." Out of the corner of his mouth, he asked of the man writhing on the ground, "Who the hell is he?"

The only one to remain calm, First Officer Nelander fielded the question.

"Someone who owes me money."

"Owes you money?"

"That's right. Get up," she ordered, narrowing her eyes. "I missed you by a good foot."

Stifling a cry, the man got unsteadily to his feet. Hand to his chest, he probed for a fatal wound. Discovering none, his shoulders sagged. She had no pity.

"Where's my money, Terrance? That which I left for Beth to use. So she could take a coach and be here when my baby was born. What'd you spend it on?"

Seth wretched, dropping his injured arm as he staggered back.

"Terrance? No."

"Terrance, yes. Mr. Terrance Windsor. Take off that damned hood."

Raising a hand, the former pirate grasped the loose material and pulled it over his head. A strand of hair stood up on end. Seth took a step forward, then reeled back.

"You son of a bitch."

Faced with the incontrovertible truth, Terrance Windsor held out a hand. No one made a move to take it. Tears welled in his eyes.

"It's not what you're thinking. I didn't want it like this."

"The hell, you say."

Terrance pointed at Barbara. "I used the money to buy a horse. We snuck outta Snow Bluff like dogs. I owed money." Still no reaction. "We had'a eat. I worked. You saw how hard I worked, Nelander --"

"Officer Nelander," came the terse correction. "To you.... scurvy dog."

She liked the analogy and smiled. It reminded the onlookers of a skull, devoid of human emotion.

"Beth wanted to come back... to be with you. She promised and I meant for her to keep her promise."

"Your timing was a little off. That was months ago; March 4th, to be exact."

"It took time. The wagon kept breaking down." He sniffed and wiped his nose with the back of his hand. "She lost hope. But all the while I kept sayin', 'We're goin' home. Back to the farm. Seth and... Officer Nelander bought it for us. It's there, waitin'. Maybe I was wrong. Maybe the land will forgive me."

"You-weren't-wrong."

His voice rose in desperation. "Don't you see? I was desperate. It hadn't worked out; none of it. That place... that tannin' factory done somethin' to me. Broke me down. I had'a get away. Come home. You said.... You said we could have the farm back."

"And you knew we couldn't wait forever."

"It wasn't forever -- months. Six months. It took me that long to get my head together. We arrived last week. Meant to come here, first, but I wanted to see it... my place. Just have a look. I never thought there'd be... anyone livin' there."

"You knew we couldn't afford to leave it empty."

"Just like I knew no one'd buy it. Not with times bein' what they are. No one has any money. You said it was mine for the askin'."

"Not for the asking. I never said that. I said you'd have to pay it off."

"And I meant to. Swear to God, I did. Put in a crop, harvest what I could. Get caught up. I got the boys to help me...." His strength seemed to fail and he slouched. "When I saw the smoke comin' out the chimney, I went ahead. On foot. Never figured to find blacks there."

"What difference does that make?"

There was no point asking the question. She only made the effort for Blind Betty and Thomas. So they would all be sure.

"You gave them *my* chance. That farm was my hope, my dreams.... My salvation. I've thought of nothing else since we started back." His hands trembled. "I'm a fair man, Nelander. I've never looked for trouble. Never was one who held that Niggertown ought to be torn down and the Negroes chased off. Live and let live. But let them stay with their own kind."

Misreading the flintiness in her eyes, he hurried on. "I'll give them a patch of land for a garden if that's what you want. They can even live on my property; build a shack so they can be nearer your place. But for God's sake, they're not like us! They don't appreciate what you've given them. They're lazy; they'll squander the land. Nothing will grow there. And before you know it, they'll invite their kind out. They're like rats. Once they get in somewhere, they overrun it. Pretty soon, they'll be everywhere."

Seaman Barbara Nelander knew a rehearsed speech when she heard one. She had no doubt those were the exact arguments Terrance Windsor had used with Matthew McConaghie and his boys. It not only appealed to baser instincts, it called to action a defense of racial superiority. The same tried and true prejudice she had heard spoken of Dutchy, the only man brave and loyal enough to have brought her word of Ned Nelander's death.

Her acute disappointment was tempered by grim reality.

"I won't stand here and argue with you, Mr. Windsor. Bitterness and failure has clouded your judgment. Working like a 'slave' in the tanning factory has given you no insight into the plight of others. You see nothing but your own needs and defend them the only way you can: by tearing others down. Innocent folk, who have done nothing to you but display a greater faith in themselves. So be it. I hereby revoke your status as pirate. You are cashiered, sir, from the service."

Moving into the yard, she waved the rifle across the arc of the horizon.

"I made a mistake in judgment and for that I apologize. You have disappointed me beyond measure. Henceforth, you are no friend of this crew." Crossing to the flagpole, she wrapped her fingers around the pole.

"We fly the Jolly Roger: a white skull and crossbones across a field of black. There is a second flag known to soar above the masts of pirate ships. It is easily recognizable though it has no image, yet is far more terrifying. It is known throughout the Seven Seas as the Black Flag. It conveys only one meaning. Death to all who cross its path. No quarter; no mercy. Take care, Terrance Windsor, for its message is meant for you."

Turning to Seth, she saluted. "Captain Ward, I respectfully request that you dismiss these cretins forthwith."

"I am honored to do so, Officer Nelander."

Moving to McConaghie's horse, he put a hand on the animal's muzzle.

"You heard the order and the warning. Go away and do not come back. Leave my property alone. Leave my children alone. Leave my people alone."

Matthew shifted in the saddle, debating whether to make a stand. As his mouth drew in a tight line, another factor was thrown into the equation.

"Git out!"

Slipping through the door, two little people, dressed in full pirate regalia, made their appearance. Between them they carried a square of dark material, roughly cut in the shape of a flag.

"Git out and don't never come back."

Peter stiffened his shoulders and rested his free hand on the hilt of his cutlass.

"Mebbe I ain't got a gun to shoot you, Mr. McConaghie, but I got something better'n that. I got bewitchment. Remember me, sir? I'm the boy who speaks to ghosts. And you know what they tolt me?"

The white's of the adult's eyes expanded as he mutely shook his head.

"No. What they tolt you?"

"That the ghost of my mama an' all the other ghosts of this land -- the Red Injuns an' the black men what have been hanged -- they're hoppin' mad. They don't like you. They don't want you here. They all joined up an' I recruited 'em to our pirate ship. They're protectin' this place. Cain't you feel 'em?"

Matthew squirmed. All of a sudden, invisible fingers probed his arms and legs; black ants crawled up his trousers. The whisper of wind became the moaning of disinterred souls. He cocked an ear. Even a white man could identify the veiled warnings of the undead.

"Make 'em go 'way," he pleaded. Behind him, his sons began scratching, fidgeting.

"Pa, I can hear 'em."

"One of 'em's got my hand!"

"Pa, let's git outta here!"

The diminutive guardians were not through. Patricia took the flag and waved it.

"This ain't just the pirate flag; it's the black flag of all the spirits round about. They don't like you, Mr. McConaghie. And they hate you, Mr. Windsor. You're a mutineer. If this land speaks to you again, it'll be to cuss you. You ain't welcome no more. Go away an' don't come back or the dead'll git you. This here is your last warning."

Terrance crossed himself in dread. Patricia mocked him by making a large cross in the air.

"The point you're missin' is that these spirits -- all these ghosts hereabouts -- is on the side of God. They're workin' for the little children -- the ones Jesus loved. He seen to it you left an' we stayed. Just so the captain an' Nelander could do His work. That," she avowed with utter sincerity, "is what this is all about. Bringin' in the sheep an' gettin' rid of the wolves."

"Pa, one's bitin' me!"

The horses shifted, impatient to be gone. They, too, felt the ghostly apparitions. Ears flattened, one reared. McConaghie put a hand to his hat, holding it down from a whistling wind which came down from the north.

"A'right. A'right, I take yer message. We're leavin'. Jes' let us leave," he pleaded. Sweat rolled down his cheeks. The tickling sensation increased his frenzy.

Hardly daring to move, he kicked the horse, backing it away with an awkward, disjointed action.

"Keep 'em away."

Peter scoffed. "Oh, they're workin' fer us, but they got a will of their own. Once they git riled, there's no tellin' what they'll do." He peered forward, staring at the enemy. "One tolt me jest the other day how he likes to reach out an' grab bad men. Draw 'em down into the grave. Jest so's he can have company." He clicked his tongue. "It's a terrible sight, seein' a grown man go under."

Douglas screamed and began beating off those invisible fingers.

"They got me, pa! They're pullin' me down. I don't wanna die."

The four McConaghies joined together, putting distance between themselves and the Wards. Ashen faced, Matthew looked over his shoulder at Seth.

"I reckon this means you ain't gonna buy no dog from me."

As an epitaph, he wrote himself a poor one.

"'spect not."

With a baleful grimace, he raised his hat.

"Tell that boy not to put no bewitchment on me. We're leavin'."

Seth shrugged. "I do not have the power."

Bill screamed. No one bothered to inquire whether he cried from the avowal or from a particularly cold hand wrapped around his throat. Bent low to make themselves smaller targets, the four departed, leaving in their stead a dust cloud swirling with the ghosts of the dead.

Terrance grasped the reins tighter, badly shaken. Afraid to stay and more afraid to leave, his mouth worked in silent plea. Nelander concluded his obsequies.

"Tell Beth I had a daughter. Her name is Paula. She thanks God her mother and father did not give her godparents such as you."

He cried and rode away, one solitary figure, pursued by devils of his own making.

They returned to the house, the captain, first officer and able-bodied crew. Sinking into a chair, Seth covered his head with his hands. Too restless to join him, Nelander asked to see the black flag. The crew duly handed it over.

"Where did you get this?"

"We heard what you were sayin'. We needed one in a right hurry."

Patricia picked up a pair of shears. "I cut up papa's Sunday suit. It was the only black cloth I could think of." Nelander raised an eyebrow. "I know I shouldn't have. I'll pay for it."

Papa finally looked up. He had aged a year in a matter of hours. Surprisingly, however, in the darkness of the room, the lines on his face disappeared and the color of his hair shone through jet black.

"You did exactly right." Although he did not think it possible, he worked a grin on his face. "It was ruined, anyway. Burned from the fire in town. That explains it."

"What?"

"Why all this happened. Why we went to the lecture and got caught in the fire. Just so's the crew would have my coat to use for a flag." Stretching his aching muscles, he rubbed a hand over his swollen face. "It explains why you bought strawberries and why we brought Blind Betty and Mute Thomas out here to settle on the Windsor's land. Why Belinda died and Peter got bewitched. Just so Jesus could work through the little children."

An explanation as good as any.

And better than most.

In the morning, the officers and crew of the *Pirate Treasure* went out into the woods and selected a tall, straight sapling. Making appropriate thanks for its sacrifice, they chopped it down and returned to the yard. Captain Ward dug the hole a respectable distance from the first, while Officer Nelander and Masters Patricia and Peter smoothed off the wood. Together, they affixed the new flag and raised it. A fresh breeze caught the material and fluttered the cloth.

Standing back, they appraised their work.

The Jolly Roger and the Black Flag. Symbols of pirates.

Guardians of faith.

Protected by God's helpers, who came in many shapes, sizes and transparencies.

# CHAPTER 31

A month went by and the Windsors, either separately or as a unit, made no appearance at the *Pirate Treasure*. Nor did people in town make reference to the black coat-remnant flying beside the figured white sheet, but their actions gave rise to speculation they were not uninformed. Either to the presence of the flags or the significance thereof.

Observing Nelander as she came out of the Post Office, Seth watched with pointed interest as a woman, whose path she happened to cross, made a polite curtsy.

"Good afternoon, Officer Nelander. Mighty hot day for August, ain't it?"

"It is, indeed, Mrs. Knight. Although it is not the temperature I mind so much as the lack of a breeze. At sea, one could almost always count on some movement of the wind, but on the prairie -- I believe that is what you call it -- a person can go a week without detecting a puff of moving air."

The woman nodded toward the southwest.

"Take heart, my dear. By this evening you will get your breeze. A storm is coming in."

"Do you think so?"

"Most certainly. I cannot say it will cool things off, but the rain is always welcome." Tightening the bonnet string tied in a bow under her neck, she hesitatingly inquired, "Will you and the Captain be at service this Sunday?"

Taking the less than subtle inquiry in stride, Barbara nodded.

"I think, perhaps, we shall. Is there any particular reason you ask?"

"We missed you these past weeks. And I thought you might not know.... We are having a church bazaar."

"What is that, then?"

"The ladies are getting together and bringing crafts to sell. There will be a picnic and afterward, some tables set out. Homemade goods offered for sale. Perhaps you have something you would like to sell?"

"To what end?"

Mrs. Knight appeared flustered.

"The men have their farmer's market where they sell produce and the odds and ends they make. Belt buckles and knife sheaths and the like. I suppose this is the ladies' way of earning a few dollars for themselves. My husband calls it 'egg money,' although few of us actually sell eggs."

"I have heard the expression." She did not need to add, *habitually used in a derogatory manner.*

"This year, we are donating a portion of what we make to the Negro Relief Fund. To help some of the poor families who were burned out that terrible night of the meeting."

"Then I shall certainly participate. Thank you for the information." Putting a finger to her cap in salute, Nelander passed by and joined her husband. "Most extraordinary. It appears men dare not take an open stand for freedom, but females are permitted to raise a Fund to assist our dark brethren."

"Women are the nurturers," he agreed, hefting a sack of corn meal onto the wagon. "Men often hide behind their skirts so not to be caught performing good deeds."

"And if a woman is not wearing a skirt?"

"Then, she ought to get dressed. I am sure there is a city ordinance prohibiting her from walking the streets in a state of nakedness."

Had they not been in public, she would have made him pay for that transgression.

"Where are the crew?"

"I sent them ahead to Dr. McTree's. They wanted to see Minerva. Hop in and I'll drive you there. If we're lucky, he'll have a pitcher of lemonade for us."

She obliged and they rode the short distance to the physician's dwelling. The front gate stood open and they were greeted by the sound of children's happy voices and the brisk barking of a dog.

Looping the reins over the fence, the couple went up the cobbled walk and knocked.

"Come on in!"

Only too glad to get in out of the searing rays, they ducked inside. Hank approached, smiling broadly.

"Welcome. Sit down and take a load off your feet."

They chose chairs in his living room and he promptly supplied the beverage, augmented by the cheery sound of ice tinkling in the glass. Nelander eyed it with some suspicion.

"Have you, too, been conjuring spells, Doctor? Ice? In August?"

"I heard that was more your line. But nothing so sinister, alas. I am sharing with you a portion of my weekly ration from the Tankard's Draft."

"You expect me to sip on ice gotten from a tavern?"

"On the chance you have had some experience with similar. Seamen are renowned for their thirst, I hear."

"I dare say I have been in more saloons than you, and an equal number of jail houses. Usually on a mission of mercy. 'Bailing out the drunks,' I believe is the expression." Grateful for the cold drink, she finished half a glass before remarking, "Why do you get a weekly ration?"

"If you are so good at expressions, I am surprised you have never heard, 'A bucket of ice a week keeps the doctor away.'"

"That, sir, does not rhyme."

"A bucket of ice a week keeps the doctor a'tweek," Seth tried.

"'A bucket of ice a week and the doctor does not seek,' is more like it," Hank laughed. "It seems the proprietor, Mr. Duggan suffers from gout. He could just as easily cure himself by watching his diet, but as he prefers my tonics to giving up fatty food, I make frequent calls to his 'death bed.' Rather than part with any of his not-so-hard-earned coin, he 'pays' me with ice. All things considered, it is a fair exchange."

"Inasmuch as he would not pay you any other way."

"Well, that is the pessimist's way of looking at it. But quite right for all that." Crossing his legs, he listened a moment to the crew outside playing. "How are you getting along?"

"You heard about our adventure?"

"I did, indeed. From no lesser a personage than Matthew McConaghie, himself."

"Why was that?"

"It seems he ran afoul of a legion of hobgoblins. They beat him up quite mercilessly. Over at your place, it was. He came in for stitches."

"Is that a fact?"

"Indeed. I understand he was on a mission of no good and paid for his sin. So did his boys. How did you fare?" he asked, critically observing the farmer.

"Let us say the 'ship' he came to burn survived intact." Seth drank more of his lemonade, then helped himself to the pitcher. "Did he also happen to tell you who he had with him to aid and abet his nefarious deed?"

"As a matter of fact, he did. I should have been more surprised than I was. Went out there with hoods on, did they? At Terrance's suggestion, no doubt."

"It was a low blow."

"Yes. It was. Dirty. But a desperate man will do anything, Captain."

Nelander took up the thread.

"A desperate man will do anything but turn on his family or his friends. I hope you are not seeking forgiveness for him?"

"Wouldn't think of it."

"I am glad to hear it, for he shall receive none. Bewitchments are not evoked lightly. I'd as soon have shot him. Came damned close."

"Heard that, too. You made quite an impression."

To ease the tension, Seth asked, "Heard what became of him?"

He meant, *Heard what became of them?* and was well understood.

"The family went begging around town. Got some handouts. No one seemed to have a job for Terrance, though. Not after Matthew got through running off at the mouth."

"How is that, now?"

"Wish I could tell you. Maybe he's afraid you'll set the spooks out after him. But I did hear Matthew's letting his wife participate in the Fund the women are collecting. Almost inspires me think you've made a convert."

Seth was clearly impressed but not quite ready to swallow the story hook, line and sinker.

"He probably thinks I'm still in the market for a dog."

"Maybe you ought to be."

He shrugged. "I don't like him."

"Any old port in a storm."

"Now you're talking like Nelander."

"A compliment, if ever I heard one."

"How much damage did they do in town?"

"Aside from the Meeting Hall, not as much as they might have. The sheriff shot a looter, you know. Drilled him through the chest. That chased the mob off."

"Local man or outsider?"

McTree tapped a finger on the arm of his chair. "Man who had enough money in his pockets to liberally pay the local physician for pronouncing him dead with enough left over for a mighty nice funeral. Don't know as anyone attended, though. Five will get you ten that the 'reverend' chiseled off the silver handles on the coffin before they laid it in the ground."

Nelander and Seth exchanged looks, speaking simultaneously.

"Outsider." Nelander continued.

"What other causalities?"

"Quite a number of burns, gashes, broken bones. Some serious."

"And -?"

"Then there was Pickering and Channing, of course. Burned to a crisp, both of them. Tangled in each other's arms. Gruesome, really. Put the fear of God in the townspeople. They weren't looking for that. Not the local folk. Bochner got 'em worked up over what the outsiders had done and they chased 'em out. You didn't read the newspaper accounts? Heard Daly got his exclusives in the *Gazette* picked up by all the exchanges. There were re-printed as far away as Philadelphia, New York and Boston."

"Haven't been here since then; just picked up the back issues at Anson's."

"Kansas isn't Missouri. Maybe people will remember that now."

"It'll start up, again."

"Yes. It will."

Grim reality caused a pause in the conversation until Nelander reluctantly broke it.

"Where did the Windsors go after Terrance didn't find work?"

"I thought they mighta gone back to your place."

"They-did-not."

"And not back to... their old place?"

"You woulda read about that, too," the officer retorted with a sour note. "Given editor Daly another chance to get his byline in the out-of-town rags."

"Can't say I know, then. Haven't seen 'em about." He paused, trying to appear pleasant. "I did hear Beth was all broken up about what happened."

"Good for her."

"No forgiveness?"

Instead of replying, Nelander got up, signaling an end to the conversation. Putting two fingers to her lips, she whistled for the crew. After a moment, they came tumbling in from the back.

"Time to go."

"Minerva's all right, Nelander. No one came after her that night," Peter stated, puffing out his chest. "I told Dr. McTree all about how brave she was."

"He did, and that's for sure. Made me mighty proud."

"She's a good dog. Speaks well for her pups," Seth agreed.

"Blind Betty and Mute Thomas getting along all right?" He nodded. "How's Mizzenmast?"

"Growing like a weed and happy as a clam," Nelander supplied, mixing her metaphors. Holding out a hand, she concluded, "Glad to see you're all right, Hank. Seth and I need a friendly 'port' in the storm."

"That makes all of us." He shook, reluctantly seeing them to the door. "Take care, won't you?"

"It's a date."

"See you Sunday," Seth concluded. "At the Relief Fund. You gonna donate bandages or some such?"

"Might just do that."

The family piled into the wagon and the captain directed Blaze to "Take us home." The horse gladly obliged and they reached midpoint between house and barn at four bells, previously known as "milking," and alternately as "chore time." Directing traffic, he saw to the unhitching while Barbara watched.

"I suppose we'll have to contribute something." Seth grunted in approval. "Can't think of what."

"That shawl you're knitting ought to be fine."

"I'll give that if you hand over that fine chest of drawers you've been working on."

Grinning at her tit-for-tat, he picked up a brush and began currying the animal as Patricia came around with a pail of milk. Overhearing the silly banter, she joined in.

"That bein' the case, I guess I can churn some butter and Peter can break out that old cheese mold."

Which formally ended the discussion on what they would not contribute to the effort, for Nelander did not knit, papa had no woodworking project and they had not made cheese in several years. That left butter as the only practical item but it would be melted in the hot summer heat before the Sunday sermon had been concluded.

It came to him after the supper dishes had been cleared and the adults retired to the living room. Setting down the newspaper he had been reading, Seth declared, "Baskets." Nelander looked up from her ledger.

"Baskets?"

"Reed baskets. Hand woven. They come in any size; some with lids, some big enough for laundry or with a strap, like the kind fisherman use to bring home their catch. We could donate baskets."

"I didn't know you could make baskets."

"I can't. But I know someone who can."

Suspicions aroused, she wiped the tip of her pen and looked up.

"Who?"

"Blind Betty. I saw dozens of them up at the house. Beautiful, they were. And all designed for a specific purpose."

Waiting for a rumble of thunder to die down as a storm blew overhead, Nelander considered.

"We're going to ask Betty and Thomas to donate baskets to the Relief Fund?"

"No, we're going to ask for some and donate them, ourselves."

"And where are we going to say we got them from?"

"The townspeople don't have any idea what skills you have. We'll say you made them. That way, we don't have to go around advertising the fact those two are working for us. If the baskets catch on, it might even be a good way for Betty to make some extra money. We could bring some into town and sell 'em off the back of the wagon. Or leave them at Anson's for him to hawk."

"He'll take a commission."

"All right; a few pennies here and there. But with some hard talk, I bet we could get him to display them for free."

"You are referring to my prowess with a deer rifle?"

"How can I be, when you missed a stationary target at ten paces? No, sir. I mean, if someone buys a basket, then they have to fill it. With items from the store. We both win. In fact," he decided, "Hector can keep the money and we'll take the value in barter. I'm sure Miss Betty and Thomas'd appreciate store-bought coffee and mill-ground flour. Maybe even a dress for her and some work shoes for him."

"I like it."

"I can make some posters," Patricia offered, coming in from the kitchen, a wet towel still clutched in her hand. "Peter can put them up around town, so's people'll know of the new merchandise at Mr. Anson's."

"That's a good idea."

Carefully folding the paper, Seth slid it under his chair.

"What do you say we go over there and ask?"

A smattering of droplets pelted the windows.

"And get wet?"

"You know, funny thing about that. I heard, though mebbe it's only a rumor, that you seafaring types don't melt in the rain. Unless working the land the way you've been has made you soft."

"I already owe you one. That makes two. You're going to be a mighty lonely man, Captain Ward, for a very long time." She joined him at the door but refused the waterproof he took down from the peg. "Oh, no, sir. You wear it. If anyone is made of sugar around here, it's you."

"How's that rhyme go?

"What are little boys made of?
Frogs and snails
And puppy-dos's tails.
What are little girls made of?
Sugar and spice

And all that's nice."

"What-is-that?"

"A poem. I'm surprised you've never run across it."

"No, you're not."

He laughed and stepped out into the storm. Nelander followed and was not heard to reciprocate his amusement. Patricia watched them go, then went back into the kitchen and made Peter re-wash a pan which she deemed insufficiently clean.

As his unwitting punishment for being made of frogs and snails and puppy-dog's tails.

Chasing one another and splashing in newly formed puddles, Seth and Barbara arrived at the former Windsor home in what would have been record time, had they not dawdled to see to it the other's clothes were thoroughly soaked. They might have frolicked up to the front porch but for the fact no light shone through any window.

"Perhaps they have gone to bed," Nelander suggested, noting the sky, prematurely darkened by storm clouds.

"No. And I'll wager they are not in the house, either." Striking himself on the forehead in a gesture of annoyance, he grimaced. "I should have thought this through a little more clearly. They hear voices and their first impulse is to get out and hide."

"Damn." And then, more forcefully, "Damn men and their evil prejudices! Why the hell is it that people are not happy unless they have someone to hate?"

"Because it makes them feel superior."

"Are their own lives so petty and meaningless they do not feel alive unless they can trample over the freedoms of others who mean them no ill?"

"You know the answer to that better than I, Officer Nelander."

"Then why are we even trying to integrate them into the community?"

"On the hope we may one day make it better. The same reason," he softly added, "that Captain Ned Nelander defended his daughter from those who disapproved her status aboard a ship they had never seen and certainly never sailed upon."

Tilting back her head, Barbara filled it with rain water, gargled, then spit to clear her mouth of the foul taste.

"Miss Betty! Thomas! It is Nelander and the captain." She repeated her call twice more before a voice, startlingly close behind caused her to spin around.

"Whe's here, suh."

Both officers from the *Pirate Treasure* caught their breaths before speaking.

"I am sorry to have driven you out into the storm," Seth apologized. "My fault. I had something I wanted to discuss and did not think to announce ourselves beforehand."

"Dat's a'right, suh. Come on in outta da rain."

Leading the way, Betty guided them toward the door where Thomas rose from a crouch. Although he held a stick behind his back, he made no attempt to conceal the weapon as they entered the home.

Creeping through the darkness, Betty lit a strand of dried grass from the embers of the cook fire and touched the flame to the wick of a homemade candle stub. Immediately, an arc of light cast a warm glow across a two foot area. Behind that, darkness lightened, separating portions of the room by persisting shadow.

"Won' yuh please be seated, suhs," Betty continued. "Yuh honor us by dis visit."

Seth sat on a chair left behind by the Windsors while Barbara perched atop the stump of a tree trunk, behind which a rudimentary back had been fashioned of interlacing oak branches.

"Thomas," the matron continued, "stir up da fire an' put in some moss so's Ah kin ketch da kindlin'. Ah make sum tea."

Adjoining her not to bother would have been the height of disrespect, so the visitors sat silently while preparations were completed. Several minutes later, after water in a quart-sized tin can boiled, Betty added dried leaves, filling the dwelling with a sweet-smelling aroma.

Allowing the concoction to steep, she poured the beverage into four crock mugs fashioned from river mud and dried in a kiln, added a spoonful of something from an open-mouthed glass jar, then distributed them. The more curious of the two, Nelander eagerly sipped.

"This is excellent. Just the right mixture of tart and sweet. From what is it made?"

"Dat be mint tea, suh. Wid a taste ob honey."

She tried again, this time nodding in agreement.

"Not peppermint, surely."

"Spearmint," Seth identified, eagerly drinking his.

"I do not know the flavor but I like it. Perhaps even better than peppermint. Is it indigenous to the west?"

Without puzzling over the meaning of the five-dollar word, the former slave eagerly responded.

"No, suh. Dis mint grows eberywhere. Better, eben, in cold climes where da frost gibes it a snap ob sharpness."

"I like it. Do you suppose you could give some me cuttings so I might grow it in our garden?"

Miss Betty appeared to contemplate the request, rubbing her long, flexible fingers over her chin before winking at Captain Ward.

"Ah don' know wedder yuh want to grow dis herb, Nelander. Der's white folk what t'inks it be used in conjurin'. Dey might take it poo' yuh cultibatin' it."

"On the contrary. Such will only enhance my reputation. And since you put it that way, I shall give it to Peter for his especial attention. Once I tell him what you said, he will devote himself to providing our table with spearmint tea. Among other things. Does it have medicinal properties, as well?"

"Yas, suh. It be berry good fo' da belly ache an' da cramps."

"Then I am all the more intrigued. And only wish I had known this before Paula was born."

Embarrassed by a discussion which should only have been held between women, Seth cleared his throat.

"Where did you get the honey, Thomas? I've spent more than a few worthless hours tramping the woods looking for a hive."

Thomas quickly signaled with his hands which his mother interpreted.

"He foun' it on a bee tree; da special kind bees look fo'." Peering back to see what else he had to say, the old woman grinned. "He says he show yuh but it be bes' if yuh let him git da honey. Dem bees gits mighty mad when dey disturbed."

Ruefully rubbing his arms, Seth shuddered.

"Never mind. I will gladly leave honey-hunting to you and pay you for a cone."

This elicited a frantic exchange between son and mother.

"He says he neber take yuhr money, Capt'n, but he be glad to bring some 'round da next time he go out."

Catching Nelander's eye, Seth plunged ahead with the purpose of their visit.

"As a matter of fact, it is money we have come to speak about. Those baskets," he continued, pointing to several hung from the wall. "You make them, Miss Betty?" She nodded. "They are of exquisite workmanship. And very useful. Just the thing a farmer or a farmer's wife is always looking for. There is to be a fund raising at church this Sunday -- the women of town are selling small items to give the residents of Little Lawrence. As a way of repaying them for some of the damage done last month during the riot."

"The captain and I thought we might donate several to the cause. And if they are agreeably received -- as the work of my own hands," she shamefully added, "we discussed the idea of selling more in town. With the credit earned, we can purchase you store-bought goods."

Blind Betty's hands trembled so badly she hurried into the kitchen and busied herself with the stove. Upset that she had said something wrong, Barbara started to follow when Mute Thomas raised a hand. Once he had her attention, he put a finger below his eye and wiggled it down his cheek. Nelander choked as tears came to her own eyes. Remaining seated, she waited for Miss Betty to control her emotions, which she did with effort.

Returning to the living room, the Negress took down several of the larger baskets, reverently handing them over to Nelander. As the white woman examined them, she received a stern warning at the same time.

"Yuh, suh, be a gift frum da Lor'. Yuh an' da capt'n do His work. But yuh rememba one t'ing, suh. Jesus, He be crucified on da Cross. Recruited into His serbice, suh, ain't no guarantee yuh be spared da same punishment."

Nelander's head snapped back.

"You will make baskets?"

"Ah will. But yuh keep da money."

"I certainly will." The vow came with a codicil. "To spend on you and Thomas. And I pray that one day you and he will receive credit for your own work and be allowed to sell them openly."

"'Mah Kingdom be not ob dis worl',' Nelander," she quoted.

"Perhaps not. But it is a world in which we must live. And try to make better." Glancing at Seth, she gathered the baskets and stood. "We had better go, now. The baby will be hungry and we have to be up early."

Raising both hands, then making a polite downward motion enjoining them to wait, Betty hurried out the front door. Ten minutes later she returned with a handful of dripping plants. Crossing into the kitchen, she carefully wrapped the roots into a small scrap of cloth before presenting them to Barbara.

"Yuh gibe des to Mista Peter, suh. Dey grows in da sun or da shade. Onst dey take holt, he can cut off da tops an' use da leabes. Yuh tell him make a poultice bag an' wear it 'round his neck." Her sightless orbs narrowed with intensity. "He put in a bit ob rosemary an' mebbe sum parsley, too. Dat be a pow'ful med'cine." A pause, then, "In a mojo bag. Yuh tell him."

"I will," Nelander responded, accepting the mint. "Thank you and good-bye."

"Bless yuh, Nelander an' Capt'n."

They dove into the rain, facing the onslaught this time instead of having it at their back. The puddles were deeper, the darkness blacker, the sky lower, but none of that effected either their progress or their mood.

Life is what you make it and somehow, they had made it good.

The church bazaar turned out to be a roaring success. After service, the menfolk set up tents while the women prepared the picnic and afterward sold their crafts. The Wards shared space with Mrs. Knight, spreading out their baskets in a neat row. Blind Betty had given them six, four large and two smaller ones with lids attached by latigo lace. They made a handsome offering and within half an hour, Barbara sold the lot and taken orders for as many more.

Counting the coins she collected, Nelander whistled through her teeth.

"Three dollars. Can you imagine?"

Seth bounced on the balls of his feet.

"Not hardly. But worth every penny. I wonder how long it took to make them?"

"I don't know but certainly time well spent." Peering out at the crowd from under the brim of her seaman's cap, she pursued, "Would these people have bought the baskets if they knew who actually made them?"

"Yes, I think they would have. But not for the price they paid you. How much are we going to give over to the Negro Fund?"

"All of it. That is what we said we would do and what Betty and Thomas expect. When we fulfill the new orders, however, that belongs to them."

"Good. I approve."

Abandoning the empty space, the pair wandered around the temporary aisles, admiring the other crafts. Some tables displayed rag dolls, others doll clothes or tiny furniture. They also found wooden cooking implements, knit potholders, bunting, infant blankets, leather sandals, mittens and a vast array of tin and wooden buttons.

The last Seth poured over with uncommon interest, finally prompting his wife to ask the reason. Instead of answering, he identified the quest.

"I am seeking a small button, preferably one of bone. With two holes drilled through. I will know it when I see it."

Spilling the contents of a canning jar across the table, he had almost given up when a cry escaped his lips.

"This is it, exactly."

Holding out the flat, roundish, white object, Barbara felt a chill come over her as its purpose became clear.

"For Peter."

"Yes. I will cut him a swatch of burlap to go with it. With a needle and black thread, he ought to be able to make...." Seth's voice died away. No sense allowing anyone to overhear. "How much?" he asked of Mrs. Bundy. She expressed surprise at his choice.

"Only one, Captain?"

"One is all I require. What did this come off?"

"I can not say I remember. It is too small to have been removed from a man's shirt and no woman would likely wear a button of that sort. A child's garment, perhaps? Or from a doll's wardrobe, although I do not think so. I am a great button collector, I confess. It may have been scavenged from almost anything. A tobacco pouch, perhaps? Are you sure you do not wish me to search for other matching ones?"

"There are no others and this will do nicely."

"I cannot say I have ever sold just one button. A penny?"

He paid the fee and pocketed the treasure, content to let of the mystery of the button remain unsolved.

At three o'clock the erstwhile Reverend Ginnis passed around the hat, enjoining the parishioners to donate a percent of their sales for the Fund. Seth laid their contribution on top and winked at Nelander.

"Now, at least we know the good ladies will have collected three dollars. If the sum be less than that, I suggest we come out shootin'."

Had he actually brought a handgun, she would have been more disposed to second the idea.

Ten minutes later, Sheriff Bochner, who had brought a metal chest for the occasion, proudly held it up for inspection.

"Twelve dollars and thirty-three cents."

A ripple of awe swept through the crowd.

"More than I ever believed!" Mrs. Knight gushed. Acknowledging the applause for her contribution of arranging the sale, she beamed with pleasure. "Lock the strong box up good, Sheriff. We don't want none of them coins fallin' out on your ride back to town."

The implication elicited good natured laughter and the lawman made a show of inserting the key.

"Not to be opened again," he promised, "until I get to Nig-- Little Lawrence!"

More applause followed and the Wards went home, stopping on the way to carry the good tidings to the other family in Lawrence, Kansas, also going by the surname "Ward." Hearing the news, Betty fell into a chair, fanning her face with a paper.

"Lor', a'mighty, suh! A fortune, if eber der was one!"

"You have yourself to thank, ma'am. Three dollars of that was yours."

"No, Capt'n, suh. Dos baskets was giben to yuh. It be yuhr money went into da collection."

"Then let us consider it a donation from the Wards," he grinned.

Rubbing her hands in glee, she matched his expression.

"Dat be nice, suh."

"And I do believe we can sell as many baskets as you can make."

"Ah a'ready sent Thomas out to fetch da reeds. He has a feel fo' dem what Ah kin weave. It be a good t'ing. Yuh cume back nex' week an' Ah'll habe dem ready. Ah make dem, suh, durin' da night. Don' want yuh t'inkin' Ah be cheatin' yuh by not workin' in da field."

"I would never think that. But there is not much to be done --"

"No, suh. Dere be waterin' an' sech. Ah do mah wo'k."

And so it would be.


That afternoon, one bone button, a patch of burlap, a strand of latigo, black thread and needle were ceremoniously delivered to Master Pirate Peter. Accepting the gifts with due solemnity, he retired to the barn where he spent the next several nights in solitude.

No formal announcement was made, but thereafter he was seen wearing a small, crudely fashioned mojo bag around his neck. Over the course of the summer, after the herbs from the garden were harvested, it was noted to have swollen in size. With it grew his confidence.

The officers and crew of the *Pirate Treasure* made no comment about the magic powers such a mojo bag might confer. They rightfully comprehended such things were not the topic of polite conversation.

# CHAPTER 32

The fall and winter proved an eventful time. On November 6, 1860, men from thirty-three states cast ballots for president. Abraham Lincoln, the Republican nominee, received a bare plurality of the popular vote, but won a clear majority of the electoral college. His victory marked the first time in the history of America that the ruling political party stood on a platform declaring "the normal condition of all the territory of the United States is that of freedom."

Two months later, in January, 1861, Kansas received approval to become the 34th state in the Union, coming in under an anti-slavery constitution.

That new sum total of stars on Old Glory was not destined to last until spring.

On March 4, 1861, two significant events occurred. One had national implications. The other did not.

In Washington, Abraham Lincoln was inaugurated as the 16th President.

In Lawrence, Kansas, Paula Ward celebrated her first birthday.

Both events were attended by family and friends of the honoree. Presumably, cake and ice cream were passed around at both parties. The man of the hour wore a formal black suit. The baby made her appearance in a white dress. Without intent, they complimented one another, color choices symbolizing the impending crisis. In one case, a toast was drunk in recognition of the other.

Holding a glass of milk to Paula's lips, the proud father declared, "All honor and glory to he who will guide our country's ship." Seconded by the equally proud mother, who acknowledged, "To the new captain of the United States, under whom we all serve."

The baby took her sip of symbolic champagne, swallowed, then blew a spit bubble to the delight of witnesses, who generally considered it, without saying so, a hearty endorsement of the sentiments.

After dinner, the guests retired to the living room where a startling array of presents had been assembled.

"Which one do you want to unwrap first?" Seth inquired of the babe. With a critical eye at the ribbon-festooned gifts, a pudgy finger indicated the largest. Nelander fetched it for her and provided assistance in vivisecting the paper.

Inside the box they discovered a silver rattle, an India rubber ball and a pair of white baby booties from Dr. McTree. After "ooghs" and "a-hahs," the shoes were tried on and as promptly kicked off, the ball placed in the pink palm and immediately tossed to the dogs, which thought it their present and began a game of chase, and the rattle madly shaken before an abandonment for the next gift.

Barbara presented her tiny daughter with a small wooden shield upon which she had fastened a dozen fancy sailor's knots. Seeing the display for the first time, Seth whistled.

"Better, even, than the one your father bought," he praised. "I am sure that Captain Ned is watching with approval as his grandchild receives that like he once owned."

"I hope so," she whispered, adding a bundle of short, soft lengths of flexible rope to Paula's treasure. "As she grows, she can practice with these. Every seaman must know his knots."

"Along with his salty language," Seth winked.

"That, she gets every other day of the year," Nelander agreed. "Along with some down-home Midwestern cussing."

"Then, we shall have a well-rounded child."

Patricia took her turn next, carefully un-scrolling a sheet of paper taken from her sketch pad. On it, she had drawn a credible likeness of the baby.

"I want her to know what she looked like on her first birthday," she explained, blushing under the well-deserved praise for her talent. "I thought about what to give her and I didn't know.... I wanted something special."

"It is beautiful, daughter. Amazing. And the colors -- so lifelike it seems as if she is in two places at once!"

"As long as she cries in only one," Peter only halfheartedly teased, offering his present. Seth unwrapped it, allowing the boy to take out the garment. "It's a pirate bib. I made it, myself. I'm not much of a hand at these things, but I thought she ought to have some official clothing in her wardrobe."

Lifting up the baby's chin, Barbara fastened the black cloth, sewn with a white skull and crossbones, in place.

"You are right, boy. Not only will it protect her from the dribs and drabs of gruel, it gives her a right to stake her claim on any treasure we find."

"I thought that, too," he admitted, scuffing his foot.

Blind Betty took her turn next, bashfully offering a small, intricately woven lid-ed basket, the inside of which had been covered with bright red felt.

"Dis fo' da babe's keepsakes. She cume wid da strawberries, yuh might say, so Thomas picked out da right color, Ah hope, fo' the linin'."

"Absolutely perfect! The first thing we shall put in it is her rattle."

"An' may one day it be filled wid bright, shiny coin."

Thomas came last, holding out a mouth organ. Looking at his mother, he pleaded with her to explain.

"Mah son neber had no way ob talkin' but he kin play music like an angel. He tell meh he feels dat chil' full ob music. Mebbe he kin teach her."

"What a special gift! Thank you, Thomas! I am sure she will be honored to learn from you. But can you really play like an angel?" The tall, mute man nodded, eyes sparkling. Nelander clapped her hands. "Will you play for us? Now?"

Slipping a harmonica similar to the one he gave Paula from his shirt pocket, he brought it to his lips and went through the notes of a song. Although a tune she had never heard, Barbara immediately felt a kinship to the notes.

"Play some more for us. Please?"

With Blind Betty's approval, he played another, tapping his foot to the tempo. The gathering did not need any further prodding and Seth quickly grabbed his wife and spun her around the floor. They cried in pleasure and encouraged the others to follow suit.

Peter boldly made a low bow before the Negress, taking both her hands in his.

"May I have this dance, Miss Betty?"

She surprised everyone by accepting and holding carefully to her date, the couple glided across the floor. Guided by Peter's eyes, they traversed the living room, circled back, then began again, faster this time as Thomas slipped into a more lively rhythm.

Copying Master Peter's elegant bow, Hank McTree presented himself to the oldest daughter of the house.

"If you're not afraid of having your feet trampled by a gentleman who has not set foot upon a dance floor in more years than I care to remember, will you have this dance with me, Miss Patricia?"

"Bet I can stomp on your feet good as you can mine," she boasted, holding out her hands. In a moment, the three couples spun around the room, occasionally bumping into one another with grunts and good natured warnings.

"Enough!" Seth finally decided, dragging Nelander toward the door. "This ship isn't big enough for such frolicking! We must go outside, to the high seas, where we shall trod the rolling waves of Ocean Kansas!"

With more room and under cover of a particularly warm evening, the couples easily fell into a graceful rhythm, sashaying back and forth, creating a loose square dance. As the music became more frenzied, they exchanged partners regardless of gender, Nelander dancing with Patricia, Seth with Betty and the doctor with the boy, until all had gone up and down the arch of interlaced hands enough times to have changed places with everyone.

Finally exhausted, they dropped onto the porch, adults in a reasonable assumption of a sitting position while the children flopped like bunny rabbits. Mute Thomas, who had found his voice at last, remained the only one standing.

The grin on his face could have launched a thousand ships.

Quicker to regain his equilibrium, for he had the advantage of a lack of years, Peter slapped his thigh.

"If that don't tie the pup!"

Nelander looked to Seth for elaboration. After nearly four years of marriage he had grown accustomed to such stares.

And hedging.

"It is a Western expression."

"That, I gathered. What-does-it-mean?"

"Why don't you ask your son?"

"I am asking you, from whom he learned it."

"Well. Tie the pup. Put a curb on enthusiasm." The logic did not appear to fit the case. He tried again. "The achievement of something difficult to perform." For his effort he received a blank face. "It means... whatever you want it to mean. 'I'll be a monkey's uncle.' 'If he ain't snake bit.' 'Damned if you do and damned if you don't.' 'Rich man, poor man, beggar man, thief; doctor, lawyer, Indian chief'.... 'I'll be dipped in gravy.'" And then, with a final try, "'Ain't I in a pickle?'"

"You don't know."

"It is a catch-all phrase. Like... 'All hands on deck.'"

For his trouble, the captain garnered himself no respite. Nelander summoned the boy by flexing the second and third fingers of her left hand.

"Master Peter: *what* don't tie the pup?"

One of the Wards, at least, had his answer ready.

"That Mister Thomas gave the harmonica to Paula an' not to me."

Which proved acceptable and reduced the grown-ups to smirking behind their hands.

"Not socially commendable, but understandable."

"Yes, ma'am. Come on, Nelander," he pleaded. "Sing to us."

The request brought immediate hand clapping and urges for her to comply. Pursing her lips, the sailor rolled her eyes.

"I fear my repertoire is entirely lacking in birthday songs."

"Then sing us something of the sea," Dr. McTree pleaded.

She grimaced. Seth poked her.

"You don't know any."

"What I know would turn your ears red, sir. An expression easily comprehended by a God-fearing man such as yourself."

He blushed but would not give up.

"Come on. Hum the tune as you go and Thomas will follow along."

The black man eagerly nodded.

"Very well. And it will serve you right if we are henceforth banned from polite company."

First humming a stanza, Nelander began the lyrics.

"What shall we do with a drunk-en sail-or?
 What shall we do with a drunk-en sailor?
 What shall we do with a drunk-en sailor
 Ear-ly in the morn-ing?

"Away, hey, up she ris-es!
 Away, hey, up she ris-es!
 Away, hey, up she ris-es!
 Ear-ly in the morn-ing.

"What shall we do with a drunk-en sail-or?
 Chuck him in the longboat till he gets sober."

Pointing at Seth, she directed the words toward him.

"What shall we do with a drunk-en skip-per?
 Lock him in his stateroom till he gets sober."

The next stanza went to Hank McTree.

"What shall we do with a drunk-en doc-tor?
 Put him in the coal locker till he gets sober."

Peter then fell in for his share of her good natured ribbing.

"What shall we do with a drunk-en bo-y?
 Hoist him to the royal yard till he gets sober."

As Patricia dove after her brother, attempting to carry out the punishment, he squealed over the refrain.

"Away, hey, up she ris-es!
 Early in the morn-ing!"

Peter managed to dodge his sister, but Blind Betty, unerring in her instincts, captured him as he raced by, stretching out his braces until hauling him in.

More clapping and foot stomping ensued until he moaned and groaned and pleaded for release.

"Tarnation!  Darned if I didn't walk into that one wid my eyes wide open!"

Ruefully rubbing his shoulder, he hoisted up the drooping suspender, then warily stepped out of harm's way. Nelander addressed the capture-er.

"All tight, Miss Betty. Now it is your turn. Something less... secular and a bit more spiritual, if you please."

Gathering her long skirts about her, the old lady accepted the request. Making some symbols in her child's hand, Thomas shook the musical instrument to clear it of spit, then ran it through his lips, playing the opening bars of a well-loved and familiar strain. She took up the lyrics as he played the music.

> "Swing low, sweet char-i-ot,
> Com-ing for to car-ry me home,
> Swing low, sweet char-i-ot,
> Com-ing for to car-ry me home.
>
> "I looked o-ver Jordan,
> And what did I see,
> Com-ing for to carry me home?
> A band of an-gels com-ing after me,
> Com-ing for to carry me home.
>
> "If you get there be-fore I do,
> Com-ing for to car-ry me home?
> Tell all my friends I'm com-ing too,
> Com-ing for to car-ry me home.
>
> "I'm some-times up, I'm some-times down,
> Com-ing for to car-ry me home?

But still my soul feels heav-en-ly bound,
Com-ing for to car-ry me home."

They all knew the song and sang with her, blending their voices in a chorus for God.

"Swing low, sweet char-i-ot,
Com-ing for to car-ry me home.
Swing low, sweet char-i-ot,
Com-ing for to car-ry me home."

They applauded for themselves, slapped Thomas on the back and congratulated one another for the uplifting end to a wonderful celebration.

Many, many miles away, but under the same moon and in a suitable frame of mind, another singer hummed the music to "Swing Low." He was a tall man, taller than any who had come before. Facing nearly insurmountable odds in bringing together a nation divided, he, too, sought divine inspiration.

Sometimes he was up and sometimes down. A man of introspection and premonition, he saw a band of angels.

Com-ing for to car-ry him home.

There was much to do before the char-i-ot came.

And yet his soul felt heav-en-ly bound.

Not a bad way to begin an administration or end a birthday party.

# CHAPTER 33

Looking over her shoulder, Seth nodded in approval.

"You have done a good job, keeping that log. Have you found it useful?"

"I will not say more than I imagined, because I knew it would be. But I never thought of it as a daily reference. Look here," Nelander indicated, putting a finger in the ledger to mark her place, then flipping back the pages. "These are the dates we planted the strawberries, and here, a record of their progress."

Changing her mind, suddenly, she set it aside and reached for a large, heavy folio. Seth glanced at the title.

"You wish me to read *A Pictorial History of French Damsels from Marie Antoinette to Present Time?*"

She chuckled before recovering her aplomb.

"No doubt you are surprised, sir, that I have recovered it from beneath our mattress. But you forget: I know your hiding places. Racier, by far," she added with a twinkle, "than a boy's pack of lewd playing cards."

Turning back the cover of the text, *Scientific Experiments in Agriculture, 1850 - 1860,* Nelander removed several loose papers. He quickly scanned them as she spread them over the desk top.

"Bar graphs?"

"Yes."

"Why did you hide them in the book?"

"Because I did not want you to see them until I had perfected the technique. I copied them from yours."

Drawing up a chair, Seth sat beside her, marveling at the meticulous work.

"Very nice. Much better than mine, in fact."

"No; they are very similar. I merely used a straight edge to draw the lines." Indicating the two years with dates, Barbara eagerly read them aloud. "This column indicates 1860, charting when we planted the strawberries, first indications of growth, blossoms and berries. The second covers the first part of 1861. Because the plants have had a year to develop their root systems and have survived one winter, they are far ahead of last season."

"So I see."

"Already they have green leaves and are beginning to bud. Here," she indicated, taking a second paper, this one a diagram labeled "Strawberry Field #2," "you can observe a pattern. You were exactly right. Those which we experimented with by using compost are far in advance of the rest. This year, I will fertilize a different patch so we may benefit next spring."

"More data for your scientific paper."

"I hope so. I am particularly interested in the patch where I laid droppings from the hen house. There has been some speculation of its benefits among strawberry growers and I will soon be in a position to validate that. With any luck, we shall have more fruit than I anticipated."

Leaning back, he rocked on the two hind legs of the chair.

"If we harvest a fair crop next month, you are going to make a believer of me."

"The proof is in the pudding. But I am beginning to feel excited. I have a long way to go before I recover my initial investment," she added, returning to her graphs, "but it will look well to see some entries here in black ink."

"How are the plants in the valley faring?"

"Better, yet; the spring growth more evenly distributed."

Seth nodded. "The sloping ground benefits from runoff so water does not pool on the flat ground as it does in a field."

"Add to that," she eagerly continued, "the fact Betty and Thomas have developed a system for watering. They carry buckets from the stream to the top of the valley, then dump them into irrigation ditches. This acts as a sluiceway, where even plants at the outer edges are hydrated. They are extremely innovative, Seth. It is a pity we cannot brag of their accomplishments."

"One day I hope we can. When people work in partnership, the results are always more beneficial than if one group plays master over others in bondage. Dismissing," he added in derision, "any so-called concerns for paternalism. Negroes are not children and if given a fair shake, there is nothing they cannot accomplish."

"And one day, you will have to tell me where you developed such enlightened sentiments when so many others feel the opposite. Surely they did not come from your parents."

Settling the legs of the chair back on the floor, he stared out the window.

"The best explanation I can offer is that I was both with them. I cannot say my father expressed any opinion on the subject at all. But in his time, there were fewer dark-skinned people in Kansas. While I never knew him to be rude, he merely dismissed the entire race as... beneath him."

"As though he had the right to proclaim himself superior."

"He had a farm and a house. It is always easy for those with property and freedom to look down on those without. Perhaps because I had it harder, it gave me more opportunity to see myself in their place."

"Not many would do that. What of your brothers?"

"Rick was a copy of his sire. He looked like him and he sounded like him. For all practical purposes, they were the same. Quiet, stern and loveless."

"And Norman?"

"Cut from a different cloth, entirely. I wonder what will become of him."

"What do you mean?"

"They say there is going to be trouble over that fort in South Carolina."

"Sumter?"

"With all this talk of secession and leaving the Union, men are riled. I read that already soldiers stationed out west have resigned their commissions and gone home."

"Surely it will not come to war."

"You have given it as much thought as I. What do you think?"

Nelander did not want to answer.

"Do you suppose Norman will come home?"

"I cannot say he has one. His loyalty is for the Army. I imagine he will stay in and go wherever they send him."

"To fight against his own brethren?"

"To fight for his flag."

She waited a long beat before asking, "And you?"

"I have not given the matter much thought." Which was a lie and they both understood it as such. Avoiding her pointed stare, he got up and put a log on the fire. "The last two weeks have been unusually warm and today it is cold."

"Yes, it is. I had thought not to burn wood in the fireplace anymore until fall. But tomorrow I will clean out the hearth and be done with it."

"I think not."

His words served to drop the temperature in the chill room.

"Why do you say that? It is already April. Winter is past."

"Which way is the wind blowing?"

"Down from the north."

"Which direction was it blowing this time last year?"

Nelander consulted her log. "Southwest." Silence turned ominous, forcing her on. "Since I am a novice in these waters, Captain, and have left Lieutenant Matthew Fontaine Maury's famous charts in my quarters, I respectfully inquire of the habitual currents around the Kansas Cape."

Doing his best to imitate a nautical officer, Ward hitched his trousers, then curled his hand into a hollow tube, bringing it to his eye for a telescope.

"Experience has taught me there is no normal, Mr. Nelander. The months of March and April are unpredictable. It is not uncommon for two weeks of spring weather to be followed by a brief but destructive return of winter."

"Rough sailing ahead, sir?"

Motioning her follow, they walked out into the yard, then through the space between house and barn, taking them to the back of the property where Strawberry Field #2 rolled out before them.

"I would not have said so two days ago, but now my instincts are aroused. Cold winds from Canada bring storms and lower temperatures."

"Snow?"

"Snow, we can deal with."

"But the crops -- the wheat and corn are already so high," she indicated. "Tree leaves are unfurling. Wild flowers color the landscape."

What she omitted from the description stood between them as a gulf. He only reluctantly filled it.

"And the strawberries are green. Another week and they will be covered with white blooms." Pacing down one of the well-defined paths, he critically observed the plants. "Snow is not the problem."

"Explain, please, sir. Will it not --?"

"Snow acts like a blanket, protecting growing plants from the worst of the cold. With the return of mild weather, it melts, leaving little harm. It is a sleet storm I fear." He stopped so suddenly she bumped into him. "That is what I dread above all else... at this time of year."

"I am listening."

"Wind and hail do major damage to crops. It beats them down; tears off the new leaves. Bitter temperatures not only set back growth, it kills by cold." Sweeping an arm to include the woods beyond, his face paled. Following his direction, Barbara beheld an arc of light velvet green. "Two days of freezing rain will wipe out all of what you see. Leaves will die, hanging from drooping branches like... battlefield causalities."

The reference, too close to their previous conversation, deepened the pall of impending doom.

"The forests will perish?"

"Older trees will; those incapable of withstanding the shock. Younger ones will eventually produce new leaves but it will take time, leaving behind an aura of... stress? You understand?"

"I do." Stepping back, she put distance between them as though giving the pair a wider avenue of protection. "And the crops? The wheat and the corn?"

"Annuals do not have the structure of a tree; no wood to support them. The roots are not deep. A hard freeze will destroy the delicate balance, leaving little capacity for recovery. In all likelihood, they will perish."

"Then it must not freeze."

He tried a smile which had closer similarity to a death's head grin.

"Spoken like a greenhorn rather than an officer."

Hands clenched, Nelander thrust a fist at the wind.

"May I not be both? Sir."

"I will expect optimism, sir, after the disaster, when we must rally the crew."

The statement stung, more the edges of a tornado than the eye of a storm. It made her reflect which part of the crew to whom he referred: the able-bodies or the commander.

"Aye, aye."

Detecting the doubt, Captain Ward shored up his own waning courage.

"We cannot prevent a storm. We must endure as best we can."

For once, Nelander's faith deserted her.

"If the cargo is waterlogged, sir, we will have nothing to sell. The voyage will be a financial disaster."

Crisscrossing rows, Seth's feet created a dull, crunching sound, not unlike those of a sailor traversing a deck strewn with hail. In the ten minutes they had stood outside, the temperature had fallen ten degrees, hardening the uppermost tips of earth. He spoke with his back to her.

"Correct me if I am wrong, Officer Nelander, for my title is honorary. I have never captained a ship at sea. But I have read enough adventure stories to draw one conclusion."

"And that is?"

"The primary object of the captain is to navigate his vessel safely into port. First, save life. Second, make a profit."

She stiffened, eyes hard and unyielding, for bitterness ran deep.

"That is true. But already in the four years I have put in on this voyage, we have suffered drought and flood and now face the deadly caprices of storm. Three disasters in the span of four years bodes ill for the continued success of the enterprise."

Spinning around in anger, flesh unnaturally flushed in anger, she thought he would scream. Instead, the words came softly, more a caress than a slap.

"Now, sir, you are talking like Terrance Windsor. Ready to abandon your way of life in the face of setback. Perhaps you erred, as he did. Neither of you are meant for the 'sea.'"

For a moment, Barbara's muscles tightened and she found it impossible to breathe. Shame crept up her neck. When it passed and her body unlocked, her head hung.

"Not an honorary title, Seth Ward, for you truly are a captain. I beg pardon, sir, and request another chance at redeeming myself. I have signed the Articles for life and mean to honor that promise."

She saluted and held the position until he returned it.

"We stand together."

"Come what will."

Meaning, quite clearly, *Through hell and high water.* Or the dry-docked equivalent, *Through drought and freezing rain.*

Two days passed and the temperature continued to drop. By April 7th, when Nelander met Seth coming in from the barn, clouds of frozen mist formed around their lips as they spoke.

"Why are you not wearing a jacket? It is too cold to be working in shirt sleeves."

He shrugged and cast a disparaging glance at the dark, low-lying clouds.

"I am trying to fool Mother Nature by pretending it is warm. That way, she may realize her error and blow in warmer winds from the south."

Nelander could not argue with his logic.

"She might consider drying up the sky, as well. We have had enough rain." One hand rubbing her neck, she ruefully considered the statement. "It seems we have been subjected to feast or famine these last several years."

Blowing on his fingers, he agreed.

"I shouldn't mind a normal spring, but we are not going to get one. How is the mulching coming?"

"Patricia and Peter and I cut as much of the wild grass as we could and spread it over the strawberries for protection. But there is only so much we can accomplish."

"I wish I had straw to offer. But there was none in reserve."

Overhead, a rumble of thunder shook the world, as though the gods lurking above had suffered a case of severe indigestion. Several seconds later a bolt of over-bright lightning streaked across the sky, eerily illuminating the nauseous underbelly. Counting the interval, Barbara grimaced.

"The storm is getting closer and headed in our direction." Shuddering, she wrapped her arms around herself. "And growing colder as we stand. What shall we do? Surely... something."

"Go inside."

He did not offer the solution she sought, and Nelander only reluctantly followed him to the house. Before they reached the porch, a spattering of freezing rain struck the earth. Stopping suddenly, she grabbed Seth's arm.

"Snow," she said.

"Snow?"

"You said it acts like a blanket, insulating the plants."

"It is not going to snow --"

"Might not ice act in similar fashion?"

He divined her meaning but saw no practical implication.

"It might; but the damage will come first from the power of the storm; ripping off the leaves."

"Not if they are already covered in ice."

"You cannot have one without the other."

"Yes, you can." Her eagerness infected him with guarded hope. "Not for a field of corn or summer wheat but the strawberries in the valley. Remember I told you about the irrigation system? How Miss Betty and Thomas created sluiceways?" He nodded. "What if we go there and pour water down the ditches, covering the plants before the worst of the cold hits? The ice coat may protect them from severe damage."

Snapping his fingers, Seth pointed to the house.

"Get the crew! Have Peter run across the field and fetch Thomas. I'll hitch Blaze. If we all work together there may just be time."

The seven, including baby Paula and Blind Betty, neither of whom desired to be left behind, met at Strawberry Field #1. Working under cold, wet and windy conditions, they formed a brigade, dispersed by age. Breaking the thin skin of ice covering the creek, the oldest of the contingent filled the buckets and passed them to the three adults. They, in turn, raced the water up the hill, passing them off to the children who dumped the contents down the ditches. The baby, under cover of a tarpaulin in the wagon, cheered them on with loud, impatient cries.

After an hour, when numb fingers occasioned her to spill a bucket, Nelander called a rest period.

"Enough."

Without benefit of fire, for the wood proved too wet to burn, they huddled together on the lee side of the wagon, attempting to use the shelter to warm their frozen bodies. Thomas signaled in his mother's hand, who translated.

"He says dis be one strange idea, fightin' ice wid ice."

The observation struck the group as funny and they laughed together.

"No stranger than fighting fire with fire," Seth noted, pulling up his collar to protect his neck. "If it doesn't work, we have wasted nothing but effort and if it does, we may yet have strawberries to sell."

His words trailed off as he glanced toward the northeast where his cash crops grew. Barbara drew closer, pressing her face to his.

"Yes, beloved," she whispered. "Somehow we will get through this."

Swallowing his fear, Seth kissed her. "God help us, Officer Nelander. You and your ship and your indomitable will."

"And you, Captain, with your faith. I love you, Seth Ward."

"And I love you, woman from the sea."

They hugged and drew strength from one another and went back to work. By the time the storm hit in full force, they had done as much as was humanly possible and hurried to the wagon, resigned, if not content, to leave the results to a higher power.

Piling in, Seth saw Miss Betty and Thomas settled in the back before realizing one of the crew was missing.

"Where is Peter?"

A limited, frantic search revealed no little boy. Repeatedly shouting his name elicited no response, for the wind gobbled all sound.

"Where could he have gone? He was here the whole while."

"Patricia -- was he not with you?"

"Yes, sir."

"Didn't he come down with you?"

She struggled to remember, then suddenly her orbs went wide. Scrambling down, she raced back up the slope of Strawberry Field.

"Has he fallen? Do you think he is hurt?"

Seth started to follow when the wise old Negress held him back.

"No, suh. Leabe her go. She find him."

"But where is he? What is he doing?"

She smiled and for a moment, no one in the wagon felt cold or weariness or fright.

"He makin' magic."

"How -- how do you know?"

Putting a hand to her sightless eyes, Miss Betty's smile widened.

"Ah sees him."

Up the hill Patricia ran, reaching the top panting and out of breath. Pausing to get her bearings, she peered through the swirling fog of low lying clouds, seeking, as Betty did. Not with her eyes but with her mind.

Following the trail which appeared to be emblazoned with phosphorescence, she came upon her brother, standing at the highest point of the valley perimeter. Oblivious to the bitter gusts whipping his jacket behind him like the wings of a bird, he held out his small mojo bag, still suspended by a cord around his neck. The girl waited until his lips stopped moving, then reverently joined him.

"Is it all right, now?" she whispered. He nodded.

"I used my powers. I called mama and the other spirits. I told them what we was doin'. Asked for help. Can you hear her?"

Turning her head into the wind, Patricia listened. Tears, like frozen gems, glistened on her cheeks.

"Yes, Peter. I can hear her; finally hear her, too."

Taking her brother's hand, the two children of the Kansas prairie, born of flesh and blood, nurtured on a father's love, taught by a stepmother's wisdom and gifted by adopted black-skinned grandparents, stared into the gathering storm. Above the dim rose a keening. Not quite human, not all supernatural.

Mother Nature.

By any other name.

Resting assured She watched over the fate of her offspring.

# CHAPTER 34

He knew it was cold by the way his feet, warmed by the protection of the woolen blanket, felt on the wooden floor. It did not register how cold until he poked his head outside and his nose stuck together.

*Damned cold.*

Below freezing. Quickly completing his business in the privy, Seth worked hard at pumping water from the well. He saw no point breaking the crust over the trough. Eventually it would melt, saving him the trouble. Far easier just to haul fresh to the livestock.

Normally, that chore fell to Peter, but this morning the captain had awaken early and fell into the boy's routine with easy familiarity. Once, it had been his responsibility to feed and water the animals, clean out the muck and milk the cow. Returning to that small age now gave him a sense that time remained fluid and all things worked out for the best.

Gently petting Blaze's muzzle in response to the friendly salutation, he scratched behind its ears before using the shovel to heft manure into the wheelbarrow. Finishing there, he laid out new straw and turned attention to the cow.

"Mornin', Bessie." He stopped, considered, then grinned. "Blaze and Bessie. Patricia, Peter and Paula. Guess we like alliteration around here." The similarity ended with Herman, but there had been a reason for that. Poor beast, resembling a hang-dog preacher. Dardanelles, he mused, represented another matter, entirely.

Setting the metal pail beneath the cow, he attempted to position his bulk down on the short milking stool. It seemed a long way down and his knees cracked. For a second he wondered why before realization struck. The stool had been designed with short legs in mind; those of a grown man were twice the length of a child's.

Blowing on his fingers to warm them, he started the task, first with concentrated effort, then from habit. Once upon a time, he could have milked a herd of cows in his sleep and if his father had owned that many, probably would have. Bessie turned her head around to stare. The large, soft brown eyes gently appraised the technique.

"You tryin' to tell me Patricia does this better?" Bessie swished her tail. "Well, don't worry. She'll be around this afternoon."

Whether the promise or the sound of his voice appeased the cow, she resumed her own contemplation. Finishing up, Seth set the pail aside and fed the barn animals before offering the same favor to the chickens. Deciding to let the able-bodies search for new laid eggs, he yawned, buttoned up his coat and braved the outside.

Ten minutes took him through the grassland to the open fields where no more than a week ago the vista had been covered with the verdure of growing corn. No longer. What he beheld this morning appeared closer to a million icicles, grown straight up instead of forming downward from the drips of a gigantic sieve.

She came up behind him, not quietly, for the crunch of frozen grass sounded as loud as a herd of grazing deer, yet he did not hear the footfalls. When she spoke, therefore, he jumped in surprise.

"Ruined?"

Betrayed by an explosion of mist expelled from his lungs, Seth did not bother grinning. He had left that expression behind in the barn with his memories.

"All."

"Can you replant?"

"It's late." And then, because they were equals, "That means buying more seed. Another expense. One we can hardly afford."

"Then we have to take out a bank loan."

He shook his head. "We already owe the bank on two mortgages. Ours and the Windsor's place."

"We can't give that up. It would mean losing your valley."

"Don't know what choice we have."

"There's no point in Mr. Provost denying us. He knows as well as any farmer that without a crop there won't be any money coming in this fall."

"He might also look at it as throwin' bad money after good. He's got stockholders to look after."

"Damn the stockholders."

This finally brought a crack in his demeanor.

"I never said they were my concern." Hands in his pockets, he walked the ruined field. "I've got some corn seed left. I'll start with that. Have to plow all this under. It's a shame. Lot of work. Had visions of an early harvest this year. Not anymore. That'll effect the price; bring it down."

"Everyone will have a late crop."

"So they will."

They walked the perimeter for something to do, then set their sights on the house. Seth made coffee while Barbara fried the eggs. They ate without bread for she had no time to make any. The crew joined them. No one spoke.

After the dishes had been cleared, Seth went for his coat and gloves.

"I'll go into town. See what's to be done. Be back by supper time."

Nelander kissed him good-bye, then stood at the door and waved as his back disappeared. Patricia joined her.

"Wind's coming up."

The stared at the two standards fluttering in the breeze, the Skull and Crossbones and the Black Flag. One promising buried treasure, the other no quarter. Both seemed a falsehood.

"Pirates," Peter stated, joining them at the archway, "don't never give up." He had changed into his uniform, complete with eye patch and cutlass. His hand gripped the hilt as though ready to face an invisible enemy.

"Not ever?" the officer demanded, more to test her own faith than his.

"No, sir. It ain't in the breed. May have to slit a few throats here an' there, but we'll get what we're after."

She wondered whether the captain were thinking the same thing. It would not give her much of a twinge to hear Seth return and announce he had sent Mr. Provost, the banker, and half his stockholders, to the Promised Land.

In fact, she decided, it would brighten her day considerably.

Patricia tugged her hand. "It's warming up, already. By noon the ice'll start melting. Peculiar thing, the ocean freezing over. It being salt water, and all. But then, pirates are used to such happenings. They're ready for anything. Never know when a Spanish galleon might be just over the horizon."

Peter shaded his eyes. "Yup. Filled with gold doubloons an' jewels. Diamonds and rubies."

"What do you expect they'll be worth?" she asked for the sake of hearing herself talk.

"A flagon of rum an' a night on the town."

This, finally elicited her curiosity.

"What, exactly, sir, does that mean?"

"Brawlin' wid the locals, a belly full of grub an' making square with the bank."

Nelander's attention deepened as she looked at the boy, wondering if he were joking and saw that he was not. Wonderment encased her. Without doubt, she and Captain Seth Ward had done a mighty fine job raising this farmer's son into a buccaneer. Not one, perhaps, of storybook legend, but a youth outstanding in his field.

Pun intended.


Seth returned with two bags of corn seed and back issues of the *Gazette.* Tossing the newspapers on his chair, he explained one but not the other.

"Didn't pay for them. Jim Daly's publishing these days without any subscription fee. Says he's making his money on advertising. I expect he's waiting for better times like the rest of us."

She did not follow through, which ended the discussion.


"It says here that President Lincoln has called for 75,000 militia on account of the trouble in Sumter. The Federal government expects South Carolina to secede and join the Confederacy any day now."

"That's too bad. I don't think anyone has any idea what that truly means."

"It means war."

"Beyond that."

Seth turned the page and ran his eye down the columns of local news.

"You might be interested in this, being a seaman. There's a whole article on wind currents and weather."

Ignoring the fact she had a vested interest in the outbreak of armed conflict, Barbara scanned the article.

"Yes," she admitted. "It is interesting. But not surprising. The winter weather swept through parts of the state, leaving others relatively untouched. How fortunate for their crops."

What else she thought Nelander reserved for herself. It was becoming a pattern.

Not one necessarily of omission, but more of "wait and see."

The frantic knocking on the door startled all within. The dogs had not warned of a visitor and thus the inhabitants were caught entirely unaware.

"Who is it?" Seth called, warily crossing from the hall into the living room. Receiving no answer, he frowned and went to stop Patricia from answering the repeated summons. Dodging his hand, she offered him a look of childlike simplicity.

"Herman and Dardanelles know who it is."

"Then, why --?" The sentence trailed off as the obvious set in. "Mute Thomas." No sense of well-being followed the identification.

The times, they were a'changin'.

Ignoring what she could not fathom, the girl raced to the door and threw it open. No war, or threat of war, could prevent her from unguardedly admitting a friend. No matter the news he carried. One look at his face, however, alleviated all concern.

All smiles and eagerness, the black man poked in his head, too well versed in the ways of the world to enter without the permission of an adult. Catching the captain's eye, he formed his lips into a wide, tooth-filled "O" and beckoned him forward.

Responding faster than her husband, Barbara sprang up, putting her own hopeful interpretation to his appearance.

"What is it, Thomas?"

Before he could answer, Seth interposed himself between the two. Clearing his throat, he assumed nominal command.

"Just a moment, here. I will handle the interrogation." Nelander's impatient foot stomping only encouraged him to continue. "Come in, sir, and shut the door behind you." The Negro complied. "Now: we surmise by your appearance you have news to impart. Is it... that Miss Betty has had some sort of accident and you need our help?" Thomas madly shook his head. "No. Well, it is that... you have taught Mizzenmast a new trick?"

Again, no.

"Ah. One of those rascally kittens has run off and you are seeking help in locating it?"

More sadly this time, a "no."

"You have come to invite us for supper?"

Thomas' shoulders sagged. Seth stroked his chin.

"This is becoming irksome. You have baskets for us to collect? Ones so large you cannot carry them, yourself?"

Nearly reducing the poor man to fits, the officer scratched his head.

"Then, can it be.... I dare not think it.... some news of the -- strawberries?" This sent Thomas into a paroxysm of hand signaling. "Ah. I have hit pay dirt. The strawberries. Covered in ice and frozen solid --"

Hand clapping replaced gestures. Leaning forward, Thomas seemed determined to wrassle out the words.

"Stop it, you bad man," Nelander warned, pushing past her husband. "Have they melted? You have seen them?"

A huge sigh escaped. Thomas nodded, accompanying the gesture by leaping out of his tracks.

"Green? Are they green? Have they survived the storm?"

*Hallelujah!*

Patricia dashed through the entranceway, Nelander on her heels, Thomas behind. Peter would have followed, but his father caught him by the scruff of the neck.

"Whoa, boy!"

"But papa captain -- the strawberries!"

"I heard."

"Are we not going to see?"

"We are. But the first officer and the able-bodied have left the 'powder monkey' behind. No excursion into the sea may be undertaken without all hands accounted for. Go and wrap the baby in her shore clothes."

For once, the excitement got the better of him.

"I am only a little boy, sir. Not qualified for such duty. I believe she is your responsibility, sir."

Wriggling free, he scampered away, hands over his ears so as not to hear the order, bellowed after.

"Belay that, boy! It is time you learned!"

Too late. Captain Ward poured, rolled his eyes, then went after Paula. By the time he emerged, baby strapped to his back, he found himself abandoned. Grunting in mock annoyance, he traipsed through the yard and into the field, having no trouble following four set of footprints, deeply mired in mud.

Guided, were he in need of direction, by the yelps preceding him, the oldest and youngest members of the *Pirate Treasure* arrived at the valley to behold a wondrous sight: two intersecting walls covered in a profusion of color so startlingly green it took his breath away. Hurrying through the open mouth of the dale, he joined the rest of the crew.

"Do you see, Seth?" Barbara cried, face pale from excitement, cheeks flushed from exercise. "They have survived!"

"Good God, so they have."

"The ice protected them -- as a blanket. As you said it would. Green. All green. Alive and thriving."

"Well, I'll be a monkey's uncle!"

"A monkey's father," she laughed, pointing to their "powder monkey." "We have made it through."

"Never doubted it."

Paula gurgled and pulled his hair. Even she knew a lie when she heard one.

# CHAPTER 35

A week later, the flowers appeared. First on one plant, then twelve, until the entire valley lay covered in white. Standing at the edge looking down, Seth drew in a deep breath through his nose, savoring the soft, sweet scent permeating the air.

"How long?" he asked, "before we have fruit?"

"Twenty-eight to 30 days after bloom."

Letting the gentle spring breeze assuage his tormented mind, he waited a long beat before asking, "How many berries can we expect?"

"Next year, when they are fully mature, one quart from each plant. Since this is only their first full season, I cannot say for sure. That we have what we have is an unexpected... blessing."

"And how many plants have we?"

"Upward of 2,500 survived. I cannot say about the ones in Field Number Two. Some are showing signs of life. They will be set back, of course. I cannot hold out hope of salvaging much of a crop there."

Taking work gloves from his back pocket, Seth wearily knocked the semi-dried clumps of dirt from between the fingers. Working his hands through the stiffened leather, his shoulder sagged.

"I must go back. The corn field is almost dry enough to re-plow."

"And then re-seed?"

"I've almost a mind to let it go like the wheat field; turn it over to the clover and wild grass and harvest it as fodder."

She did not have to ask what that meant. No corn and no wheat meant no income from the crops upon which they relied for income.

Without a substantial cash flow, they could not hope to keep their land, much less the home upon which it sat.

"Do you need some help?"

"I need a miracle." Sorry that he spoke so unguardedly, he tried to put a better face on the situation. "No. I have Peter with me. He's a good boy. He can break up the clods."

"Patricia and I can do that, too."

"No. I would rather you...." But he did not know what he would rather. "Are you going to put out fertilizer?"

"What I've been gathering from the hen house."

"We should have had more chickens. About a thousand of them. That ought to just about do it."

"You'd be pretty sick of fried eggs by now."

He did not answer and Nelander let the joke slip away. Watching him go, she had to stay a hand. For the first time in many months, she felt the call of the sea. Wind and waves, the creak of pulleys and the snap of sails reminded her of what she loved and understood.

Squatting down so that her hands brushed against the grass and the moist earth, she thought of her father with an ache of regret and nostalgia.

"What am I to do, Captain?" came the low, tortured inquiry. "How would you handle this, Ned Nelander? You taught me that where there is a will there is a way. What way, sir? We owe the bank so much money. Come fall, there will have to be a reckoning. Mr. Provost will want his money. I spent my savings on a pipe dream. Almost half is wiped out. Even if we harvest strawberries, who has the money to buy them? The people in Lawrence have no cash to spend on luxuries. I thought I had planned it all out, but I had not considered that."

Unlike Belinda Ward and her companion spirits, Captain Ned Nelander had nothing to say. At least not in a way his seaman daughter understood.

Rising slowly from her crouch, Barbara trudged back the way she came, leaving one pair of footprints on the land. It could be said she left her mark, but had fallen short of making one.

Last year there had been a party with flapjacks and an invited guest. This year, as the sea of white ripened slowly into red, expectations were more guarded and far less demonstrative. Ironically, as their needs increased, celebrations ebbed in the opposite direction.

Early Saturday morning after a quiet breakfast of biscuits and coffee, Nelander began her offensive.

"I shall require the horse hitched. The crew and I are going out to the valley to pick strawberries."

"You are going to be too tired to walk home?"

Ordinarily she would have railed at the tone, but Seth had been sullen and cranky of late, feeling the burden of an uncertain corn crop mount as the days passed.

"No, sir. But I do not think the three of us can carry several large baskets of fruit back from the field."

A grunt served as an apology.

"You are going to pick, then?"

"We are."

"And sell them -- where? To whom?"

"Tomorrow is Sunday. There is another bazaar at church. I will offer them there. That has always been my plan and I intend to stick to it."

"And are you going to take chits on it? No one in Lawrence has any money."

"I shall see who has a few pennies to spend on a treat. If no one does, I will bring them home."

"And do what with them?"

"Feed them to the pigs."

"But we ain't got any --" She silenced Peter with a stare.

"We 'do not have any,'" came the stern correction. "Kindly use proper grammar. I have let you lapse too long. Henceforth, I will make amends." His lower lip protruded.

"Pirates don't speak the Queen's English."

"In that, you would be surprised. Many of them were educated and spoke well. You will kindly follow that example." Surprised at her own terse rejoinder, Barbara debated mitigating the demand then dismissed her own repentance. "Master Patricia, get the reed baskets and be certain to line them with towels so we do not damage the bottom row."

"Yes, sir."

Slipping from the table, she grabbed her brother by the arm and guided him away. Finding themselves alone, the black mood thickened, forcing Nelander to rise.

"I will prepare some bread and cheese for your noon day meal."

"Don't bother. I will eat at supper."

"Suit yourself."

She might have followed his example but for the fact she would have the children with her. A man and a woman might fast as a means of sulking, but it would be wrong to force that deprivation on innocent parties.

Quickly preparing the remainder of the biscuits and rolling a thick slice of cheese into a towel, she held the crew back until Seth harnessed Blaze, then ushered them outside. Taking the reins herself as a means of asserting some control over a life rapidly spinning out of hand, she made one final reconciliation by waving good-bye. She did not expect Seth to return it and when he did, the day brightened considerably.

*Enough,* he had transmitted and *enough* she accepted.

Enough for the present.

Tomorrow would be a new story. And the week after that a chapter.

Thomas and Betty were waiting for them. As the wagon rolled to a stop, the Negress took Paula from her traveling basket and cradled the babe in her arms.

"Dis be a fine mornin' fo' pickin', Nelander. Der's plenty what's ripe; an' sweet, too," she added with a grin. "Ah taste one fo' to see if mah nose tolt me right. Der's mighty good. Da bes' Ah eber had."

Appreciative of the praise, the officer forced a smile. She need not have, for the old woman could not see the expression, but it restored a sense of normalcy to the morning.

"Thank you. I hope others feel the same. Patricia, Peter, begin at the top, one on either side. Pick only those berries which are the reddest. If you find some which still have white, leave them. We do not need more than a peck or two for tomorrow."

Nodding their understanding, the pair dispersed, eagerly scampering up the hill to begin their task. Allowing them half an hour to assemble a small quantity, she inspected their work, declared it in accordance with her wishes and began filling her own basket. By midday they gathered at the cheek to check one another's progress and to partake of their meal.

Offering a slice of cheese and biscuit to Peter, he drew back, shaking his head.

"I ain't hungry."

Immediately annoyed at what she perceived to be a copy of his father, Barbara pressed the food on him.

"What do you mean, you aren't hungry? You are always hungry and I want you to eat --"

His grin disarmed her but only temporarily.

"I ete about two hundred strawberries!"

The proof of his assertion lay on his red lips and stained cheeks. Taking stock, Nelander recoiled in horror.

"Those are not for eating! They are to be sold. How in God's name are we to make any money if you eat all the crop? We won't have any money to pay the bank."

Reacting at first as though he thought her teasing, then realizing his mistake and what he had done, tears came to his eyes.

"I didn't mean to.... I didn't think.... Ain't papa gonna sell the corn?"

Overcome by anger, Nelander spoke without reflection.

"There isn't going to be any corn. It is too late. The cold weather will strike before the corn has a chance to ripen. He only planted it on a hope. And not a very good one."

Wailing in misery, Peter jumped to his feet, started wildly about, face flushed as more tears spilled down his eyes.

"No one told me!" Beating his chest, he cried, huge sobs wracking his spare body. "I didn't mean to do anything wrong!" Clenching a fist, he waved it in the air. "Damn you! Damn you all!"

Before she could stop him, he ran off, oblivious to the calls for him to stop. Reaching the crest of the hill, he paused once to look back, then disappeared from sight. Torn between following him and letting him go, Nelander grasped a hand to her head.

"Oh, God, what have I done?"

Flinging her navy cap across the narrow stream, she gritted her teeth and prepared to rise before Blind Betty put out a hand to prevent her.

"Let him go, Nelander."

"I can't. I don't know what he will do. I shouldn't have said anything --"

"Mebbe not; mebbe so. But da fac' is, yuh did an' der's no takin' it back."

"I never meant to hurt him. I should have warned them what the strawberries mean --"

"So, now he knows. Now we all knows."

The fact that Betty and Thomas also had no idea of the nature of the Ward's dire predicament slowly registered. Biting her lip until blood flowed, the seaman-turned-landlubber withdrew, head swirling with frustration and sorrow.

"I'm sorry. I'm so sorry. Forgive me. Never mind what I said. Patricia -- "

The girl backed away, the whites of her eyes reflecting a different sort of horror.

"Don't touch me. I ate them, too. I'm just as guilty as Peter."

"No, child, no. It was my fault. You didn't know."

"I wanted to have fun. This was a big day. Now," she finished with a hurt sniff, "it ain't."

The purposeful use of an incorrect word did more than anything else to inflict damage on the adult.

Dragging one foot behind her, then stamping it on the ground, she huffed in defiance.

"I'm going to get papa."

Not "captain papa," or "the captain," but "papa." Just plain papa.

Stuffing both hands in her overalls, the child began a long, slow trek away from the valley and the forbidden strawberries and the sailor who had come into her life so suddenly. A rejection of them all came with a curt kick at a lump of earth.

"An' I'm gonna take down that Jolly Roger."

She did not have to add that the Black Flag would remain flying. In both warning and defense against a new common enemy.

Barbara Nelander watched her go, having no idea what to say or how to handle the situation which had so suddenly blown up in her face. As much as she tried, the anger welling inside would not quell. In frustration, she addressed the older woman beside her.

"Now what, mother?" Blind Betty added wind to her sails by guffawing. More than a chuckle and less than an outright belly laugh, the reaction seemed entirely out of place. The younger seethed. "I see I have amused you. Would you care to enlighten me as to the reason?"

"Yuh call me 'mudder' but yuh don' mean dat."

"I meant it as a term of respect --"

"Possibly. But da word don' habe no meanin' to yuh. Dat's why Ah laughed."

"How can you say that when I am a mother? -- three times over," she added and meant it.

"No, suh. Yuh cain't be a mudder 'cause yuh neber been a chil'."

"What does that mean? Do you suppose I sprung on this earth fully grown?"

"Ah don'. But Ah 'suppose' yuh neber been treated like a chil'. Mos' all yuhr life, yuh been a grown-up. Tell me dat ain't so." Nelander had no reply. "What age yuh be when yuh wen' to sea?"

"Five."

"So frum dat day to dis, yuh been carryin' 'sponsibility on yuhr shoulders."

"That is so."

"Yuh ain't been wid no chil'run. Yuh don' think like no chil'. Yuh don' see da worl' da way dey do."

"But... I have worked hard to see Patricia and Peter do have a childhood."

"An' so yuh habe. But yuh jes' puts a separation 'tween yuh an' dem. Yuh been worried 'bout money. Yuh t'ink 'bout it night an' day. It eatin' yuh up inside. Dat an adult worry, Nelander. Yuh keep it to yuhrse'f; yuh an' da capt'n. Yuh put yuhrse'f in dem young'uns place but yuh still t'ink like a big person. Den when yuh discober dey don' t'ink like yuh, der's a blow-up."

"I tried to apologize --"

"Like one adult to anudder. Yuh cain't get down to where dey are, so yuh ask me to 'splain it by callin' me mudder. But what yuh mean is, 'Now what, Miss Betty, suh?' Yuh ain't one mudder axin' another -- yuh's one seaman askin' another how to bring da crew back in line."

"All right: how do I do that?"

Betty laughed again and pointed across the stream.

"Furst, yuh go an' fetch yuhr cap an' put it back on yuhr head. Den yuh set down an' eat."

"I am not hungry."

The old woman clapped. "Dat good. Now, yuh talkin' like a chil'. Mad an' spoiled."

"All right. I-will-eat. What next?"

"Nex', yuh go back to work. Pickin' strawberries."

"But what about -- the crew? Shouldn't I go to them?"

"Yuh let dem work it out in der chil'run's mind."

A flush crept into Barbara's face.

"But Patricia is going to take down the flag."

"So, what if she does? Dat gonna change innythin'? Yuh gibin' up on da pirate ship?"

"If they don't want it...." Her fists clenched as she tried to convince herself. "It's just pretend, anyway. You're right. It doesn't matter to me."

"No, suh. Dat's not what Ah say. If da girl takes it down, she'll put it up, ag'in. In her own time. Time yuh can't decide fo' her. Time da capt'n can't decide fo' her."

"If it comes down, it will never go up, again."

"Good, ag'in. Now, yuh're talkin' like a chil'. Yuh been hurt an' yuh wanna hurt. Pretty soon, yuh'll be don' to der lebel. Goin' backward. Den mebbe yuh kin see da way dey see."

"And-do-what?"

"Gibe 'em space to grow. Gibe 'em da sky to soar through. Dey ain't gonna turn on yuh, Nelander, suh. Dey take it down, dey'll put it back. Yuh unnerstan' pride. Chil's got it, jes' da same as a grown-up. Dey go up a peg, yuh cume down a peg. Den, yuh know yuh're back on course."

Goose bumps spread down Nelander's spine.

"You, Betty Ward, are officer material." She saluted, then realizing the woman could not see, gently took her hand and guided it along her arm. "I bow to your convictions and superior knowledge."

"I ain't neber been an off'cer, but Ah am a mudder. Mebbe der's sumthin' of one in da odder. Now, go an' fetch yuhr cap an' do like Ah tolt yuh."

The seaman started to comply, then twisted her face into a question mark.

"How did you know I threw my cap? You did not see me do it."

"It's all part ob bein' an off'cer, suh."

"Yes, sir." Barbara forged the stream and retrieved her cap. Placing it on, she stared into the blue expanse. "And I am damned glad I was raised by Ned Nelander and not by you. I thought him a hard taskmaster; you are worse."

Which was meant as the ultimate compliment and taken for just that.

## CHAPTER 36

Barbara Nelander picked as many strawberries as she thought she might sell on the morrow and carefully set the baskets into the wagon.

"Can I give you a ride home?"

Wearily rubbing a calf muscle, Betty considered, then gratefully agreed.

"Dat be kind."

"And Thomas? Will he come?"

"He be along in his own time."

"But we have done as much as we can do for one day."

"He stay behind to say a little prayer ober da plants. As a way ob t'ankin' dem fo' da berries. An' den he sit a spell. Watchin' ober 'em. He stays ebery day till da night falls. Dat's his job," she proudly added.

"I appreciate that. And you?"

"Ah tend da garden. An' weabe da baskets."

"Don't you ever rest?"

"Ah res' when Ah goes to heaben."

Which settled the point. Helping her up onto the seat, Nelander took the reins and carefully guided Blaze through the valley and up into the hills. They traveled a half mile in quiet solitude, each tending her own thoughts, when the driver caught sight of a small figure on the horizon. Leaning forward as if to bring the image into sharper focus, she identified Patricia. The child stood in the open field, hands by her sides, back positioned away from the wagon.

Hesitantly slowing down, Barbara debated hailing the girl, then decided against it. Clearly, Patricia had an awareness of their presence. If she wanted to draw their attention, all she need to was wave. The fact she did not implied no desire to summon them closer.

Contrarily, by permitting herself to be visible, the act seemed a peace offering of sorts. Clutching that as a hope, Nelander picked up the pace, taking care not to maneuver too close. They passed as ships in the night, both with figurative fog lamps burning, neither giving an indication they had any but a passing interest in the other.

After leaving Betty at the farmhouse, Barbara abandoned the road, cutting through the hills. She had originally determined to steer clear of the girl's position, but without being conscious, found herself following a direct line of confrontation. Arriving at the site where she had originally seen Patricia, great the disappointment to find it abandoned. Sadly urging Blaze forward, a movement caught her eye. Reigning in the horse, the wagon stopped.

Pretending to have detected something wrong with the animal, the woman alit, busying herself by lifting a foreleg and inspecting the frog for pebbles. Finding dirt lodged along the hoof, she grabbed a stick cleaned the hoof. Thus legitimately occupied, she did not hear the child come up.

"Peter's digging, again."

Startled by the statement, Nelander's head jerked up.

"What?"

"In the ground. Just like he used to."

"Oh, dear God."

"Papa's gone after him. He brought the harness."

"No."

Falling back against the wagon, she gasped for breath.

"It cannot be."

"I seen him, myself."

Casting aside the stick, Nelander indicated the conveyance.

"Get in. We will go to them."

"Papa don't need no help."

The challenge stung.

"All right. Papa Captain doesn't need any help. Will you go home with me?"

"Reckon I'll walk."

Accepting the rebuke, Barbara resumed her place and moved the wagon ahead at a crawl. Patricia followed. After one hundred yards, she hurried to catch up and with an easy grace, hopped into the back. Beside the baskets of strawberries. Neither spoke.

At the edge of the crest overlooking their farm, Nelander noted both flags still flying. Heart in her throat, she picked up the pace, praying that after they arrived, Patricia would leave them be. But she said nothing and as they reached the yard, the girl slipped out. Grabbing the baskets, she took them inside. Barbara walked Blaze to the barn, unhitched him, then went through the motions of currying as she had been taught. Half an hour later, she stepped back into the sunshine.

The Skull and Crossbones and the Black flag fluttered in the breeze.

Point.

Giving no indication she saw a pair of bright eyes watching from behind the curtain, she crossed to the bell. Gauging time from the sun, Nelander rang the bell eight times. Four o'clock. Post meridian. The afternoon being self-explanatory. Because of the light.

Counter-point.

All part of growing up. Or growing down. Depending on one's stature.

Seth and Peter returned an hour later. Just as Nelander rang the bell. One time. Five o'clock.

The harness hung limply from the adult's hand. Peter trotted by his side.

"Go on in," he ordered. "And get washed up."

"Yes, sir."

Dialogue which might have been exchanged between any Kansas farmer and his son.

Waiting until the boy disappeared, the man approached the woman.

"Peter was digging."

"Patricia told me."

He shifted positions, swinging the harness lazily by his side.

"It's not what... we thought."

A beat, then, "Isn't it?"

"He wasn't digging up ghosts." The pulse of a heartbeat. Two. "He was looking for buried treasure. Gold doubloons. To pay the bank."

Her throat constricted.

Another prayer answered.

"Did he find any?"

"No. But you and I found something more precious."

He held out his arms and she fell into them, hugging with all her might.

"Love. And understanding."

Seth kissed Barbara, then held her back at arm's length.

"I was going to say something completely different, myself." Playing along with his tone, a raised eyebrow offered permission to continue. "Not all shipboard quarrels result in mutiny."

"No. A few... reddened eyes and some harpoon jabs to the vital organs, narrowly avoided. But nothing fatal."

"I am sure Captain Ned Nelander knew that."

"Yes. After consultation with Belinda Ward."

"Interesting, how they conspired against us."

"No, Seth. The 'conspiring' was done by we of mortal frailties. The 'fraternizing,' if you will, came from above. And not a moment too soon."

"Shall we have supper, then?"

Tongue in cheek, she appeared to consider.

"Oh, I don't know. I ate for three at noontime." Then, as quickly added, "Yes. We shall. I'll fry some beefsteak if you break out a flagon of rum. I think this calls for a celebration."

"Shall the four of us drink ourselves silly?"

"Flat under the captain's table."

And so they did. Or a reasonable approximation of same.

In the morning, the Ward family dressed for church. Arriving ahead of the congregation, they set up their table, prominently displaying the strawberries to be offered for sale after service. The booth became an instant topic of conversation as the arriving parishioners gathered around to stare at the unexpected offering.

"What's that you got there, Captain?" Hector Anson inquired, pawing through the bucket of fruit with interest.

"Strawberries," came the laconic reply.

"For sale?"

"That's right."

"Where'd you get 'em?"

"Grew them."

"In Kansas? Didn't know strawberries'd grow in Kansas."

"They grow fine, Hector."

"How much?"

"Ten cents a pint," Nelander supplied.

"Do I git to sample some before I buy?"

"No."

"Sure," Seth overruled, nodding at his wife. "One ought to be enough."

Selecting the largest he could find, the shopkeeper nibbled on the end, rolling the pulp around his mouth.

"Sweet."

Others elbowed closer, watching, then demanding a taste for themselves. After observing the way potential customers handled the delicacies, Nelander took to dispensing them herself, offering whichever berry happened to fall under her fingers. In the thirty minutes before Reverend Ginnis opened the doors, they had provided a taste to everyone, including several boys who went through the line twice, professing innocence when accused of the crime.

For the effort, the Wards sacrificed a portion of the stock and earned what Seth described as "Good will." Nelander would have chosen others, but did not feel at liberty to express them in so close a proximity to the church.

After sitting two hours on the benches, listening to a layman extemporize on the holy theme, "It is better to give than receive," then suffering through the self-appointed minister's plea, "Not to withhold your spare change from the collection plate," they gratefully returned once again to the great outdoors.

Resuming her place behind the booth, Nelander discovered that a quarter of her strawberries had mysteriously disappeared. Distressed at the loss, she stared angrily at those passing by, trying to ascertain who had come late and might therefore have had the opportunity to steal.

"Damn bastards," she muttered, forgetting or rather overlooking her previous determination to refrain from cursing. "Steal from their own mothers if they had the chance. It was Matthew McConaghie, or one of his boys, unless I miss my guess."

"Could be. But don't say anything. We don't have proof."

"He's over there licking his fingers. I doubt he's lapping off yolks from raw eggs or just finished chewing on last year's sweet potatoes."

Catching the miscreant's eye, Seth nodded agreeably. The man tipped his cap. Nelander seethed.

Women set themselves up at their own tables, displaying an unusually varied amount of items for sale. Unlike the usual arts and crafts, however, many of them had brought different items: tables and chairs, lamps, crockery, even some picture frames. Taking stock from a turn around the area, Seth returned with a grimace.

"Ugly."

"What do you mean?"

"What they're selling. These people aren't looking to make 'egg money.' They're offering furniture outta their own homes, hoping to make enough to buy food. Most of them don't have ten cents to call their own."

She said nothing. Eventually, a small group formed around her table, each carrying baskets or small wooden crates. Jostling one another, they picked over the strawberries, adding varying amounts to their containers.

Mrs. Knight filled a particularly large burlap sack and handed over her money.

"Ten cents," she offered. "For a pint."

"You have at least three quarts there, Mrs. Knight. That's sixty cents."

"It isn't, anyway. Why, I dare say there is not even one quart here, let along three. I hope you are not trying to cheat me."

Nelander attempted to carry the argument by showing the shopper several lines she had marked on one of her own baskets.

"Look: this is my measurement for a quart --"

"It may be yours but it is not mine. And who is to say which of us is correct? I have lived in Lawrence all my life, and I am accustomed to having my word taken as fact. Whereas you, if you excuse my boldness, are a stranger. Perhaps where you come from, measurements are different. But if you are going to sell strawberries by the pint and quart, they ought to be *Kansas* pints and quart."

Finished with the extraordinary declaration, the customer awaited final disposition of her case in the court of "I Am Always Right."

Averting her face, Nelander scanned the church yard, working slowly toward the crude, clapboard building itself. Smaller in size yet no better constructed than the Meeting Hall which had burned to the ground, she debated whether to stand on principle or bow to the demand no one, least of all Mrs. Knight could believe a fair one.

Uninspired by her surroundings and with less charity than common sense, she returned to her customer with a wan smile.

"Twenty cents it is and I regret any misunderstanding. I really *must* get Captain Ward to explain the difference between a Canadian and an American quart."

Although the statement fell short of an apology, Mrs. Knight accepted it with grace. Dipping her bonneted head, she smiled and merged into the crowd. Seth sidled up, affectionately patting his wife on the arm.

"You handled that nicely."

"You mean, I gave in without smacking her over the head."

"That, too."

"Stranger, indeed," Nelander spat. "I have lived here upward of four years, married a local man and had his child. What does it take to be considered 'one of the girls'?"

He guffawed, spewing spittle over the fruit, which in no way decreased its value.

"I am afraid you will never be that. Fill out your sails, does it?"

"Yes, but not in the way you mean."

They stood another hour, exchanging pleasantries and accepting compliments on their crop from people passing by. Some offered a trade in exchange for berries; others simply displayed wistful faces and walked away without making an offer. By the time most families had reluctantly repacked their household goods and left, they had collected a sum total of seventy cents. Grasping the coins in her hand, Barbara worked the muscles in her jaw.

"Not exactly what I had hoped for."

"We may have better luck in the farmer's market. More people from town frequent those stands."

"Are they better off than those who come to church?"

He shrugged. "Some are."

"Those who aren't farmers?"

"They aren't all, you know. There are shop keepers and tradesmen. And then, of course, there is 'Reverend' Ginnis. And Sheriff Bochner."

"All people who depend on the farmers. And they are distressed."

Without the heart to disagree, Seth piled the remaining fruit into the wagon. Crimson juice, looking suspiciously like blood, leaked through the wicker, staining the sides and leaving red rings on the table. Shooing away a contingent of flies, Barbara wiped it down and prepared to join her family when she caught sight of Matthew McConaghie meandering in their direction. Steeling herself for an unappreciated confrontation, he surprised her by politely tipping his broad-rimmed hat.

"Afternoon, Miz Nelander."

"Good afternoon to you, Mr. McConaghie."

Awkwardly shifting his weight, then hooking his thumbs under a wide leather belt, he took pains not to make eye contact.

"Wasn't sure you'd speak to me."

Surprised at the softness of his voice, she did not let it disarm her natural suspicions.

"We all make mistakes. You had prompting. No lasting harm came of it and I am content to let bygones be bygones."

"I was wondering.... You didn't sell all yer strawberries."

"No. I did not."

"What you gonna do wid 'em?"

"Sort out the bruised fruit and eat it, I suppose. Try to sell the rest in town tomorrow or the next day."

"Long ride into Lawrence."

"Yes, it is."

"Thought I might save you the trip."

She did not bother to explain there were plenty more strawberries where these came from.

"What did you have in mind?"

"A trade. Captain Seth... he mentioned awhile ago he were interested in a dog. Got one I might be willin' to part with in exchange for them berries you got left."

She had hoped for an offer of money and hardly concealed the disappointment.

"We got two pups from Dr. McTree." The suddenly crestfallen expression made her regret the statement. "What kind of dog have you?"

"Hound dog. Six months old. He's likable 'nuf, but he jest won't hunt. Seth, he ain't much of a hunter, is he?"

"No, he is not."

"Thought mebbe you could train him as a guard dog. Keep 'em in the barn; eats a mite, though. More'n I care to feed 'im. You don't take 'im, I'll have to let 'im go up in the hills somewhere. Or shoot 'im."

"I wouldn't want you to do that."

Again, an awkward silence before he spoke.

"Don't much like to think on it, myself. Them dogs is sorta like my family. Worth more'n the boys, sumtimes, I think. But times bein' what they are -- an' a bad dog, he's like a rotten apple. Spoils the others. They git in bad ways, then none of 'em'll hunt."

"What, exactly, do you hunt, Mr. McConaghie?"

"Possum; coons. Rabbits. Squirrels. Whatever goes in a pot."

"I was thinking more like human beings." He stiffened. "I hear there are those who make a living chasing runaway slaves."

"Not many do that in Lawrence."

"Why is that?"

"Too many... nigger lovers."

"Like my husband?"

"Everyone knows how he feels."

"And how do you feel?" Matthew sucked in his cheek. "Is that what the dog won't hunt? Niggers?"

Breaking out into a toothy grin, the man leaned forward so that she felt his exhalations on her cheek.

"Miz Nelander, iffn I wanted to collect bounty on runaway blacks, I wouldn't need no dogs to do it."

She could make no sense of the declaration.

"What do you mean?"

Without being able to see McConaghie's eyes squint, Nelander registered the vibration as he cleared his throat to spit. A thin brown stream of tobacco juice landed within an inch of her foot. She would not have moved it out of harm's way to save her life.

"They's free fer the pickin'. If you know where to look."

"Do you know?"

She thought she heard him chuckle. The sound rankled her temper, yet she stifled the impulse to shove him away.

"All right, Matthew. I will take your dog. In fair trade."

Pulling back his head, the man's eyes flashed. She would have given much for the power to read his mind.

"I thought you might. It's a good bargain. See you hold onto him, now. If you know what's good fer ya."

An implied threat. Not the first. And not, she suspected, the last.

"Does he have a name?"

"Squash."

She could not have been more surprised if he had said "Emancipation." Or "Black Republican."

"You have him with you?"

"I do."

Motioning her to wait, he slithered away, a big man moving with unexpected agility. Crossing to his own wagon, he reached into the back and withdrew a scrawny dog, all black except for two swatches of tan over its eyes. Cradling it under his massive arm, he returned and offered it. Uncertain she had made the correct decision, Nelander held back.

"It has no collar -- no lead. How am I to keep it from jumping away and going back to you?"

"Now, that'd be a bad bargain, wouldn't it? Me givin' away a dog only to have it... escape. You'd have to come after it."

"Indeed, I would -- for I hate to be cheated."

He winked. "I'll be lookin' fer you, then. See that you come alone an' you an' I kin bend the elbow over a glass of whisky."

"Oh, I will not come alone. None of the Wards ever travel by themselves. Or haven't you heard? We've accompanied by spirits. Those who know how to protect what's theirs."

McConaghie stepped off, licked his lips, then thrust the dog into her arms. Grabbing for a basket of strawberries, he dumped the half full one on top of the other, then carefully rearranged the fruit so as not to spill any. When satisfied, he dipped his head.

"You come callin', lookin' fer the dog an' you kin collect this basket at the same time."

"Better yet, you can pay me now for it."

"I a'ready paid 'nuff. That animal's got breedin'. He's worth twenty dollars."

"He doesn't hunt."

"Mebbe you'll have better luck."

Balancing the basket, he turned away. She addressed his back.

"Why is he called 'Squash'? Seems to me a black dog outta be called 'Midnight.'" *Or 'Nigger's Toes,'* she thought but did not say so.

But Matthew McConaghie had finished talking. Seeing he would not return, Seth joined her.

"What was that all about?"

"I have no idea."

"What's with the dog?"

"He traded me for the rest of the strawberries."

"Why? Seems to me he ate enough of them without paying. What prompted him to want the rest?"

"I don't know that he did."

"What's that supposed to mean?"

More carefully examining the pup, Nelander flipped back one of its ears, then cradled the unresisting beast in her arms to inspect its underbelly.

"It occurred to me it might be diseased; distemper or rabies."

Making an expression of distaste, Seth took it from her. The animal shoved a wet nose in his palm and he reluctantly petted it.

"No. Not that I can tell. What did he say?"

"It eats too much."

"Probably right." The dog wagged its tail. "We don't need another dog."

"No. But he wanted us to have it. I didn't feel right, not taking it."

"Maybe it bites. He was hoping we'd let Paula play with it and it'd sink its teeth into her hand."

Squash licked Seth's fingers. It did not behave like a dog with a temper.

"Maybe it understands English and its been trained to tell him all it hears. We better not let it out at night."

"Do you mean that?"

"No."

But she almost wished she did.

# CHAPTER 37

"Stop the horse. I'm getting down."

Seth did as directed, casting a worried look at his daughter.

"What's wrong?"

"You're going to slow."

"Well, excuse me, Master Patricia. I had no idea you wished to rattle the bones of your baby sister. I could 'get a move on,' I suppose. Race like the wind; Nelander's cap flying off; Peter tossed from the back. My posterior splintered by the wagon seat. Would that suit?" He poked his wife who sat beside him. "Had you any idea your child was a speed demon?" He gleefully answered his own question. "She gets that from you."

"Certainly not from a Kansas farmer."

He grunted and pulled up. Spreading her arms, Patricia jumped to ground, landed gracefully and bolted ahead, soon vanishing into the tall wild grasses.

"Gone to catch a whale, I suppose. Were we ever that young?"

"Yes. And in many ways I'd like to think we still are."

"Oh." He jabbed a finger at his son. "You going, too?"

"I didn't bring my harpoon."

Slapping the reins, Seth directed Blaze forward. They continued at a leisurely pace. Half an hour later, the wagon pulled into their yard. A large sign had been posted on the flagpole.

> Fresh, Sweet
> **Strawberries -**
> This Way!

Following the red arrow beneath the words, they discovered a second sign.

> You Are Getting
> Closer
> To Fresh, Sweet

**Strawberries!**

Scrambling down, the Ward family eagerly followed a second arrow.

**Strawberries!**
Only
Ten Cents
A Pint!

Other signs, depicting large, red berries, some alone, others in a cluster set off by a profusion of green leaves, whet the taste buds. Eagerly going from sign to sign, they found themselves in the clearing behind the house.

There, they beheld a table, decorated with a red and white tablecloth. Atop it were scores of small, reed baskets. Just the size to hold a pint of strawberries. The proprietor, a gangly girl wearing a red apron stood behind her wares. Smiling pleasantly at her customers, she gave them a welcome smile.

"Greetings, folks. Fresh strawberries for sale! Just picked this morning, with the dew of a Kansas day still on their sweet outsides. Just the thing for a Monday morning breakfast. Makes a mighty good topping for a mess of flapjacks, Miss. And you, sir; bet you haven't ete strawberries like this since you was a boy. Jest ten cents and you've got jest enough to eat! And you, young man -- strawberries is better'n peppermint sticks, inny day."

"What -- what is this?" Nelander gasped.

"My stand."

"You are going to sell strawberries from the house?" Her heart sunk. "But no one comes out here."

Patricia rolled her eyes.

"Not from the house. This is only a demonstration. Look." Holding out one of the baskets, she showed them how her plan would work. "You saw what happened at church -- everyone dug through the big baskets, trying to find the biggest fruit. They squished some, tossed others aside. That 'ain't' good business. Then, most was like Mrs. Knight -- they had no idea how big a pint was. Or they was quarrelin' about how some got more'n they did. They can't say that if all the baskets are the same."

"Where... did you get these?" Nelander demanded, picking one up and examining the loose weave. Already guessing the answer, she could not equate what she saw with the obvious fact.

"Blind Betty."

"She made these up in a morning?"

Patricia scoffed and proudly shook her head.

"No, sir. She's been working on them for months. I bet I've got upwards of five hundred."

"Five hundred baskets?"

"Five hundred pint baskets."

"You arranged this ahead of time?"

"We all have a hand in this, don't we? Captain Papa had the valley and you had the idea. Master Peter is gonna be the procurer. I'm the huckster."

Seth blushed and winked at Barbara.

"Perhaps you ought to call Peter the --" She interrupted him with a laugh.

"I don't know. 'Procurer' sounds right to me. And you, Master Patricia -- the huckster?"

"Yup. I'm the one who talks it up. I'm also the artist," she proudly added. "I made the signs. Got dozens of them. Peter's gonna put them up all over town. To alert folks what we have for sale."

"In Lawrence?"

"No, sir. I know times are bad there and people are hard up. But I heard you and the captain talking -- about how the freezing weather and the ice went through Kansas in a pattern. Last time I was in town, I asked around. Spoke to Mr. Anson. He's a gossip," she explained. "Talks to everyone. He told me that Olathe and some of the other towns close by weren't hit like we were. We're goin' there."

"We are?"

"On Tuesday. Tomorrow, we're picking. As many as are ripe. Then we're piling up and taking the strawberries on the road. Going from town to town until we sell 'em all. Then we come back for more and start all over again."

"You determined all this by yourself?"

"I figure it's like charting a course. Pirates island-hopping. Lookin' for a place to bury their treasure. But in our case, we're looking for a place to sell our treasure. Convertin' our jewels, you might say, into spendin' money."

"Patricia... I had thought about that, too. But such a long way in the hot sun.... The fruit will spoil."

The girl squared her shoulders, jutting out her chin to appear in command.

"A good officer is always prepared for emergencies. Always thinking ahead. Isn't that what you taught us?"

"I did."

"I may not be an officer, yet, but I aim to be one day. Just like you and the captain. What we need, sir, is ice."

"Ice?"

"To keep the strawberries cool."

"The is only one place to get ice in Lawrence and that is at the Tankard's Draft. It is sold at a premium."

"No, sir. There are two places. Remember Mr. Duggan's gout? He pays Dr. McTree a weekly stipend in ice. The last time I was in town --"

"You made a deal with the doctor?"

"You bet. He said he'd rather have strawberries than ice, so I made a trade. He'll be waiting for us bright an' early Tuesday morning. I figure we can spread the ice out over the tarpaulin, then lay some towels on top. Then we put the strawberries on top. That ought to keep 'em fresh for a day or so until we get 'em sold."

Puffing out her chest, she finished the Grand Scheme. "I know Captain Papa and Peter have work to do in the cornfield, but you said the strawberries'd only be ripe for a month or so. I a'ready spoke to Thomas. He'll tend papa's crop best he can while we're away."

Seth removed his hat and fanned his flushed face.

"You planned all this by yourself?"

"Me and Miss Betty and Thomas."

"When did you start this planning?"

"It was Miss Betty who had the idea about the pint baskets. She knew what was comin'. Started making them over the winter; in between times

when she wasn't makin' baskets for you to bring in town. An' Thomas --
he volunteered to work the corn field. I've been painting the signs for a
month." Wiping her hands together, Patricia declared, "Well, that's about
it. What do you think?"

Peter had the answer ready.

"I think you're a damn good pirate!"

Which pleased everyone and set the tone for their new adventure.

It went like clockwork. Arriving early Tuesday morning at Dr.
McTree's, the Wards paid him his fee in fruit and collected the ration of
ice. Under Patricia's watchful eye, they spread it over the back of the
wagon, added a legion of white towels and placed their precious cargo on
top. Following the map created by Mr. Anson, they hit the smaller towns
less effected by the freeze, setting up shop at farmer's markets or near
obliging places of commerce.

Peter posted the signs, then ran up and down the streets, advising anyone
who would listen there were "Fresh strawberries, the best you ever ete!" to
anyone who would listen. Nelander and Seth set up the table and filled the
baskets, making sure the biggest and plumpest berries were displayed to
best advantage. Patricia cajoled prospective customers.

"Strawberries! Jest picked strawberries! Sweet and juicy! Get 'em while
you can: goin' fast!  Only ten cents a pint an' that's a bargain if I ever
heard one!"

Amazed to be offered such a delicacy, people rushed toward their stand,
eager to be among the first to bring back treats for the table. The idea of
displaying the berries in pre-filled containers proved an instant success, not
the least because each purchaser gained not only a quantity of strawberries,
but a "quality, reusable basket, to boot."

By the end of four weeks, after most of the produce had been picked and
sold, the captain of the *Pirate Treasure* discovered a sign posted on the
front door.

"Council Meeting today at six bells. The presence of all Officers and
Able-Bodied Crewmen required. By Order of First Officer Nelander."

Washing face and hands at the pump, he changed his shirt, combed his
tangled mass of dark hair, then set himself on the porch to await the

appointed hour. Blind Betty and Mute Thomas arrived just as he got up to ring the bell.

"Evening."

"Good ebenin' to yuh, suh. We ain't late fo' da meetin'?"

"Right on time."

Betty grinned and held up a basket.

"Ah didn't know what da occasion, but Ah fixed us some suppa. Got sum nice greens frum mah own garden."

The pride evinced in her voice brought tears to his eyes.

"That's fine. Real fine."

Allowing her to pass before him, the men followed. Inside, Nelander and the three smallest seamen were gathered. Taking the basket from Betty, Barbara set it aside for later consumption, then indicated everyone be seated. They obliged with a festive air of expectation.

"Thank you all for attending. The meeting is hereby called to order." Rapping the back of a spoon on the coffee pot served as official notification. "It is my wish, first and foremost, to thank all of you for your extraordinary contributions to my somewhat haphazard experiment. Without your skill, ingenuity, hard labor and most of all, your enduring faith, we have managed to grow a whale out of a minnow."

"She means," Peter loudly whispered to Betty and Thomas, "a grizzly bear outta a gopher."

Both analogies were vivid and perfectly clear.

Hefting a large gunny sack onto the table, Nelander spilled the contents. Coins rolled out, some spilling onto the floor. Waiting until the "accident" had been cleared, she indicated the contents.

"This is the total of our earnings. In the interest of accuracy, not one penny has been added or removed. I wanted you all here to help me count the... spoils."

Directing that coins of like denominations be piled into easily addable stacks, the extended family went to work. With an eye toward the passage of time, both Patricia and Peter rang the bell once before they had completed the work. Across the table lay a veritable treasure chest of money.

Prohibiting herself from making a premature and thus exaggerated speculation, Barbara directed the gang, further separating piles into ten dollar increments. That done, they merged groups into those which equaled one hundred dollars. A unified gasp of breath proved how easy they were to add.

"Three hundred, eighty nine dollars and fifty cents."

Not the five hundred dollars she had been hoping for, but considerably more than the seventy cents collected at the church, when it appeared they had reached the end of the line.

"A fair amount," Captain Ward declared, voice unsteady. "Enough to pay the bank and save both farms." The declaration brought more tears and a wave of raised fists. "Next year, with decent corn and wheat crops, we can spend our strawberry money to get caught up. And have some to put aside -- for the first time in the history of this ship." For a Kansas man not prone to unbridled optimism, his avowal solicited foot stomping and cheers. "By God, well done!"

Reaching for his wife, Seth hugged her, planting kisses on her face. Only reluctantly releasing her, he kissed his children, then bowed to their friends.

"Mother Betty, may I kiss you, too?"

"Ah would consider that a great honor, son."

Engulfing her in his arms, Seth kissed her wet cheeks, then offered his hand to Thomas.

"Brother, we could not have done it without you."

Extending his hand, the black man shook with the white, both of their chins quivering with emotion. Lips moving without sound, Thomas appealed to the older woman.

"He says," she interpreted, "you da bes' brudder he eber had an' da bes' man he eber knew."

"Thomas Ward, I bestow the same sentiment to you, sir. And you, Betty Ward, the best mother Barbara or I ever had. We thank the Lord for His blessings in bringing us together. I have not always been a believer of His working in 'mysterious ways,' but on this occasion, I am willing to bow my head in thanks."

Clasping hands, the family of seven copied his example, baby Paula between her mother and grandmother. After a silent prayer, they took the basket of food and retired to the porch, where six of the gathering partook of a feast, home grown on a freed people's farm.

As the moon came up, shining soft, Nelander rose for one final declaration. Reaching under her chair, she produced a packet of papers. Clearing her throat, she handed the first to the boy.

"Master Peter, in recognition of services above and beyond the call of duty, I, as first officer of this pirate ship, pronounce you warrant officer. That, my lad, is an officer below commissioned rank -- but a promotion over able-bodied."

Accepting his certificate, eyes wide, he made a stiff salute.

"Thank you, sir."

The next went to the girl.

"Master Patricia, in recognition of services above and beyond the call of duty, I, as first officer of this pirate ship, pronounce you a full-fledged Navigator."

"Thank you, sir."

"Thomas Ward, you, sir, are to be an Able-Bodied Buccaneer."

Clasping the document to his heart, he saluted, a large, happy grin dominating his features.

"Betty Ward, you, sir, are promoted to ship's doctor -- which means," she added with a glance at Peter, "our official cook, healer and spiritual confidant. In honor of my best friend, Mister Dutchy, who had more courage than a ship full of sailors."

"Dis be fine, suh. Ah now be Betty Dutchy Nelander Ward. Three new names fo' an old woman who neber t'ought to habe another den dat she born wid."

"And you, Seth Ward," Barbara Nelander concluded, "in recognition of your extraordinary seamanship and steadfastness in time of great peril, and with great love, I assume the right of maritime law by hereby promoting you to Captain of the Fleet. Your special duty is to maintain discipline -- and faith." Handing him the certificate, she saluted with the pride of one born and bred to the sea. "And now, as befits the wondrous occasion, a toast."

"With rum?"

"Yes, Peter. With rum."

She went inside and brought back an unopened bottle of Black Jack rum and six glasses. Breaking the seal, she poured a small amount into each. After the crew took theirs, the new Captain of the Fleet took it upon himself to offer the benediction.

"To all those who sail the briny seas, whether they be the Atlantic, the Pacific or the oceans of Kansas. And to Captain Barbara Nelander."

The revelation came as a shock and she staggered backward, mouth agape.

"No, no...."

"Yes, indeed. Was that not always your wish? To be a captain in your own right? You have proven yourself on this and many battlefields. You have addressed the present with courage and innovation and by so doing, you have given us -- and the ship upon which we sail -- a future. By the right of maritime law which you have assumed, I, too, claim, in so honoring an officer of the highest integrity and courage."

Captain Nelander.

The second to claim such a distinction.

The first to have done so on land as well as sea.

Beyond the sailor's moon a cluster of stars broke through.

Bestowing their blessing on Strawberry Fields.

And the pirate ship which sailed upon them.

The End

GSFE

ALSO BY: S.L.KOTAR AND J.E.GESSLER

A character based historical 1950's courtroom based murder mystery entitled "**The Hugh Kerr Mystery Series**"..

- Book I          **The Conundrum of the Decapitated Detective**
- Book II         **The Conundrum of the Absconded Attorney**
- **Book III        The Conundrum of the Sins of the Fathers**
- **Book IVThe Conundrum of The Two-Sided Lawyer**
- **Book V         The Conundrum of the Clueless Counselor**
- **Book VIThe Conundrum of the Loveless Marriage**
- **Book VII        The Conundrum of the Executed Defendant**
- **Book VIII       The Conundrum of the Jettisoned Jury**
- **Book IXThe Conundrum of the Perjured Pigeon**
- **Book X         The Conundrum of the Haunting Halloween**
    - **Party**
- **Book XIThe Conundrum of the Tuneless Tunesmith**
- **Book XII        The Conundrum of the Meddling Motorcar**
- **Book XIII       The Conundrum of the Blundering Bear**
- **Book XIV       The Conundrum of Shooting Fish in a Barrel**
    - 
    - **To Be Continued!**

Next a series is "New Beginnings" a 1950's medical drama.

- Book I          **The Believer**
- Book II         **The Heretic**
- Book III **Arrow Song**
- Book IV **Peas In A Pod**
- 
    - **To Be Continued!**

**"the ReproBate saga"** is a character-based series in the 1860 American Civil War

- **Book I**      **Beneath the Rose**
- Book II      **skull and cRossBones**
- Book III      **Redefining Bastions**
- Book IV      **thicker than Blood**
- Book V      **prioR Battles**
- Book VI           **Requited Blasphemy**
- Book VII           **The waR Between**
- Book VIII           **To Richmond or Bust**
- Book IX      **carrying Battlescars**
  - **To be Continued**

"the Hellhole saga" is a character-based series from the American West

- Book I      **First Draw**
- Book II      **Audition for a Legend**
- Book III      **Strange Bedfellows**

**"The Kansas Pirate Series"** is another character-based series from the American West

- Book I      **Pirate Treasure**
- Book II      **Strawberry Fields**
- Book III      **The Drinking Gourd**

Stand-alone novels include:

- **Catman** *He was every man; he was no man*

- **ONE** Science Fiction space travel

- **Shepherd of the Kingdom** a modern-day horror classic

Non-Fiction

"**The Kepi Magazine**," A publication specialized in the Civil War and 19th century life.:

- **The Kepi Volume I and II**
- **The Kepi Volumes III and IV**

www.ingramcontent.com/pod-product-compliance
Lightning Source LLC
Chambersburg PA
CBHW030400180626
46812CB00005B/1863